SWEEPERS

SWEEPERS

A NOVEL OF SUSPENSE

P. T. DEUTERMANN

ST. MARTIN'S PRESS
NEW YORK

Design by Maureen Troy

Library of Congress Cataloging-in-Publication Data

Deutermann, Peter T.
    Sweepers : a novel of suspense / by
    P. T. Deutermann.
      p. cm.
    ISBN 0-312-15669-3
    I. Title.
   PS3554.E887S95   1997
   813'.54--dc21   97-5772
                                   CIP

First Edition: August 1997

10 9 8 7 6 5 4 3 2 1

This book is dedicated to all the honest cops,
throughout the country,
who try their very best to keep us all safe.

ACKNOWLEDGMENTS

I wish to thank Lt. Bruce Guth and the members of the Fairfax County Homicide Section; Comdr. M. T. Hall of the Navy JAG Corps for organizational advice; the expert on optical weapons, who must remain nameless; Drs. Brooks and Parks for medical pathology reference; Suzanne Olmsted for Doberman lore; Nick Ellison for intense moral support; and George Witte for careful editing. The names and functions of some government entities have been altered deliberately, as have some police procedures and forensics parameters. Any errors and omissions are, of course, mine. Any resemblance of the characters described herein to actual persons, living or dead, is purely coincidental. Nothing in this book is meant to represent the policies or views of the U.S. Department of Defense. This is, for the most part, a work of fiction.

SWEEPERS

PROLOGUE

Marcus Galantz tilted his head back, pushed his nose above the surface of the water, and took a silent breath. He bumped the top of his head against the underside of the mangrove trunk and then realized the airspace was getting bigger here in the root cage. Ebb tide, finally. He discarded the breathing reed, breathing normally for the first time in two hours. He didn't bother to open his eyes, knowing that he would hear the boat long before he would ever be able to see it in the darkness of the river. He reached out to touch the mangrove roots, which felt like smooth, slippery bones extending from the tree above down into the alluvial muck of the riverbanks. There was only one drawback to a mangrove root cage with a space large enough to admit a human, but so far he'd been lucky.

He submerged again and listened. The Swift boats would go quiet and darken ship when they drifted back down the river for the pickup, their huge diesels silenced. But they always kept their radar on. Without the engine alternators, the radar drew power from its battery-operated motor generator, which emitted a high-pitched whine through the boat's aluminum hull, a sound that could be heard for some distance underwater. He listened. Still nothing. He surfaced silently, aware that there might be a VC patrol nearby, probing the banks for him. Nighttime in the Rung Sat belonged to Charlie, although there weren't as many as there had been two nights ago.

He shifted his feet in the muck, making sure he hadn't been sinking an ankle into a root tangle. A few noxious bubbles percolated up through the black water and broke soundlessly near his face. With his right hand, he made a fingertip inventory of the root cage, feeling for the gap that occurred where two roots diverged, about thigh-high in the cage. To get out, he must submerge, turn sideways, and push down through the gap. He would then swim out underwater, homing on the bearing of the motor generator's whine, until he reached the boat.

His hand encountered the opening. Right. There. Okay.

He settled back against the landward side of the cavity and concentrated on his breathing. At one point, he thought he detected soft footfalls above, faint vibrations stirring the mud banks, a rhythmic sense of pressure.

C'mon, boat.

With the two big Jimmies shut down, the only sounds in the cramped pilot-house where Tag Sherman sat came from the sweep motor grinding away inside the radar display unit. It was one of those bottom-of-the-well, pitch-black nights on the Long Tao. The surface of the river itself was indistinguishable from the motionless curtain of sodden night air and the black line of steaming vegetation on the near banks. Near banks, hell, Sherman thought. The Long Tao was only a hundred yards wide here just below the S-turn. The scale of the radar screen reproached him—he had it on the two-hundred-yard scale. Much too close to the bank. Ambush city.

He squirmed in the driver's chair of the sixty-foot-long gunboat, his khaki trousers sticking to the seat. He had to sit almost sideways to keep his head hunched over the hood that shielded the amber radar screen to his right. His left hand rested loosely on the engine start buttons. He could hear and feel the subtle movements of the rest of the Swift boat's crew through the thin aluminum superstructure. Above the pilothouse, just behind his head, he sensed Gunner's Mate Second Kelly shifting around in the cage of the twin 50 machine-gun mount, training the heavy black barrels in a gentle sweeping motion from side to side, the roller path of the cage so heavily greased that it made little sucking sounds when the guns moved. Back down behind him in the cabin, Radioman Second Ryker would be kneeling on the starboard-side bench seat, hunched over an M60 machine gun stuck through the little window, his headset wire stretching over to the HF radio set. Gunner Jarret, desperate for a cigarette, would have the port side covered with an M16 set on full auto, a backup magazine taped to the bottom of the service clip. Engineman First Keene would be on one of the bunks down in the tiny, stuffy cabin beneath the pilothouse. As the off-duty driver, Keene technically was supposed to be sleeping, but more likely he was fully awake, sweating in his combat gear and cradling his beloved captured Kalashnikov.

Back on the fantail, Boatswain Second Yanckley would be sitting on an upended mortar crate, pointing the Hotchkiss gun to starboard, a full-pack white-phosphorous round loaded in its 81-mm mortar tube and a prodigious chew stuck in the side of his mouth. Sherman grinned in the darkness. With the turretlike armor-plated jacket and a steel helmet big enough to accommodate both his sound-powered phones and his large, many-chinned, round head, the bosun would look like a big armor-plated toad back there on his ammo crate. But with that mortar, Yank was the Man: He could hit a palm tree at a thousand yards, as a few Victor Charlies had learned just before they went to see Baby Jesus in a cloud of superheated white phosphorus. Or maybe over here it was Baby Buddha.

Sherman took a deep breath and let it out quietly. The stinking wet air gave his lungs little satisfaction, and there was a persistent metallic taste on his tongue. He screwed his ears on even harder, trying to sift out any human sounds coming through the pilothouse doors on either side from the nearby reed beds and palmetto grass. With the engines shut down, they were unable to maneuver, and they had drifted in much closer to the shoreline than was wise. He could smell the banks of the river now that the ebb tide had begun in earnest, the muddy, earthy smell of an ancient swamp, threaded now with the stink of Agent Orange and the sewery effluvium coming down from Saigon, some twenty miles upstream.

Ordinarily, they would keep themselves precisely out in the middle of the river, but not tonight. They were drifting on purpose, fully darkened, all electronics running on the batteries, while they slipped downstream at the whim of the Mekong tidal currents. Their mission tonight was a SEAL pickup. Three nights ago, they had come roaring up the Long Tao through this same area, making lots of noise, lights on, the big 39 boat throwing up a powerful wake, which chased the monkeys off the banks and caused the smaller crocodiles to grunt in irritation and slither into the water. One mile above the S-turn, they had slowed to idle speed and then, when darkness fell, shut her down, going dark and quiet, to begin the slow drift back toward the insertion point at the top of the S-turn.

Tag could still conjure up an image of the SEAL sitting all the way at the back of the boat, perched on top of the mortar ammo locker in the familiar costume: an olive green floppy hat and T-shirt, khaki swim trunks, flip-flops, and a knife strapped to one ankle. No guns, radios, flippers, masks, or anything else. And no talk. And no face—just eyes. The man's facial features had been obscured by the floppy hat and heavy daubs of green and brown paint, but Tag remembered those eyes: bright, dark, intense eyes, looking right back at you. Tag and his crew had done six SEAL insertions in the Rung Sat over the past year, and he had never heard one of them speak more than about three words.

Sherman shifted his flak jacket and scratched his neck where some insect had just achieved a blood meal. He tried to remember if he'd taken his malaria pills. The interesting thing was how surprisingly normal these guys looked, as opposed to being huge, bandoliered macho monsters. Like this guy they were picking up tonight: He had been listed on the mission brief sheet as Hospital Corpsman First Class Galantz. He was not quite Sherman's size: five eight, maybe five nine, 150 or 160 pounds. Average-sized

American military guy, maybe a little more muscle than most, but other than that, altogether unremarkable—except for the way he sat back there, still as a statue, totally self-contained.

The insertion drill was always the same: After making a big, noisy deal of transiting through the intended drop zone, they'd shut everything down and drift back with the current under the cover of darkness. Sometime during the drift, they would feel the stern tip ever so slightly, indicating the SEAL had gone over the side. Sherman shuddered at the very thought of going into the black waters of the Long Tao, a venomous stew of toxic leeches, sea snakes, mangrove pythons, and, of course, the crocs. They must call these guys snake eaters for a reason.

Three, sometimes four nights later, they would execute the same maneuvers for the pickup. If the guy was a no-show, they would try once more the following night. After that, he was on his own. Or dead. Or, worse, much worse, a prisoner. The VC were afraid of the SEALs, and reportedly, they would skin one alive and take a month to do it if they ever captured one.

Sherman expanded the radar display scale out to a half a mile and scanned the glowing details painted on the radar screen, orienting himself on the bank features leading into the S-turn at the top of the screen. The whine of the motor generator dipped momentarily when he made the display adjustments. After eleven months, he knew the river pretty well, and he could tell where they were with one quick glance at the radar. There was no point in looking through the windows. As the driver, he had to sacrifice his night vision in favor of the Decca radar screen, like an airplane pilot flying on full instruments. He shifted the scale back to two hundred yards. The Decca was a beauty of a radar. At this scale, he could make out individual logs as they bumped along the undercut banks.

"Boss?" said Yank, speaking on the sound-powered intercom.

"Yeah?" Sherman pulled the mouthpiece up to his lips. He kept his eyes on the radar screen and wiped a curtain of sweat off his lower face to keep from shorting out the phones.

"Ain't we awfully close here? I can hear the freakin' frogs."

"Yeah, well, you wanta paddle? We do a drift ex, we go where the river takes us. Just let me know when our guy is back, and we'll *didi-mau* the hell out of here."

"I hear that," Ryker chipped in.

"Okay, knock it off, everybody," Sherman ordered. "Only targets make noise in the Rung Sat at night."

The circuit went quiet. Sherman knew everyone was tense, and the urge to talk was strong. But sounds carried on the river. The radar showed that they were only fifty, sixty feet away from the right bank. He flipped on the fathometer just to make sure. The orange water-depth marker flickered at thirty feet. About right. He shut off the fathometer and wiped off some more sweat. Another thirty, forty minutes and he'd call it off, which was the decision Yank undoubtedly had been trying to provoke with his question. But they had to give the snake eater a decent shot at getting back. There was no telling where he would come out of the weeds, or in what condition.

After a year of operations, and despite what the Saigon propaganda boys said, all the Swifties knew that the Rung Sat at night was Charlie's country. It was an area of dense mangrove swamp, encompassing the bulk of the jungle twenty miles on either side of the Long Tao and extending from Saigon to the sea. It was mostly water, littered with small hummocks of semi-dry land. By day, the American Army helos and the Navy's Swift boats owned the Long Tao and the surrounding bayou channels. By night, however, it was all up for grabs. Charlie came out of his spider holes and island tunnel complexes to move his endless ant columns of guerrilla logistics. Precious rice and dried fish went north to the cadres fighting up-country. Ammunition, weapons, wounded, and replacements moved south. All movement in the Mekong Delta at large meant boats—usually small sampans powered by ancient French outboards, which the VC piloted in the darkness through the twisting network of side streams and mud flats. It was the American gunboats' mission to prowl the rivers at night like big gray water spiders lurking out on the river, spiders with magic Decca eyes. Ordinarily, the Swift boats would skulk along the main channels, waiting with muffled engines until a sampan got itself smack out in the middle of the river. Then the gunboats would thunder to life and swoop down, searchlights stabbing out to transfix the small boat with its four or five occupants. The lights would be followed by the hellish roar of the twin 50s tearing men, supplies, and the boat to pieces, until the wreckage disappeared under the bows of the gunboat. Then, searchlights off, reverse course, and tear up the banks on either side with the 50s and the big mortar to keep any support troops' heads down. After a minute or so of suppression fire, slow down and retrieve some evidence of the kill—bits of boat, clothes, body parts, boxes of supplies bobbing in the water. Body parts were tough: This had been going on for long enough that the crocs now knew what all the noise meant. Body parts, you did with a boat hook, and there were times you relinquished the boat hook if a big-enough croc clamped onto it at a critical moment.

The crews of the Swift boat were not briefed on what the SEALs were doing out there in the Rung Sat, but everyone in the division had a pretty good idea. Word was that these guys would lay up in the trees for a day and a night, watching the bad guys, identifying the officers, and then slip into the VC hideouts at night to knife the officers. Sherman shuddered again. He could not imagine what kind of guy could do that. Yes, you can, he thought. Just remember those eyes.

• • •

Galantz submerged again, listening for the whine. And there it was—very faint, but definitely there. To the right, upstream of his tree. Now he had to wait until the whine drifted closer, because he'd be swimming underwater, and he didn't want to misjudge the distance and have to surface like some noisy fish out there within Charlie's AK-47 range. He pushed his face above the surface again, lots more room now, and began deep breathing. Then, just to be sure, he felt for the gap again, leaning down, his chin touching the surface of the water, reaching with his left hand for the top of the gap. There. Good. And then he felt something, a sensation of pressure from just outside the root cage, something moving in the water. In the split second of recognition, there came an excruciating clamp of pain on his left hand, pain so intense, he nearly blacked out with the effort to stifle his scream. And then the croc started tugging, trying to pull his meat prize out of the mangrove cage. Galantz pulled back, saw a white-hot flare of pain before his eyes, and got his head underwater just in time to release the scream, a horrible burbling sound that he hoped would be muffled under the water even as he set his legs and grabbed out at the slippery roots with his right hand for a purchase. But he knew what would happen next. The croc would start rolling to convert the clamping bite to a detached gobbet of meat. Letting go with his right hand, he surfaced for a final breath, bent down, face underwater, and grabbed the croc's muzzle. Hooking desperate fingers into the fold of skin behind the jaw, he set his legs and pulled back, straining hard, trying to get enough of the croc's head into the root cage so he could stand up, get another breath, and then force the croc's head up against the opening, pin it, and get to his knife.

The croc pulled back, and he thought his left hand was going with it, but then he managed to grab one of the croc's front legs and pull hard, leveraging the pull with his leg and thigh muscles, and this time he got the croc's head through the bars. His left hand was numb, dead, along with his forearm, maybe almost gone even, except the croc was still there. He was a dead man unless he got this croc off his hand. Keeping his left leg pinned against the cage, he used his right knee to jam the croc's head tighter into the upside-down Y-shaped top of the gap, fighting the instinctive urge to recoil when he felt the tip of the croc's head push into his groin. He was just able to snatch a breath before the croc started to thrash, never releasing the bite but trying now to get its head out of the mangrove. Galantz clamped even harder with his right knee while searching desperately for the knife strapped to his right ankle, his left leg a rigid, thrumming column of muscle and bone, his right leg cramping with the strain of keeping the croc's head jammed, but then he had the knife and was stabbing, stabbing hard into that relatively soft hide beneath and behind the croc's jaws, pushing with all his strength, feeling the steel tip bumping on bone and gristle, and feeling the croc's thrashing tail beginning to pound the water outside, making noise. Die, goddamn it. I can't stand noise; the VC will hear it. But then there came an enormous underwater roar and an almost overwhelming squeeze of pressure that made him forget the croc and his arm and his mortal struggle under the mangrove.

At that instant, Sherman felt the deck under his feet squeeze up toward his seat as if a great fist had punched up from the bottom of the river, jamming his knees against the console, and then his helmeted head was banging off the overhead and he was going ass over teakettle onto the deck as a huge red and roaring wall of water shot up just in front of the boat, accompanied by a bellowing blast out of the river.

"Mine!" he yelled. The boat was wallowing around like a drunken pig, no longer as light in the bow as she had been. Through the crash of the water plume on the bow, he heard the boom of the big mortar on the fantail and then night became blinding day as Yank's white phosphorous round went off right in front of them on the banks, close enough that he could feel the heat through the open door. The 81 was echoed by the stuttering blast of the after 50-cal as Yank went into action against the bank, joined almost immediately by the forward 50's.

Tag groped for the console, punching hard at the engine start buttons as he struggled to get upright. The welcome rumble of the engines was drowned out by the forward 50's getting seriously into it. The flash from the 50's revealed enough of the bank to determine the boat's position. The ebb tide had been building fast, and he could see mangrove roots that looked like half-submerged prison windows in the flash of the heavy machine guns. For a heart-stopping instant, he imagined he saw a white face in the water. Reflexively, he grabbed both engine control handles and pulled them all the way back, causing the boat to lurch astern as the 800 hp of General Motors finest dug in, extracting her from the lethal riverbank even as a second mine went off, but this time about thirty yards in front of them. Sherman saw the dull red glare underwater just before another thick column of water erupted, rising impossibly high. But the boat was going full astern now, and the bank had already receded into the darkness, visible only as the point from which the boat's 50-cal tracer rounds were ricocheting up into the night sky. After nearly a year on the rivers, his guys knew exactly what to do—lay down a withering fire on both banks long enough for him to get them all out of the kill zone.

After fifteen seconds of backing out into the river, he yelled a cease-fire over the phones. He reduced the backing bell and then shifted to ahead, spinning the steering wheel full over, turning downriver. The sudden silence was startling, and his eyes were stinging as he realized that the pilothouse was filled with gunsmoke. He kicked out to clear his feet from a couple of inches of hot powder casings that were rattling around on the deck and burning his ankles.

"Station check," he barked into the phones. His throat was so dry that his voice cracked, and he felt his heart pounding and his hands shaking. No matter how many times, it still scared the shit out of you.

"Fifty-one, no casualties," Kelly called from up above. "I think I got rounds in the chamber and I *know* I got a hot gun."

"Fifty-two, no casualties," the bosun's laconic voice announced. "Clear bore. I'm outta fifty and I'm reloading the eighty-one." Nothing, not even mines, phased Yank.

"Radio's okay," Ryker squeaked in his high-pitched voice. He laughed nervously. "But I think Jarret crapped his pants."

There was a moment of silence on the circuit as Sherman gathered his thoughts while he continued to turn the boat.

"Fifty-one, clear 'em through the muzzle," he ordered. "Radio, check on the snipe. He was down in the hole." No more radar, so he was flying blind out here. He flipped on the fathometer. He could keep her in the middle using the compass and the fathometer.

"Snipe's okay," Ryker called back immediately. "Says we got water coming in, though. He's linin' up the pumps. We bookin' outta here, boss, or what?"

Sherman thought for a moment. They had been very, very goddamn lucky. Two mines, and they still had the engines and the props. If the hull was holed, it was up forward, away from the engine compartment. His right knee and his head hurt like hell, and he suspected everybody had some minor injuries. But there had been no machine gunners waiting to shoot his aluminum-hulled boat to ribbons from spider holes in the banks. Or if there had been, the Swift boat's immediate response with the 50's had kept the bastards down. Two loud bangs overhead made him jump as he climbed sideways back into the twisted chair.

"Bores clear, Fifty-one. What about the snake eater?" This from Kelly as he jacked open the gun's chambers to make sure they were physically empty.

"Screw the snake eater," Ryker offered. "I think it was me shit his pants. That was too goddamn close." He was trying to keep it light, but Sherman could detect the fear in his young voice. His realized his own hands were still trembling.

"And Fifty-two here," said Yank. "The eighty-one has a willie peter, locked and loaded. Ready for bear. Tell Jarret to gimme some more fifty-cal."

"Okay, girls, let's get it together," Sherman snapped, trying to get some strength and authority back into his own voice. The boat was definitely settling by the nose. "We're gonna go down the river," he said. "See if we can get this bitch to that sandbar at checkpoint Kilo."

"What about the SEAL?" Kelly asked again. At that moment, the starboard diesel engine misfired and then started to run ragged. Sherman swore and punched the right-hand shutdown button, and the engine died with a grudging rattle. Shit, he thought. Bet we busted a fuel line. He energized both engine compartment bilge pumps to keep fuel from pooling and starting a fire. The port-side Jimmie kept humming.

"The SEAL's on his own for now," Sherman replied. "Right now, we've got our own probs. Yank, you stay at your gun. Watch behind us for shooters. Kelly, get inside and help the snipe with those pumps. Send Jarret back aft to open the engine compartment doors, tell me what we've got going back there. We need to get Baby here onto that sandbar before she sinks on us."

Sherman pushed the useless radar display unit out of the way and tried to think. They would drift away from the ambush area even without engines because of the ebb. The compass showed he was pointed east, which was roughly downriver. But it was still pitch-black, and he wanted to be out in the middle and not about to bump up against one of the banks.

What about the SEAL? Kelly had wanted to know. Obviously, the enemy had known they were out there. And known they were drifting. Which meant they probably knew there was a pickup going down. Which might mean the SEAL had been discovered, and perhaps made to tell them when the boat was coming back. Or maybe they just knew the pattern. Have to mention that in the debrief. He turned the wheel to take them across the river, watching the depth gauge as he did so. He snaked the boat back and forth across the river until he found the deepest part, then pointed her back east on the compass. From where they had started, they should run aground on the sandbar at the dogleg sometime in the next hour, by which time another boat should be coming in to assist. What about the SEAL? Well, the SEAL was probably dog meat by now. Sherman concentrated on the flickering red light of the fathometer and saving his boat. Too bad about the SEAL, but another boat would go back again tomorrow night and try again. That was the deal. You didn't just leave a guy out there in the weeds.

CHAPTER 1

Rear Adm. Thomas V. Carpenter, Judge Advocate General of the U.S. Navy, was perplexed as he stared up at his aide over his half-lens reading glasses.

"A cop? A Fairfax County homicide cop? Wants to see me?"

His aide nodded. "Yes, sir. He just showed up here, with an escort from the security office. Says he needs to talk to you. Won't say what about, Admiral."

Carpenter leaned back in his chair. "Well, hell's bells. Send him in. But first get Captain McCarty. I want—"

"The executive assistant is on his way, Admiral."

"Yeah. Okay. Good. Soon as he's here, bring 'em in."

The aide left the office. Frowning, Carpenter swiveled around in his chair to look out the windows. His office was a large square room, paneled and carpeted, with shelves of legal books lining two walls, a conference table with leather-trimmed armchairs, an ancient leather couch, and three upholstered chairs arranged to face his desk. Behind his desk, a steel flag stand displayed the American flag and his personal two-star flag denoting a rear admiral of the staff corps. Carpenter was one star short of having an office out on the prestigious E-ring.

There was a knock on the heavy mahogany door, and Capt. Dan McCarty, his Pentagon executive assistant, came through the door. McCarty, with twenty-nine years of service, was tall and thin, and he wore square horn-rimmed glasses that made him look bookish.

"A Fairfax County homicide detective, Admiral? You finally shoot one of those budgeteers?"

"That's a thought," Carpenter growled. "There's some who desperately need it. But to answer your question, I haven't the foggiest. Let's get him in here. I have to see the Secretary in thirty minutes."

The executive assistant opened the door and beckoned to the aide, who escorted the detective into the office. Carpenter was struck by how well dressed he was: expensive-looking three-piece suit, polished shoes, a flash of cuff links. Mid-thirties, and in good physical shape. His stereotype of the scruffy-looking, coffee-stained, potbellied, cigarette-smoking TV homicide detective took a serious hit. This guy looked like a real pro. The policeman introduced himself as Detective McNair of the Fairfax County Homicide Section, sat down on the couch, and took out his notebook.

"Admiral," McNair began. "You are the Judge Advocate General of the Navy, is that correct?"

"That's right. I'm the JAG. I work for the Secretary of the Navy. I run the Navy's legal corps, and provide military law counsel to the Navy."

"Yes, sir." McNair nodded. "I've come to see you at the recommendation of the Defense Investigative Service. We're working a situation, and frankly, we're not sure what to do with it. It involves a Navy admiral. Sort of, I mean."

Carpenter leaned forward. " 'Sort of,' Detective?"

McNair closed his notebook. "I guess I'm not being very clear. Last Friday night, a woman had a fatal accident in a town house out in Reston. At least it looks like an accident at this stage of our investigation. She apparently fell down a flight of stairs—from the main floor going down to the basement. She broke her neck in the fall. A neighbor found her Saturday morning. Her name was Elizabeth Walsh."

"Sorry to hear it. But you said 'apparently'?" Carpenter was still in the dark.

"Well, sir, she definitely broke her neck. What we're not to sure about is the genesis of the fall."

"So this is a possible homicide? Is that what you're saying?"

"Remote possibility, Admiral," McNair replied. "There's some, ah, disagreement in the Homicide Section as to what we really have here."

"Disagreement," Carpenter said, looking over at his executive assistant.

"And why, specifically, should the Navy care, Detective?" asked McCarty, getting right to it.

"Yes, sir. I was coming to that," McNair replied. "As I said, we're not sure that this is anything but an accident. But on the possibility that it was not an accident, one of the things we checked for was a possible motive. If she was killed, say, pushed down the stairs, and I'll admit that we have no direct evidence of that, but if she was, then we have to ask why?"

" 'Cui bono'?" McCarty said. "Who benefits from her death?"

"Yes, sir. Exactly. And someone does. Her lawyer told us there was an insurance policy—a big one. Two hundred fifty thousand, to be precise. The beneficiary was one—" He consulted his notebook. "One Rear Adm. W. T. Sherman. The Defense Department phone book says he's assigned here at the Pentagon, on the staff of the Chief of Naval Operations."

Carpenter drew a blank on the name. He looked over at his executive assistant again, his eyebrows raised in a silent question.

"He's fresh-caught, Admiral," McCarty explained. "Last year's selection list. He runs the Surface Warfare Requirements Division in OP-03. I think he's been on board for about a year as a flag officer. Before that, he was the executive assistant to the Chief of Naval Personnel."

"Oh, right," Carpenter said. "Got it. I remember him. Now, this insurance-policy business. This makes Admiral Sherman a suspect of some sort?"

"No, sir. There's no crime, at least not so far. Like I said, there is no *evidence* of a homicide. There are some, um, forensic ambiguities. Which is why I'm here talking to you instead of going directly to interview Admiral Sherman. Basically, I'm here to ask a favor. Would you arrange a meeting between Admiral Sherman and us? An entirely informal meeting?"

Carpenter was starting to get the picture. "You mean as opposed to a formal police interview? Something we could call a conversation, say? So that we don't have it getting out that the Fairfax County Police Department is interviewing a Navy admiral in connection with a possible homicide, when all you have are—what was it—'forensic ambiguities'?"

"Yes, sir." McNair nodded.

Carpenter sat back in his chair. "Let me speculate further," he said. "You went to your commonwealth attorney, told him you had a feeling about this case, and said you wanted to talk to Admiral Sherman. The CA told you to be very damn careful about pulling in a flag officer when you didn't have any sort of case. Said he didn't want any federal heat about harassment, or to listen to legions of federal lawyers raising hell because something got loose in the press."

"His very words, sir," McNair said admiringly.

Carpenter nodded. "Detective, we appreciate your discretion, and of course we'll be happy to cooperate. I'll speak to Admiral Sherman right away, and I'm sure we can work something out—as long as you can assure both of us when we meet that he is not suspected of any crimes. I will be present for this meeting, and I'll want the right to shut it off if I think it's going astray, all right?"

"Yes, sir," McNair said. "I have no problems with that."

"I'll have my aide get back to you this afternoon, Detective."

McCarty remained behind after the aide shut the door.

"I'm amazed," Carpenter said.

"That they would be so discreet?"

"Yes. I mean, admiral or no admiral, we're all citizens first. If there's been a homicide out there in civvy street, they'd have every right to go see him, or ask him to come down and see them."

"Well, he did say that they're not sure they even have a homicide."

"I guess I'm glad. Our friendly hometown newspaper would love a little morsel like this. Okay, Dan, call this guy Sherman and have him come up and see me this afternoon. And get me his bio."

"Would you like me to handle this one, Admiral? Or maybe the Deputy? Keep you at arm's length and all that?"

Carpenter thought about that for a moment. "We might do that eventually. But let me see his bio first, see if I know this guy Sherman."

At 5:30 that afternoon, Captain McCarty brought Carpenter a manila folder. "This is the bio on Admiral Sherman," he said. "The picture was taken when he was a captain, but he doesn't look much different."

"That'll change," Carpenter observed as he opened the file.

"He's waiting out front, Admiral. If you'll buzz me when you're ready . . ."

"Just give me a minute to look at this and then you can bring him in."

While McCarty waited, Carpenter looked at the photo for a minute before scanning the career biography. The photo was that of a very young-looking officer with the sharp eyes and the taut-skinned face of an athlete. The face was composed in an expression of watchful authority that bespoke command at sea. He wore five rows of awards and decorations, which indicated he had wartime service in Vietnam. The insignia worn over the ribbons indicated a surface-warfare specialist.

He scanned the bio page. Naval Academy, class of '66. First ship was a destroyer in San Diego. Then a year and a bit in the gunboat Navy, down in the Mekong Delta. Fun times, that must have been. Then department-head school in Newport, a second tour in another destroyer in San Diego. Then graduate school up at Monterey. Exec in yet another destroyer, then off to the Bureau of Naval Personnel in Washington. "Ah," he said out loud. "The Bureau. He was a detailer." Both of them knew that being a personnel assignment officer was one of the surer routes to the flag-selection board-room. After seeing the Bureau of Naval Personnel item, Carpenter barely scanned the rest of Sherman's record.

"Okay," he said. "Professionally good enough to get that first job as a detailer, and politically good enough to get another one. I wonder who his patron saint was."

"He was executive assistant to Adm. Galen Schmidt," McCarty said. "Just before Admiral Schmidt's ticker trouble forced him to retire."

Carpenter nodded. "Schmidt would have made a great CNO," he said. "And young Sherman would not be coming to see me if Schmidt were the CNO today. Okay, he's something of a pretty boy, and I distrust pretty boys. Jealousy, I suppose. Bring him in, please."

McCarty smiled and left the room, returning a few seconds later with the officer in the picture.

"Sorry about the delay, Admiral," Carpenter said in a formal tone. "The Deputy SecNav called precisely at seventeen-thirty." It was a small lie, but he expected Sherman to be adept enough to swallow it.

"No problem, Admiral," Sherman replied.

"Thank you, Dan," Carpenter said to his executive assistant, who nodded and left the room. "Admiral Sherman, it's a pleasure to see you again, especially as a flag officer. Congratulations." Carpenter smiled as he said it, but he watched to see if the younger officer understood that the JAG was reminding him who was the senior officer in the room.

"Thank you, sir," Sherman replied. "Even after a year, I'm still getting used to it."

"I'll bet you are. Please sit down."

When Sherman had taken one of the chairs in front of the desk, Carpenter walked him through the morning's visit from the police.

"I'm sure Dan told you that this concerns the Fairfax County Police. I had a visit today from a homicide detective. They are investigating an apparent accident that involved a woman having a fall in her town house in Reston."

"In Reston?" Sherman asked quickly. Carpenter saw a look of alarm cross Sherman's face. He leaned forward before Sherman could say anything.

"The woman died of her injuries. An Elizabeth Walsh." He stopped when he saw the alarm in Sherman's face change to shock. "You didn't know about this? Was she someone close?"

The color was draining out of Sherman's face. He appeared to struggle for words.

"I—yes. I didn't know anything had happened," he stammered. "I—we—we used to date. I've known her for three years or so. When did this happen?"

Admiral Carpenter suddenly felt as if he had been caught off base. Automatically, he looked around for his executive assistant, then shook his head. "This apparently happened three days ago. Friday night. The homicide cop showed up here this morning. They're investigating her death. I guess because she died by misadventure—you know, as opposed to dying in a hospital with a doctor present. I think the cops are called anytime there's an unexplained death."

"But what—"

Carpenter felt genuinely embarrassed now. He should have thought of this—that no one had told this guy. McCarty should have checked. "He said that there was no direct evidence of foul play. But they pulled the usual strings, and they found out that she had a life-insurance policy, a pretty big one. And apparently you're the beneficiary."

"Me? Life insurance? Elizabeth?" Sherman was shaking his head. "So I'm a suspect of some kind? In a murder case?"

"No, no, no," Carpenter said, waving his hand. "That's why they came to see me first. There is no murder case. There's apparently no evidence of foul play. I think they just want to talk to you." Sherman was obviously in a state of emotional shock. "Look, you want a glass of water or something? Coffee? A drink maybe?"

Sherman was still shaking his head, his eyes unfocused. "No thank you, sir. I saw her—what, three weeks ago. I can't believe this."

"Yes. Damn. I am very sorry. I just assumed . . . well, I don't know what I was thinking. But back to the cops. You know how they are—they go with what they've got. They have to investigate. You're apparently the only human tied in some fashion, however indirect, to her death, so they want to talk to you."

"But what—"

Carpenter interrupted him again. "It's not what you're thinking. I think they're just running down their standard-procedure checklist. And the guy who came to see me said they disagreed among themselves if it even *was* a homicide."

Sherman got up, then sat down again, his hands flailing a little bit, as if he still couldn't grasp it. "Elizabeth and I dated for nearly three years," he said. "I'm divorced, you know. Well, hell, of course you don't know."

Carpenter nodded encouragingly. He felt like a clod for just dropping the bomb on this poor guy.

"But we saw each other in a pretty meaningful way until about six months ago. We—she—finally realized that our relationship wasn't going where she wanted it to go. She's a bright, attractive woman. She wanted to get married."

"Ah. And you did not, I take it."

"Right, sir. First time around cured me of that. And that's something I had told her from the very start. Anyway, we agreed to part company. Only fair thing to do, the way I saw it. But we missed each other. From time to time, we got together. We did well together. But the long-term relationship essentially was over. Now we're just good friends, as they say. And I knew nothing about any insurance policy."

Carpenter waited.

"I mean, I guess we *were* just good friends. Hell, this is terrible." He put his hands up to his face and rubbed his cheeks.

Carpenter got up and went over to the window, giving Sherman a minute to compose himself. Then he came back and sat down.

"What he wanted to do is to meet with you," he said. "Informally. I told him I would arrange it, but only if I could be present. I also told him I would shut the meeting off if it started to look like anything but a friendly chat. I recommend you agree to this, and that we do it soon, like tomorrow. You understand that they don't have to do it this way, right? They could just call you downtown or wherever the cops are headquartered in Fairfax County. But I think they're actually trying to be discreet. Since you're a flag officer, that is."

Sherman nodded, although it was obvious that his thoughts were spiraling elsewhere.

"So why don't I have my office coordinate with your office on the calendars, and then we'll get this over and done with, okay?"

"Yes, of course," Sherman said. "And I appreciate your intervention, Admiral."

Carpenter nodded and stood up. Sherman remained seated until he realized the meeting was over. He stood up as well.

"I'm sorry for your loss, Admiral," Carpenter said. "And I apologize for just dropping a bomb like that."

Sherman nodded but said nothing as he left.

Carpenter scanned Sherman's bio again while he waited for Sherman to get clear of his outer office. Something about the Vietnam assignment had ticked his memory, but he could not quite put his finger on it. He buzzed for McCarty, who came in with his ever-present notebook at the ready.

"Dan, get back to that cop and set up a meeting for tomorrow. Coordinate with Sherman's office. Plan for thirty minutes maximum. He and the woman were close, by the way. He didn't know anything about this. Took the wind right out of his sails."

"He knew her and didn't know the woman had died? Damn. I guess I should have checked."

Carpenter was silent just long enough to let his EA know that he agreed with that observation. "Yeah, well, those things happen," he said finally. "He agreed right away to talk to the cops. Didn't seem to care about them, or the insurance business. More upset at what had happened to the woman. Said he was divorced and that they'd been dating for a couple of years and then broke it off, friendly like." Carpenter stood and gathered up his cap and briefcase.

"Let me get my hat and I'll walk down the hall with you," McCarty said. "I assume you're going to handle this one personally?"

That mental twitch about the bio bothered Carpenter. "Yes, I think so. For now, anyway."

"Yes, sir. Have you briefed the CNO on this issue?"

They walked through the outer office and into the corridor before Carpenter, not wanting to talk about this in front of the staff yeomen, replied. "No. Not yet. I want to see how this meeting develops. If it's a firefly, the CNO doesn't need to be bothered. If there's something to it, we'll need more facts before I approach the throne. Which reminds me. I'd like to have one of our staff attorneys present. Just in case that cop wasn't telling the whole truth about the purpose of this little séance. Like if it turns out

Sherman needs a lawyer. I'd like to have someone there who can be in on it from the git-go."

McCarty had his notebook out again. "Somebody who could defend him? Or someone who will hold his hand and keep us in the loop at the same time?"

Carpenter smiled the way he did when his aides read his thoughts with such facility. "The latter," he said. "And somebody who is perhaps under-employed at the moment."

McCarty smiled. "Oh-ho. A certain lady commander perhaps," he said as they went down the stairs to the second floor.

"As always, you're way ahead of me, Dan," Carpenter said, laughing now. Even the normally taciturn McCarty managed a brief smile before he remembered something else. "Oh, Admiral, one last scheduling matter for tomorrow. Warren Beasely's relief has reported—from NIS."

Carpenter stopped as they reached the second-floor landing leading into the A-ring. "This the guy we heard about? Von something?"

"Yes, sir. A civilian named von Rensel. Wait till you see this guy. He's huge."

"He's not a fat guy, is he?"

"No, sir. Just big. Not tall, either. But really big. He scared Chief O'Brien when he showed up this morning. Didn't say anything, just stood there at the chief's desk until she turned around. I thought O'Brien was gonna faint."

"Beasely was such a damn wimp," Carpenter said. "This guy look like a player?"

"Yes, sir, I'd definitely say so. And in all fairness, Beasely was not a well man."

"Yeah, I know, but the net result was that I couldn't use him the way I wanted to. Okay. Put this von Rensel on my calendar. And get the word to the lady commander, as you call her."

"Yes, sir, I'll put a call into IR this evening. I'm assuming you just want her there to observe the meeting?" McCarty asked. "Karen Lawrence is an investigations specialist, not an investigator." Carpenter gave his EA a sideways look, inspiring McCarty to backpedal a bit.

"I mean, I know she's very good at what she does," he added hastily. "But her specialty is reviewing other people's work, not doing investigations herself. Unless—"

"Unless I can get her interested in something long enough for her to pull her damn request for retirement papers," Carpenter said.

McCarty shook his head at that prospect. Comdr. Karen Lawrence was an expert lawyer who reviewed Navy field investigation reports to see if they had been conducted thoroughly, properly, and effectively. She was very, very good at it, having that rare ability to sense from the field reports when an investigation had missed something crucial, either because the field investigator was less than competent or because local command authorities were trying to hide something. The problem was that her husband, a wealthy Washington lobbyist, had died very unexpectedly of a heart attack about a year ago. Thereafter, she had simply lost interest in what had been shaping up as a brilliant career in the JAG Corps. Four months ago, she had put her papers in to take retirement on twenty. Admiral Carpenter wanted very much to change her mind about getting out, but he had had no luck at all in persuading her.

"I mean, I understand what she's probably going through," Carpenter said. "But as the JAG, I have to take the Navy's point of view, not hers. With all these sexual harassment cases and the even bigger problem of female integration, I need to keep any lady lawyer who's as sharp as she is."

"Yes, sir, I understand. I'm just not too optimistic this will do it. If there is a homicide investigation, she'd be out of her competence."

"Well," Carpenter said as they reached the Mall entrance, "maybe put the new NIS guy into it. If it's out of *his* competence, then send him back and tell them to try again."

CHAPTER 2

Comdr. Karen Lawrence arrived in her office at eight o'clock, thirty minutes later than everyone else. She had come in early to work out at the Pentagon Officers Athletic Club before work. Since Frank's death, she had felt the need to get out of the house early in the morning, and the 7:00 A.M. athletic-club session offered a good excuse, not to mention the advantage of lighter traffic. But most important, it got her through that emotionally treacherous morning hour when they used to prepare for work together. *Together* was a nonword these days, and having to live alone again was unexpectedly painful.

The Investigations Review Division of Navy JAG was on the D-ring of the fourth floor of the Pentagon. The office was typical of the Pentagon these days: An office suite designed to hold three officers in 1945 now held eight in a warren of modular furniture enclosed in crumbling ten-foot-high plastered walls. Each staff legal officer had approximately an eight-foot-square cubicle. The division boss, Captain Pennington, had a slightly larger cubicle in one corner, under the only window.

Karen said good morning to the staff yeoman and fixed a cup of coffee.

The yeoman waved a telephone message slip at her as she reached her cubicle. "Presence is requested, Commander," she called.

Karen walked back over to pick up the slip, then returned to her cubicle. She flopped down at her desk, patting a damp lock of her dark red hair back into place, and scanned the message: "See Captain McCarty when you come in." Great. No subject, no hint of what he wanted. She looked up as Captain Pennington stuck his head in.

"Good morning, Karen. I hear the EA wants to see you."

Word travels fast, she thought. "Yes, sir. Good morning. Any idea on what it's about?"

"Nope. It was on the office voice mail, six-thirty last night. I told them you hit the athletic club first thing in the morning, so you're not late or anything." He looked at his watch. "As long as you're up there in about the next five minutes."

"Appreciate that, Captain," she said. She hesitated. "I hope this isn't another shipping-over lecture."

"I don't think so, Karen," he said. "Although the offer is absolutely still open." They looked at each other for a moment, and then he raised his hands in mock surrender. "Okay, okay, I know. We've been down this road. Better go see the EA."

She smiled briefly at him to show that she wasn't angry. Pennington had been a peach of a boss for the past two years, and she knew he was sincere in wanting her to pull those retirement papers. But she had made up her mind. She would reach the magic twenty-year point in six more months. She had taken the emotional plunge a month after Frank died, then waited a little while longer to put her papers in. Nothing had happened in the interim to change her conviction that it was time to go. Her professional career drive had just evaporated after Frank's heart attack, especially considering the circumstances surrounding that event. She was determined not to be a hanger-on, just for the sake of keeping busy or for the chance to put another gold ring on her sleeve. In the Judge Advocate General Corps, reaching commander signified a successful career; making captain meant an unusually good career. She was ready to settle for success.

Notebook in hand, Karen headed for Admiral Carpenter's office up on the fifth floor. When she arrived, she found that she was not the only visitor to the front office. There was a civilian who looked like a cop sitting on the couch. Another civilian, a very large man, was standing by one of the windows, his back to the room. A youngish-looking one-star rear admiral was sitting in the single armchair. He gave her a fleeting glance of appraisal when she came in but then went back to a folder he had been studying.

The presence of the two civilians puzzled her, unless they were Naval Investigative Service types. But they looked like real civilians, and they were too well dressed to be NIS. The big man was huge, tree-trunk huge. She wondered if he was Warren Beasely's relief from the Naval Investigative Service. She had heard some scuttlebutt that they were sending over a real character. The other guy looked like a cop. She walked across the front office and knocked on the EA's open door.

"Come in, Karen," McCarty said, indicating with his hand that she should close the door behind her.

"Good morning, sir," she replied.

"Right, it probably is. You see that one-star out there?"

"Yes, sir."

"That's Rear Adm. W. T. Sherman. OP-32: director of the Surface Warfare Requirements Division down in OP-03. Last year's flag-selection list.

The civilian on the couch is a Fairfax County detective. Homicide cop, no less." He watched for her reaction.

"Homicide cop?" she said, pleased with herself for picking him out as a policeman. "Somebody shoot somebody?"

"Not quite," McCarty said. "At least we don't think so. But that guy came in to see the JAG yesterday. He asked for a sit-down with this Admiral Sherman. The JAG wants you in there as the duty fly on the wall. I won't say any more, so as not to influence what you see and hear. You'll be introduced as a headquarters staff attorney, okay?"

This was vintage Carpenter, she thought, nodding. Whenever something out of the ordinary popped up, the JAG would bring in a neutral observer from the staff. When the meeting was over, the staffer, who was never told what the meeting was supposed to be about, would be asked for his or her take on things. "Got it, Captain," she replied with a smile. "And who's the Mack truck out there?"

"That's *the* Mr. von Rensel from the NIS. Wolfgang Guderian von Rensel, to be precise. Warren Beasley's relief, at long last. I can't wait to hear the admiral's reaction to him."

" 'Wolfgang von Rensel' ? Now, there's a good Irish name."

"Yeah, right. Somebody told me his nickname is Train. He's been in the building before. Naval Intelligence, I think. Anyway, you may get to find out if this meeting develops into something. The admiral apparently told him to hang around for this meeting."

"Ah," she said. Vintage Carpenter again.

"Exactly," McCarty said.

A lighted button on his multiline phone had just gone off. He stood up. "Okay, let's rock and roll," he said, picking up the phone and hitting the intercom button for Admiral Carpenter's desk. "We're ready, Admiral," he said. He listened for a few seconds. "Yes, sir, she's here. And Admiral Sherman. Right."

He hung up the phone and they went back out into the front office reception area. Admiral Carpenter's aide came out of the inner office and asked them all to come in. Admiral Sherman went first, followed by the policeman and the EA. Karen saw that von Rensel had turned around from the window. His great size not withstanding, he was an unusual-looking man. He had a high forehead with receding, very close-cut black hair. His alert brown eyes were faintly Oriental in shape, and a large Roman nose presided forcefully over thin lips and a prominent chin. He looked directly into her eyes and smiled, until she realized with something of a start that he was waiting for her to precede him into the room. She recovered and nodded a silent hello before walking ahead of him into the admiral's office. Out of the corner of her eye, she thought she detected an amused expression on his face.

Admiral Carpenter was standing at the head of the conference table. "Morning, everybody," he said, and made the introductions.

Carpenter began by recapping the problem. "Admiral Sherman, this matter concerns an accidental death, as we've previously discussed. Detective McNair would like you to help him with his inquiries."

"How can I help you, Detective?" Sherman said. He was not smiling, and he focused intensely on the detective.

McNair cleared his throat before beginning. "Admiral Sherman, this concerns a Ms. Elizabeth Walsh. I assume the admiral here has told you what happened?"

Karen saw Sherman's face tighten. "Yes. He said that she had an accident of some kind in her house and died from her injuries. Is that correct?"

"Yes, sir. That's what it looks like to us right now. We understand that you, uh, knew Ms. Walsh?"

"Yes." He looked down at the table for a moment before continuing. "Ms. Walsh and I were friends for three years. She and I were . . . dating. Until about six months ago."

"And may we ask, sir, why you stopped dating?"

Sherman hesitated, and Carpenter stepped into the conversation.

"Detective, I think we need to know where everybody stands before Admiral Sherman answers that. Could you please explain where you are in your investigation and what Admiral Sherman's status is?"

McNair opened his notebook. "Last Saturday morning, the police were called in when Ms. Walsh's neighbor, a Mrs. Klein, reported that she had found Ms. Walsh lying at the bottom of the stairs going down into her town house basement level. It appeared to Mrs. Klein that Ms. Walsh had fallen down the stairs, and that she was deceased. Mrs. Klein was very upset."

Karen watched Sherman as he listened to the detective recite the grim facts. She realized from his expression that the relationship between Elizabeth Walsh and Sherman had gone well beyond dating. Von Rensel was also studying Sherman's face.

"The Homicide Section was called in as a matter of routine," McNair continued. "As you probably know, we are required by law to investigate any unexplained death. We arrived at the scene within an hour of Mrs. Klein's call. Mrs. Klein had a key, and she had let the EMTs in. There was no sign of violence in the house, no sign of forced entry, or that anyone else had been in there other than Ms. Walsh and Mrs. Klein, who stated that she had not seen anything missing or out of order. The medical examiner's preliminary judgment as to the cause of death was a fractured cervical vertebra—a broken neck. Time of death was probably early Friday evening."

"And she just fell down the stairs?" Sherman asked. McNair gave him an appraising stare, which made her wonder if this was more than just a friendly little chat after all. She realized at that moment that the detective had not answered Carpenter's other question about Sherman's status.

"Well, sir," McNair replied, "there was one of those plastic laundry baskets at the bottom of the stairs. It looks like she was carrying it downstairs and maybe tripped. Hard to tell, really."

"Laundry?" Sherman said, frowning.

"It was clean laundry," McNair said. "You are familiar with the layout of the town house." It was a statement, not a question.

"Yes, I am," Sherman replied, staring back almost belligerently.

"Could you tell us where you were on Friday evening, Admiral Sherman?"

"Detective," Carpenter interrupted. "An answer to my original question, if you please. Is Admiral Sherman a suspect in a homicide investigation?"

"No, sir," McNair answered immediately. "This isn't really a homicide investigation. If it becomes one, we'll of course have to start over. We can do the Miranda bit if you'd like, Admiral." Sherman started to shake his head, but then he looked to Carpenter for guidance. Carpenter nodded, indicating to Sherman that he should go ahead and answer their questions.

"Friday." Sherman thought for a moment. "Friday, we were preparing for internal Navy budget hearings. I was here—I mean here in the Pentagon—until, oh, I'd say twenty-thirty. Sorry. That's eight-thirty. Then I drove home. I live in McLean."

" 'We,' meaning you and members of your staff?"

"Yes. My deputy, Captain Gonzales, and two OP-32 branch heads—Captains Covington and Small."

"And home is at nineteen Cheshire Street, the Herrington Mews complex, is that right, sir? Off Old Dominion?" McNair was letting him know that he had done some checking.

"Yes, that's right. The traffic was pretty much done by then; it takes about forty minutes from the Pentagon to my house."

"So you were home by nine-fifteen, nine-thirty?"

"Yes, somewhere in there. Then I changed clothes and went up to Pucinella's. That's a restaurant about a ten-minute walk from my house. I had dinner there and went home, where I remained for the rest of the night."

"Did you pay with a credit card, by any chance?"

Sherman paused. "I think I used cash. Oh, I see—if I'd used a card, you could verify that I was there, and at what time. Sorry. But I'm a regular there. They'd probably remember. Now, my turn. Why do you ask?"

McNair frowned but then said, "Sir, as I told Admiral Carpenter yesterday, we have no probable cause to suspect foul play here, although there are some minor forensic ambiguities. It's just that the only lead to other persons we turned up in our preliminary work was that Ms. Walsh had a life-insurance policy naming you as beneficiary. Did you know about that policy, sir?"

Sherman shook his head. "Not until Admiral Carpenter told me about it yesterday. Elizabeth and I didn't talk much about personal business affairs. No, the insurance policy is news to me."

The detective looked straight at him. "The death benefit is two hundred and fifty thousand dollars, Admiral."

Revelation of the actual amount cast a hush over the room. Sherman's eyebrows went up, but then he said, "I'd trade it back for Elizabeth."

Good answer, Karen thought. And yet, despite his quick reply, even Sherman appeared to be surprised by the sum of a quarter of a million dollars. "I knew nothing about this," he said. "I wonder—"

"Yes, sir?" McNair had his notebook open and pen poised.

"Detective, Elizabeth Walsh and I had an intimate personal relationship for a little under three years. That relationship ended on my initiative— when it became evident to me that she wanted to get married." He stared down at the table for a moment. "For reasons I won't go into, I was not prepared to remarry, so I began to put the brakes on. I'd been married before. It turned out badly. I had told her from the start that I did not want to remarry—ever. Elizabeth is—*was*, I guess is the appropriate word now— a lovely woman. She would have made a very fine wife for someone." He paused again for a moment, his lips pressed together, while he looked down at the table. Then he continued.

"We parted amicably, and we even saw each other socially from time to time. I think both of us kind of hated just to let go. I was about to speculate that maybe she'd had this policy from her previous marriage, then changed the beneficiary while we still had prospects, and simply forgot to do something about it. I don't know. I can't offer any other explanation."

"Yes, sir," McNair said. "To your knowledge, was she seeing anyone else after the two of you broke up?"

"Not to my knowledge, but then, I wouldn't necessarily know. I didn't ask. Besides, I'd just been promoted, and the pace of my work here has increased considerably."

"And when did you last see Ms. Walsh, sir?"

"About three weeks ago. We went to a benefit dinner for the Wolftrap Farms concert center. But other than that, I don't know anything about her current social life. Mrs. Klein would probably know more about that."

"And your own personal and social life, sir?"

"I took my OpNav division in the middle of the budgeting cycle. I don't have a personal social life at the moment."

Karen saw a wry look pass over Admiral Carpenter's face at this answer.

McNair studied his notebook, as if searching for more questions. Carpenter finally spoke. "Detective, have we covered the ground here?"

McNair nodded. "Yes, sir, Admiral, I think we have. Again, I appreciate your cooperation, Admiral Carpenter, Admiral Sherman. If we have anything else, we'll be in touch. But right now, I think I've got what I need."

"Well, then, everyone," Carpenter said, standing up. "We're adjourned. Lieutenant Benning will escort you back to the South Parking entrance. Admiral Sherman, I appreciate your assistance this morning."

Everyone stood. Karen did not know whether she and von Rensel should leave or not, but Carpenter gave them a sign indicating they should stay. Sherman remained standing by the conference table as Carpenter walked over to his desk.

"Sounds to me like that's all back in its box," Carpenter said. "Commander Lawrence, any observations?"

Karen consulted her own notebook for a moment, aware that Sherman was looking at her. "Nothing of significance, Admiral," she said finally. "Except that I'm not convinced that they're finished with this."

Carpenter paused in the act of slipping his jacket over the back of his chair. "You think it's not over, Karen?"

"Her death is ambiguous, Admiral," she said. "On the other hand, if they had some clear evidence of a homicide, we wouldn't have been meeting here in this office."

Carpenter nodded thoughtfully, then glanced over at von Rensel. "Comments?" he asked. But von Rensel just shook his head. Carpenter turned back to Sherman.

"You okay with this?" he asked. "What do they call you, anyway? Bill?"

"Actually, Admiral, it's Tag. Short for my middle name, Taggart. I used it at the Academy to make sure all the Southern upperclassmen knew it wasn't William *Tecumseh* Sherman."

Carpenter smiled briefly. "Damn straight," he said. But then his face sobered. "Look, I know this has been unpleasant, if not a shock. A lady friend dead. A homicide cop nosing around before you've even had a chance to absorb the news. I'd recommend you attend to your personal affairs and let us handle this. In that regard, I'll ask Commander Lawrence here to pull the string in a few days, make sure there aren't any loose ends. If nothing else, that will put them on notice that Navy JAG is between you and them. That okay with you? Or do you have a personal attorney you'd rather consult?"

"No, sir, I don't. Not for something like this. I'd appreciate any help I can get. I do have one question."

"Yes?"

"Has the CNO been informed of this matter?"

Carpenter shook his head emphatically. "No, no. I didn't feel that was appropriate at all. He would just have asked me for the facts on the case, and of course we have no facts, to speak of anyway. Once we're sure it's all cleared up, I think the less said the better, don't you?"

"Yes, sir. I appreciate your discretion."

"Very well, Tag," the admiral said, pointedly eyeing his in-basket. "Thanks again for helping out with this."

Sherman nodded and left. Karen gathered up her notebook.

"Just a moment, please," the admiral murmured after the door closed. He took a red pen to something in the folder, drew several lines on the paper, and then tossed it into his out basket before looking up.

"Mr. von Rensel, given a two-hundred-fifty-thousand-dollar prize, and acknowledging that you're coming out of the gate cold, what's your take on this?" he asked.

"I believe the cops think it *is* a homicide," von Rensel replied. Karen was surprised at the clarity and precision of his diction, which hinted at a level of education beyond that of most of the NIS people she had met. "Before this meeting, McNair wasn't sure about how to approach Sherman. Now he'll check his alibi. If it holds up, then they'll have to regroup. That insurance money is a natural pointer."

Carpenter nodded thoughtfully. "And Karen, what's your take on Admiral Sherman?"

Karen was expecting to be asked to comment on what von Rensel had just said. Carpenter's question had surprised her: Admirals did not normally ask commanders for their opinions about other admirals.

"Based on first impressions," she replied, "I don't think Admiral Sherman killed his girlfriend. Assuming she was killed at all, that is." She glanced over at von Rensel. "I think he was sincere about trading in the money if he could get her back."

Carpenter stared at her for a moment. "Two hundred and fifty thousand tax-free dollars. But, yeah, I think you're right. Okay. Karen, I want you to run a very quiet probe for me. I want to know what else the cops found in the house that's making them itchy, and I want to know something about William Taggart Sherman. See, contrary to what I told the young admiral, I *did* tell the CNO about this. The CNO has one cardinal rule about possible scandals: He doesn't like surprises. Really doesn't like surprises. So, yes, I let the CNO know. He told me to forget about it."

"Forget about it?" Karen was surprised.

"Yes. Forget about it. As long as I could assure myself that there was ab-so-lute-ly nothing to it."

"In other words," von Rensel said, "check it out."

Carpenter grinned. "Exactly. Although, of course, he never did say that, did he? Now, Karen, I take it you're not exactly overwhelmed with work down there in the IR Division these days, right?"

Ah, here it comes, she thought. "As the admiral is aware, I've put my papers in," she replied sweetly.

"Right. So I am. Okay. I'll be asking Captain McCarty to have a word with your boss, Captain Pennington. But I want both of you to go check this thing out for me—low-key. Go see Sherman, tell him that you're going to snoop around to see what the cops are doing. Then go see the cops and tell them you're going to check out the dashing young admiral. Mr. von Rensel here can help you with any outside resources, such as the NIS or any other law-enforcement agencies if you need them."

"In other words, we play both sides against the middle," von Rensel said.

Carpenter gave him a speculative look. "You could say that."

"But we report only to you," Karen said.

"Exactly."

Karen had one more question. "So, I am not in any way representing Admiral Sherman?"

"Representing? Whatever gave you that idea, Commander? You work for only one admiral at a time in this business." And then, with a little wave, he dismissed them.

Karen took von Rensel to see Captain Pennington. Pennington was in his cubicle, but they had to wait for a few minutes until he got off the phone. She had expected a flurry of questions from von Rensel on the walk back to the IR offices, but he had said nothing at all. She was amused at how the flow of people in the corridor parted around him like skiers avoiding a tree.

"Goddamned people up in OSD," Pennington complained as he hung up the phone. "They want another meeting on the Tailhook report. Lord, I'm getting tired of that word. Okay, Karen, what did the great man want this time?"

Karen slipped into a chair and crossed her legs. Von Rensel remained standing, literally filling the doorway. "Something a little different," she said. "A private matter involving a flag officer on the OpNav staff. Admiral Carpenter wants me to do some off-line work."

"Ah. Another one of his little secret missions. Mr. von Rensel, you're probably used to this. By the way, mind if I use a first name?"

"It's Wolfgang von Rensel," the big man said. "In high school, they called me Train. It was a football nickname."

"Train," Pennington said, savoring the image with a grin. "Perfect. Train it is. Anyhow, this JAG plays a lot of things pretty close to his vest. Likes to work the back channels, set things up before he makes any significant moves, especially when it concerns flag officers. Your predecessor here was unfortunately not very adept at that kind of work."

"Having pancreatic cancer might have had something to do with that," von Rensel observed.

"Yes, indeed, and we're sorry that he passed away. But Warren Beasely was not the kind of guy this JAG had in mind for the liaison job. I'm told that you, on the other hand, are not unused to working off-line?"

Train smiled noncommittally. "I think Admiral Carpenter and I reached an understanding during my reporting-aboard call, Captain," he replied. "I hope to make myself useful. I was pleased to find that he seems to know exactly what he wants from people."

"Oh, yes, he certainly does that. You may not be aware that he's short-listed for a judgeship on the Court of Military Appeals. So he's being especially careful these days, which is probably why he's having Karen look into whatever this is all about."

"Oh, supposedly Captain McCarty will be in touch with you about all this," Karen said.

Pennington sat back. "Ah, the chain of command. Better late than never, I suppose. Okay. Mr. von Rensel, since you're replacing Beasely, you might as well take over his cube. The yeoman will set you up."

"Thank you, Captain," von Rensel said. He nodded at Karen and backed out of the captain's office, being careful not to knock any walls down. Karen remained behind.

"So," Pennington continued. "In the meantime, you will be acting on private instructions. As before."

"Yes, sir," Karen said. She had done one other investigatory assignment for Admiral Carpenter, involving an element of the Tailhook scandal. He had sent her after information on three individuals, but she had never learned how that information had been used or what, if anything, had happened to them, or why he wanted it in the first place. That also was vintage Carpenter.

"And no shipping-over lectures?" Pennington asked gently.

She smiled. "Not this time. Although I suspect he has some high hopes that this kind of assignment might change my mind about leaving."

"I can't imagine the admiral being so devious," Pennington said with a straight face, and then they both laughed.

"I'm not going away mad, Captain," she reminded him. "I'm just going away. The Navy's been terrific. Oh, okay, not always terrific, but certainly far more interesting than doing corporate law or political flack work here in D.C. It's just that with Frank gone, the fun's gone out of it. I'm forty-four years old, no kids, no family to speak of. Going on with the career just seemed . . . pointless."

Pennington nodded sympathetically. "The only observation I can offer is that your Navy work could at least fill the void for a while." He paused to let her consider that, but she said nothing. "Okay. Get on with whatever he's got you doing this time. And I'll pretend to be appropriately surprised when McCarty calls down."

She gave him her best smile. "Thanks, Captain."

She checked her voice mail when she got back to her cubicle, but there were no messages. Frank had often called her during the day, usually leaving a mildly obscene message or a two-line joke on her voice mail. And yet, try as she might, she could not quite sustain a perfect halo of love and remembrance around her late husband because of that nagging detail that nobody wanted to talk about: why Frank had been at that hotel in the first place. The question that would not go away. And the roaring silence that followed whenever she asked the question, along with the inescapable conclusion that perhaps her whole marriage to that congenial, successful, and ostensibly loving man had been a sham.

She sighed and placed a call to Sherman's office. She was put on hold. Then there was a click. "Admiral Sherman."

"Admiral, thank you for taking a moment. I wanted to let you know that I'll be calling the Fairfax County Police this afternoon to see what I can find out about their investigation. Basically, my tasking is to find out if they are going to continue with it or declare victory and go home."

"That sounds reasonable, Commander," he said. "It wasn't exactly clear after the meeting what they were going to do."

"No, sir, it wasn't. Anyway, I'm going to be in contact with them, low-level sort of thing. They may choose, of course, not to give me the time of day."

"That would tell you something, wouldn't it?" He was silent for a moment. "Look," he said. "I'm going over to her house this evening." There was another short silence on the line. "To Elizabeth's house," he continued. "Elizabeth Walsh. I've got this need to see where it happened—her accident. I don't know if that makes any sense—"

"Yes, actually, I do understand, Admiral," she interrupted. "Frank, my husband, had a heart attack in a hotel lobby." She heard a sharp intake of breath, although Sherman said nothing. "I got to him in the hospital, but he never . . . surfaced, as they put it. A week later, I found myself standing in that hotel lobby. There was nothing to see, of course, but I felt that need just to, well, go there."

"Yes, exactly. I can't explain it, either," he said. There was a thread of relief in his voice. "Elizabeth and I weren't married, of course, but we were pretty close. I'm having trouble with this notion that she just fell down the stairs. Anyway, if you're going to try to get some info on what happened, you might want to see the, uh, scene, as it were."

She tried to think if there was any reason *not* to go there. Then she agreed.

"Okay," he said. He gave her the address. "That's in Reston. Do you live in northern Virginia?"

"Yes, sir. Great Falls."

"Oh. Okay. I live in McLean." He gave her directions, then told her he still had a key.

That was interesting, she thought. She wondered if the police knew that. "I can find it," she said. "What time will you be there?"

"I'm supposed to be at Mrs. Klein's house—she's next door, on the left, as you face it—at seven this evening. Let me give you her phone number."

She copied it down. "Will Mrs. Klein be going into the house with you, Admiral?" she asked.

"She might, although I haven't asked her. But I thought that would be a good idea. Or maybe you can. I don't know. But I'm just thinking I shouldn't be in there by myself just now."

"Yes, sir, that probably wouldn't be a good idea."

There was another moment of silence. "Right. Okay, I'll see you there. I'll be in civvies, by the way."

"Yes, sir. I'll see you there."

She hung up, wondering if she should tell von Rensel about this. She looked out of her cubicle, but he wasn't in sight. She asked the yeoman where Mr. von Rensel had gone.

"Anywhere he wants," the yeoman said with a grin. "Actually, into the check-in pipe, Commander. Building pass, parking pass, OpNav security briefing, then Crystal City for the other stuff. Probably be back tomorrow— if he's lucky."

Okay, so much for that, she thought, wheeling her chair back into her cubicle. We'll just have to go meet the admiral on our own.

Train von Rensel waited patiently in the line for parking passes down on the Pentagon concourse. After nearly twenty-five years in the federal and military bureaucracy, he was resigned to the all-day routine of checking into a new organization. As the line shuffled forward, he reviewed his first meeting with Admiral Carpenter. The old man had pulled no punches about his disappointment with Train's predecessor. Only the onset of a terminal disease had prevented Beasely from getting fired outright back to NIS. Train had been just as direct: NIS had sent Beasely in the first place because, at the time, NIS had been at war with OpNav, as the Navy's headquarters staff was known. Carpenter had then shared his perspectives on the new political situation.

"Your boss and I have made a deal. NIS and OpNav need to bury the hatchet somewhere besides between our respective shoulder blades. In effect, we've signed a peace treaty—shared computer network and database systems, much closer coordination between their investigations and our field attorneys. Your assignment is part of this. Your boss promised me a player. You'll work directly for me. You'll be stashed in Investigations Review, which is about as bland as we get here in JAG. Does that square with what you've been told?"

"Yes, sir. I've been detailed to be your freelancer, with complete access to the top people in NIS."

"And I see you've worked in Naval Intelligence, with a secondment to the FBI. So I can presume you know your way around town?"

"Reasonably well, Admiral. Always learning new and interesting things, though."

Carpenter had smiled at that response. Any Washington old hand who thought he had seen it all was, by definition, not yet an old hand. This business with the homicide cop was another matter. Commander Lawrence was right: That cop didn't really appear to want the admiral for the death of Elizabeth Walsh; otherwise, the meeting would have been in a much smaller room with much brighter lights. And yet they obviously felt that the Walsh woman had met with more than just an accident. And that homicide cop was interesting: not what Train would have expected from a county police force, even in the upscale northern Virginia area. He would have pegged McNair for an FBI guy, or maybe even Treasury.

He looked at his watch. This was Tuesday. Whole thing would probably blow over by the end of the week, which is when he might, if he was lucky, also be done with admin check-in. And he had thought NIS admin was bad.

Karen arrived early in Reston, having misjudged the traffic, and parked across the street to wait. The town houses were tastefully done, with sculpted front gardens and mature trees interspersed with faux gaslights. Sitting alone in the car, watching commuting husbands and wives driving by on their way home, she felt the familiar wave of depression approaching.

Karen had been born and raised in the Washington, D.C., area, moving around the city and its suburbs as her parents' careers prospered. Her mother had been a special-education teacher who worked in both the private and public school systems. Her father, now drifting peacefully in a Chevy Chase nursing home, had been an attorney with the Federal Power Commission for thirty years, which is how Karen had come to meet J. Franklin Lawrence.

Marriage to Frank had come much later in life than she had ever planned, after she had already spent ten years in the Navy's JAG corps. She had been thirty-four, Frank exactly ten years older. He had been divorced for three years when they met at a weekend barbecue at her parents' place in Chevy Chase. Frank had been interesting, funny, wealthy, and desperately lonely, although it had taken some time for him to reveal that. She had just been selected for lieutenant commander and assigned to the Navy headquarters staff at the Pentagon for the first time. She had met several really great guys in the Navy over the years, but by the time she met Frank, she was profoundly aware of what the typical Navy marriage entailed: months of separation, perpetual money problems, and increasingly intense career pressures. Frank the civilian had been a perfect fit. Her only real disappointment was not having had children, but they had both agreed from the outset that neither their careers nor their respective ages would be very suitable for child rearing. She had been old enough to keep her own counsel on this subject, and she had to admit that their well-to-do lifestyle had assuaged whatever sense of loss she had experienced along the way. Now that Frank was gone, she reluctantly acknowledged an almost guilty sense of relief that she was not facing the prospect of raising teenagers without a father.

She looked at her watch. It read 6:45. She felt somewhat conspicuous sitting alone in her car on a residential street at twilight, flanked by a row of town houses on either side.

She really missed the after-work routine, and she realized how much she had been just going through the motions over this past year. She looked over at the single dark town house, one in from the corner, and thought about Elizabeth Walsh, coming home of a Friday evening, settling into her own routine, resigned perhaps to living alone but probably missing the dashing, young Admiral Sherman, and then falling down the damn stairs and breaking her neck. What a way to end the week, she thought irreverently. Damn, I've been in Washington too long.

She wondered about the new guy from NIS, von Rensel. Bet he could run an effective interrogation, she mused. All he would have to do would be to stand up and stretch a couple of times and I'd sing like a bird. She checked her watch again. She wasn't quite sure if von Rensel was supposed to be her partner in this matter or just a backstop. She would have to find out how well he knew his way around town and the Pentagon. McCarty had mentioned something about his having worked in the Office of Naval Intelligence.

Von Rensel was completely different from Sherman, who was a tall, dark, and handsome type, if ever she had seen one—the picture of a Navy success story. Right. Here he was, in his first year as a flag officer and involved, however tangentially, in a Fairfax County homicide investigation. Congratulations on that fine promotion, Admiral, sir; may we have a few minutes of your time?

She looked at her watch again. Eight more minutes. He would probably drive up at the stroke of seven. She wondered again about Elizabeth Walsh, what she had looked like. And why there was not even a mention of a family in the admiral's biography. What had he said at the meeting with the police—that he had told her from the start that he did not want to get married? No, he had said "*re*marry." "I did not want to remarry, ever." So he had been married once. She wondered about all that vehemence. A flare of headlights in her mirror announced his arrival, and she got out of her car.

"Commander," he said formally.

"Admiral Sherman," she replied, nodding. She had almost saluted. He locked his car and they went across the street. As they approached the corner town house, its front door opened and a short elderly lady with bright white hair came out and down the stairs. She met Sherman at the sidewalk.

"Tag," she said emotionally. They embraced for a moment, then stepped apart so that Sherman could make introductions. Mrs. Klein looked over at Karen and nodded a greeting; then she looked back at Sherman with an unspoken question on her lips.

"Commander Lawrence is a Navy lawyer," he explained. "She is going to try to find out what the police have found out. I want to go into Elizabeth's house. I still have a key. When we're done, I'd like to come back and talk to you—unless you want to come with us?"

"No, Tag," Mrs. Klein said, shaking her head. "I don't want to go in there anymore. The police have been there. They just took down all that awful yellow tape this morning. This is just so terrible. I can't believe it happened. I miss her so much."

"I know, Dottie. I do, too. We won't be long. I just had to come see. I'm having a hard time accepting all this."

Mrs. Klein kept shaking her head from side to side. She fished a handkerchief out of her sleeve. "I just don't understand. Why her? She was so young. And such a good person. It doesn't make any sense. But you go ahead. I'll make us some coffee."

"Thanks, Dottie."

Mrs. Klein walked back up her front steps and went inside. Sherman produced the key to the adjacent town house and went up and unlocked the front door. The mailbox was stuffed with what looked like mostly junk mail, with more on the foyer floor, and he gathered it up before stepping inside. Karen followed him in. He turned on the light in the front hall. The air was slightly musty, with a faint hint of perfume.

Karen looked around while he turned on some more lights. Fairly standard town house layout: carpeted stairs on the left going up to the second floor. A hallway straight ahead, leading back to the kitchen, and a spacious living room to the right. She noticed that the living room was devoid of the clutter of everyday life, which meant that, like many city commuters who lived alone, Elizabeth Walsh had probably lived in her kitchen. She followed him back through the living room and dining room and into the kitchen, which had a breakfast nook overlooking a walled garden in back. He was walking around the kitchen, turning on every light. She had been right: The kitchen table was stacked with mail and magazines, a phone, and Day-Timer book; there was a small and very cluttered desk and a television.

"It even *feels* empty," he said, sweeping his eyes around the room. Karen felt like an interloper. "Yes, it does," she said. "I can wait in the living room, if you'd like, Admiral."

"No," he answered quickly. "No. I'm not sure why I'm doing this. I guess I don't really believe it yet." He looked at a door next to the refrigerator. "That goes downstairs."

Karen didn't know what to say to that. After a minute of looking around the kitchen again, he went over to the door, opened it, and flipped on the light.

"What's down there?" Karen asked, already pretty much knowing the answer.

"Finished basement: family room, fireplace, wet bar. Storage rooms, utility room."

"And the laundry?"

He turned to look at her with a peculiar expression on his face. "Well, no, not really. I mean, yes, there's a laundry room down there. But she didn't use it. Couldn't see the sense of hauling clothes up and down two flights of stairs, so she had one of those over/under washer-dryer units put in upstairs about a year after her divorce."

She frowned, remembering his reaction when the policeman had mentioned laundry. "So why was she carrying a laundry basket full of clothes?"

"Yes," he replied, frowning. "Why indeed."

He turned away and started down the stairs, with Karen following reluctantly behind him, unsure of what they would see down there. He flipped on a second light switch at the top of the stairwell, which turned on recessed overhead lights downstairs. He stopped halfway down when he saw the chalk outline of a human figure on the carpet below, just beyond the landing. No mistaking what that was, she thought as they resumed their way down the stairs. Karen noticed that the stairs were steep but fully carpeted, with handrails on either side. There was a long green scrape mark on the left side wall about halfway down, and a dent in the wallboard that had been circled in chalk.

The basement smelled faintly of chemicals, and she saw traces of what she assumed was fingerprint powder here and there around the room. While Karen waited on the next to the last step, the admiral stepped around the chalk outline at the bottom of the stairs. He appeared to be trying not to look at it. The outline did not appear to Karen to be large enough to contain a human. But she remembered how Frank had looked in the CCU, his sleek lobbyist figure shrunken into the metal bed, nested among all those ominous tubes and hoses, as if to make himself small for the dangerous journey that was coming. There was an empty green plastic laundry basket parked on one end of the couch. Next to the basket, there was a pile of clothes in a tagged clear plastic bag. A second, smaller plastic bag held a pair of slippers. Sherman walked over to the couch and examined the bags.

"This really doesn't make a lot of sense," he said finally.

"Are those her slippers?" Karen asked, pointing to the second bag.

Tag looked at the other bag, then looked harder. Then he swore.

"What?" Karen asked.

"She hated those slippers. She never wore those slippers."

"Are you sure?"

"Yes, damn it. I bought them for her. Christmas present, two years ago. They were too big, wrong style, wrong all the way around. Even the soles were too slippery for the carpet in this house. She made a joke out of it to protect my feelings, but it was one of things, before we really knew each other, just a dumb present. But the thing is, she never wore them. If they found her wearing those slippers, something's way out of whack with this picture."

Karen followed the admiral out of the house ten minutes later. She had decided to wait in her car while the admiral went in to talk to Mrs. Klein. She was disturbed by what he had said in the basement and was beginning to wonder about what was going on. He had shaken off his funk after finding the slippers and gone through the house like a man possessed, leaving her standing in hallways while he went through each room on all three floors, turning on every light in the house. He didn't say anything the whole time, but she could hear him muttering occasionally under his breath. He was obviously thinking what she was thinking, and what the detective was probably thinking: The "accident" might have been staged. Except the detective would certainly not know about the slippers. The admiral would have to tell them about that. So what had twitched their antennae? The fall itself? Those stairs were steep, although well lighted, carpeted, and with railings on both sides. One could certainly trip or stumble, even with an armful of laundry. But she should have been able to grab something on the way down.

Karen also wondered about the admiral's distracted look when he had arrived this evening. He looked far less confident and commanding than he had seemed in the conference room this morning. It was as if he had come here tonight preoccupied with something over and above the weight of this somber visit. But it probably was just the emotional stress of returning to the place where his lover—his ex-lover, she reminded herself—had died. She could relate: The hotel lobby where Frank had been stricken was not a place she would ever go again.

He came out of Mrs. Klein's town house after ten minutes, walked over to his car, and stood next to the driver's window, putting both hands on top of the car. She got out and walked back to his car. She waited while he gathered his thoughts.

"Now I don't know what to do," he said finally. "McNair apparently picked up on the bit about the laundry. And Dottie says she was wearing those slippers, or that they were down there at the foot of the stairs. I guess there's probably a logical explanation for all that, but I can't put it together. Do you suppose these are the forensic ambiguities McNair was talking about?"

Karen shook her head. "They couldn't know about the slippers. The laundry, maybe."

"Right. But laundry isn't really forensics. And my fingerprints will be all over that house."

"Which is perfectly logical, given your past association with Ms. Walsh."

"Yeah. But there must be something else."

She decided this would be a good a time to remind him. "Sir, as I told you, Admiral Carpenter has asked that I follow up on their investigation. Perhaps I can find out what the rest of those forensic ambiguities are."

"And tell them about the slippers?" he asked, looking sideways at her.

"Well, yes, sir, I think we should. Oh, you think they'll attach significance to the fact that you came here tonight?"

"They just might."

She shook her head. From her perspective, it was a perfectly normal thing for an ex-lover to do. "I disagree, sir," she said. "But I do think they ought to hear about the slippers from you, or from you via me. If they think this is a murder, they'll be back to see Mrs. Klein anyway."

"And find out I was here, and maybe what we talked about."

"Yes, sir."

He nodded. "You're right. See what you can find out tomorrow, and please keep me informed. Now I'm going home. I've had a long day with a depressing ending. No offense intended, Commander."

She tried to smile, but there was that bleak look in his face again. Still waters, she thought. Be careful. You know nothing about this man. But then he gave her a sudden, almost intuitive look that said, I know what you're thinking, and then he did smile. It transformed his face, revealing an unexpected charm. "Thanks for coming tonight, Commander. I mean that. Call me when you have something."

"Yes, sir. Good night."

She smiled to herself as she started up her car. "Call me when you have something," he'd said. It was almost amusing, how he just assumed she was working for him. Admirals did that, she had noticed: They automatically assumed that everyone in the room was acting in support of the Great Man at the head of the table. She would call the police first thing in the morning and see if she could arrange another meeting with McNair. As she drove away, she glanced back at the Walsh house, and she realized Sherman had left all the lights on. The windows blazed out at the dark street as if to defy the lingering presence of death inside.

CHAPTER 3

At 10:15 on Wednesday morning, Karen Lawrence met with Detective McNair in Fairfax. He offered her coffee, but she declined; they sat down in his office.

"So, Commander Lawrence. What can we do for you?"

"As I said when I called, Detective, I'm working for Admiral Carpenter. He asked me to act as liaison between you and your efforts to solve the Walsh, um, situation and Navy headquarters."

McNair kept a neutral expression on his face. "And the reason for establishing this liaison, Commander?"

Karen looked right at him. "To be perfectly frank, Detective, I think Admiral Carpenter wants to know right away if Admiral Sherman becomes a suspect in a murder case."

"I see," McNair said with the hint of a smile now. "Forgive me, when someone says they're being perfectly frank, I usually expect quite the opposite. So you are not working for Admiral Sherman, then?"

"No. I work for the JAG, Admiral Carpenter."

"Tell me, that insignia on your sleeves means you're a lawyer, right?"

"That's right."

"So, if this Admiral Sherman tells you something in confidence, is that privileged information? You know, lawyer-client privilege and all that?"

"No. I'm not representing Admiral Sherman in the lawyer-client sense. I'm not operating 'of counsel.' I'm operating as a staff officer on the Navy headquarters staff."

"Okay," McNair said. "When you called this morning, I went in to see Lieutenant Bettino. He's the boss of the Homicide Section. I explained about this liaison proposition, and he said he could understand the politics of it. But he needed to know *what* you were. If you were Sherman's lawyer, then we wouldn't talk to you, of course, until we either charged him or gave it up for Lent. But, secondly, he didn't feel we needed a whole lot of help with this case as things stand."

"Are you saying you would prefer there not be a parallel Navy investigation?"

"Yes, I guess I am. I mean, of course the Navy can run any kind of investigation it wants on any of its personnel. You've got jurisdiction over naval personnel. But we'd prefer that any such investigation or related activities not interfere with anything *we* might have going down in our jurisdiction."

Karen understood the implied warning immediately and moved to put his concerns to rest. "First, we wouldn't think of interfering with your investigation, Detective. And, second, since Ms. Walsh died in Fairfax County and not aboard a naval installation, our position is that you have exclusive jurisdiction. Besides, we're not conducting an investigation. I'm here to—"

"Yeah, I know," he interrupted, sitting back in his chair. "To establish liaison. So, let's stop beating around the bushes here. You know we're not going to reveal every little detail of what we're working here with this case. But what I hear you saying is that you'd like a little heads-up, we decide to make Sherman for the perpetrator. Is that about it?"

Karen decided this was the time to show him that they wanted a little more than that. "Not exactly," she said. "We might be more useful than that. Let me fill you in on something." She told him about going to Elizabeth's town house the night before with Admiral Sherman. He nodded slowly while she talked, taking it all in but keeping his face a blank mask. He was indeed a pro, Karen thought, but she did get a reaction when she told him about the slippers. He reached for his notebook and wrote something down. He appeared to think for a moment when she was finished.

"Lemme ask you," he said. "Did Sherman authorize you to tell us this?"

" 'Authorize'? Wrong word. I told him that the police ought to know about this, and he agreed."

"Why did you go with Sherman last night?" he asked.

"He asked me to. Personally, I think he thought it would look better if he had someone with him. There were no indications that the house was a crime scene when we got there. That's not a problem, is it?"

"Nope," he replied. "Did he appear to key on anything else when he went through the place?"

Karen shook her head. "No. He went through the entire house, but I don't think he was looking for anything specific. He appeared to be, I don't know, trying to exorcise the place in a way. He turned on all the lights, went into all the rooms. I had the impression that he suspects something's not right with the picture, but he also realizes that if he yells murder, he's the only guy you're looking at. I think the man feels he's in a box."

McNair thought about that for a moment. Then he looked back up at Karen. "Do you think he's clean?" he asked.

"Yes, I do," Karen replied immediately. "Absent any physical evidence to the contrary. Based on what you said about the time of death—early evening, Friday—he was either in the Pentagon or at that restaurant. Did that check out, by the way?"

He looked at her for a moment, as if gauging whether or not he should answer the question she had just casually slipped in.

"The restaurant, yes," he said grudgingly. "Like he said, he's a regular. They remembered him being there. We haven't talked to his office yet."

"Perhaps I can help with that." She handed over one of her cards, with Sherman's deputy's name and number written on the back. He slipped the card into a pocket in his notebook and then sat back, looking at her again, a speculative expression on his face. Karen waited. McNair appeared to be one of those cops who could be perfectly polite, even solicitous in his approach to people, but who still exuded the stoniness born of dealing with murder and murderers. Finally, he nodded.

"Okay," he said. "Let me try this again, see if I get it right this time. You will stay close to this Sherman guy while we're working this thing. You'll pass along to us any information of interest that develops. In return, we will keep you informed as to how our investigation's shaping up. You want advance notice if we decide to move against Sherman, but you also want us to get off him just as soon as we feel there's no case to be made. How's that?"

Karen gave him her brightest smile. "Admiral Carpenter has told me to ensure that your investigation is fully facilitated by the Navy, one way or the other."

He nodded again. Karen almost thought he was going to offer his hand so they could shake on it, but he didn't. He surprised her with another question instead.

"Tell me something, Commander. Does this guy Sherman think you're on his side on this?"

Karen felt the slightest tinge of a flush start around her throat. "Admiral Sherman wants to clear this up as quickly as we do, Detective," she replied.

He nodded again, the ghost of a smile on his face. "Damn," he said. "And I thought we cops were the masters of evasion."

Karen struggled to maintain her composure as he continued to stare at her. He had understood the setup only too well. Then he got up, signifying they were done. He handed her one of his own cards. She realized that he was almost an inch shorter than she was, but bigger than she remembered. Indeterminate age, maybe late thirties. Metallic gray eyes. An iciness back in there. A basically hard face under all that professional courtesy.

"We'll be in touch, Commander," he was saying. "Anything comes up you think is useful, there's the number."

"Thank you, Detective," she said. "I guess I do have one more question: As things stand now, do you think Admiral Sherman murdered his ex-girlfriend?"

He raised his eyebrows. "Hard to tell just now, Commander. I'm not sure what the slippers signify, if anything. But we'll sure let you know if that's what we conclude."

"Now who's the master of evasion?" she said, but he only smiled politely and escorted her back out to the reception area.

Karen tried to shrug off the Judas feeling as she drove back into town. Sherman was a flag officer. He didn't get to be a flag officer without knowing how the system worked. He had to suspect at least that Carpenter would be working his own agenda, which would not necessarily parallel Sherman's best interests. As the JAG, Carpenter would have his eye on protecting the Navy. And she was not, in fact, his lawyer. So legally speaking, there were no confidentiality aspects to their conversations. So there really wasn't a problem here, right? Right. So why did she feel she was betraying the man?

She mentally reviewed what she thought were the elements of her tasking: gain Sherman's confidence, tell him that she had a line into the cops and that she would alert him to anything shaking from those quarters. In return, he would tell her—what, if anything? Well, like going to Elizabeth Walsh's house last night, where the slipper business had come up. She sighed as she drove down Route 50 toward the Beltway. Time for a workout. She would call Sherman's office from the athletic club to see when he had a hole in his schedule after lunch. Then the hard part: She would have to back-brief Carpenter and talk to von Rensel—she hadn't spoken to him yet today.

Ten minutes after one o'clock, Karen entered the OP-32 outer office, with a salad plate in hand. The yeoman got up and knocked on Sherman's inner office door, stuck his head in, and then held the door open for her. Sherman was finishing a sandwich at a small conference table. His office was similar to Admiral Carpenter's but smaller and with less prestigious furniture. He did not get up, just waved her over to the table.

"So, how did it go out there with the *Polizei*?"

She took a moment to summon her thoughts while she unwrapped her plastic fork and opened a carton of milk. She took a bite of salad.

"Well," she said, "it was pretty short. I told him about your visit to Ms. Walsh's house, and the slippers—that she would not have been wearing those slippers."

"And?"

"McNair didn't really react one way or the other, but he did make a note of it."

"Did he seem to care that I had gone there?"

"No, sir. They're apparently not treating her house as a crime scene. In a way, it's kind of strange what they're doing—or not doing, I mean. The slippers, the laundry, the basket: All of that would have been held in a lab somewhere if this was a homicide investigation. And there would have been police seals on the house. Frankly, I don't think there's anything going on. Or if there is, McNair didn't reveal it."

"You're probably right," he said. "Did you get any hint of what those forensic ambiguities were?"

"No, sir. But I'm almost beginning to think that that term is a euphemism for somebody's hunch."

He nodded thoughtfully and finished his sandwich. Crumpling up the paper plate, he leaned back in his chair. "Do they understand that I'm a little reluctant to be Freddy Forthcoming as long as they're acting as if I'm possibly a suspect of some kind?"

"Yes, sir. But, Admiral, I don't think you are a real suspect."

"Then why won't they just say so? The longer they keep this up, the bigger my political problem in OpNav becomes."

"Cops don't work that way, Admiral. They don't tell outsiders anything they don't have to. Besides, the converse is true: If you were a viable suspect, they would be acting altogether differently."

He nodded again and looked away for a moment, as if making a decision. "I need to tell you something," he said. "But it has to remain in confidence for now, vis-à-vis the cops at least. Are you okay with that?"

She thought fast. Here it was: the confidentiality issue. From the cops, he'd said. Did that mean from Carpenter, too? She stalled for time by miming that her mouth was full.

"Admiral," she said finally, "if you're about to tell me you're an ax murderer, then, no, that's not going to be possible." She thought about qualifying that, but she said nothing more. Somewhere along the line, she was going to have to face this problem. But he did not seem perturbed by her answer.

"No, nothing like that. I'm a hatchet man, myself." He smiled at her then, and she felt a little less uncomfortable. But then his expression sobered. "Something happened last night that I think bears on this whole situation. There's a story behind it, going back more than twenty years. I'll give you the basics, and then see what you think."

"This bears on Elizabeth Walsh's death?"

"Yes, I think so. And unfortunately, it may corroborate my own misgivings about what really happened to Elizabeth."

"I'm all ears," she said, finishing her salad and packing up the plate and wrapper.

Sherman nodded and went to his desk. He sat down and put his palms up to his face and rubbed his cheeks.

"Last night, I went home to change before going over to Elizabeth's. Went through the mail. Usual stuff—bills, catalogs. And one letter." He paused and gave her a long look between his fingers. "A threatening letter."

"A threat? What kind of threat?"

"This relates to something that happened in Vietnam—when I was a lieutenant. An incident that I suspect the Navy would not want to have come out, even after so many years. So for now, I won't disclose what it was. But because of what happened, a certain individual swore revenge—against me. And he apparently understood the old rule about revenge being a dish best savored cold."

Karen was baffled. "And that's what this letter was about? Revenge?"

"Yes. Back in the early seventies, this man told me he would get even with me for something we—I—had done. But he said he would wait until I had something of value to lose. And that when he came back, he would give me one warning."

"Which is what this letter was."

"Yes. It wasn't signed, but it has to be him. Galantz."

"Galantz?" Karen wished she had had her notebook out, but was unsure she should go digging for it just now.

"Yes. Galantz." He spelled the last name for her. "Hospital Corpsman First Class Marcus Galantz. Last known duty station was as a member of Seal Team One."

"A SEAL! Oh, dear."

He paused and rubbed his face again, then looked across the room at the far wall, his eyes focused out about a mile into space, his lips pressed together in a flat line. She was beginning to understand his concern. A threatening letter from a SEAL. Lovely.

"What did the letter say?" she asked finally.

"It said, 'Sherman: Time to settle up. Things of value, remember? Walsh was the first.' "

"Uh-oh."

"Yeah."

"Admiral, we have to get this letter to the police. This changes everything. It also means that Elizabeth—" She stopped, seeing the sudden flash of pain on his face. "I'm sorry, Admiral."

He nodded but did not say anything for a moment. Then he continued.

"At first, I didn't know what to do. And I'm not sure I'm ready to bring the police into this. Or at least I wasn't sure until I went to talk to my sea

43

daddy, Admiral Galen Schmidt. You may remember him: He was Chief of Naval Personnel in early '93, when he had to quit because of heart problems. He'd been my mentor ever since my first Bureau tour back in the late seventies. He's retired and living in McLean now, not far from my house."

"Yes, I remember him. Everyone said he was a prime candidate to be the next CNO."

"Yes. Great guy. Anyhow, after getting that letter and going to Elizabeth's house, I went to see him. I told him about Elizabeth. He knew her, liked her a lot. I also told him about the letter, and most of the story behind it."

Which you won't tell me, she thought. But that detective will surely want to know. "He wasn't familiar with the incident back in Vietnam?"

"Very few people are, and probably no one still on active duty. It was all news to him. Long story short, I asked him whether or not I ought to tell the cops about the letter—because of what it implies about Elizabeth's so-called accident. His advice was that I should tell them."

"But?"

"But I've got two problems with that. First, I'm not sure I'm ready to open that can of worms, especially outside the Navy. Or even inside, for that matter. And second, I no longer have the letter."

"*What?*"

He got up and started to pace around the office. "When I got home from Galen's house, I found my front door unlocked—not open, but definitely unlocked. I never leave my door unlocked. In fact, it locks itself when I pull it shut. I thought about calling the cops—you know, maybe somebody in the house. But instead I went in and checked the place out. Nothing was missing. So I secured for the night, then took some paperwork upstairs. Only later, around eleven-thirty, when I was ready to go to sleep, I thought about bringing the letter in. I went back downstairs and discovered that's what was missing—the letter, the envelope, the whole thing."

"Wow. You think somebody, maybe even this Galantz guy, broke into your house and retrieved the letter? After he was sure you had read it?"

"That's exactly what I think, yes."

Karen thought about that. If that was the case, then the admiral had to have been under surveillance.

"This is stalking, you know," she said, speaking the thought that had just come to her mind.

"Stalking?" he asked, frowning.

"Yes, sir. There's a whole new area of criminal law covering exactly this kind of thing. Where there's a persistent threat of a criminal act but nothing's happened to the stalker's target yet. There are federal and state laws against it."

"I'm not sure an ex-SEAL bent on revenge will be worried about breaking the law. Especially this SEAL, since he doesn't officially exist."

"Excuse me?"

He sighed and sat down again. "I've already told you more than is probably wise, Commander. May I call you Karen?"

"Of course, sir." His request was not improper. Most admirals throughout the headquarters called staff subordinates by their first names. In return, subordinates were graciously invited to address the admiral by his first name: Admiral.

"HM1 Galantz was officially listed as MIA. I happen to know personally that a few years later, he was alive and back in the States. But, once again, I can't reveal how I know that, and I'm not sure anyone else knows that. Like I said, this is very complicated."

He had said he didn't want this story to get loose either outside or inside the Navy. "At the risk of sounding impertinent," she said, "why are you concerned about this story getting out inside the Navy?"

He gave her a long, speculative look. There was some steel in that look, which made her feel she might have overstepped some bounds. But then it receded and he nodded. He got up and started pacing around the office again. "Fair enough," he said. "I've got to keep reminding myself you're on my side."

Remembering McNair's comment earlier that day, she almost replied to that, but he was already going ahead.

"I'm a fresh-caught rear admiral. To everyone who's a captain and below, flag rank is the apotheosis of the career ladder. The man with the stars. But the truth is, I'm really not even promoted yet. I'm frocked. I can wear the uniform, I have the responsibility, and I can enjoy the title. But until someone who's currently on the flag registry dies or retires, I have to wait to make my number. I even get paid as a captain. People think this is a fluke of the Defense Manpower Act, with its grade quotas. But the truth is, I am, like every other new flag selectee in any of the services, very much on probation."

"How long does this go on?"

"For nearly two years. I probably won't be promoted to O-7 until about the time I go off to my second assignment as a flag officer."

She nodded thoughtfully. "So the association of your name with a homicide and a long-buried, potentially embarrassing incident back in Vietnam could mean you'd be invited to retire instead of going on to that next assignment."

He nodded. "Precisely. And, as you might imagine, there happens to be an infinite supply of eager young captains ready and willing to take my place." He looked at his watch. "We're about out of time. You'll need a while to think about this. So do I. And now, of course, you have to figure out what to tell Admiral Carpenter."

She felt a sudden flush on her face as she looked up at him. There was a hint of amusement in his eyes. "Karen, look," he said gently. "You're the king's eye here. We both understand that. All I'm asking is that you keep what I've just told you close-hold while I make up my mind what to do with it."

"I'm not sure I understand," she said.

He nodded again, acknowledging her confusion. "With all the trouble the Navy's been having lately, the last thing we need is for this particular story to come out. Which means we're going to want very much to solve it in-house. Which also means we're probably going to need some NIS help to find this guy. The complicating factor is that my superiors are absolutely going to panic at the prospect of another Navy scandal. So for me, this is a political problem as well as a personal problem."

"Yes, sir, of course." *What the hell am I going to do with this?* she wondered. And then she realized she might have the answer right there in her office: von Rensel.

He was pacing again. "I'll call you. Probably tomorrow. I have to go to Elizabeth's memorial service tonight." Once again, she detected a thread of anguish leaking through all his highly professional, controlled composure.

"Would you like some moral support, Admiral?" she asked, surprising herself.

He stopped short. "Would you? I mean, I know that's a lot to ask. Especially after your—"

She gave him a steady look. "Yes. I swore I would never face another funeral service after Frank's. But they tell me that the best cure for grief is to help someone else. Where is it and when?"

He gave her the details and was thanking her again when there was a knock on the door and his deputy stuck his head in with the news that the fourteen-hundred briefing team was ready. Karen got up at once, nodded to the admiral, and walked out past the team of officers waiting to present the budget briefings. She hurried back to her office.

Karen looked for von Rensel, but he was signed out at lunch. She got on the phone with the Bureau of Personnel, the enlisted Records Division, and asked for an archives retrieval on one HM1 Marcus Galantz. The clerk put her on hold in order to access a computer. When the clerk came back on, she said that there was an archived record but that there was a special hold on it.

"This individual's a Vietnam-era MIA. You'll have to get clearance from the Office of the Secretary of Defense, and then you can E-mail me a written request indicating the clearance authority." She gave Karen a number in Crystal City. Karen thanked her and hung up. Should have known I couldn't do that with just a phone call, she thought. And then she thought about getting the front office to make the calls for the records. But that would mean explaining why she wanted them, and Sherman had asked her to keep that information close-hold for the moment. But maybe she *should* tell Carpenter; he was her boss, not Sherman.

She sat back in her desk chair. Back to that problem again: Whose side am I on? Her tasking was to find out what the cops were up to, and then to keep Carpenter and, apparently, the Navy hierarchy from getting any nasty surprises. And a nasty surprise now appeared to be a distinct possibility. As best she could tell, Sherman was not entangled in the Walsh matter as a possible killer—that is, assuming he was telling the truth about all this.

She shook her head. Going in circles here. Go back to your tasking. Find out what the cops are doing, what they are thinking. I did that. So go tell Carpenter. But to deal with this other matter, Sherman would have to meet with the detective again, this time without any interference from the higher-ups in JAG. She nodded to herself. If Sherman would meet with the cops, she could put off telling Carpenter anything about the stalker—at least for now. She called the number in OSD and began the clearance process.

Train von Rensel came by her cubicle as she was finishing up the E-mail request for the records, and she waved at him. When she had transmitted the request, she went over to his cubicle. He looked like an adult sitting at one of those tiny school desks on parents' night at the elementary school, as if afraid to move for fear of breaking something.

"All checked in?" she asked.

"Sort of. I have to go back to NIS to finish some check*out* stuff, if you can believe it. Over here, I've got one more security clearance brief, and I'm on some eternal waiting list for a locker at the athletic club, but otherwise, I think I'm real. How'd your meeting with the Fairfax cops go?"

"Why don't I buy you a cup of coffee?" she asked. He raised his eyebrows, looked around, and then nodded. He got up carefully, trying not to bump into any of the partition walls. They left the office together and went down to the nearby snack bar, where she told Train about her meeting with the police that morning and then what she had learned from Sherman. When she was finished, he stirred his coffee with a wooden stirrer and frowned.

"Really?" he asked. "A SEAL?" He looked sincerely concerned.

"Yes, a SEAL," Karen said solemnly.

Train nodded slowly. "Your admiral's dead meat," he pronounced, then just looked at her.

"That's it?" she asked, not sure if he was joking. Oh God. He wasn't.

"Probably," he replied soberly. "Tell me what he said again."

She gathered her thoughts for a moment. She had not expected this reaction. Then she went through the whole thing again. Von Rensel sat there like a stone Buddha, unmoving, with those intense brown eyes locked on hers in perfect concentration. When she was finished, he took a long drag on what now had to be cold coffee.

"Well," he said, "if some SEAL has materialized out of the mists of the Vietnam War to come after Sherman, the admiral is in serious trouble. It would help if we knew what this was all about."

"He may yet tell me—us. But so far, he's holding that back. He feels the Navy wouldn't want it resurrected, whatever it was, and he definitely doesn't want to tell the cops."

"He may not have any choice. What actions have you taken so far?"

"I've summoned Galantz's service records from the federal archives. But first, I had to request clearance from the POW/MIA task force over in OSD."

"He's listed as an MIA?"

"Apparently."

"Uh-oh."

"What?"

Train paused before replying. "Let me get back to that," he said finally. "How much of this have you told Carpenter?"

"None of it. I haven't reported back to him yet. My plan was to tell him nothing about this SEAL business until Sherman sorts out what he wants to tell the cops. Sherman's very worried about surfacing a scandal. Apparently, his own political exposure as a new flag is substantial. I guess the SEAL angle complicates all that, of course."

"Sure does. I think you're right: The best move for him is to go back to the cops."

"He's leaning that way, too." She nodded. "We're going to have to tell them about this."

He looked at her. "We?"

She nodded. "Well, Sherman seemed to think the cops would need Navy help finding this Galantz guy. Of course I immediately thought of NIS."

Train nodded. "Sherman's instincts are probably right on target. After Tailhook, the Naval Academy drug thing, a CNO committing suicide—they'd dump him in a heartbeat."

"Yes. The way I see it, the only people who can help him with a stalker are the cops, so I'm hoping he might be willing to tell them the Vietnam story. If by doing that, he comes off the 'suspect' board, then maybe he can ground any possible lightning bolts from the heavies here at headquarters."

"Fair enough," Train said. "He didn't get to be a boy admiral without having keen political instincts." He looked around the snack bar, which was moderately crowded. "Right," he said. "Let's go take a walk."

"A walk?"

"Yes. Like down to that center court area. I like the looks of all those trees and park benches. And exterior walls with no ears."

The center court of the Pentagon was a combination arboretum and snack bar area, offering a three-acre surprise in the midst of the fortresslike poured-concrete walls of the Pentagon building. There were green lawns, flower gardens, a few dozen varieties of large trees in spring bloom, and chairs and benches placed along the walkways. In another month, the snack bar in the center, fondly called Ground Zero by legions of Cold Warriors, would open for lunch, allowing the 27,000 inmates of the Pentagon a half an hour of fresh air and mental respite from the crumbling concrete pile surrounding them.

There were a few dozen people out in the court, and Karen thought the two of them, this great bear of a civilian and a Navy female commander, must present an incongruous image. She was used to being stared at by men, but she wondered now if they were looking at her or at him. Train led them to a park bench near the center, where they sat down. For a moment he just stared down at the sidewalk, saying nothing.

"Okay. NIS investigator talking now. Two ways to look at this. Either our Admiral Sherman is indeed the target of a stalker, who may or may not have iced the admiral's ex-girlfriend, or—"

"Or?" Karen suddenly felt uncomfortable with the direction of Train's logic.

"Or he's making it all up. And *he* pushed the Walsh woman down the stairs. For that insurance policy. Two hundred fifty large constitutes a reasonable motive in these here uncertain economic times."

"But he has an alibi. A verified alibi for the time of death."

"For the *presumed* time of death. And it wasn't really verified in any ironclad sense. That restaurant on a busy Friday night? Look, the Walsh matter—bottom line? He had a motive: the money. There was opportunity: He has a key to the house. He had full knowledge of her place, her domestic routines. She would gladly have let him in without a second thought. He had the means: He could have easily surprised her, pushed her down the stairs. And now the mysterious letter from the even more mysterious SEAL? We have only his word for it. His house was broken into, but did he report it to the cops? No. Were there busted windows or jimmied doors? No. And now, most conveniently, there is no letter. If I were the Fairfax cops, and I heard this little fable, I'd be thinking that this is smoke he's blowing my way, a classic case of offense/defense. The killer doesn't run from the cops, he runs *toward* them, all anxious and sincere. He feeds them stuff, lots of distracting stuff. Throws crap in the game—the slippers, the laundry downstairs instead of upstairs, and now this mysterious letter."

"Damn," she said.

Train leaned back and rubbed his hands together, making a sound like sandpaper. He had very large hands, with ridges of callus on the edges of his palms. "The Fairfax cops might, in fact, have something," he was saying. "They might well be feeding out some rope and hoping like hell that Sherman gets cocky and wraps it around his own tricky neck."

Karen thought about what he said for a long moment, then shook her head. "I don't get that sense of it," she said. "Obviously, there's more to this story. He wouldn't tell me anything about what happened back in Vietnam to start all this. Says he can't tell, in fact."

"How convenient for him."

"Or it could be true. I don't know. I was just coming into the Navy when that war was ending. He's made it to flag rank, but I get the impression he's paid a personal price for his career success. Remember what he said about never wanting to remarry? I saw some pictures of Elizabeth Walsh in that house. She was extremely attractive, and yet he bailed out the moment she started even talking about marriage. Not because of her but because of what *he* went through the first time he was married. There must be some emotional wreckage somewhere back there in his wake. That's why I'm going to go with him to this memorial service tonight. Now, what was that uh-oh all about?"

Train was quiet for a moment. He looked around at all the spring greenery, his face an impassive mask. "I may be wrong," he said. "But the Bureau told you Galantz was an MIA. If Sherman is telling the truth—that is, he knows Galantz was in fact alive *after* he had been declared MIA—then Galantz may be doubly dangerous."

"I don't follow."

"Yeah, I know. Let's do this. See if you can set up a second meeting with the cops. Maybe do it in Sherman's house, or anywhere that's not their turf, okay? You say you have a records-retrieval request in?"

"Yes. They said it will take a few days."

"Okay. But if he's an MIA, his record may not be in deep storage. I'll join you for this meeting. In the meantime, I've got to check on something; then maybe I can explain what I meant about his being doubly dangerous."

"And you think we shouldn't tell Admiral Carpenter anything about this letter?"

"For now, that's correct." He looked straight at her. She was struck again by the incongruity between his physical size and the intelligence gleaming out of those eyes. "This could involve some heavy stuff," he said. "I hope not. I hope our boy admiral is totally innocent."

"I'm guess I'm confused," she said.

He nodded slowly, and she sensed that there was some latent energy stirring in him. "Karen," he said, "no offense intended here, but you might be getting way out of your depth. I know I'm the new guy on the block and that I'm probably sounding presumptuous, but I strongly recommend you go slowly, very slowly, and carefully in this matter, okay?"

She swallowed because her throat had dried up suddenly. She felt a chill that was out of place amid all the vernal warmth and light of the center court.

Karen arrived promptly at Saint Matthew's at 6:25. The church was a small-ish Methodist brownstone, and its entrance was set practically onto the sidewalk along Glebe Road in Arlington. There was a small, heavily wooded graveyard next door, but there did not appear to be any preparations in place there. She went in and found Sherman, who was also still in uniform, sitting in one of the back pews, as if unsure of how he might be received by the small crowd of Elizabeth's coworkers clustered up front. Karen was relieved when an elderly gentleman slipped into the pew behind theirs as the service opened and squeezed Sherman's arm. Sherman introduced her to Adm. Galen Schmidt. Five minutes after the service started, Mrs. Klein arrived.

Karen could sense Sherman's discomfiture, and she felt a sudden lump in her own throat when she realized where she was. The absence of a coffin in the center aisle of the church only highlighted the stark fact that Eliza-beth Walsh was indeed gone. She knew only too well what that felt like. She wondered if Sherman was adding the what-if mantra to the sorrow of his own loss: If I had not run away from this woman, would she still be alive? Or worse: Is she dead now because of something that happened in a far-off place a very long time ago? That would be a tough one. Train von Rensel's warning came fleetingly to mind. Looking out of the side of her eyes, she still couldn't picture this intense man as a murderer. And yet Train's logic made some sense.

The service was secular and short. When it was over, Karen remained seated in the pew while Sherman talked quietly to Mrs. Klein and the el-derly admiral. Galen Schmidt was of medium height and spare frame, with a congenial, handsome face that she remembered from when he had been Chief of Naval Personnel a few years back. But now his hair was snow white and he had a porcelainlike complexion. Although he looked as if he was nearing his mid-seventies, Karen knew he couldn't be much past sixty-three or -four, so that heart condition must be pretty serious. People started to leave, and Sherman herded his small group out the front door.

"Nice service, Tag," Admiral Schmidt said, adjusting his raincoat and looking at the scudding overcast. Karen stood behind them as she slipped on her own black Navy raincoat. Schmidt said he was going to get right home before the rain hit. "You going to be okay tonight?" he asked Sherman.

51

"I think so, Galen. Thanks for coming. Besides you and the ladies here, I'm afraid I was the odd man out. I don't really know any of those people."

"They're not who you came to say good-bye to, Tag. Chin up. Life goes on. Commander, Mrs. Klein, nice to meet you all. I am sorry for your loss, Tag. Come see me in a day or so."

"I will, Galen. Thanks again for coming out tonight."

Schmidt shook hands with everyone. Karen noticed that the bones in his fingers felt like bird bones, featherlight, almost fragile. Sherman waved as the old man steamed off down the sidewalk toward his Cadillac, and then he looked around, as if trying to remember where he had parked his own car. Mrs. Klein made her own hasty departure, and then it was just Karen and the admiral standing on the sidewalk as the rest of the other people came out. Everyone seemed to be concentrating on the first raindrops spattering on the steps. The admiral was not wearing his raincoat, and there were a few stares, but no one came over to them.

"Damn it, I knew it," he said above a sudden gust of wind.

"You go ahead, Admiral," she said. "I'm parked in the next block."

"Right. Look, I've decided I do want to talk to that detective."

"Good," she replied, holding on to her hat. Then she remembered von Rensel's suggestion. "How about doing the meeting at your house instead of in the Pentagon? Tomorrow night?"

"Okay," he said. "Would you set it up? And call me in the morning? Oh, and thank you for coming tonight, Karen." Then he was jogging away down the sidewalk as the rain began in earnest. Karen followed with her head down, reflecting on how everyone was always anxious to get away from a funeral. Her mother had organized a service for Frank out in Chevy Chase, and she had dreaded leaving the church when it was over. Probably because they then had to go to the cemetery. Elizabeth Walsh had spared them that trauma by donating her body to medical science.

She looked back to see if Sherman had reached his car, when she heard the dissonant sound of a motorcycle coming toward them. She looked up the street and saw the bike and its rider approaching down the inside right lane, pursued by a small vortex of rain and traffic mist. The motorcycle looked like a fat wingless wasp, shiny and black, with chrome exhaust pipes, an oversized headlight, and only a small windshield. Its engine was running rough, battering the evening air with a painfully loud staccato that seemed incongruous in this neighborhood of older homes and nicely fenced yards. The helmeted rider, wearing a sleeveless, black T-shirt and dark jeans, looked too spindly to be piloting the big two-seater machine. As the bike drew abreast of where the admiral was fumbling with his car keys, she suddenly realized that the rider had his visor raised and was looking right at Sherman.

Karen, who had stopped about thirty feet away, saw the admiral look back at the rider and then freeze. He whirled around as the bike went by, but it was already accelerating along the right lane in a cone of smoky spray. Karen stood there for a second and was about to start forward, but the admiral was scrambling to get his car door open, as if anxious to pursue the bike and its rider. But it was not to be: The stream of rush-hour traffic made it impossible for him to get out of his parking place, and she saw him thump the steering wheel in frustration. The rain became heavier, and she hurried to reach her own car. She looked back once more and saw the admiral push his way into traffic, provoking an angry constellation of brake lights and horns behind him.

She got in and struggled out of her dripping raincoat. The rain drummed hard on the roof, and she decided just to wait it out for a few minutes, turning on the engine to get the defroster going. So what the hell was that all about? she wondered. She had had only the briefest glimpse of the rider's face. The predominant impression was thin: thin face, narrow hatchetlike head, a hank of greasy-looking black hair down one side, the flash of an earring. But there was no doubt that he had been looking at the admiral, almost as if he had been willing the admiral to see him.

Mystified, she switched on her car phone, got out McNair's card, and placed a call to his office. She got his voice mail. She asked if it would be amenable to meet with Admiral Sherman at his home in McLean at 6:00 P.M. tomorrow night and said to call her if this would work. As the rain squall passed, she began watching the traffic for an opening. She made a mental note to close the loop with von Rensel first thing in the morning. She would also have to figure out how to put off any questions from Carpenter for one more day.

As he piloted his Suburban carefully through the evening rush-hour traffic on I-95, Train von Rensel made a mental inventory of some things he needed to do before the lovely lady commander got herself too much further into the Sherman matter. A disappearing letter from a disappearing SEAL who was also supposed to be an MIA—he shook his head.

Assuming the good admiral was being honest, Train felt that his first comment in the snack bar had been the simple truth. Navy SEALs have the reputation of being the baddest of the bad in the Special Forces world, where bad inferred supreme competence rather than a capacity for malice. If a SEAL had been declared missing in action and then had reappeared back in the States some time afterward, still being carried as an MIA, then there was a high probability that he had found himself a new government job.

Fortunately, Train still had one contact in that organization all the spooks loved to hate, the Federal Bureau of Investigation. Dr. McHale Johnson was a senior scientist in the Computer Operations and Machine Intelligence

Division of the FBI's Washington laboratories, or at least that's what he said he was. Train had first met him during an NIS counterintelligence operation connected with the Walker cryptography spy ring. Up to that point in his career, Train had been under the naïve impression that there were rigid rules governing the boundaries of counterintelligence operations, with the FBI solely in charge of domestic counterintelligence, while another agency dealt with security issues beyond U.S. borders. McHale Johnson quickly had disabused him of this quaint notion, demonstrating repeatedly that both federal agencies had their own interpretations of this rule. During a subsequent Joint Intelligence Board debriefing on the Walker case, a board member from that other agency had tried to pin Train down as to whether or not he had seen any evidence that the FBI ever operated off the reservation. Train had testified solemnly that he had seen absolutely no evidence of any violations of this rule during the investigation. Since then, McHale Johnson had been available for informal consultations from time to time. The FBI kept score.

But first, he needed to be convinced that this wasn't some kind of smoke-blowing exercise on the admiral's part. He was a little bit surprised that Karen Lawrence would be so ready to believe such a story. On the other hand, she was a commander and Sherman was a flag officer. He had long since learned never to underestimate the capacity of naval officers to put the star-wearing elect of the military congregation up on exceedingly high pedestals.

Train stared out at the stalled river of evening commuters. Being that he considered himself a Washington-area native, he should be used to this. Born in 1949, he had been the only child of Gregor von Rensel and his wife, Constance. He had grown up on the family's riverside home near Aquia, Virginia, which was about thirty-five miles south of Washington.

His father, a Washington attorney, had been on MacArthur's staff during World War II. He had followed MacArthur to Tokyo when the war ended, and he'd spent two years on the Tokyo Occupation Staff. Despite being part of the hated army of occupation in that devastated city, Gregor found himself quite taken with the Japanese approach to life. When he came home to the Washington area in 1947, he met and subsequently married the daughter of an American banker, Hiram Worthfield, of the San Francisco Worthfields, who had himself taken a Japanese wife long before the war. Wolfgang had been born two years later, growing up on the family estate at Aquia until his ninth year, when his mother contracted breast cancer and then died a year later.

The Worthfield family, conscious of Gregor's old-world attitudes about raising their only grandchild, prevailed upon him to accept two young Japanese retainers from their own San Francisco household, Hiroshi and Kyoko Yamada. Kyoko had quietly become Train's surrogate mother, while her husband, Hiroshi, took over as groundskeeper, chauffeur, and general factotum. Hiroshi had generally ignored young Wolfgang until the child's twelfth year, at which point Gregor von Rensel, aware of impending puberty, had had a quiet word.

With patience and quiet persistence, Hiroshi had infiltrated Wolfgang's nonschool hours, skillfully bringing the prepubescent boy into his orbit and teaching him the essential arts of manhood. To the young Wolfgang's eyes, Hiroshi was an aloof, taciturn, stoical man of little apparent humor who was inexplicably starting to take up a lot of his time. But over the next three years, the rapidly growing teenager was exposed to the best concepts of the Japanese upper-class traditions: a strong sense of honor, an awareness that there was such a thing as duty, and the importance of personal integrity. Hiroshi had come from a military family and had received extensive military training in anticipation of the impending U.S. invasion of the home islands. When the time came to instruct his new master's son in the duties of manhood, he imparted a high regard for personal self-sufficiency, including extensive and daily instruction in the martial arts.

Content with Hiroshi's work, Train's father insisted on boarding school as the next step, then prelaw at the University of Virginia. It had been Train's idea to try military service, and he served for thirteen years in the Marine Corps, first as an infantry officer, and then, after time out for law school from 1975 to 1978, as a Marine Corps JAG officer until 1983.

Two factors drove him to resign his commission in the Marines: the increasingly complex demands of managing his financial affairs after his father's death in 1982, and the fact that he had developed a passion for the art of investigation, following an assignment to prosecute a widespread contracting-fraud ring with foreign government industrial-espionage overtones in 1980. He put away his major's uniform in late 1983, and he split the next eleven years between the Office of Naval Intelligence and, later, the Naval Investigative Service. He operated increasingly as an independent investigator, to whom his superiors often turned to handle those politically sensitive cases that needed as much discretion as detective work.

He sighed as the traffic restarted and then groaned immediately to a stop again. Although Train was one of the very few people out on the interstate who did not have any particular deadline by which to get home, the house at Aquia was increasingly his little island of tranquillity along the Potomac— a tranquillity he sincerely hoped was not about to be disturbed by the appearance of a rogue SEAL. Maybe he could ask around the NIS operations directorate tomorrow, talk to some of the people who'd worked with the SEALs, see if anybody had ever heard of this guy.

CHAPTER 4

Karen called Admiral Sherman's office the next morning at nine to relay the message about the proposed meeting. McNair had agreed to meet with Admiral Sherman at his house, as requested. The yeoman put her on hold and then came back on the line.

"Admiral asked if you can come down here, Commander. Says something's come up."

She agreed and hung up. Now what? She looked around to see if Train von Rensel was in yet, but then she remembered he had to go back over to NIS to close out some files. She gathered her purse and headed down the corridor to Sherman's office.

"Good morning, Admiral," she said, waiting to see what had precipitated his request for her to come down.

"Developments," he began, after they had exchanged greetings. "OP-03 himself, Vice Admiral Kensington, apparently wants to see me. His deputy just called down ten minutes ago. I suspect it has to do with this Fairfax police visit. I'd like you to go with me."

"My, my," she said. "Word gets around."

He smiled ruefully. "Indeed it does. That flag-protection network people are always talking about. Sometimes it works too well. I found out earlier that Admiral Kensington had sent down for my bio. Do you know Kensington?"

"No, sir. Other than who he is."

"Yeah, well, he's a surface nuke. His full name is Vice Adm. Richard Millard Kensington. No nickname, except the occasional play on Millard. Spend about five minutes with him and you'll see why. Archetypical nuclear-trained officer. All business, all the time. Whenever he talks to the division directors, he speaks from a collection of three-by-five index cards."

Sherman's yeoman knocked and stuck his head in the doorway. "Admiral Vannoyt's office called down, Admiral. 03's available, sir."

"Available. I love it. I guess it beats yelling down the passageway for me to get my bucket up there," Sherman said, getting up and reaching for his jacket. "Rear Admiral Vannoyt is Kensington's deputy," he told Karen as he opened the door for her. "When the summons from Kensington comes down formally through Vannoyt, it means this is not going to be a social call. Which is why I wanted someone from JAG in the lion's den with me. That okay with you?"

She smiled bravely. "Wouldn't miss it, Admiral."

"You lie well, Commander. What is it the Army guys say? 'We're behind you, Major. Way behind you, if we can manage it.'"

Vice Admiral Kensington's E-ring office was comfortably appointed, as befitted a senior three-star. A window wall gave a fine view of the Pentagon heliport four floors below, beyond which sprawled the marble-dotted hill-sides of Arlington Cemetery, visible in the middle distance across Washington Boulevard. The view reminded Karen of that poignant sixties poster, an aerial view showing the Pentagon in the foreground and Arlington cemetery in perspective, under which were the words THE PENTAGON AND ITS PROD-UCT. There were two couches, several leather armchairs, and a large mahogany conference table. At the end away from the windows was a very large mahogany desk, behind which sat the austere figure of Vice Admiral Kensington. He was wearing his jacket fully buttoned, an affectation that had to be very uncomfortable. He was obviously a tall man, and he had a humorless, stony face that reminded Karen of a cardinal she had seen once in a Shakespearean movie.

Admiral Vannoyt remained standing and announced Sherman's presence. Kensington was concentrating on a staffing folder and did not look up for several seconds. Karen, standing to one side of Admiral Sherman, watched the interplay among the three flag officers. Vannoyt focused at a point some-where behind and over Kensington's head, his face expressionless, his phys-ical position indicating a clear distance between himself and Sherman. Then Kensington looked up, first at Vannoyt and then at Sherman. He ignored Karen completely. He had piercing gray eyes and he stared directly at Sher-man with the unblinking gaze of a fire-control radar.

"Admiral," Kensington said in a dry, nasal voice. "Are you in some kind of difficulty?"

"I'm not entirely sure, Admiral," Sherman replied, which surprised Karen. His answer sounded evasive.

"Sure enough to be working with counsel from the JAG's office, Admi-ral," Kensington replied, flicking a glance at Karen. "I have two questions: What's it all about? And why am I finding out about it from my executive assistant and not from you?"

Good questions, Karen thought. She saw Vannoyt move over to a chair and sit down, bringing Sherman's little joke about being behind you, way behind you, to mind.

"I didn't come tell you about it because I have very few facts, Admiral," Sherman replied. "You've stressed the importance of facts many times. But, basically, a woman with whom I had a relationship for a few years was found dead in her home last Friday. The police investigated, made a preliminary determination that her death was accidental, but then they learned that she had named me as the beneficiary in a life-insurance policy. They came calling via Admiral Carpenter's office Tuesday morning to talk about it. To my knowledge, that's it. I'm going to meet with them again tonight to make sure there are no more questions. Commander Lawrence here is from Navy JAG, and she is acting as liaison with the police."

"Then why do you need a lawyer, Admiral?"

"Commander Lawrence isn't acting as *my* lawyer, Admiral. She works for Admiral Carpenter."

Kensington finally looked directly at Karen for a second, giving her the feeling she was being exposed momentarily to dangerous radiation. He then trained back on Sherman. "Commander Lawrence is not a trial lawyer," he said. "She is an expert in investigations review. Why her?"

Whoa, Karen thought. Not many secrets left in this little box. Kensington's EA had been doing some homework.

"She was Admiral Carpenter's choice, Admiral. And I suspect it's because if there's anything going on right now, it's a low-level investigation. The police are not talking about a crime. As I said, we're meeting with them tonight. If they decide otherwise, *and* if they name me as a suspect, then I'll probably go hire a civilian attorney. Commander Lawrence is sort of a neutral adviser at the moment. I don't think I need any more help than that. For what it's worth, I was still here in the office at the time when they think this happened."

Kensington looked down at his desk for a moment. Karen wondered if he had one of his three-by-five cards there with his questions on it. But then he looked back over at Sherman, locking on again with those glittering gray eyes.

"Any interaction between a flag officer on the Navy staff and homicide police is a matter of concern. To me, to the CNO. Please make sure I am apprised of how this matter is resolved, Admiral. On your initiative, please, and not mine."

"Aye, aye, sir," Sherman replied, hesitating just long enough to make it clear he didn't like the way he was being treated. But Kensington had already refocused on the staffing folder. Vannoyt was tipping his head in the direction of the door. They followed him out.

"Commander, if you will excuse us for a moment," Vannoyt said pointedly. Karen said, "Of course," and went out into the E-ring corridor. Vannoyt took Sherman into his office and closed the door. She noticed that the yeomen were all concentrating very hard on their paperwork, and then she remembered that Kensington's door had been open through all of that. A minute later, Sherman came back out and joined her. As they walked back toward the OP-32 office in silence, Sherman's face was grim. She resisted an impulse to put a finger in her collar and unstick it from her neck. The brief session with Kensington had made her appreciate the congenial atmosphere of IR, and she had not even been in the line of fire. She wondered if Vannoyt's last-minute discussion had been about taking her into Kensington's office. The three-star had generally ignored her, as if to show the one-star that she should not have been there in the first place. Sherman didn't say anything until they reached his office.

"Okay. Six o'clock at my house in McLean. It's in that cluster of town houses off Old Dominion just before you reach McLean. Number nineteen on Cheshire Street, second left after you come in the main entrance. The numbers are visible."

"Yes, sir. I'll be there."

He paused, and then his face relaxed a bit. "Curious?"

She smiled. "A little. I'm guessing he was not pleased to see me in there."

"Correct. Vannoyt reminded me that flag officers never indulge in antagonistic interpersonal relations. And when they do, the help waits outside, thank you very much. More along that line."

"I'm surprised he didn't just tell me to wait outside."

It was his turn to smile. "The fact that they didn't was intended as a message to me. By all means, if you're in trouble, bring your lawyer in. That's really what Vannoyt wanted to make sure I understood." His expression grew serious. "We need to reach some kind of resolution with these people tonight if we can. That whole little scene was a political warning shot across my bow."

"Yes, sir, I could see that. But resolution will depend on how forthcoming the police want to be."

"Forthcoming homicide cops. Well." He looked less than hopeful. Then she remembered Train.

"Oh, and I've asked Mr. von Rensel to be there tonight."

"Why? I want to limit disclosure, not expand it."

"You said we would probably need some NIS help with the Galantz problem. He's a senior investigator with the NIS, working directly for the JAG."

"I see." He paused, staring at nothing for a moment. "I guess we'll have to. It's just that this adds yet another person in the loop. Oh, well, I'll see you this evening, I guess."

As she walked back toward her office, she wondered if he understood that he, too, would have to be a little more forthcoming about what had happened in Vietnam. She was also wondering where he really stood with his bosses. Presumed innocent or presumed suspect? He had been concerned right from the beginning about this story getting out in flag circles before the issue was properly defined, and now she had had a taste of why he was worried. She would have to fill Train in on what had happened in Kensington's office and alert him to the fact that Sherman had been reluctant about folding NIS into this picture.

Karen and Train arrived at Sherman's house nearly twenty minutes later than she had planned, thanks to an overturned pickup truck and trailer at the north end of the GW Parkway. He had followed her to McLean in his car, a large fire engine red Suburban, which he parked behind her in front of Sherman's town house.

There did not seem to be any lights on in the town house, so once again she found herself waiting outside a strange front door. After her excursion to OP-03's office, she had spent the rest of the morning harassing the Bureau about getting the records on Galantz. Train von Rensel had not returned until just before she left the Pentagon to make the meeting at Sherman's house. She had not had time to back-brief him on the meeting with Kensington before they had to get on the road.

Von Rensel's open skepticism about the admiral's story of the disappearing letter irritated her. She resented the inference that she would be getting way out of her depth if the mysterious SEAL really did exist. She also wondered if von Rensel's reaction to the admiral's story had anything to do with simple male competitiveness. She was getting the feeling that the big man was interested in her, although she couldn't put her finger on why she felt that way. She had seen men do this before, getting competitive just because she was involved. Train wasn't really her type, if there was such a thing, but still, he was interesting in some indefinably exotic sense. Sherman was an extremely handsome, smooth, and obviously very successful naval officer; Train, a great bear of a man whose watchful demeanor did not seem to quite square with his physical size. She smiled in the dark at her silly mental meandering. She had always been interested in men, but now, in her newfound widowhood, she had turned inward, unwilling to expend the energy required for a new relationship. The disturbing possibility that Frank might have been meeting another woman in that hotel, however much she suppressed it, had unsettled her self-confidence. She had been ruthless about tamping down that subject every time her subconscious mind wanted to surface it. But she really did wonder every once in a while what she had done, or failed to do, that would have led Frank to seek out another woman's companionship. Maybe I just got lazy, she thought. Or at least complacent. But then her independent self would react angrily: Why should I assume it was my fault if Frank was unfaithful?

Headlights appeared in her mirror as Sherman showed up in a big Ford sedan. She got out of her car as von Rensel got out of the Suburban.

"Sorry to keep you waiting," he said, locking his own car. "There was a last-minute flap."

"At least we didn't keep the detective waiting," she said. "Admiral, this is Mr. von Rensel of the NIS. You were introduced at the first meeting, I think."

The two men shook hands, visibly sizing each other up. "Mr. von Rensel, thank you for joining us," Sherman said. "If we're going to need NIS, it'd be good for you to be in on this from the beginning."

"Hope we can help, Admiral," Train replied, but he left it at that.

Sherman nodded, looking around, and they walked across the street to the front steps of his house, which was a large and fairly elegant three-story affair. Once inside and settled in the living room, Sherman looked at his watch. "McNair should be here in just a few minutes. We're agreed I should tell him about the SEAL, as little of the history as I can get away with, and what happened the other night, right?"

"Yes, sir," Karen said. "And then I think we should try to find out what they're really doing. Is this a homicide? Is there an investigation? Like that. In the spirit of your telling them everything, McNair should be a little more forthcoming."

"And you've briefed Mr. von Rensel here?"

"Yes, sir. And I've called for the records on Galantz."

"They'll want to see those."

"Yes. Another opportunity for a quid pro quo."

He looked at her, nodding thoughtfully. But she could tell his mind was elsewhere, probably on what he was going to say to the detective. The doorbell chimed.

"Action stations," he said, then got up to let him in. McNair came in, shucking a trench coat. He looked a little like a prizefighter in a three-piece suit, she thought, and she noticed that he frowned across the room when he saw Train. The admiral was making introductions.

McNair looked at Train again, as if acknowledging the presence of a fed. When they were finally all situated in the living room, the admiral kicked it off. "First, I should tell you that Commander Lawrence and I have talked about the nature and extent of my cooperation with you."

"Is Commander Lawrence acting in the capacity of your lawyer, Admiral?" McNair asked immediately. Karen was amused by the way they talked as if she was not even in the room.

"No. Commander Lawrence is officially acting on behalf of the JAG. At the moment, I have not sought counsel. One of my main objectives for this meeting is to find out if I *should* seek counsel."

McNair nodded, as if this was the most reasonable position in the world.

Sherman leaned forward. "I haven't requested counsel because you have indicated that I am not suspected of any crimes. As I said, I've kicked this around with Commander Lawrence here, and she has advised me to co-operate fully with your, um, inquiries. I have a new development to bring to your attention, which is the other reason I wanted this meeting. But first I'd also like to get confirmation that nothing's changed as to where I stand in this thing."

Karen watched with interest. She was sure that McNair would have expected to conduct the meeting. It was interesting to watch the admiral turn the situation around.

"Admiral Sherman," he said, "we've been over the pathologist's report with respect to the estimated time of death. We've verified where you were during the most likely window of opportunity. We're satisfied that you were where you said you were, and that you could not have been in Ms. Walsh's house at the presumed time of death. You are not a suspect, per se."

"Has a crime been committed?" Karen asked.

"Perhaps we can let the admiral tell me what he wants to tell me, Counselor," McNair suggested. "Then we can talk about a crime."

Karen was about to argue when she saw the admiral nodding. She deferred. Train stood by a window, remaining silent.

"Fair enough," the admiral said. "As I believe you know, I—we, actually, Commander Lawrence and myself—went to Elizabeth's house Tuesday night. I wanted to call on Dottie Klein. She and Elizabeth were very close. I also wanted to see the house. Somehow, this whole thing wouldn't be real unless I could go there. That probably sounds pretty strange."

McNair listened attentively, his notebook open.

"So, anyway, as Commander Lawrence has told you, I noticed something odd about the scene, or the scenario, perhaps. Beyond the business about the laundry basket. The slippers. I gave her those slippers as a present, but the fact was, she detested them. One of those awkward things, a present that didn't work. But the key point is, she *never* wore them."

"Yes," McNair said. "Commander Lawrence mentioned them. But if she never wore them, why did she keep them?"

"I'm guessing because they had been a gift from me. Who knows. Like I said, one of those awkward things. But I was very surprised to see them down there. Dottie said it looked as if she had been wearing them. Then, of course, there's the problem of her taking a laundry basket of clothes to the basement level. I can't think of a single reason for her to do that."

"Yes, sir," McNair said. Karen thought she heard a trace of impatience in his voice. I've heard all this. Cut to the chase, please. Sherman seemed to catch it.

"Okay. Before I went over there, I came home first to change. I found something in my mail that was pretty upsetting." He went on to tell McNair about the letter, what it said, about later going over to see Galen Schmidt, only to come home and find that his front door was unlocked, and that when he had gone looking for the letter before going to bed, it was gone.

McNair made some notes. "The door was definitely locked when you left, Admiral?"

"Yes. It's set to lock itself. You can take a look if you'd like. I would have to make a special point of unlocking it, which of course I never do. This is McLean, but hardly a crime-free area."

"And you are positive the letter was gone when you got back?" McNair asked.

"Yes. Although I didn't realize it until after I had gone up to bed. I did some paperwork upstairs, where I have a small study. Then I decided that I'd take the letter into the office, so Karen here could see it. I came back downstairs to look for it. It must have been after eleven. I'd left it on the kitchen counter, with the rest of the mail, before going to see Admiral Schmidt. I'd put the envelope in the trash with the junk mail. I couldn't find either one when I looked."

"Anything else in the house missing?"

"No. I checked that as soon as I got into the house. As best I can tell, that's all that was taken."

McNair consulted his notebook. "So you think this guy has come back after all these years to get revenge for something that happened back in Vietnam, and that he's started the game by mailing you a warning letter. Then he watched your house to make sure you got the letter, and then, when you left, broke into the house, retrieved the letter and the envelope, and left the door unlocked so you would know he'd been here?"

Karen saw a trace of embarrassment on the admiral's face. "I don't know what else to think," he said. "I'm very upset about what's happened to Elizabeth, and I'm beginning to conclude that her fall was no accident. I'm also worried that whatever happened to her might be my fault, at least indirectly."

McNair leaned forward. "This thing in Vietnam. You're implying that something happened over there that would inspire a guy to come back after more than twenty years to do something to you, that something including maybe killing your girlfriend?"

Sherman studied his feet for a moment before replying. Then he looked up. "I guess I am," he admitted.

"It would make your hypothesis a lot more credible if we knew what that incident in Vietnam was all about."

"I'm sure it would. But it involved some highly classified operations. All I can say is that I can fully believe it." Sherman looked down at the rug again for a moment. "I know. That's not much to go on."

McNair gave him a look that made it quite clear he was in full agreement with Sherman's last remark. "See, Admiral, it's not just us," he said. "To open a homicide investigation, especially if there's a new element, we have to convince our lieutenant—and maybe a judge—that we want to do some searching. Now if we just had that letter—"

"I know," Sherman interrupted. "But it's gone. Maybe the postman might recall sorting it. I don't know. But as to what happened in Vietnam, it's classified. I can't tell you any more than that."

"*Is* there a homicide investigation in progress?" Train asked from his perch by the window.

There was a sudden silence in the room. McNair opened his mouth but closed it without saying anything. Karen decided to make her move. "Detective McNair," she said, "in our original meeting, you mentioned certain forensic ambiguities. The admiral here has been concerned that, over and above the slippers problem, if he told you about this letter, it would make Elizabeth Walsh's death seem less like an accident and more like a possible homicide. The problem is, up to tonight, the only person you are talking to is him. He's told you as much as he can. What can you tell us about those forensic ambiguities?"

McNair thought about that, and then he nodded.

"Okay," he said. "Our first take was accident. Lady fell down the stairs, landed wrong, broke her neck. Medical examiner's preliminary report said the same thing. We caught the fact that the laundry room down there didn't appear to be used very often, if at all. But she could have been carrying that stuff down to store it, and using a laundry basket to carry it. Who knows. There was no apparent forced entry, no physical evidence of personal violence, other than that which could have reasonably been caused by the fall. Abrasions where you would expect them. And later, postautopsy, nothing in the pathology reports indicating assault, poison, drugs, rape, or anything like that."

"You did an autopsy?" Sherman asked. Karen had seen him wince at the word.

"Yes, sir. Standard procedure in an unexplained death. Unless the victim's doctor can come in and give us a reasonable explanation, an autopsy will normally be performed. But, like I said, that didn't give us any indication of homicide."

"So what were the ambiguities?" Train asked.

"Well, it's like this. When there's no obvious cause of death, we assume misadventure, or accident. But we also look at it from the other perspective:

If this *had* been a homicide, what kind of evidence should be there? Well, first of all, some physical evidence of someone else being in that house. So just to make very sure, we had our crime-scene unit come in and do a standard sweep." He leaned back in his chair for a moment before going on.

"Let's put aside fingerprints for a minute. Let's postulate, for instance, that someone who knew what he was doing broke in, waited for her, and, surprised her, say, and then pushed her down the stairs. He probably wouldn't have come in the front door—too exposed. More likely, he'd use the back door or a back window, say from that garden. Either way, there should have been some physical traces of that garden in the house—grass, dirt. And the back porch paint is old and dried out. There should have been some tiny flakes of that paint in the carpets. None of the windows had been kicked in, right? The back door lock is a Baringer. They use a peculiar steel alloy for their keys. If somebody had picked the lock, there should have been physical evidence of foreign metal-alloy particles in that lock, or in any of the locks. Stuff like that."

"But there wasn't?" Train asked.

"That's right."

"This sounds like a pretty thorough examination," the admiral said. "But I don't understand the premise. If this was an accident, none of this evidence would be there in any event."

"Ah, yes," McNair said, leaning forward. "But from a forensic perspective, that place was hinky. Like fingerprints? Well, we did find fingerprints—hers, Mrs. Klein's, and, incidentally, even some of yours, Admiral—but only upstairs. Remember what I said about physical evidence a minute ago? That there wasn't any? We didn't get a single fingerprint lift downstairs. None. Zero. Zip. And you know what else? Mrs. Klein, the nice old lady who says she goes over there all the time to have coffee, shoot the breeze, whatever? Mrs. Klein says she always comes over via the back porch. They're connected. She even has a key. Her porch paint is like Miss Walsh's: sunbaked, flaking, but a different color."

"I don't understand," Sherman said.

"Except for the very obvious trail she left when she found the body, there were no other signs of that paint in the Walsh kitchen, or in any of the rugs on the main floor. In fact, there wasn't much of anything in those rugs. Very little dirt. And no sand or bits of moss from those bricks in her front walk. Assuming Miss Walsh came home via her own front door that afternoon, there should have been something, see?"

Karen twisted anxiously in her chair. This was beginning to sound like something far different from the cut-and-dried accident they had been talking about all along.

"Admiral," McNair continued, "this may be painful to hear, but there was something wrong with Miss Walsh's clothes, too, besides what you told us about the slippers."

"Her clothes?" he asked, obviously baffled now.

"Yes, sir. We found none of the things on her clothes that should have been there after a working day in the office—no dandruff, no loose hairs, no foreign fibers on the seat of her slacks from an office chair, no ink smudges on her fingers, no residue of toner from a copy machine or a laser printer on her hands or sleeves. Now you know most Washington people can't spend a day in the office without touching a Xerox copy of something, right?"

"Yes, of course."

"And in addition to all the stuff that collects after a day in the office, there's the ride home on the Metro. She took the Metro, didn't she? There was a fare card in her purse."

"Yes, she did. Park and Ride from the West Falls Church station."

"Well, okay. You come home Friday at rush hour, it's back-to-back, belly-to-belly, right? But her street clothes were clean—much too clean. No one else's hair. No traces of another human being anywhere on her collar or her raincoat. We checked."

"Like somebody had vacuumed them?" Karen asked. McNair gave her a look, as if to say she had just incriminated herself.

"Maybe. Or the clothes she was wearing weren't the clothes she wore to work."

"How about her shoes?" Train asked.

McNair smiled. "Bingo," he said softly. "Oh, we found shoes aplenty up in the closet, but none that showed evidence of having been worn to the office that day and then exchanged for slippers."

Karen let out a long breath. "So can't you check with the people in her office, find out what she was wearing that day?"

"We did," replied McNair. "Slacks, blouse, sweater. But no one re-members exactly which ones, which colors. One guy said gray; another guy said dark. They were mostly men in the office. You know how it is, Commander: Men never notice a woman's shoes. And you review investi-gations, right? You know how poorly even eyewitnesses' statements correlate."

Karen knew only too well. "Yes, I do. How about her vacuum cleaner?"

"New bag."

"Ah," she said, understanding what he was trying to say. "So the evidence in this case is backward. It's the evidence you *didn't* find that's bothering you."

"Sherlock Holmes," the admiral muttered. "The dog that didn't bark."

"That's correct, Admiral," McNair said, nodding. "So your news about the slippers is, unfortunately, entirely consistent. But until you told me about this letter, it was still ambiguous. What was this guy's name, Admiral?"

"He was a hospital corpsman—a medic, as well as a SEAL. HM1 Marcus Galantz."

McNair blinked, almost as if the name meant something to him. But then he asked the admiral to spell it for him, and he wrote it in his notebook. Then he asked another question. "Since Mr. von Rensel is here, can we assume the Navy's working on this Galantz angle, Commander Lawrence?"

That came out of nowhere, Karen thought quickly. "On getting his old service records, yes," she replied. "Beyond that—" Beyond that, the Navy didn't yet know about Galantz.

"The records may be of use, and they may not," the admiral interjected. "My guess is that they'll end abruptly in 1969."

McNair stared at him, his expression making it clear that the admiral could not go on with all this secrecy.

Sherman looked back at him for a moment and then got up, walked over to a front window, and stared out at the growing darkness. McNair, as if sensing a critical moment, remained quiet, watching him. Then he spoke.

"Admiral, it's becoming pretty clear that something happened to Elizabeth Walsh, something that was not an accident. We're reasonably satisfied that you didn't go over there Friday night and do something to her. Now you've given us another lead to pursue, but you're leaving too much out. We need your help. We need to make this guy real."

And to get you entirely off the hook, Karen thought.

The admiral remained at the window, his back to them, for almost a minute. "Okay," he said finally, so quietly that Karen wasn't sure she had heard him. Then he turned around, and she was startled by the pain in his eyes. "Okay. This'll take a while."

He returned to his chair and sat down, his eyes slightly out of focus as the memories came flooding back. Then he told them the story of the aborted SEAL pickup and that terrifying night on the river.

"Did they go back the next night?" Train asked.

Sherman hesitated. "No. They didn't. Saigon naval headquarters called it off. They concluded that the SEAL never made the rendezvous and that the VC probably had him, which was why there was a mine ambush waiting."

"But they were wrong, weren't they, Admiral?" Train said. The two men stared at each other for a long moment. Then Sherman looked away and exhaled. "Yes. They were wrong. Because three years later, the SEAL came to see me. I was finishing up my department-head tour in a destroyer and was actually home for a change. But I remember it. God, do I remember it. He was a memorable guy. I was sitting in my dining room, working on some overdue fitness reports."

It had been after ten o'clock on a rainy February night, one of the few such nights in San Diego's unvarying pattern of monotonously beautiful weather. Sherman had been downstairs in the dining room when he thought he heard the front door open. He remembered sitting up and thinking, What the hell? I locked that door. There had been a gust of wind and the sudden sound of rain, and then suddenly a figure was standing in the entrance to the dining room, just outside the cone of light from the chandelier. Sherman absorbed a vague image of jeans and a wet black windbreaker, but the face—the face looked familiar. Only this time, there was no brown and green paint. Just those eyes. Actually, just one eye.

"Remember me?" the figure asked in a husky, strangled voice. There was something wrong with his throat. There was a small swatch of gray bandage where his voice box should have been, and a livid scar.

Sherman had been speechless, glued to his armchair, trying to comprehend what he was seeing. A very dangerous-looking one-eyed man, was standing motionless in his dining room, dripping rainwater on the rug.

"How—who—"

"Oh, you remember, Lieutenant. You know who I am. Or who I was," the man said, advancing closer to the table, into the light, appearing to get bigger as he did so. He was not visibly armed, but there was no mistaking the menace in that mutilated face. And then Tag Sherman knew.

"You're—you're the SEAL."

"Yeah, the SEAL. The one you left behind. In the Rung Sat."

Sherman could only stare at him, trying to remember what the division commander had said—what, exactly? He couldn't recall the words, other than him saying, "You did the operationally right thing, aborting the mission." But by then, the SEAL had come even closer to the table, and with a sweeping motion of his left arm, he scattered Sherman's paperwork. That's when Sherman saw the glove, the black glove with a glint of stainless steel at the left wrist. What was his *name?* he'd asked himself. Galantz, that was it.

Galantz perched on the edge of the dining room table, making it creak, and leaned down to stare directly into Sherman's eyes. His face was pale, gaunt, hollow-eyed, with taut skin, a bony forehead fringed with only a stubble of close-cropped black hair. The right eyebrow was flat, but the left was bisected by an ugly red and obviously unstitched scar running from his voice box up into his jaw and then exiting across the left cheek up into his scalp, transecting the puckered skin of his empty left eye socket. Sherman had been able to smell the wet clothes, overlaid with the rising scent of his own fear.

"See this?" the SEAL asked, pointing to his face and throat with his finger. "One of your fifties did this. Ricochet round. While you girls were busy running away, shooting that stuff indiscriminately all over the riverbanks—where I was hiding, waiting for you. And this"—he brandished the bulky black glove in Sherman's face—"this is where I had to amputate my own hand after a croc bit most of it off."

He leaned even closer to Sherman, who remained frozen in his seat. Sherman had to crane his neck just to look up at this man, whose single eye burned in his face like the headlight of that proverbial oncoming train.

"It had lots of time to get infected, Lieutenant," he whispered. "Five nights in the mangrove roots, while I tried to get down out of the Rung Sat and into the harbor. Couldn't quite make it, though, because the Cong knew I was running, see? And I couldn't go into the main river because by then the crocs could smell the arm. All that heat and mud and humidity. They call it gangrene. Stinks real bad. I'm a medic. Know it when I smell it. Crocs love rotten meat. So finally one night, I found a tree stump and chopped it off at the wrist with my trusty knife. This knife, right here." Out of nowhere, he brandished a heavy dulled steel knife, then deliberately put it down on the table right in front of Sherman. It looked bigger than he remembered it, when the SEAL had had it strapped to his ankle. It made an audible *clunk* when Galantz laid it on the table.

Galantz had leaned back then, staring down at the knife, and continued his story. "I clamped off the artery with a piece of string and then that night I bellied into a VC camp and killed some people so I could get to their fire and cauterize the stump. Didn't happen to have any anesthetics, by the way. It hurt a lot. But I did what I had to do. Stuck that bloody stump into the fire and bit a piece of bamboo right in half waiting for it to cook. I gotta tell you: I did scream. But the screaming sounded better than the barbecue noises, you know?"

"We were in an ambush," Sherman had said, feeling his stomach grab. His voice seemed to be stuck in his throat, which was as dry as sand. "There were mines. We had standing orders to withdraw. We came back the next night." And then he remembered: No, they hadn't.

The SEAL had just looked at him with that one baleful eye. "Sure you did, Lieutenant. But you know what? I was three klicks from the main river by then, trying to lick my wounds with my tongue swelling out of my mouth, hiding out inside the hollow trunk of a dead tree that was full of that Agent Orange stuff. And trying to figure out if that was my eyeball dangling on my left cheek or just another leech. And that was just the beginning. It took me *five weeks* to get back to friendly territory. Five weeks of crawling around in the Rung Sat, no compass, no landmarks, no food, no clean water, moving only at night, going the wrong goddamned way *every* goddamned time. And killing people. Lots of people, you know? Anyone who got any-where near me ate steel. This steel, right here. Men, women, children— anyone. Five bloody weeks until I got into the outskirts of Saigon. And then I got arrested by the White Mice, who put me in a Chinese jail for a year in Cholon until they found somebody who would buy my ass out. All thanks to a bunch of chickenshit Swift boat guys. Like you."

"I did what I had to," Sherman had protested. "They were setting off mines. Lose the boat and nobody gets out. I'm sorry it happened. But we had no choice."

The SEAL had stared down at him with that one glaring eye, his ravaged face twisting in contempt.

"What do you want?" Sherman whispered.

"Want?" The SEAL leaned forward again. "I *want* revenge. I *want* to stick this knife through your hand and into this table here so you don't go anywhere. Then I *want* to go upstairs and rape your wife and blind your kid, and then I *want* to come back down here and open up your belly with this knife and strangle you with your own guts. That's what I *want*."

The knife had been lying on the table the whole time, right in front of him, but Sherman was transfixed in the chair, a watery feeling in his stomach, his mouth still arid. And then with the swiftness of a rattlesnake, the man had him hauled up out of his chair and bent over the table, his right arm pinned behind his back by the SEAL's knee in a bone-cracking arch, his face pressed down on the table by the SEAL's left forearm, the edge of the table pressing hard against his windpipe. He could barely breathe, and then he felt, rather than saw, the cutting edge of that knife resting across the bridge of his nose about one millimeter from his eyes. The SEAL's voice hissed in his ears.

"What do I *want*, Sherman? I *want* to pop your eyeballs out and make you eat them while the nerves are still attached. I *want* to drive twentypenny nails into your skull and wire them to your car battery. I *want* to jam your mouth open with a bent fork and put a black widow spider in there and piss her off. I *want* lots of fun shit for you and yours, Lieutenant, but guess what—I've learned to wait for what I want. I've learned to be a patient man. I'm going to wait some more. I'm going to wait until you have accumulated some things of real value. And then I'm going to make *you* pay for what you and your crew did to me, no matter how long it takes. You were the skipper, so you're the Man. You'll never know when I'm coming. Until I tell you. And I will tell you, you son of a bitch. You will get one warning."

His air shut off by the table's edge, Sherman's vision had gone red and his ears were roaring ominously. He had barely heard the small voice from the edge of the room. "Daddy?"

The SEAL had come off his back in an instant, leaving Sherman to slide off the table and onto the floor like a sack of potatoes, his mouth working but nothing coming out, all his muscles putty. Out of the corner of his eye, he could see that Galantz had grabbed his son, Jack, and was holding the petrified child off the floor with his good arm, growling at him like a wild animal, as if he was about to dash him against the wall. Sherman had tried desperately to move, to get up, but he had been perfectly helpless, gagging on the floor, his nearly dislocated right shoulder preventing him from even beginning to get up.

And then suddenly, it was over. The terrified child was sobbing in the corner of the dining room, and Sherman was pulling himself across the floor to get to him. His wife had slept through it all, even when little Jack had begun to wail like a banshee in his arms. It had taken him an hour and a half to calm the child and get him back to bed. He had not awakened his wife. There seemed to be no point in her being terrified, too. He had gone back downstairs to get some brandy to steady his shaking hands and to close the front door, which was still standing wide open in the rain. He had nearly lost it again when he found the knife lying on the dining room table—a little reminder that it had all been real.

A little message from the SEAL: I don't need the knife anymore. But you might.

Now Sherman's eyes refocused and looked over at McNair. "I was mostly ashamed when it was all over. Ashamed for what we had done back there in the Rung Sat. Ashamed that I had been scared to death in this guy's presence. Ashamed that I had been helpless to do anything when he had my son up against the wall like a rag doll."

Karen remembered to breathe, and she swallowed hard. McNair, who had been listening intently, reopened his notebook.

"This was when, Admiral? And you're sure this man's name was Galantz? Marcus Galantz?"

"In 1972. February. And I'm sure about the name."

"And you're sure this was Galantz?" McNair asked again, his face a study in concentration. Sherman said yes. Sherman looked drained, as if the memories had emptied him of all energy. He was slumped in his chair like a teenager.

"Well, this of course makes a difference," McNair said. "The fact that he came back proves he lived through what happened out there in Vietnam."

"If he was that disfigured, he should be easier to find, don't you think?" Karen asked.

Train shook his head. "That was 1972. Cosmetic surgery has come a long way since then." He turned to Sherman. "Admiral, is there a possibility that he was still in the Navy then? That he was on active duty?"

"I don't think so." He took a deep breath, as if trying to make the memories go away. But then he looked over at McNair. "I've told you this story because now I'm more convinced than ever that she was killed. Elizabeth, I mean. But the Navy would not take kindly to having this story get out."

"It's been over twenty years, Admiral," McNair said. "Why would it be such a big deal if it comes out now?"

Sherman rubbed his face with both hands. "We left one of our own behind, Detective," he said. "In the armed forces, that's a big deal. You don't abandon your wounded, and you sure as hell don't leave a guy out there just because headquarters makes some assumptions. You go back and get him. Guy's count on that, in return for which, they're willing to fight and die."

"I understand, Admiral," McNair replied. "But if Miss Walsh was indeed murdered, that takes precedence, don't you think? What I'm saying is that you did the right thing in telling me this. I promise to be discreet about this matter. Although, now that I think about it, we may have a small bureaucratic problem here."

"Which is?"

"The department has several cases that *are* clear-cut homicides."

The admiral nodded slowly. "I think I understand. Cases where there is direct evidence of a crime, as opposed to evidence that isn't there."

"Something like that," McNair said. "Our lieutenant isn't convinced about this, although he doesn't know what you've told me tonight. But right now, from an evidentiary point of view, this one's still sort of a reach."

Sherman looked perplexed. "But—"

"Don't get me wrong. I mean, we can work this thing, okay? But it will help a lot if the Navy can help us locate this Galantz. Turn him into a living, breathing human, instead of a missing letter and a story from some twenty years back."

Everyone looked over at Train.

"As soon as we have anything at all, I'll get it to you," Karen offered. "And I'm sure Mr. von Rensel can turn on some Naval Investigative Service assets."

"That would help," McNair said. "We need something tangible here. Otherwise—"

The admiral was rubbing his face again. Karen's heart went out to him. His face had taken on an ashen hue with the inescapable conclusion that Elizabeth Walsh had been murdered. Train remained silent.

"Is there anything else you want to tell me, Admiral?" McNair asked.

The admiral shook his head. "I can't think of anything, other than to reiterate the need for discretion."

"I understand," McNair said. "And I need to reiterate the need for full disclosure, Admiral. If nothing else, it will save us all a lot of time."

Karen stood up to indicate that the interview was over. McNair got the message and stood up as well, thanked the admiral for his cooperation, retrieved his coat, and left. Karen saw him out, then came back to the living room. Sherman was still sitting there in the armchair, staring at nothing, his chin in his right hand.

"Well, did we do any good?" he asked finally.

"I think so," Karen said. "He's certainly got something new to think about."

"We all do," Train said. "We've got to find this guy."

Sherman let out a long breath. He looked as if he'd been through a mental train wreck. "You tell me how I can help you with that, Mr. von Rensel, and you've got it. For the Navy's sake, it'd be better if you guys found him than the police."

"Admiral, I'll get on this right away," Train said, getting up. "Commander Lawrence and I will meet first thing tomorrow."

"And go see Carpenter?" Sherman asked.

Karen, feeling she knew more about the political sensitivities than von Rensel, intervened. "Not yet, Admiral," she said. "I think we have all the authority we need to turn on NIS help right now." She was hoping Train would just leave it at that for the moment, and apparently he understood.

"So do I," he said. "Karen, I'll see you in the morning."

After Train left, Karen came back into the living room. The admiral was still just sitting there, looking emotionally sandblasted. Karen suggested that a drink might be in order.

An hour later, they were sitting in a booth at a small Greek restaurant. Afraid that he would sit there and polish off the bottle of scotch, she had suggested they go get something to eat. And after watching him down a good-sized drink, she had even volunteered to drive. He had been silent during the drive down to the restaurant. She had tried to divert him from his visibly grim train of thought.

"Admiral, what's done is done. And we may still all be wrong here. Even the cops feel they're backing into a homicide. She really may have just fallen."

Sherman was quick to shake his head. "No," he said. "Elizabeth was a competent woman. She was less of a klutz than I am, and I'm pretty agile for my age. She'd lived in that house for ten years. Those aren't treacherous stairs. Now this letter, and then the business with my front door, and what we've learned about the forensic gaps in her house. I just can't swallow all that as coincidence. Maybe if I'd just been there . . ."

She toyed with her salad, waiting while he wandered mentally in the what-if thicket again. "Sorry," he said. "I was just kicking myself in the ass again. I guess I missed a good thing when I told her no."

"Told her no?"

Sherman recapped the story of their relationship, how they first met, and how well it worked out up until the point where Elizabeth began steering conversations around to the logical next step.

"I told her no. I was married once before and it was an unqualified disaster. Although that all seems a lifetime ago now."

"I'm sorry to hear that," she said. "Would it help to talk about it?"

He started to reply but then hesitated, as though unsure of her. "It's not a pretty story," he said at last. "Are you sure you want to hear it?"

"I apologize, Admiral," she said immediately, afraid she had overstepped the bounds of junior-senior propriety. "I—"

"No, don't apologize. And let's put the admiral-commander stuff aside for a moment here, Karen. After what we've learned tonight, I need your help. I need your legal expertise. I need your brains, now more than ever. This is no longer admiral-commander territory. But there's history, history that bears on what happened between Elizabeth and me. I guess what I'm saying is that I just can't toss off a cavalier answer. And the other thing is, I wouldn't want this to be discussed with anyone else. I've already disclosed too much to the police, I'm afraid."

She thought about that. He was obviously referring to her real loyalties vis-à-vis Carpenter. But, as a woman, she was also very curious as to what could have happened to make a marriage to this attractive and intelligent man go off the tracks.

"Yes," she said. "I do want to help you. But you must understand something: Except as a very junior officer, I've never been anyone's lawyer. Anyone's advocate. I've been a professional second-guesser for most of my career. My specialty is to sit in judgment over other people's investigative efforts. That's not the same as being an experienced investigator or trial attorney. And, as much as I do want to help you, I'm in an equivocal position here: I work for Admiral Carpenter. So if you're about to tell me something he shouldn't hear, you probably shouldn't tell me."

"I understand that," he said. "At this point, I probably should go into JAG and ask for formal counsel. But you were there in Kensington's office: The moment I do that, there'll be red rockets going up in the flag community, which, as best as I can tell after a few months of being a member, would happily cut its losses where someone in my situation is concerned. I've worked for nearly thirty years to get this star. I'm not ready to just throw it away because the admiral herd is getting antsy."

"Yes, sir." She smiled. "Now tell me as much of the history as I need to know."

He signaled the waiter and asked him to bring them another glass of wine.

"I grew up a navy junior," he said. "When my dad was a commander in a heavy cruiser based down in Norfolk, he was killed in a shipboard accident. He was an Annapolis grad, so naturally I gravitated to the Academy. With some help from his classmates, I got in on a presidential appointment."

"Yes, sir," she said.

"Well, I graduated in 1966. Did the not-terribly-bright thing of getting married on the same day."

"Had you known her long?"

"Yes. Since high school. We'd been sort of circling each other in the eighth grade. When Dad was killed, she became terribly important. When I went into the boat school, she went off to American University. For the first year, my plebe year, none of us was allowed to date. But her letters kept me alive. And we saw each other during Christmas holidays, and later, after my summer cruise. After that, we dated steadily for the next three years. It was all so, I don't know, convenient. Comfortable. Reliable. She was pretty, bright, and fun. I was nothing much at the Academy, did okay in academics but was otherwise undistinguished. She helped to define who I was: the guy with this good-looking girlfriend."

"What was her name?"

"Her name was Beth. Actually, her name was Marcia Kendall. Beth was a name she adopted in the third grade, and that's what everyone called her. Her father was a history prof at the Academy, in what we called the 'Bull' department: English, history, and government." He caught her look. "Yeah, well, Canoe U. has always been a little bizarre in its nomenclature. If you didn't go there, you probably can't understand how inbred Annapolis and the whole Naval Academy scene was."

"Sounds like a typical college town."

"Probably. Except that Annapolis also happens to be the capital of Maryland. But the mids are oblivious to that little fact. Anyway, back then there was only one academic major, and that was naval engineering. Everybody did the same thing, the same summer cruises. Marched to class. Same plebe year BS. You couldn't whine or complain about the regimen or discipline to anyone. But I had Beth."

Karen sipped her wine.

"She'd been around the Academy as long as I had, so she knew the score. Knew what I was going through. Anyway, we got married, graduation day wedding number thirteen—thirty minutes, guests in, ceremony, guests out, swords up, swords down, next couple, please. But even on the assembly-line basis, it was romantic—the chapel, the big organ, the guys holding crossed swords, the whole bit. And we were free—free of the Yard, the walls, our parents, all the chicken rules and regs. I knew my old man would have been very proud. I had done it—carried on the all-important tradition. It was a day to remember."

"And then?"

"And then a month to get across the country, report in to the fleet, and experience our first collision with reality. We set up housekeeping in a little cracker-box house in San Diego, three tiny bedrooms, two baths, a living room and a kitchen, and the all-important two-car garage. All the houses the same, and all eight feet apart. Three cars in every yard. And then I went to sea. And I mean, I *went* to sea. My first ship was gone seventy percent of the time. Vietnam was starting to come to a boil in the fall of 1966. Hell, when I left the Academy in the summer of 1966, I don't think I even knew where Vietnam was. But off we went, out to WESTPAC, to the Seventh Fleet, and that was the big time, the Navy's first team.

"Back in San Diego, Beth had Jack—that's my son—in January 1967. Seven months after graduation, but who was counting? And that's when the trouble began, I think. She was pregnant, on her own, and trying to live on ensign's pay, which in those days was two hundred and twenty-two dollars a month. And then I heard about the Swift boat program, and naturally I volunteered. At first they said no. I was Academy, a regular officer, bound for department-head school. They were sending only extended reservists to the boats. But then they changed their mind, and off I went to gunboat school in Coronado."

"How did she feel about that?"

"About what you'd think. The training lasted two months, which was ironically the longest straight period of time I'd been home in over two years. But then I shipped out with my boat crew to the Philippines for two months, and then went in country for a year. I saw Beth once during that year—in Hawaii during our one R-and-R period."

"So, two years of arduous sea duty, a new baby, then—what, fourteen months of overseas duty, with one week in Hawaii to make it all up?"

"You got it. Except it was five days, not a whole week. R and R was actually almost painful for the married guys. We tried like hell to carry it off, but it didn't really work. You knew on day one that there were only four days left. You could almost tell how many days a couple had left by the looks on their faces. I was jet-lagged, and she was desperately tired, something I didn't really anticipate. There was a lot I didn't notice. Like too many of us at that age, my focus was on me. *My* career. *My* adventures in Vietnam. *My* prospects for the next assignment. *My* future in the Navy. And there was another problem: little Jack. The baby was hitting the terrible twos, and giving new meaning to the term. If Jack comes visiting, watch him every minute. He would hit and hurt other kids. He broke stuff. He ran off and hid when you came to find him. He disrupted the nursery school, when we could afford one. He went through baby-sitters by the dozens. Of course, Beth didn't tell me any of this during our one week in the Hawaiian paradise. Jack was 'difficult at times' was all I got."

"Was the child ADD?" she asked. "Or was it a psychological problem?"

He smiled. "We didn't even know about attention deficit disorder, or dyslexia, or any of that stuff. People were just fairly blunt about it: The Shermans had a bad kid, that was all."

"It is amazing how ill-prepared we humans are to raise a child," she mused, turning her wineglass in her hands. "We train for everything else but just fearlessly jump into the baby scene."

"Did you have kids?"

"No. By the time I married, children were pretty much out of the question, really. We married rather late in life. I was thirty-four, Frank was forty-four. Children would have just messed things up. At least that's what I kept telling myself."

"We play the hand we're dealt," he said softly. "Sounds like you made some better choices than I did. Still want to hear this?"

She nodded.

"Right. Well, when I got back from Vietnam in 1970, I had a three-plus-year-old little horror and a wife with the beginnings of a drinking problem. Once again, I didn't really notice. I was off to the next rung on the ladder. *My* career, *über alles*. We sold the house, shagged off to Newport, Rhode Island, for department-head school—that was six months—and then back to San Diego for my department-head tour. Oh, great: more sea duty. Not exactly the most stable family life. I was finishing up that tour—that was, I guess early 1972, when Galantz came calling. Jack was about five. By then, Beth was using fruit juice laced with vodka just to get through the day, and I was just starting to wonder how this would all come out—especially Jack."

"Did you get help with Jack?"

"Well, yes and no. We used some Navy counselors at Balboa hospital, but they were dealing with seriously disturbed kids—schizophrenics, kids with severe learning disabilities. To them, Jack was a discipline problem—not a mental problem, but behavioral."

"They know a little bit more about that today."

"I wonder," Sherman said. "But in our case, there were two problems. The first was the old who's-in-charge problem. Beth ran the household when I was away at sea, which was most of the time. Then I'd come home for a couple of weeks and try to take over. Kids are smart: They learn to divide and conquer. But Jack posed a legitimate question: Whose rules did he have to follow? Did everything change just because Daddy was home?"

"I've heard other Navy people talk about that. And the second problem?"

"Five years ago, I would have said it was hers. But in retrospect, it really was mine. That's one of the things Elizabeth showed me. Basically, I didn't much like my son, so I abdicated. Jack became Beth's problem child, not mine. I seized on the excuse that it didn't make sense for me to come home at irregular intervals and change all the rules. By leaving her in charge, I could simply back out of the problem. I had an operations department and a career to worry about. Mommy can be in charge on the home front. Mommy can own it. Again, in retrospect, pretty lousy for her."

Karen looked down at the table for a long moment. She was struck by the fact that his wife and her replacement had almost the same names. The waiter came by and cleared away the dishes and asked about dessert. Both declined and asked for coffee.

"How did she handle it?" she asked.

"She didn't. Jack defeated her. He was wary of me, and he learned not to push things when I was around. But he just plain defeated her. I wasn't much help. I think I lost respect for her because this kid had her number. And, of course, because of the drinking. Anyway, we went off to our first shore-duty tour, up at the graduate school in Monterey. Other guys took advantage of graduate school to get reacquainted with their wives after a couple of sea-duty tours. I was first in my class instead. I simply took advantage. I think that was when Beth lost hope."

"Surely you're being a little hard on yourself, aren't you? Most divorce stories I've listened to have two sides."

"Perhaps, but I've had years to think about it. Upshot was that after three more assignments, it all finally came apart. We were divorced in 1981, when I was en route to my first ship command. Jack was almost fifteen, and solidly hooked up with the teenaged hoods in school. *D* student. Not stupid, mind you, just rebellious, uncommunicative, cigarettes, then dope. Beth was sustaining herself on nearly a bottle of vodka a day. I had to be sent home from the Mediterranean one time to straighten things out when the neighbors got the social workers into it. Not the sort of thing up-and-coming commanders in the Navy are supposed to have to deal with."

"What happened to Jack?"

"He bummed his way through high school, graduated, and then got picked up for some low-level stealing with his gang. Because Jack was the youngest, he was offered a shot at the county's youthful offenders boot-camp program. It was a brand-new thing back then, but, amazingly, Jack took to it. They contacted me toward the end of his program and asked if I could pull some strings, maybe get him into one of the services. The Marines, of all people, took him."

"Are you in touch with him nowadays?"

After a slight hesitation, he said no, prompting Karen to wonder what he was holding back.

"No," he repeated. "Not since he was in Marine boot camp. He told me in the one and only letter I ever got from him after the divorce that he had been selected for the Marine recon battalion—that's their Special Forces group. But then something happened in his third year, and he apparently was discharged early. I never found out what it was. Jack and I have had no contact since then. I'm sure I'm the bad guy in his life's story."

"How do you feel about that now?" she asked, looking at him over the rim of her wineglass.

"Sad, I guess. He *is* my son. I feel a duty to love him. But I still don't like him."

"People can change. Have you ever tried to find him?"

Another moment of hesitation. Some evasion there. But it was such a personal and painful story, she was ready to forgive any omissions.

"For my own sanity, I have to consider it ancient history," he said. "Long story short, these experiences are what conditioned my response to Elizabeth's marriage overtures. I know now that the whole mess was mostly my fault—for being gone, for being too centered on my career. The career worked; the marriage didn't. Now I know what I do best."

She cringed mentally at the bitterness in his voice and decided not to say anything for a minute. When she did, she was being very careful. "I think," she said, "that most of us get one free shot at the love-and-marriage prize. You had a wife and child, but the marriage did not succeed. I had a good marriage for almost ten years, or at least I thought it was good, but then he just . . . died. I never did get to play mommy. I've been up and down the emotional hill over that, but the reality is, that chapter of my life is simply closed. That's the main reason I'm getting out of the Navy on twenty."

"What do you mean, at least you thought it was good?"

Damn, she thought. I didn't mean to let that slip out. "I told you that Frank died in the lobby of a hotel down in Washington. It was a residential hotel. I could never get a satisfactory answer from anyone who was close to him in the office as to why he had been there. In fact, the harder I tried, the quicker the shields went up. His junior partner finally told me just to leave it alone, for my sake more than anything else."

"Wow. And you had no idea?"

"None whatsoever. I've often wondered if I simply got too complacent. I know I'm a reasonably attractive woman. But Frank was wealthy and influential, if not downright powerful in the energy-lobbying industry. You know Washington. What is it, seven eligible females for every one male? Power is stimulating."

It was his turn to hold his tongue. But then he smiled at her. "You are more than just reasonably attractive, Commander. Notice I used your rank, so that was an official observation, not personal."

She smiled back at him and there was an awkward pause.

"So what's next for you?" he asked, opening the way for her to talk about something else. She realized then how smoothly he had steered her off his own story.

"I have no idea. Frank made a lot of money as a lobbyist, so I'm financially secure. Once my release from active duty comes around, I'm probably going to close up the house in Great Falls and do some traveling. See what happens next, I guess. If I was twenty-one, I'd probably be trying to plan everything out. Now I'm just going to roll with it, see what happens."

"Sounds very sane, Karen. But be careful. What might happen next is the male version of an Elizabeth Walsh will move into your life. That's one of things I've learned: Life doesn't just leave you alone just because you feel like sitting out the next few dances." He stopped. "Christ. I can't believe Elizabeth is gone. I miss her." He paused to collect himself. "Well, enough of my sad story. What do we do next regarding this police matter?"

"We get the records on Galantz over to the cops. Train von Rensel will turn on an NIS search."

"Von Rensel, yes. I think NIS is going to be crucial in this. Okay. And when next you see Carpenter, perhaps you can tell him that the cops and I are on the same side for now."

The penitent was gone. The admiral was back. "Of course, sir," she replied. If he caught the change in her tone, he gave no indication of it. He was looking at his watch. "Reveille beckons. Thanks for brokering that meeting tonight. I think having you in the room probably predisposed that guy to be nicer than he had to be."

She nodded. "I think you did the right thing in telling him the story behind the Galantz problem. As soon as the files come in, I'll fax an extract to McNair so he can see that this is, or was, a real person."

"He's real enough."

"I believe it, Admiral."

He paid the bill and then excused himself to use the bathroom before they left. She waited by the front door. When he came out, they walked out to the car. " 'Train'?"

"He said it was a football nickname. He's very different from most of the NIS people I've encountered. Not the typical ex-enlisted guy playing at gumshoe. He has a law degree, and he has worked in the counterintelligence world at ONI. Oh, and with the FBI, too, I think. He appears to know his way around."

"Going after Galantz, he'd better," Sherman said as they reached her car. Only then did she remember Train's warning about the ex-SEAL. She unlocked her car with the remote key, which activated the interior light. He made as if to open the door for her and then stopped. She was about to ask what was the matter when she saw what he was staring at. There was a medium-sized syringe, its steel needle glittering in the light, lying in plain view on the driver's seat.

They both stared down at the syringe. What was this evil-looking thing doing in her car? Karen wondered. She looked quickly around the parking lot, as did Sherman. Only one of the cars in the lot appeared to be occupied, and that by a young woman trying unsuccessfully to control three squalling children. A thin, sloppy-looking young man came out to the car, unwrapping a fresh pack of cigarettes. He got in the car, cuffed one of the kids, and then drove off.

"Okay, I give up," Sherman said. "Where the hell did that thing come from?"

"And how," she said. "This car was locked. I think I want to call a cop."

"I agree, I guess."

"You guess?"

"What if it's loaded with heroin or cocaine or something? And it's in your locked car?"

That got her attention. She looked back down at the driver's seat and felt a small tingle of alarm. A syringe. An empty syringe, from the looks of it. The plunger was depressed all the way into the barrel. She felt helpless. Call a cop? Or reach in there, pick it up, and throw it into that Dumpster over there? Where *had* this thing come from? She looked up at Sherman, who was obviously having the same thought that she was: Galantz. This was just like the note.

The cabin light in the car went out, as if the car was tired of waiting for them. The admiral reached forward and opened the door. The light came back on.

"You're sure you locked it?"

"I'm sure. I always lock it."

"Just like I always lock my front door. So whoever did this was able to open the door without damaging it. Just like the front door of my house."

"I still think we should call the cops," she said again. "Get word to McNair, or at least a patrol car."

He reached in and picked up the syringe, touching only the edges of the flange nearest the needle. He smelled the needle, then withdrew the plunger a bit, again touching only the edges of the upper flange. She could see a tiny speck of red on the bottom of the barrel, below the zero line. He handed it to her gingerly, pointing out the speck.

"Do you suppose that's blood?" she asked.

Suddenly, there was a blaze of bright headlights as a car came diagonally down the parking lot and headed directly for them. Only when it had pulled up right next to her car did she realize that it was a police car. She suddenly felt very vulnerable, standing there in the parking lot, in uniform, with a syringe in her hand. Two police officers got out and walked casually around the nose of the cruiser to the driver's side of her car.

"Evening, sir. Ma'am. Got a problem here?" the taller one asked, eyeing the syringe. The other cop, a woman, was peering into Karen's car with her flashlight.

"Yes, we do," Sherman said. "I'm Admiral Sherman. This is Commander Lawrence. We just had dinner in that Greek restaurant there. When we came out, we found this lying in the front seat." Karen handed the syringe, point up, to the policeman, who took it and held it the same way Sherman had been holding it, by the edge of the top flange.

"We got a call that some Navy guy was shooting up drugs in the parking lot," the cop said, looking first at the syringe and then at Sherman. The policewoman had moved to the other side of the car and was pointing her flashlight into the backseat area. Karen tried to remember what she might have back there.

"Well, I guess I can understand that," Sherman said. "We were just about to call you guys. This is Commander Lawrence's car. It was locked when we went into dinner, and there's no sign of forced entry."

"Yeah," the cop said. "Can I see some ID there, Admiral? Commander?"

Sherman fished his wallet out and flashed his Navy ID card. Karen fumbled in her purse for her wallet. She was angry to see that her hands were trembling. The policewoman came back around the rear of Sherman's car and shook her head at the other cop.

"Give me an evidence bag, will you, Carrie?" he said. "One with one of those test-tube dealies in it. So, you found this thing where, exactly, Admiral?"

"Right on the driver's seat. We saw it after Commander Lawrence activated the remote lock system and the interior light came on. It was out in plain view, as if whoever put it there wanted to make sure we saw it."

"And you're sure you locked the doors, Commander?" The cop sounded as if he was starting to get bored with it all. The policewoman was back with an evidence bag. The cop handed the syringe to his partner, who dropped it gingerly into a tube in the evidence bag and took it back to the cruiser. The cop took out his notebook.

"Yes, positive," Karen said. Sherman asked him if he knew Detective McNair in the Homicide Section.

The cop stopped writing in his notebook and gave Sherman a suspicious look. A car went by, the driver slowing to gawk. Karen suddenly felt very conspicuous in her uniform. She could only imagine how the admiral felt.

"McNair? Sure. What's he got to do with this, sir?"

"We just finished a meeting with him. This syringe may relate to a case he's working, one that involves me. Can you make sure he knows about this?"

The cop put his finger in his notebook to hold his place and gave Sherman a perplexed look. "This something we should do right now, Admiral? Call the homicide people?"

Sherman shook his head. "No, I don't think so. Well, actually, I don't know. I'm involved in a stalking situation, which may be related to a possible homicide. That's where McNair comes in. I know, this isn't making much sense."

The other cop came back with a clipboard full of forms and handed them to the first cop. "You want a Breathalyzer kit?" she asked. "If not, I'll go ahead and clear us."

The first cop shook his head, and she went back to the car and got on the radio. The first cop took down their identification data. When he was finished, he put away his notebook.

"Well, okay, Admiral. We'll turn this thing in as a suspicious-incident report, and I'll make sure a copy gets to McNair and company. I'll forward this item to the police lab for analysis. You understand, Commander, it's your car: If there're drugs in this thing, you both may have some explaining to do."

"I understand," Karen said.

"Thank you, Officer," Sherman said. "Please don't forget about McNair."

The cop nodded as he climbed back into the cruiser. Karen suddenly needed to sit down and got into the Mercedes. Sherman walked around to the passenger side and got in. For a moment, they just sat there. His face was in shadow when he spoke.

"We were being watched," he said. "That cop car was here too quickly. Whoever put that thing in the car waited for us to come out, then called the cops."

She swallowed but did not reply. She started the car, turned it toward the main entrance, and then turned right onto Old Dominion. "That's a scary thought," she said. "But the good news is that nine-one-one calls can be traced. Even if it turns out to be a pay phone, the call and the syringe are the first tangible evidence that something's going on. This should also help to convince McNair that Galantz is real."

"Maybe," he said after a moment. "But I can see his problem: He has only my word for it that I got that letter. And he could make the case that I could have put that syringe in your car. That would explain how it got there without forcible entry."

"But you were with me the whole time," she protested.

"Think about it" was all he said as she turned in to his town house development.

Karen did think about it as she drove home. Train von Rensel had inferred something similar earlier. But why would the admiral commit murder? She had seen his house in McLean. Money as a motive to kill his ex-girlfriend seemed implausible to her. And Mrs. Klein had been first and foremost Elizabeth's friend, and she wouldn't be nice to Sherman if he had been some kind of bastard toward Elizabeth Walsh.

The admiral's story about his marriage was depressing. She wondered about how many of the chosen few who made it to the top in any American profession could tell similar stories about what happened to their families along the way. The difference with this guy was that at least he seemed to have the capacity to be embarrassed about how it had all turned out, and he could admit that he bore a large share of responsibility for the wreck of their marriage.

She turned right on Springvale Road, and headed out toward the river, adjusting her mirror against the lights of a car behind her. She had met several senior naval officers with similar marriage histories who callously chalked it off to their having picked the wrong wife. The real bastards were the ones who happily let their wives slog through the sea-duty separations and the diapers and the teenager crises all by themselves while the Great Men climbed the ladder at sea, only to dump their wives in favor of new trophy wives to match the trophy stars. Sherman didn't seem to be one of those. And it must have been especially hard to know that his only son was out there somewhere, incubating a major psychic cyst.

She turned left on Beach Mill Road at the French restaurant and started down the winding hill. The car behind her was still there, not tailgating exactly, but staying right with her, its dazzling headlights making it look as if it was right on her bumper. She remembered the admiral's comment about being careful and tried not to take any particular notice of the car following her. Beach Mill Road was only about a lane and half wide along here, and it wasn't as if he could pass. Another two minutes down the road, she put her turn signal on and slowed. The car came right up behind her then, its lights filling all the mirrors.

All right, jerk, hold your horses; I've got to make this driveway and then you can go play Richard Petty. Probably one of the local Masters of the Universe with gonads on fire to get his Porsche out of second gear. She made the turn, going slower than usual just to spite him, and the car roared past. She tried to see who or what it was, but it was long gone in a howl of expensive valves.

She drove down the winding driveway to the house, warmed by the sense of security she felt every time she came down this tree-lined drive. The house was a two-story *Southern Living* design, suitably scaled up to fit into the mansion decor of Great Falls. It had graceful white balustrade porches enveloping three sides on the ground level. There were ten acres altogether, which included a separate two-car garage, a six-stall horse barn, and a small riding ring set within the moss-covered foundations of an enormous old hay barn, all framed by the graying remains of an ancient apple orchard. The rest of the property was divided into three pastures. The property bordered on a narrow strip of state park that formed the Virginia banks of the Potomac River. On still spring nights, she could hear the river from the porch.

She parked in the garage and then diverted down a branch of the driveway that led to the small horse barn to see her three charges. Actually, only one was hers, a steady Morgan mare named Duchess. The other two residents were boarders, one belonging to a neighbor who rarely came to see the creature, and the other to a high school student who lived farther up

Beach Mill in what the locals called a "mansion graveyard," a cluster of huge homes sited much too close together on a hill overlooking Beach Mill Road. The student, a pretty sixteen-year-old named Sally Henson, took care of all three horses in return for a break on her board bill.

Karen peered into the near paddocks, but the horses were apparently hanging out in one of the darkened fields, glad to be out of the barn now that winter was over. She took a quick look around the barn, flipping on the aisle lights briefly, but everything seemed to be in order. Sally was conscientious. The sounds of insects and tree frogs were amplified in the confines of the aisleway. She turned out the lights, then returned to the house via the garden pathway, a bricked walk that led through a sixty-foot-long, eight-foot-high boxwood hedge passage. She was reassured by the scent of new boxwood leaves and the loamy perfume of freshly mowed grass permeating the night air. There was a bright moon backlighting the low cloud cover and diffusing the shadows among the apple trees and the spreading oaks in the near yard. The house seemed artificially still in the moonlight as she walked up the steps of the front porch.

A quick peek through the front windows failed to reveal any lurking bad guys. She heard snuffling behind the front door, and she quickly unlocked it to let Frank's elderly Labrador, Harry, out for a late-night tree-watering mission. She reassured the alarm system, then stood out on the porch while the dog ran around, making his usual federal case out of which tree was going to be honored this evening.

Watching the old dog snuffle around the dark yard, she felt a familiar weight of depression at the prospect of living alone again. It didn't help that, in all likelihood, Frank had dishonored the last years of their marriage. An image of Admiral Sherman came to mind, sitting in his living room, rubbing the sides of his face with both hands as he struggled with the ghosts of his scary past. Sherman was a handsome, physically fit, intelligent, and successful man about her own age. But she felt no particular attraction toward him, other than a growing reservoir of sympathy. In her younger years, before Frank even, that kind of man would have had her attending to her makeup. But now all he had were his stars, and a nice, big, empty town house in McLean with which to share them. She called the dog, but, like an old man with selective hearing, Harry ignored her, intent on pursuing some scent into the bushes.

Over the past few years in the Pentagon, she had watched in amazement as each new crop of flag officers seemed to redouble their efforts to impress, coming in at seven and going home at seven, as if those shiny new stars meant they suddenly had to shoulder the cares of the entire Navy. By his own recounting, Sherman had spurned what had been probably his best shot at a second chance to have a life partner, at least in part because of the demands of his career. And now some vengeful ghost from a long-lost war had apparently come back to make his life truly meaningful. What a deal. She looked at her watch. It was just past eleven.

"Harry, get in here," she called.

As she turned back toward the front door, she heard the sound of a car going by out on Beach Mill Road. It seemed to slow as it went by her front gates, its headlights creating a strobe effect through the double row of tree trunks parading along the driveway. The dog stopped for a moment, as if to listen to the car, but then reluctantly came in. It's not him, Harry, she thought. But thanks for looking.

CHAPTER 5

Early Friday morning, Karen had decided on an abbreviated workout, and she was coming back toward the Pentagon athletic club's building from a two-mile run when she saw a small knot of runners clustered around a grassy knoll, about two hundred yards from the athletic club's entrance. She finished her cool-down exercises and then jogged over to where the small crowd was gathered. She was surprised to see that they were watching Train von Rensel, who stood like a stubby oak tree, alone in a space about fifteen feet square. He was wearing a martial arts outfit consisting of a white short-sleeved cotton jacket, white cotton trousers, and canvas tennis shoes. He had a narrow red-and-white cloth wrapped around his forehead and, with both eyes closed, was gripping a thick curved wooden stick shaped to look like a Japanese sword. The stick was about four feet long, three inches thick, and made of what looked like rosewood.

As she came up on the small group of watchers, Train was executing a carefully choreographed set of maneuvers with the wooden sword, moving almost in slow motion, while stamping out a metronomic rhythm with his feet, first one foot, then the other. He resembled one of those sumo fighters in the way he moved, a careful exertion of great physical mass, but without all the fat rolls. With every other stamp, he pronounced a low grunt in what sounded to Karen like Japanese, while simultaneously executing the next move. Train's concentration appeared to be complete, and he gave no sign that he had seen Karen or was even aware that people were watching. Finally, he gave a huge shout and whirled around in a complete circle while holding the stick straight out at waist level with both hands. Even though it was just a stick, everyone watching instinctively moved back a few more feet as the huge man began to execute a swift series of what were obviously fighting moves, vertical and horizontal slashes, each followed by a defensive posture against an imaginary attacker, then another thrust, a jump, a slash, a crouch, a lunge, another defensive position, then a running attack, each move punctuated by an unintelligible cry. He continued this drill for about three minutes, at the end of which his close-cropped head and face were pouring with sweat and his chest heaving under the straining jacket. With a final shout, he jumped into a two-handed position, arms and knees bent, legs spread, the stick held vertically in front of him and his eyes focused directly on it. Then, eyes closing, he began some breathing exercises, after which he extended his arms straight out and lowered the point of the stick. With arms fully extended now, he began a turn, the point of the heavy, thick staff describing a menacing eye-level circle through the crowd. Karen's shoulders ached in sympathetic pain as he did it, because he was no longer gripping the stick with his fingers, but, rather, holding the butt end extended between his flat palms, which were pressed together, a position that obviously took great strength. At the end of the circle, and with his eyes still closed, he growled and then did something with his hands that made the stick jump, spinning first around one forearm and then the other, like a drum majorette's baton. Moving ever faster, Train flicked it around his shoulders, along his forearms, behind his head, the thick staff making a wicked hissing sound in the still air, his massive hands a blur as he spun it, stopped it, balanced it, and then chopped it into a different motion or direction with almost casual flat-handed strikes. This exercise went on for almost sixty seconds, to the utter fascination of the crowd, and then ended abruptly with the stick held once again motionless, vertically in front of him. He raised his right leg and stomped the ground like a pile driver and shouted out a single word. Then he bowed to his imaginary opponent, put the stick down on a rectangular piece of canvas on the ground, and, still ignoring the people watching, reached for his towel as if he had been doing nothing more unusual than a few casual jumping jacks on the lawn.

Karen sensed that the people around her didn't know whether to applaud or simply to exhale. As people drifted away, Karen pushed her way forward.

"Morning, Counselor," he said through his towel. "Didn't know you worked out so early."

"Every day," she said. "And what, pray tell, was all that?"

"Just a stick drill," he replied. "I use it to unwind after working the weights."

"That's some stick. May I see it?"

"Help yourself," he said, reaching down and picking it up. He offered it to her butt-first. She was surprised to feel how heavy it was. "It's heavier than it looks," she said. "Why the sword shape? I thought kendo used a plain staff?"

He grinned as he began to gather up his gear. "That's not kendo. Kendo is stick drill. This is just my version of kenjutsu, which is sword drill. Nothing mystical—just exercise. And the stick is shaped like a sword because of this." He took the heavy stick back from her hands, held one end, twisted it slightly, and withdrew a glistening full-sized Japanese fighting sword. She blinked in surprise. A Marine standing nearby exclaimed when he saw the sword.

"Would you hold this, please?" he said, handing it to her. She grasped the handle with both hands. The sword was beautifully balanced, and the steel surface of the blade appeared to be marbled in various colors. Train fished an oily rag out of his gear bag, took the sword from her hands, and proceeded to wipe down the entire weapon.

"How'd you finish it up with Sherman?" he asked. "He reveal any more about this Galantz problem?"

"We went down to a local restaurant and had dinner. He told me some of his personal background. Look, I'm going to cramp up if we just stand here. And—"

"Right," he said, understanding. There were too many people around, some still gawking at his unusual athletic getup. He gathered his gear and the sword, then indicated they should walk toward the small tidal channel on the other side of North Parking.

Karen told him about the syringe. That got his attention.

"In your car? In your locked car? And then the patrol car just shows up as you're standing there?"

"I know," she said. "It means we were being watched."

"And tracked. From his house down to the restaurant. Damn, Karen, this changes everything, I think."

"You *think?*"

"Well, technically speaking, Sherman could still be making this all up. I mean, the logical explanation of how that thing got in your car without a break-in was that somebody with recent access put it there—namely, him. Was there some interval of time during which he could have called in that patrol car? Some time between the end of dinner and going out to the car?"

"No," she said. Then she hesitated. "Wait. Yes. He said he was going to use the bathroom. I waited out by the front door. But—"

"But what, Karen? That's as plausible an explanation as some mysterious stalker."

She shook her head in exasperation. "Why are you so anxious to pin this stuff on him?" she demanded.

"Why are you so ready to believe everything he says?" Train retorted. "Just because he's an admiral?"

"No, damn it!" she said, glaring at him. But then she frowned. "Oh, I don't know. I just wish you could have heard him tell the story of what happened to his marriage. I just can't find any motivation on his part to make all this up, or to do something to Elizabeth Walsh. I'm beginning to think he's being set up somehow."

Train didn't answer, just turned around, steering them back toward the POAC building. He stopped when they were about to go through the door, stepping aside to let people go by.

"I'm going to pull the string on this Galantz guy with some contacts at the FBI. And elsewhere," he said. "I have a bad feeling about a guy who's supposedly an MIA but who isn't missing. That syringe was a nasty touch. I'll see you up in the office."

He left before she had time to answer. He seemed either angry or concerned, and she couldn't tell which.

Train fumed at himself as he tied his tie for the second time in front of the foggy mirror of the locker room. He should not have said that out there, that bit where he asked her why she was so anxious to defend this guy. Besides, he knew the answer. She was Navy, he was an admiral, and a Studly Dudley one at that. Plus, she was not a trained investigator. He was willing to bet that she was simply falling under this charmer's spell. As opposed to your charming personality? It has nothing to do with that. Not at all. Hah! It didn't help that she looked positively ravishing in that damp tank top.

But after this syringe business, the SEAL story had some more legs, and he had not been kidding about a bad feeling. He gathered up his gear bag and the sword case, closed the temporary locker, and headed downstairs. Suppose what Sherman was saying was the truth, that some badass had come back from the grave to get revenge. Was the syringe a warning? Or the next step? Have to talk to McHale Johnson at the FBI, he reminded himself as he crossed the wide pedestrian overpass between North Parking and the Pentagon building.

As soon as Karen got back to her desk, she called the front office to get an appointment with Admiral Carpenter. Twenty minutes later, Captain McCarty called back and asked why she needed to see the JAG. Respecting Admiral Sherman's apprehensions, she asked only that the front office confirm that she could call on Mr. von Rensel and the NIS regarding the Sherman case. McCarty was obviously perplexed, and he asked why she was asking. As he remembered it, the JAG had already assigned the new guy from NIS to the Sherman case. Mentally holding her breath, she explained only that the police might need help in tracking down an ex-enlisted man in connection with the Sherman matter. She was careful not to allude to Navy Special Forces or to Vietnam. She left it at that, hoping that the EA would be sufficiently distracted by the press of business not to probe further. She knew she was taking something of a chance, but if and when the business with Galantz got out, she wanted to be able to say that she had asked about involving the NIS, especially if her bosses raised hell about not being informed right away. McCarty said impatiently that he would look into it and get back to her. She hung up, hoping that it would stop with the EA. She might sneak one past McCarty, but Carpenter missed nothing.

She finished off her morning coffee, still feeling a bit nervous about the bureaucratic games she was playing with this case. She also wanted to talk to Train von Rensel some more, but she was a little bit miffed with him over his persisting suspicions about Sherman. And what had he meant by that crack about her readiness to defend Sherman? But five minutes later, Train came through the door, smiled and waved at her, and went to his own cubicle, carrying his gear bag and that big stick under his arm like a toy gun. His suit was obviously tailor-made, but there was no disguising the fact that he was about the biggest man she had been around in a long time. Despite herself, she smiled back. Then her phone rang.

"Navy JAG, Commander Lawrence speaking, sir."

"Commander. This is Detective McNair with the Fairfax Police Department."

"Good morning, Detective." This was fortuitous. She had been about to call him to see if he had been given the syringe. She looked to see if she could get Train on an extension, but he was already on another line.

"Not very, actually," McNair was saying, which got her immediate attention. She could hear the sound of other voices in the background. "I'm at the home of a retired Navy admiral in McLean. Guy named Galen Schmidt. Name ring a bell?"

It certainly did. The old gentleman at the memorial service. Sherman's sea daddy. "Yes, it does. What's happened?"

"Sorry to inform you, but he's no longer with us. Looks like a heart attack. Housekeeper found him this morning. She says he had a bad heart condition. His doctor's here, along with a rep from the county medical examiner's office. Like I said, apparent heart attack, although they're not done yet."

"Oh dear. I'm sorry to hear that. But—"

"Why am I calling you? Well, see, we found a pad of paper on his desk with Admiral Sherman's name on it. And Elizabeth Walsh's. Something about a memorial service. The word SEAL, with a circle around it. And a question: TELL THE CNO? Looks like notes, maybe taken during a conversation, or afterward. Any thoughts?"

Karen thought for a moment. "I believe Admiral Schmidt was Sherman's professional mentor before Sherman made flag. And he was at the memorial service for Elizabeth Walsh Wednesday night. From what I saw, they were very close. Damn, does Admiral Sherman know about this?"

"I hope not," McNair said pointedly.

Karen was taken aback by the detective's inference. "I see," she said, groping for words. "Okay, I guess I can be the bearer of bad tidings." She hesitated. "Detective, tell me something. Are there any indications, uh . . ."

McNair picked right up on it. "That this is anything other than a heart attack? No. We're not doing a crime scene or anything, unless one of the docs comes up with something hinky. Any particular reason for asking?"

"I don't know. It's just this syringe business last night."

There was a moment of silence on the phone. "And what syringe business is that, Commander?"

He didn't know? "The police were supposed to forward some kind of incident report to you. You haven't gotten it?"

"I'm drawing a blank, Commander. I am the police, remember? What're you talking about?"

Karen told him about the events of the previous night, following their meeting at Sherman's house. McNair was silent for a moment.

"Okay, Commander," he said at last. "That's all very interesting. I'll make sure I retrieve that incident report. Will you see if you can find out when Admiral Sherman was here last? At Schmidt's house? The housekeeper confirms that they were close friends. But we'd like a precise time."

"Yes, I will. I'll go see him right now. Has the Navy been informed officially?"

"Not by us. Like I said, right now it's a heart attack. Housekeeper says there's no immediate family." He paused for a moment, and she heard pages in his notebook ruffling. "Let's see, wife died of cancer ten years ago. They had one son, who was lost in a submarine accident in the early sixties. It looks like there's no family, so maybe Admiral Sherman is the next-closest person. I'm assuming Schmidt had a lawyer, so we'll track him down and find out."

"Well, you should probably notify the Bureau of Naval Personnel. Hang on a moment." She grabbed a DOD phone book and looked up the number of the Casualty Assistance Calls Office and gave it to him. "He was prominent enough that the CNO and other people at that level are going to want to know. Especially if—"

"If what, Commander?"

She realized she had made a mistake.

"Nothing. They should just be informed. I can do it if—"

McNair interrupted her. "Especially if what, Commander?"

She hesitated. "I'm not sure. It's just that this is the second person tied in some way to Admiral Sherman to die in a week's time. I'm worried about what's going on. Things happening out there in the fog."

"So are we, Commander," McNair said gently. "But this one does look pretty much like an old geezer with a heart condition fulfilling his destiny to flop and twitch in the night. We'll hang around until his physician pronounces, and then we'll be back in the office. Maybe that syringe report'll be there by then."

"Okay, I'll go inform Admiral Sherman. Thanks for the heads-up, Detective."

She hung up and sat back in her chair. "Flop and twitch." These cops! She kicked herself mentally for bringing up Sherman's name in connection with her suggestion to inform the Navy. Right now, the admiral was supposedly operating in full-cooperation mode with the police. On the other hand, given Train von Rensel's lingering suspicions, she was beginning to wonder about what the hell she was dealing with here. Maybe it wasn't such a good idea to be keeping things from Captain McCarty and Admiral Carpenter. Then she remembered that she had promised to go tell Sherman about the admiral's heart attack. She looked at her watch. It was going on 9:30. She put a call into OP-32's front office and waved to Train, who was off the phone, to come over to her cubicle. He got his coffee mug and ambled over. He smiled at her. Almost without thinking, she smiled back.

"Admiral's at the athletic club, Commander," the yeoman said when she got through. Karen thanked him, hung up, and told Train about Admiral Schmidt. Train's good humor evaporated. "And he said heart attack? No more of those forensic ambiguities?"

"That's what he said. Admiral Schmidt's own doctor is there. I saw the admiral at the service Wednesday night. Classic heart-condition appearance."

Train nodded thoughtfully. "Want some company on your mission of bad news?"

"Let me call CHINFO first," she said. "They'll alert the rest of the flags here in the building."

Fifteen minutes later, they found the admiral coming out of the weight room, which, at midmorning, was not crowded. He must have been really pushing it, she thought. His face was taut and shiny with perspiration, and there were red splotches on his cheeks and throat. His gym clothes were also soaked, and he was rubbing his upper chest and face with a towel when he caught sight of them.

"Gonna be a sweaty workout in those street clothes," he said with a weary grin. Karen and Train were conspicuous in their office attire.

"Good morning, Admiral," she said. "We need to talk for a minute."

"Fire away," he said, wiping himself down again. He took a deep breath and whooshed it out while bending over. He had the physique of a man in his mid-thirties and was in prime condition. If Train looked like an oak tree in his Japanese jacket, the admiral looked more like a professional triathlete.

"Okay," he said, straightening up. "Got both lungs back in synch. But now I need to walk that session off. Mr. von Rensel, good morning."

"Yes, sir," Train said as they fell in with the admiral, who headed down the main hallway of the club. Train was glancing at Karen, as if to say, When are we going to tell him? They reached the back exit door and stepped outside into the warm-up area. Karen stepped to one side so as not to obstruct the people coming and going from the building. Sherman, still needing to walk, frowned, but then he looked at her face.

"So what's the matter?" he asked.

"I got a call from the police this morning," she began.

"Ah. That syringe business?"

"No, sir. It was Detective McNair, and he was at Vice Admiral Schmidt's home in McLean."

"Galen?" he said, staring hard at her. "Galen Schmidt? What's happened?"

She took a deep breath. "I'm afraid he's had a heart attack. He . . . he didn't survive it. His housekeeper found him this morning and called nine-one-one."

"No!" he exclaimed. "Damn and blast. He was just—I mean, Wednesday night. At the memorial service. He was fine. He's—are you sure he's gone? Mrs. Murray couldn't revive him? She was trained for that. The housekeeper, I mean." He looked from her face to Train's, as if hoping one of them would say this wasn't true.

She shook her head. "I'm afraid not. I'm guessing it happened after she went home. The reason Detective McNair called me was because he found a notepad or piece of paper that had your name on it. And Elizabeth Walsh's. And something about a SEAL."

"Right. Sure," Sherman said. "That's what I went over to talk to him about. Tuesday night. God, this is like losing my father again. Just a great guy, Karen. Damned heart just gave out. He'd been a heavy smoker. *Goddamn it!* I better get out there. Mrs. Murray will be a wreck." He had begun walking around in a little circle, his body demanding a cooldown but his mind obviously hurtling elsewhere. For a moment, she thought she saw the makings of tears in his eye.

"I'm very sorry, Admiral," she said softly. Train was staring down at the concrete.

"Yeah. Damn. Not a good week here. First Elizabeth, now Galen Schmidt. Not a good week at all. And damn that cop. Making you come tell me."

"I volunteered," Karen said, looking at Train. See, she wanted to say, is this the reaction of a murderer?

Sherman was staring down at the ground when he thought of something. "So why were the homicide cops there?"

"Apparently for the same reason they showed up at Elizabeth's: unexplained death. Standard procedure. But they weren't doing a crime scene or anything like that."

The admiral shook his head wearily. "*Goddamn it!* I'd better get over there. I'm going to clear my afternoon calendar." Then he stopped and shook his head. "No. I can't. I've got that White House POW/MIA delegation meeting. Well, I'll just have to be late." He looked at them. "Sorry, I'm all over the place. Thanks for bringing me the word."

He turned around to go back into the club, and they followed. "McNair hadn't heard anything about the syringe business last night," she said to his back. "I told him about it, and he said he'd chase down the report."

He nodded over his shoulder. "Okay. I've got a couple of hours before my meeting. I'm going to go out to Galen's house. There's no surviving family, and I probably ought to take charge, at least for the moment. I know he's got a cemetery plot down at the Naval Academy. I guess I'd better call his lawyer, Terry Harris, too."

He gave them a dismissive wave and went back inside the club. Train indicated they should wait outside for a moment to give him time to get ahead of them. They stepped back outside, making way for the procession of runners entering and leaving the building. There were several thousand military personnel working in the Pentagon, all of whom were required to work out. This made the POAC a crowded place.

"Pretty good shape for a flag officer," Train said. "He looks more like a Marine brigadier than a Navy guy."

"He looks like he just got hit by a Mack truck," she replied. Train said nothing.

"You still think he's hiding something?" she asked, giving Train a challenging look. "I mean, I don't think that was acting. Besides, first his exgirlfriend, and now his closest personal friend? Both dead in a week's time? What're the chances of that being coincidence?"

"Slim to none," Train agreed. "But we'd better wait for the cops to finish with their investigation out there. What was that about a POW/MIA meeting at the White House?"

"I don't know. Why?"

"Galantz is supposedly an MIA. Maybe Sherman can get the POW/MIA Task Force records, if he's in that loop."

She nodded. "I'll ask. But not right now, I think."

"You're probably right. That cop comment on all this coincidence?"

She turned to walk back into the POAC building. " 'That cop' does not reveal what he's thinking all that well," she said. "But I got the impression that he was at least intrigued by the association."

Train snorted. " 'Intrigued by the association'? You've been in the JAG Corps too long, Counselor."

She ignored that remark. They walked up the front stairs and out onto the pedestrian overpass. "I'm going to harass the Bureau of Personnel some more," she said. "We need to get those Galantz files."

"How much of this have you passed on to Admiral Carpenter?" he asked.

Karen hesitated. She was not yet sure enough of Train von Rensel's relationship with the JAG to reveal why she had held back the Vietnam story from the front office. Once more, she wondered if all this evasion was prudent.

"None of it, actually. I've asked Captain McCarty, his EA, to confirm that I can count on your help marshaling NIS assets—to find an ex-enlisted guy who might have something to do with Sherman."

"But you held back on the Vietnam river story? And the syringe?"

"Yes." She looked straight ahead as they entered the cavelike North Parking entrance and went through security.

He stopped just inside the main doors, forcing her to look at him. "I assume you have your reasons, okay? But, that said, I recommend you get to Carpenter and tell him everything. And I'll want a copy of that Galantz file. I'll run some traps within NIS. And one more thing."

"What?"

"You need to start being careful. Very careful."

"Why? What do you mean?"

"Two people are dead, Karen. One sounds a lot like homicide; the other's an open question—for now anyway. But both of these people were close to Sherman."

"And?" But then she knew.

"And, you're getting close to Sherman. Now's maybe not such a good time to be close to Sherman, okay?"

"Oh."

"Yeah. Oh. Let's get back to the orifice."

Karen finally got the call to go see Admiral Carpenter at 3:30. After Train's warning, she had called the front office again for an appointment. The chief had put her on call for the afternoon. Apparent.y, the JAG was handling a flap about a breaking drug scandal down at the Naval Academy. Wonderful, she thought. The CNO will have been foaming at the mouth, which would put the JAG in a really swell mood.

In the intervening hours, she had mulled over the issue of how much of what she had learned in the meeting with the cops and at dinner she should tell Admiral Carpenter. But she had promised Sherman not to reveal what he had told her over dinner, and she still could not see any relevance between his failed marriage and his current situation. Admiral Sherman, at least in her mind, deserved some consideration, assuming that he was the target of a stalker. But what if Train was right and Sherman was involved somehow in the death of Elizabeth Walsh? What had Train said? "Sherman could still be making all this up"—that was it. Well, I know how that three-star was acting. She thought the word *shabby* just about described it. She and Train had reviewed the case file again after lunch, but there were too many loose ends for any effective brainstorming. Just about when she had decided to ask if he wanted to go with her to see Carpenter, Train had signed out for the Navy Yard and left the office.

She entered the JAG's office three minutes after getting the call. The admiral was sitting in his desk chair, his back to the door. He, too, was talking on the telephone. Karen wondered irreverently if he was talking to the yeoman on the other side of the door. She made a noise to alert him that he was not alone, and he acknowledged her presence with a wave over his shoulder. A minute later, he hung up and turned around. "Okay, Commander. I can give you ten minutes. Bring me up-to-date on the matter of William Taggart Sherman."

Karen took a look at the expression on his face and decided to tell him everything. It took twenty minutes, not ten. She detailed the events of the past week, since the first meeting on Tuesday. She told him about the meeting with the police at Sherman's house, the session with Admiral Kensington, the mysterious threatening letter from the SEAL, the syringe incident, and now the news of Galen Schmidt's heart attack. The only part that she deliberately left out was the story behind Galantz and the dinner conversation about Sherman's marriage. She was halfway hoping that Carpenter would be satisfied to absorb the big picture and not worry about details. But of course the Vietnam story was his first question.

"Why would this individual be after Admiral Sherman? What is this stuff about an incident back in Vietnam?"

Karen hesitated. "Admiral, he asked me not to reveal that part of it. At least not within the 'Navy hierarchy,' as he calls it. I think he's afraid that the story might create a scandal if it got out now."

Carpenter frowned. "He did, did he? The 'Navy hierarchy'? And yet you just told me he shared this story with the *civilian* police?"

Karen colored but did not reply. He looked at her and nodded. "Right. I forgot. He's a pretty boy. Okay, let's stop with the games. Sherman is a flag officer, but you work for me, not him. Besides, a basic rule of life applies here: When you're in trouble, you don't hold things back from your lawyer. Ever."

"But are you his lawyer, Admiral?" she asked. And then she caught her breath when she realized how impertinent that question might sound.

Carpenter surprised her with a quick grin. "Good point, Commander. But in a sense, I am. I'm the JAG. I'm the whole uniformed Navy's lawyer. Not to be confused with the Secretary of the Navy's general counsel, who is the Navy Department's lawyer. But practically speaking, I'm 'of counsel' to that flag-officer hierarchy that Sherman's still so afraid of. Hell, he's still acting like a captain. If he wasn't such a brand-new flag officer, he'd have known to come see me a long time ago. Now, give."

She recounted the facts of the Vietnam story, and of the night visitation in San Diego. She was surprised when he interrupted her.

"What was the name again? Galantz?"

"Yes, sir. HM1 Marcus Galantz."

Carpenter was writing down the name. "And he was a SEAL?"

"Yes, sir. That's one of the reasons I am definitely going to need Mr. von Rensel's help. I'm waiting for Galantz's record to come back from the archives. Oh, and Admiral Sherman feels that, given the circumstances, Galantz was probably listed as MIA."

"He does, does he? Why isn't von Rensel in here with you right now? Does he know all this?"

"Yes, sir."

"So, where is he?"

"He's over at NIS right now, sir. He and I—" She ran out of words.

"You and he what? Disagreed? Let me guess, you think Sherman is being screwed over, and von Rensel thinks he's guilty of something. Am I right?"

She swallowed and nodded.

"Tell me something," he said. "What was his recommendation regarding this bullshit about keeping back information from the Navy hierarchy?"

"He told me that I should tell you everything."

Carpenter nodded with satisfaction at her answer, but he did not comment out loud. Instead, he went back to Sherman's situation. "And the good admiral has no proof of the letter, or of that long-ago nocturnal visit from this supposedly MIA SEAL, right?"

"Yes, sir. That's true."

The admiral turned in his chair, his face scrunched up again in a frown as he stared out the windows at nothing.

"For what it's worth, Admiral," Karen said. "I don't think Admiral Sherman is making this up. Or that he's involved in the death of Elizabeth Walsh. Nor do the police, as best I can tell."

Carpenter wheeled the chair around slowly to face her. "And this feeling is based on what facts, precisely?"

Karen paused before replying. "Admittedly, just a gut feeling, I guess. He didn't have to tell us about the discrepancies he noticed at Elizabeth Walsh's house. Or, for that matter, the mysterious letter, or the incident back in 1972."

"Unless he's a really clever devil. He is a flag officer, after all."

Karen managed to keep control of her face, but Carpenter caught the effort. "You can think it, Commander," he said with a frosty grin. "But you'd better not say it."

"Aye, aye, sir," was all she could manage, glad to have the tension broken.

"Okay. What I was getting at, of course, is that by offering up some morsels, he could be running a game on the cops—a dangerous game to be sure, but a game nonetheless."

"But what about the syringe business?"

"It was in your locked car, after you and he had taken a ride to the restaurant. Do you *know* that he didn't just plant it, make a quick call to the cops from the restaurant, and then go through some charade with the patrol cops, all in order to make it look like someone was watching the two of you?"

This is just what Train was saying, she thought. "That's all possible, I suppose," she said. "I've made a note to see if the cops can tell where that call came from. I'm pretty sure they caller-ID all nine-one-one calls as a matter of policy."

"Okay, you do that. Now, tell me precisely what Mr. von Rensel is doing with all this. And why you think you need NIS's help."

"Because Galantz is—was—a SEAL. SEALs work in the unconventional warfare area—which has ties to the world of intelligence. Mr. von Rensel used to work for the Office of Naval Intelligence. And with the FBI on foreign counterintelligence cases. I believe NIS is better equipped to translate Galantz's service record information into a productive search than the cops are. Besides, I think—"

"Yes?" He was giving her that stare again.

"Well, actually, Admiral Sherman thinks that it might be in the Navy's best interest to have the first look for Galantz. A Navy SEAL who's gone off the reservation could be pretty embarrassing—especially if it looks like something's been covered up."

Carpenter nodded thoughtfully. "Well, now, in this day and age of Navy scandal *du jour*, that's a valid point. The Navy is under siege, Karen. Admirals who draw lightning go home. I want a copy of that personnel file as soon as it comes in."

"Yes, sir." She made a note.

"Now, do you know very much about Mr. von Rensel?"

"Just what's on his bio. When we talk about this case, he gives me the impression he's not convinced that Admiral Sherman is . . . is, um, entirely innocent."

Carpenter nodded again. "He thinks like a cop. Okay. Tell him I said that he and NIS are hereby formally tasked. I'll make sure their head shed gets the word. And, Karen, listen to him from time to time. His reputation is formidable among the senior NIS people. Now, new subject. You mentioned something about OP-03 himself taking an interest in this little problem."

"Yes, sir." She went on to describe in detail the meeting in Admiral Kensington's office. "I think that's part of what Admiral Sherman is nervous about."

"I'll just bet he is. Vice Admiral Kensington isn't bashful about making his feelings known. Okay. Let me offer you some more advice. I know you have your papers in and all that, but please take care when you get around the so-called flag-protection circuits, especially in the surface Navy world. If you have any more contacts with Kensington or his executive staff, make damn sure they know you're working for *me* and not for Sherman. Admiral Vannoyt didn't seem to know that."

"That sounds ominous for Admiral Sherman."

Carpenter gave her that flat stare again, reminding Karen that flag officers did not take kindly to commanders who presumed to know anything about that world. "Let's just say, Karen, that this whole situation has taken Admiral Sherman, who is, need I remind you, a frocked captain, a long way out of the politically conventional channel. You don't even want to be in the same *ocean* with him if a thunder lizard like Kensington trains the business end of those three stars around on him. Got it?"

Karen recognized the dismissal. "Yes, sir. Thank you, sir," she said, getting up, but Carpenter was already back on the phone, making his next call.

Fifteen minutes later, Captain McCarty let himself into the JAG's inner office.

"You buzzed, Admiral?"

"Yup. Sit down. Let me tell you a story."

When Carpenter was finished, McCarty sat back in his chair, closed his notebook, and rubbed his fingertips together slowly. "I'm damned sorry to hear about Galen Schmidt," he said finally. "There were a lot of people who had high hopes he would be CNO."

"I was one of them. But getting back to this mysterious SEAL story— what's this sound like to you?"

McCarty thought for a moment. "It sounds like the lumpy-suit crowd up the river."

"Bingo. Which is why I want you to pull the string with those people whenever Karen Lawrence gets this HM1 Galantz's personnel files in from the archives. I told her to get us a copy of his file. Oh, and give me the cheat sheet on our archive database; I'm going to check something out."

"We can have somebody do that for you, Admiral."

"I know, but I can work a computer, and I'm not exactly sure what I'm looking for. Back to Langley—I want you to go over there, back-channel, and ask if they've ever heard of this Galantz guy. Maybe get somebody in their general counsel's office to broker a meeting."

McCarty made some notes. "You think they would tell me?"

"Don't know. Sometimes, with those gomers, it's what they won't discuss that tells you what you want to know. Go see them. See how they react, what their attitude is—stonewall, indifference, or even, heaven forbid, some cooperation."

"That would be a first. And I presume we don't want to sidebar first with our own DNI?

"Precisely. The Navy Intelligence wizards would feel obligated to act like they knew the answer; then they'd just go ask Langley themselves. And Langley, as a matter of professional courtesy, tends to give the military intelligence people diddly-squat. Especially now that they're being coerced into cooperating with the great unwashed hordes over in the FBI. No. Go direct."

"Got it. Would it not be wise for you to direct Mr. von Rensel personally on this matter?"

Carpenter shrugged. "Not initially. Let's see what he's made of. See if he has it figured out. If he's as good as they claim, he ought to know which wires *not* to grab, unlike Karen Lawrence, who, I'm afraid, has fallen some-what under the dashing young admiral's spell."

McCarty nodded thoughtfully but did not reply.

"What?" Carpenter said, recognizing the signs that McCarty was not en-tirely in agreement.

"I'm not sure," McCarty said. "I just have this feeling that this one might get away from us. That maybe we ought to pull Karen out and let von Rensel run with it. I mean, we've either got an admiral or an ex-SEAL committing murder. Karen's an admin specialist. She's never worked any-thing like that."

"I think she's finding this pretty interesting. Remember the objective."

Captain McCarty closed his notebook. "Yes, sir, I understand," he re-plied. "But I can't tell if you want Karen Lawrence to succeed and thereby be enticed to stay, or if you're just testing her."

"Bit of both, I suppose, EA. We'll have to promote her to captain if she stays, so I guess I need to know if she can work off-line in a real investigation instead of just second-guessing other people's work."

"But if this Galantz problem turns out to be spooked up, then will you pull her off this thing?"

Carpenter studied the blotter on his desk for a moment, somewhat an-noyed at his EA's persistence. "Don't know. My job is to keep the Navy's skirts clean, not hers. One step at a time, EA. Get thee to Langley."

McCarty nodded and stood up. "On my way. But my take is that she's going to bail, no matter what."

After McCarty left the room, Carpenter picked up the phone, but then he put it back down again. HM1 Marcus Galantz. He was pretty sure he recognized that name. But what the hell was going on here? An MIA. He made a note to look at that record when it came in. Marcus Galantz. He sighed. This better not be what he thought it was. On the other hand, there was still plenty of time to control this situation. And McCarty was worrying about nothing. He couldn't imagine that Karen Lawrence was in any danger.

· · ·

The Galantz files had arrived while Karen was in with Carpenter. She riffled quickly through the package. There were three folders, one containing his enlisted service record, the second his medical record, and the third, a single card of microfiche, which should contain his leave and pay records. She stopped to examine his Page Thirteen, the chronological listing of assignments and administrative actions. The final entry caught her attention. Galantz had been officially declared missing in action on 1 June 1970 by direction of the Chief of Naval Personnel.

An official MIA, she thought. Wait a minute. There should have been an investigation conducted by his parent command, Naval Forces Vietnam, following his disappearance in the Rung Sat zone. It would have been a JAG investigation, which meant it should have been forwarded to Navy JAG for final review. To the very office you're working in, she reminded herself. So their own archives ought to have a copy. She kicked herself mentally for not thinking of this before.

She put a call into OP-32. First, she verified that the admiral had returned to the Pentagon from Admiral Schmidt's house. Then she left a message with the duty yeoman that she would be in her office until eighteen hundred and that she had the Galantz file, and that it had a picture. Then she made copies of the file for the front office and called one of their yeomen to come down to pick up Admiral Carpenter's copy. Then she waited. The IR office was empty. Train von Rensel had apparently not returned from the NIS headquarters over in the Navy Yard. Everyone else appeared to have gone for the day.

Thirty minutes later, the OP-32 yeoman called back and asked her to come down to Admiral Sherman's office. She locked up and hurried down there.

"Appreciate your hanging around, Karen," Sherman said as his deputy went out and closed the door behind him. "Actually, if that record isn't classified, perhaps we could go somewhere else. Otherwise, my staff is going to have to hang around. They can't secure the divisional spaces if I'm still here."

"Yes, sir, of course. The JAG spaces are already secured. Let me think—"

"How about the Army-Navy Club? It's fifteen minutes by Metro. We could have a drink and discuss what we're going to do with this information. I need one after this afternoon."

Thirty minutes later, they were ensconced at a corner table in the second-floor lounge of the Army-Navy Town Club. Karen showed him the three parts of the personnel record, then let him peruse it for a few minutes.

Sherman extracted the print of the official black-and-white photograph from the record and put it down on the table in front of him. He spent some time studying it. The picture had been taken of then Hospital Corpsman Third Class Galantz in 1963, which meant he had been advanced quickly to HM1 by the time of the incident. It was not a very clear picture, having been printed from a microfilm frame, but a steely determination was evident in the man's face. He looked almost Eastern European, with close-cropped unruly black hair and intensely dark, if not black, eyes.

"Did you see that last entry on the Page Thirteen?" she asked.

"Yes," he said slowly. "Formally declared MIA."

"Do you remember precisely when he came to see you that night in San Diego?"

"Yes, I do. It was February 1972."

Karen nodded. "I'm embarrassed to say I thought of something earlier today," she said. "His parent organization should have done a command JAG investigation when he first went missing. A copy of that investigation should ultimately have come up to Navy JAG for final review. I did a quick search of the Navy JAG archives index for investigation reports dating back as far as 1970, and, in fact, I have found something, or at least an index listing of something. I can't get it until Monday, but there's definitely something on file in our archives."

"That's terrific, Karen," he said, his face lighting up. He looked as if he had seen ray of hope. She realized that he had probably begun to doubt his own memory of those events long ago. Then she pressed ahead with the first of the two questions she really wanted to ask. "Do you believe now that Elizabeth Walsh's death was a homicide?"

He sighed again and then nodded.

Karen was silent for a minute. Then she took a deep breath and asked the other question that had been on her mind since talking to Train.

"First Elizabeth," she said slowly, her voice almost indistinct in the rising background noise of the lounge. "And now Galen Schmidt. Your lady friend, and then your mentor." She looked over at him, waiting for him to understand. He frowned and then put his drink down. She thought she saw his hand tremble.

"Galen? Are you suggesting—"

"Admiral, I don't know what to think," she said hurriedly. "Other than that's a lot of coincidence. Two people dying, unattended, within a week, both connected to you in a significant and personal way."

"Judas Priest!"

She leaned forward. "The police are saying that Admiral Schmidt's death showed no evidence of being anything but a heart attack. And his own doctor participated in the examination, and *he* says it was a heart attack. A not-unexpected heart attack. It's just—"

He was nodding slowly. "Yes, I see where you're going with this. And you're right, perhaps more than you know. Galen Schmidt was more than a mentor. I followed him to a sea job from the Bureau. He was my personal pillar of strength when my wife finally hit bottom with the drinking. He kept me from making all the political mistakes ambitious officers usually make. Even when he had to retire, I kept going back to the well. It's fair to say that he became the father I lost when I was growing up."

Karen nodded. "But the question is, if someone did something to Admiral Schmidt in order to hurt you, he would have had to know about this relationship."

He shrugged. "That wouldn't be difficult, I guess. It was well known in my professional circles that Galen Schmidt was my sponsor when I went up for flag." He paused thoughtfully. "You're right: It's a reach. I can understand his being able to discover Elizabeth. But I can't see an ex-enlisted man knowing about the inner workings and hidden mechanisms of the flag-selection process."

She thought about that for a minute. The waiter came by and the admiral raised his eyebrows in her direction, but she shook her head. He did the same and asked for their tab.

"But just suppose," she said, "just suppose that Admiral Schmidt became a target of opportunity, that Galantz has been planning and plotting for a long time, but that part of the plan was to murder Elizabeth, and then see what you did. And when you went to Galen, especially the night you got the warning letter, the admiral became the next target."

She watched as he thought this through, but then he surprised her. "If that's true, you'd better start watching your back," he said. "And I guess we'd better have another sit-down with the Fairfax cops. I hate to say it, but maybe they better take another look at Galen Schmidt's heart attack."

She felt a chill of apprehension as Train's words of warning echoed in her mind. She had been with Sherman when he visited Elizabeth's house. And at the church. And at the restaurant. And someone had made the phone call to bring in the police when the admiral found the syringe. She looked up. He was watching her intently. She tried hard to keep her face composed, but either Sherman was being stalked or he had to be the killer. But why?

She shuffled the service records in front of her. "We have to ask the police where that nine-one-one call came from," she said, stalling. "The one summoning a cop car to that parking lot."

"Yes indeed."

"But only if the syringe and what was in it was important," she pointed out. "I mean, it wasn't likely that the cops would have arrested you for doing dope in the parking lot, an admiral in full uniform."

He considered it for a moment. "So maybe we were not the focal point of that phone call?"

"Right. It may have been the syringe."

He shook his head in exasperation. "We're going in circles. I guess we're just going to have to wait to see what the cops come up with. I think we should try to meet with them again, say Monday. No, not Monday. Galen's funeral is Monday afternoon in Annapolis. Tuesday, then."

"I'll call McNair Monday. I'll ask about the source of the phone call, and what's come back on the syringe."

He nodded, then looked at his watch. "Is von Rensel working this?" he asked, pointing to the records.

"Yes. I spoke to Admiral Carpenter this afternoon."

A trace of alarm went through his expression "You spoke to Carpenter?"

Karen wished she had not brought that up. "Yes, sir. I had to in order to get NIS tasked. Officially, that is."

"I see. And I suppose he wanted to know what's behind the Galantz story."

She hesitated, not knowing how much to tell him about the conversation in Carpenter's office. "Yes, sir. I . . . I told him that you were concerned about this story getting out—the public sensitivity."

Sherman gave her a long look and then sighed. "Okay, I guess there was no way around that. Thanks for trying."

"He said he would respect your wishes to keep this close-hold," she said, lying.

The admiral smiled again. "Sure he did. Well, I guess we'll see. I'm still not used to the idea of Galen's being gone, which is more important than my professional worries. Anyhow, the weekend cometh. I don't suppose the police will be working this over the weekend."

"Should I call if something comes up?"

"No, I don't think so. Oh, you can always leave a message. But I'll be out of town until late Sunday. If you have anything to report, call me at home Sunday, why don't you. Otherwise, I'll be in the Pentagon Monday until about eleven hundred; then I'll be headed down to the Academy for the service." He paused. "Do you want to come to the service?"

She was taken off guard. "Well, I—"

"It's going to be a pretty big deal. The CNO and most of the bigs will be there. Full military honors. CNO's office is handling the arrangements." He paused. "It's just that things seem to be happening when you and I are together."

She must have assumed a strange expression, because he was suddenly backpedaling. "That didn't come out right, Commander. Karen. What I meant was—"

It was her turn to smile. "I think I understand, Admiral. If someone is watching us, we might be able to see who it is if we make the effort to look."

"Yes. That's what I meant. If that makes you nervous—"

It seemed to her that he was the one being nervous. "I have a suggestion," she interrupted. "Let me see if I can get Train von Rensel to come along, too. He keeps reminding me that he's the trained investigator. He might see something we don't."

He stood up. "Good idea. Let him see this record, and that picture. It's old, but it's a start." She stood up as well and gathered her purse. The admiral continued. "Maybe we ought not to tell the cops too much about von Rensel. Let him work the web independently. If he and NIS can ferret out Galantz, perhaps we can take care of this problem in-house."

She thought about that as they walked out of the lounge. "Well, I think that's a good idea, up to a point. I mean, McNair knows he's in the picture. And we already told them we'd try to get some NIS help. But if Train can get a line on Galantz, then we probably need to let Carpenter decide when to bring in the police."

"Of course," he said quickly. "Let me call us a cab back to the Pentagon. Then I'll walk you to your car."

CHAPTER 6

Late Sunday morning, Karen was reviewing her tax forms when the light of the beautiful spring day streaming through the study windows overwhelmed all her good intentions and drew her outside. She walked down to the barn and spent a few minutes talking to Sally, but then the extension phone in the tack room started ringing. It was Detective McNair.

"Commander, good morning," he said. "Sorry to bother you on a Sunday, but we need to find Admiral Sherman. No one's answering at his home, and a patrol car reports his car's gone. Any ideas?"

"He's out of town. Let's see, he told me he'd be away until this evening, I think. I don't know where, though. Has something happened?" She almost said had something *else* happened.

"Well, yes and no. Remember your syringe? The lab report came back on it late Friday. The thing is, we need to get Admiral Schmidt's body into the ME's lab. There's something we need to check out."

Karen felt her heart sink. "Don't tell me: There *is* a connection between that syringe and Admiral Schmidt's heart attack."

"Whoa, now, Commander. You're getting way ahead of us. We just need to check some things."

"Are you talking about doing an autopsy?"

He paused, as if trying to decide how much he could tell her. "Well, a partial one. Normally when the deceased's own doc pronounces, we don't do an autopsy. But we need Admiral Schmidt's blood type, and a sample, if we can get it. There was human blood and a residue of potassium chloride in saline solution in that syringe."

"I'm sorry, I don't follow."

"An injection of the right amount of potassium chloride into a vein can stop a heart. Admiral Schmidt died of a massive heart attack."

"Oh my God."

"Yeah, well, we're still speculating at high speed here. But someone left a syringe in your car, a syringe that hadn't been cleaned or rinsed out. Almost as if someone wanted us to make this connection. Potassium chloride, Sherman, and the old man's heart attack."

Karen found herself nodding into the telephone handset, at a total loss for words.

"Commander?" McNair said at last.

"I'm here. I just don't know what to say, other than Admiral Sherman and I had a conversation very much like this Friday night. We were trying to figure out why in the hell someone called into nine-one-one to report a Navy guy doing dope in a parking lot. We wondered if it was really about the syringe and not him."

"Well, we pulled that string, too. Asked the nine-one-one dispatchers to check their logs to see where that call came from."

"And?"

"No joy in Mudville. The caller-ID function was disabled because the phone company is changing around all the northern Virginia area codes. They've been taking segments of the caller-ID system down after nine P.M."

Karen was silent again. Damn. So it could have been Sherman making the call himself. Sally stuck her head into the tack room and mimed good-bye. She had a folder of show entries under her arm. Karen waved back and then remembered the Galantz records.

"Oh, we have the SEAL's archived records," she told McNair. "They came in late Friday afternoon. There's a picture, although it's many years out-of-date, and taken when he was very young."

"We'll want anything you can give us. And I think maybe we need to meet again."

"Yes, I agree. So does Admiral Sherman. But he wants me to go with him to the service in Annapolis on Monday afternoon."

"He say why? Or would that be normal?"

Karen hesitated, then explained their reasoning, leaving out the fact that Train would also be going along. It was McNair's turn to hesitate. Finally, he agreed to the logic, although he seemed to question the prudence of it.

"Look, Commander, this guy's stalking Sherman. If that was him calling nine-one-one, then he's seen you. If he's bent on knocking off people close to Sherman, he may target you next. He seems to have no problem finding out who's who."

"That thought's occurred to us, Detective."

"Yeah, I suppose it has. Well, let me get onto this other problem. If Sherman calls you, can you let him know what's going on? We're scaring up a court order to do the partial autopsy. Fortunately, there aren't any grieving relatives, so we plan just to do it. Hopefully, we'll beat the embalmer. Oh, by the way, there is the outside possibility that the Navy may have to do their ceremony around an empty box Monday."

"Oh, wonderful. You get to tell the CNO's office."

"Yeah, I know. But we need to schedule that meeting. I don't like the way this thing's shaping up. Technically, if Schmidt was iced, this qualifies as a serial kill."

"On that optimistic note—"

He laughed. "Yeah. Right. We'll be in touch. Watch your back, Commander."

Karen hung up and walked out of the tack room and into the empty aisleway, the skin on her back tingling just a little. Sally had left, and the horses were turned out. She stood for a moment in the shadows of the aisleway, thinking about what McNair had said: "Watch your back." There it was again. The barn was empty, and the concrete aisleway felt cold and threatening in comparison to the bright rectangles of warm sunlight framed by the doorways at either end.

She started to walk back up to the house. Where the hell was Sherman? she wondered. Not that there was anything for him to do at this juncture. The police would have the old man's body taken to the medical examiner's lab whether Sherman liked it or not. And what if it turned out that the syringe was indeed an instrument of murder? Then what? Harry the watchdog was curled up in a black ball by the entrance to the hedge passage, soaking up some sunlight. He opened one eye as she walked past, the tip of his tail twitching in greeting.

"Come on, Harry," she said. "I need some lunch." But the old dog didn't move, apparently preferring to soak up maximum heat from the patch of sunlight. She was surprised: The *L* word usually took priority over anything else Harry had on his schedule.

"Okay for you, dog," she said over her shoulder, and then she headed up the path toward the house. She decided to call Train von Rensel.

Train was roughhousing on the front lawn with two of the Dobermans when Hiroshi appeared on the porch with a portable phone.

"Who is it?"

"A Commander Lawrence, Train-sama."

Train dismissed the dogs, who scampered off across the front lawn, heading toward the river wall. He wiped his face and upper chest with a towel. After an hour of sword drill in the bright April sunlight, he was ready for a shower. He was surprised to be hearing from Karen Lawrence, especially after the chilly tenor of their working relationship at the end of the week.

"Counselor," he said into the phone, plopping down on the front steps. He wasn't quite sure how to address her. First names would have been appropriate after a week in the same office, but they hadn't really hit it off that well. On the other hand, he wasn't going to call her Commander.

"Hi," she said, neatly stepping around the same problem. "I'm sorry to bother you on a Sunday, but McNair just called."

"That sounds ominous. Let me guess: The syringe connects to the old man's death."

"Definite maybe," she replied. "McNair was being coy. But they now want to do a partial autopsy. And they want to talk to Admiral Sherman again, but he's out of town for the weekend."

"Official trip? Or personal?"

"I don't know. He told me Friday night he was going to be gone for the weekend."

"Friday night?"

"Yes. I went by his office late Friday, with the Galantz personnel files. We went over to the Army-Navy Club for a drink and to discuss next steps."

Train didn't know what to say to that. Drinks at the Army-Navy Club? How cozy.

She must have sensed his disapproval. "It wasn't a date, for crying out loud," she said. "It was Friday evening. Nobody in his outer office can leave until he does, so we left. I don't know why I'm explaining this to you."

"You are absolutely right," he said. "You want to socialize with the admiral, that's your business."

"It wasn't socializing," she insisted. "We went through Galantz's record. There's a picture, an old one, but at least a picture. The admiral recognized him right away. Oh, and he wants me to go to the funeral for Admiral Schmidt tomorrow. I suggested you also go along, separately. If someone's watching us, maybe you can spot the watcher."

The admiral was wasting no time, Train thought. Take the lady to an emotional scene like a funeral, build on that sympathy. Why was he even wasting his time thinking he might—oh, the hell with it.

"That's probably a good idea," he replied. "What are the arrangements?"

"I'm not sure yet. The funeral's tomorrow. I'll have details in the morning."

"Okay, thanks for calling. I'll see you in the office." He hung up, cutting her off. He went back out into the front yard. Okay, let's get squared away here. Forget Karen Lawrence, redhead extraordinaire. Focus on this case. The cops wanted to take another look at the old man's body. So some badness had turned up in the syringe, which logically would imply that Admiral Schmidt had been helped along to the other side. He had to admit that he couldn't think of a reasonable motive for the boy admiral to kill his girlfriend and his sea daddy. Okay, so let's assume Galantz is real.

He began some tai chi exercises. If Galantz had indeed survived the Rung Sat experience and made it back to the States, then he was not working at

Burger King. He'd made the threatening appearance in Sherman's house in 1972—over twenty years ago. Where had he been for all those years? *What* had he been? Must get to McHale Johnson, sooner rather than later.

Sherman called Karen later Sunday afternoon. "Oh, good," she said. "Have you spoken to Detective McNair?"

"Yes, I have," he said, sounding annoyed. "It seems the police have been very busy. They've taken Galen Schmidt's body in for an autopsy, and I've just had a second call from McNair."

"He called me earlier. Looking for you. Did they—"

He sighed. "I'm afraid so. The remains had been embalmed, and apparently, that makes a chemical analysis almost impossible. But he confirmed that at least the blood type is a match with the residue in the syringe."

"Oh dear. And was there potassium chloride?"

"There's a problem with that. Apparently when someone dies, the body's own cells release quite a bit of potassium into the bloodstream, enough to mask the quantity needed to stop a heart. Their toxicology people are going to try. I think they called it some kind of differential analysis, but it will take some fairly sophisticated tissue studies. Unofficially, the ME told McNair it would be a waste of time."

Karen didn't know what to say. Now Galen Schmidt's death was forensically ambiguous, just like Elizabeth Walsh's. "Does this mean Galen was killed?" she asked.

Sherman's voice betrayed his anxiety. "The blood *type* matches. Now they'll have to do DNA matching to see if it's actually his blood. I have to tell you, Karen, this is beginning to get to me."

She could certainly sympathize. "What about the funeral?" she asked. "Will they get the remains back to the funeral home in time?"

"Yes. That's all back on track. But this other business . . ."

Karen felt the urge to fill the sudden silence. "McNair wants to meet as soon as possible after the funeral, Admiral," she said. "May I suggest Monday evening?"

"I suppose," he said. "Oh, and he asked about NIS. I told them what you said Carpenter said—that NIS was coming in."

"Yes, sir. I talked to Mr. von Rensel earlier this afternoon. He'll be there in Annapolis."

"Good," he said distractedly. Karen wasn't sure he had even registered what she had just told him. Poor man. He paused for a moment. "Because if the higher-ups try to squelch this investigation, I'm gonna take it public."

"Well, yes, I understand that, Admiral. But wouldn't that do you even more damage, politically, I mean?"

"I suppose it would, Karen," he said. "But if this guy killed Galen Schmidt—not to mention Elizabeth Walsh—just to get at me, then to hell with it, okay? I'm ready to get this bastard before he does another one. Especially given his probable motive for doing it."

She was startled by the sudden ferocity in his voice. This was a side of him she had not heard before. "You can't blame yourself for what's happened, Admiral," she said.

"Thanks, Karen," he said. "Maybe I'll call Admiral Carpenter and reinforce that notion. Maybe first thing tomorrow."

That's not a good idea, Karen thought quickly. Carpenter was already conscious of the ripples spreading among the flag community in Washington over this matter, starting with the cinder block Vice Admiral Kensington had pitched in the political pond. "Why don't you let me work that problem, Admiral. I think if you called him you might, uh . . . " She wasn't sure how to phrase it. He did it for her.

"Might show some desperation, huh? And then he might decide just to pull the plug and let me sink or swim by myself. Did you tell him about our little séance with Kensington?"

"He'd already heard about it, Admiral."

Sherman laughed, making a harsh sound. "Why am I not surprised?"

"Admiral, I think Admiral Carpenter has his heart in the right place here. He's going to move on this matter, not sit on it."

"You're probably right. Well, I think I'm going out and do a ten-mile run somewhere. I need to think."

"Yes, sir," she said. "What time will you leave for Annapolis?"

"I've got a car laid on for thirteen hundred. Why don't you meet me at the Mall entrance. Maybe we'll have some developments by then."

She agreed and hung up. She thought about calling Train back, then decided against it. That pregnant silence after she had mentioned the Army-Navy Club had made her angry. He had no right to judge her—about anything. So why do you care? He's just a civilian, and an odd-looking one at that.

She went out to the front porch to enjoy the late-afternoon sun. Two things were bothering her. Train's abrupt demeanor on the phone hinted at professional disapproval. If she was working for Carpenter, what the hell was she doing going places with this guy? But over and above that, she still sensed that Train was interested in her, and, somewhat to her surprise, she felt herself responding to this interest. And if that was true, then maybe some of his antipathy toward the admiral was not entirely professional. She smiled to herself as she saw Sally's car turning into the drive for the afternoon feeding. Train might even be jealous of Sherman, which was a bad joke: That poor man had bigger problems on his plate. She headed down to the barn to help Sally with the horses.

CHAPTER 7

Karen was surprised at how small the Naval Academy cemetery was as she waited behind and slightly below the main ceremonial group surrounding the canopied grave. The cemetery was located on a gentle hillside across a wide creek from the main campus, occupying five wooded acres on the Severn River. Fortunately, it was not raining, because the crowd was far too large to fit under the two temporary blue-and-gold canopies that had been erected facing the grave site. Several three- and two-star officers had shown up for the service in the Naval Academy chapel. She wondered idly if their attendance was because they knew Galen Schmidt or if it was because the Chief of Naval Operations himself was attending.

She shifted her feet on the cold grass, trying to keep her heels from sinking into the spongy lawn. She found it fascinating that Sherman, who was probably the human being closest to Galen Schmidt, had been relegated to a back row of the flag officers' section by virtue of the fact that he was just a frocked one-star. The same thing had happened in the chapel. It must be strange, she thought, to have nearly every facet of your professional life dictated by your lineal number in the Naval Register.

Now the Navy band was assembled on one side of the grassy hillside, playing appropriately funereal music while the admirals and retired admirals stirred uncomfortably on their folding chairs. The rest of the funeral audience, nearly two hundred officers and even some enlisted men, remained standing. The grave itself had been bordered with sections of incongruously green AstroTurf, and the casket was perched on a chrome-plated frame above the hole in the ground. Up higher on the hill, there was a smaller crowd of onlookers, comprised mostly of tourists who happened to be visiting the Academy and a few dozen midshipmen. There were some civilian youngsters standing to one side who looked like military dependents, attracted by all the stars and big black cars.

That morning, she had tried to check in with McNair, but he had not been available. Train had come in at 8:30, and she'd filled him in on the itinerary for the afternoon. He took it all aboard and then got on the phone to Admiral Sherman's office to assure the admiral that NIS was moving on the case. He then made a copy of the Galantz personnel file and transmitted that to the NIS database administrator. Throughout the morning, he treated her with almost-exaggerated civility, which she found a bit frustrating. This tension between us is going to have to stop, she thought. And somehow she knew she would have to make the first move.

Karen got a surprise at midmorning: The archived investigation report on the Rung Sat incident was locked out. She had called Train over when she saw the banner on her screen.

"What's that mean? Unavailable?" Train asked, looking over her shoulder.

"I don't know," Karen said. "But there was an index listing. Damn thing has to be somewhere."

"It may be a security problem," Train had said. "Given what these guys purportedly were doing, I suspect any records related to SEALs are long gone."

"What exactly were they doing?"

He thought about that for a moment, then shook his head. "I can't tell you," he replied. "But it wasn't social work. Anyway, does it matter? We've established Galantz was a real guy and that he did go MIA. That corroborates at least part of Sherman's story."

"How will that help to find him?"

"It won't."

The band stopped playing, and there was a long silence as the chaplain mounted a platform and approached the podium to begin the traditional interment ceremony. The day was partly cloudy, and it was cooler than she had anticipated. Her uniform shoes did little to keep out the damp cold of the cemetery grass. The chaplain said something, and everyone stood, removed their uniform hats, and bowed their heads. She searched for Sherman again in the sea of dark blue uniforms, feeling a pang of sympathy for him. His usually outgoing expression was now a cold mask, devoid of any visible emotion. He appeared to be staring at a headstone monument to his right, as if unwilling to watch the bronze casket be lowered forever into the cold ground.

About two hundred feet off to her right, she could see the burial crew clustered at a discreet distance around a bright yellow backhoe. She looked away and then looked back. Train von Rensel was in their midst, dressed in oversized overalls, just like the rest of the crew. He appeared to be carefully scanning the crowd in and around the cemetery. As she stared at him, their eyes met briefly across the open ground, but he gave no indication that he had seen or recognized her. The fact that he would not acknowledge her made her feel uneasy.

Just after three o'clock, Captain McCarty knocked once and let himself into Admiral Carpenter's office. The admiral was on the phone, as usual, and he waved McCarty over to a chair. A minute later, he hung up. "So, what did you learn at Langley?"

"I learned absolutely, positively nothing," McCarty replied, opening his notebook. "My contact in their general counsel's office put me together with a woman—if you can call her that—from the Technical Operations Directorate. You should have seen her—a dead ringer for Mrs. Khrushchev. A walking, talking, personality-free zone. Came in, sat down across the table from me in some kind of interview room, got her breath back after the effort of walking, and gave me what sounded like a fully rehearsed statement."

He consulted the shorthand in his notebook again. " 'My name is Madeliene Parker-Smith. The Directorate of Technical Operations has no records pertaining to a Navy Hospital Corpsman Galantz. Any interdepartmental association of military personnel with the Directorate would be a matter of record and would involve the concurrence of both the Department of Defense and the individual's military personnel agency. No record of such concurrence exists.' We have spoken."

"Did you get a chance to explain the possible circumstances by which they might have come across Galantz in Saigon?"

"No, sir. She delivered her speech, pushed some kind of a button under the table, and suddenly I had a brace of rent-a-cops standing next to my chair. I was escorted back to the badge lobby."

"Well, well, well," the admiral mused, rotating his chair to face the windows, his fingers laced together behind his head. "They knew you were coming to see them about Galantz, specifically?"

"Yes, sir. I'd given them HM1 Galantz's name and serial number. They knew."

"And had that answer ready."

"There stood Madeliene the Immovable, like General Jackson's Virginians at First Manassas: a veritable stone wall."

The admiral swiveled back around. "So in a sense, we have an answer. This Galantz must have been spooked up. The question is, When?"

McCarty nodded. "On the other hand, Princess Happy may have been stating the bald truth. The Tech Ops people have never heard of the guy."

"Yeah. Okay. Let me pull the string one time at my level. Maybe I need to go see my dear friend, the Director of Naval Intelligence, after all. Sometimes spooks will trade secret signs and totems only with other spooks."

"And what shall we pass on to Karen Lawrence?"

"Nothing. Which, in terms of facts, is what we have. Just some educated cynicism based primarily on our combined sixty years of experience in dealing with those people. We might as well try for the facts one more time before we worry her pretty little head about it."

"Aye, aye, Admiral," McCarty said in a tone that suggested he was not entirely in agreement. Carpenter eyed him over his reading glasses.

"Always a safe answer, Dan," he pronounced.

After McCarty had left the office, Carpenter picked up the phone to his yeoman. "Get me through to Admiral Kensington," he said. "On secure, please."

As the band broke into the Navy hymn, Karen had trouble controlling her eyes. The stately, dolorous, yet hopeful chords carried across the grassy slopes of the cemetery with such power that even the civilian tourists up on the hill stopped taking pictures to listen. So she was startled when she saw Admiral Sherman starting to rise out of his chair. He appeared to be staring at something up on the hill. As she strained to see what or who it was, she caught a movement among the grave diggers standing around the backhoe. Train. He had apparently also seen the admiral's sudden interest in something or someone up on the hill, and he was moving behind the backhoe, as if to go up the hill. She looked back at Sherman, who was standing now, causing the flag officers seated on either side to look up. Feeling a sudden fist of apprehension grab her heart, she looked back up the hill, half-expecting to see a man with a rifle. But there was just the same small crowd up there, so what on earth was he looking at? There, standing next to a group of midshipmen in uniform: a kid. No, a young man, not a kid. Scrawny figure. Black motorcycle jacket opened over a white T-shirt. A cigarette hanging from his lip in impudent mockery of the somber proceedings down the hillside. As Karen looked on, the young man apparently made eye contact with Sherman, because he grinned at the admiral. There was no mistaking it: an almost ugly flash of teeth. But then the midshipmen up on the hill moved across her line of sight, and he was gone. She looked back at Sherman, who was now sitting back down. Baffled, she looked for Train. He was no longer in sight.

Forty minutes later, Karen and the admiral were heading back into Washington in his official sedan. She was anxious to ask him what it was that had attracted his attention up on the hill. But then she decided that she had better talk to Train first.

"I'm very sorry for your loss, Admiral," she said. The words sounded trite. She glanced over at the driver, a civilian from the Defense Department motor pool. "But we still have some business with the Fairfax County, um, people. They do want to meet."

"Well, not tonight," he said immediately. "I'm still too upset about losing Galen. How about tomorrow? Although I shouldn't even say that without looking at my calendar. Damn it."

She waited for a few minutes. "I'll talk to them. Perhaps we could meet off-line again, maybe in Great Falls this time," she proposed. "Perhaps at my house. Same deal as last time, after working hours. That would be better than your having to go to Fairfax."

"Fine," he said distractedly. He was staring out the right-rear window, his mind a thousand miles away.

"I'll call them this evening, then," she offered. "Tentatively for tomorrow evening, say nineteen hundred?"

"Fine."

At 5:30, Rear Admiral Carpenter walked down the C-ring to the offices of the Director of Naval Intelligence, Rear Adm. Kyle St. John Mallory. He smiled as he reached the door and glanced at the name board. What was it about the intel world, he wondered, that seemed to attract these pretentious-sounding names?

"Come in, Thomas," said Admiral Mallory, who came around his desk to shake hands. He was a tall, slim, and perfectly bald officer, and he was known for affecting British mannerisms and dress, even to the point of insisting on the traditional British pronunciation of his middle name as 'Sin-Jin.' True to form, he was wearing an off-white Royal Navy cardigan sweater that was about two sizes too big for him over his uniform shirt and trousers. He was senior to Carpenter, thus the instant familiarity and first name.

"Kyle," the JAG responded, shaking hands and then taking a chair as the DNI's executive assistant withdrew, closing the door behind him. Mallory took the adjacent chair and offered coffee. Carpenter demurred.

"Are your fields working?" Carpenter asked, glancing up at the odd-shaped black boxes perched in the ceiling corners.

"They'd bloody well better be," Mallory replied. "Whose ears might be about to burn?"

"Those people up the river."

"Ah. Just a moment, then, please." He turned to reach the intercom on his desk. "Full SCIFF, if you please, Petty Officer Martin." He waited, looking expectantly at the intercom box.

"Full SCIFF, Admiral." A low humming sound filled the room, and the panel of floor-to-ceiling windows behind the DNI's desk went opaque.

"Thank you," Mallory replied in an almost-singsong voice as he switched off the telephone console and turned back around to face Carpenter. "Funny you should mention that lot. But by all means, you first."

Carpenter cocked an eyebrow at him, then proceeded to tell the DNI about his probe regarding an ex-SEAL. He did not reveal the full context of his inquiry, but he did tell Mallory that the case involved homicide and that the ex-SEAL was a likely suspect. He also mentioned that the individual supposedly had gone MIA back at the end of the Vietnam War. Mallory nodded patiently as Carpenter described the Technical Operations Directorate's initial answer.

"Well, that explains something," he said when Carpenter was finished. "The deputy director of the *Defense* Intelligence Agency rang me up this morning. Seems those people were coming through channels, for a change. Wanted the Navy, the *whole* Navy, one presumes, to cease and desist making any further inquiries regarding one"—he got up and went to his desk to retrieve a piece of paper—"one Hospital Corpsman Galantz. That your fellow?"

"That's him. And that's very interesting. First, my guy hits the old stone wall. Never heard of this individual, they tell him. Now you say they're warning us off?"

Mallory said nothing, but just raised his eyebrows expectantly, as if waiting for Carpenter to answer his own question. But the JAG just sat there, ostensibly thinking.

"This may have been as simple as a mild rebuff for going direct, Thomas," the DNI prompted finally. "Was there some reason you did not bring the, um, inquiry through our office?"

"Yes," Carpenter said. "There's a client privacy problem. This involves another flag officer." Almost as an afterthought, he added the fact that the CNO had been apprised.

"Ah, I see," Mallory said, his peevish expression revealing that he did not see at all.

Carpenter ignored it. "I need to find this Galantz individual. We have reason to believe he may have survived his MIA status and is now here in the Washington area. Oh, and did I mention that the Fairfax County Police are involved?"

"You said homicide," the DNI said, resuming his seat. "What assets have you put on this problem?"

"I have a new NIS operative on my staff. A guy called von Rensel."

"Ah, yes, we know Mr. von Rensel," Mallory said. "He's not famous in the intelligence community for being a team player, I'm led to understand."

"From what I've heard, it was team playing that brought Navy Intelligence the Walker spy ring and that Korean thing," Carpenter retorted. "Anyway, I plan to turn him loose to see what he can find. What I came to ask you to do was to pull the string with those people. Spook to spook."

Mallory didn't like the crack about the spying cases. "I rather think their warning preempts any good that I might be able to do," he said. "Going spook to spook, as you so quaintly put it."

Carpenter gave him a level look. "This matter has the potential to embarrass the Navy flag community, Kyle. I need to find Galantz, or, which I suppose would be equally useful, prove that he does *not* exist—that he went MIA and stayed that way. I guess what I'm saying is that I need you to tell them that we can do this the easy way or hard way."

"Oh dear," Mallory protested. "That sounds like a threat. Do you know how those people usually react to threats from other government entities?"

"I'm not sure I give a damn," Carpenter replied. "Since the Fairfax County cops are involved, I can always just turn the whole thing over to CHINFO, let him invite the Washington press corps in for a chat. That way, those people can exercise their newfound expertise at doing damage control right here in River City."

Mallory rolled his eyes. "And then I get to explain to the CNO why this thing got loose, is that it, Admiral?"

Carpenter got up. "You're the official pipe into the cave of the intel bears, *Admiral*. My lawyerly instincts tell me if Galantz went MIA and then was resurrected somehow, the American version of the Lavender Hill Mob was probably involved. Basically, I'm proposing to give our client one free shot at extricating himself from this tar baby. But my bottom line remains the preservation of the herd. Just make the call, okay, Kyle?"

Mallory frowned and pursed his lips. "Very well, I will make the call. But there's something else they said in *their* call. Do you perchance know what a sweeper is—in their vernacular, that is?"

"Nope. Although I would assume it has to do with cleaning up a mess."

"Rather more elaborate than that, Thomas. As you know, those people have the need from time to time to take—how shall I put this?—to take extreme measures connected with their line of work."

"This is news, Kyle?"

"I suppose not. But the people they engage to perform these distasteful functions are not nice people. Not gentlemen, shall we say."

"Understood. And the point to all this is—"

"The point is, Thomas, that from time to time, these ungentlemanly people themselves require the imposition of disciplinary measures. Think about it. Think about what kind of people would be good at imposing disciplinary measures on the wet-work mechanics. That is the function of the so-called sweepers. Which makes the rest of their message rather important."

Carpenter stared at him. "And that was?"

"That they don't acknowledge the existence of this fellow Galantz. But that if he did exist, he might be involved in certain extracurricular activities, and that, because of *what* he is, they are of the opinion that they are best equipped to look into that problem, not us. One assumes that will happen sooner rather than later, but one never knows with those people."

"Forgive me, Kyle, but I still don't get it. If Galantz is one of their wet-work mechanics, as you call them, and he's gone wrong, why don't they get one of those—what'd you call 'em, sweepers? Why don't they put one of those guys onto the problem?"

"Well, nobody over there is speaking in declarative sentences, Thomas. But you may have touched on the heart of the problem. My guess is that this fellow Galantz *is* a sweeper."

Karen was not surprised to find Train waiting in the otherwise-empty office when she got back to the Pentagon at 5:30. He was now dressed in his regular office clothes. The rest of the JAG offices along the C-ring hallway were dark, except for the workaholic Appellate Defense Division, where they always worked late.

"Counselor," Train pronounced when she came through the door.

"Well if it isn't Igor, the grave diggers' assistant," she replied brightly. She was secretly glad to see him, if only because the empty corridors of the Pentagon after working hours were a mildly spooky place. She slung her purse over the back of the yeoman's chair and sat down. "So what was Admiral Sherman jumping up about toward the end of the ceremony? I saw you take off."

"Some kid on a motorcycle. He was standing up there on the hill among all the tourists and midshipmen. It looked to me like Sherman recognized him, which is why he stood up. By the time I got up the hill, the kid was jumping on a big Kawasaki two-seater and hauling ass. Never really saw his face. Any ideas?"

Karen shook her head. Something was playing at the edges of her memory, but she couldn't surface it. "No ideas," she replied. "I was going to ask Admiral Sherman about it, but he was really down about the old man's death."

She dialed into the voice-mail system, and there was one message, from Detective McNair, requesting a meeting as soon as possible—like tonight. She told Train about the message and that Sherman wanted to put it off a day.

"Homicide cops don't like to wait," Train said. "Better call Sherman."

She put a call in to OP-32. The admiral was in conference, having left orders not to be disturbed. Karen hesitated, then told the yeoman to tell the admiral that the Fairfax business meeting had to be tonight. She said she would remain in her office until he was able to return her call.

Train slouched down in a chair by the office door. Karen thought he looked like a big old bear trying to balance on a rock. A treacherous part of her brain began to speculate on what a hug might be like from such a bear. He killed her thoughts with the observation that he wasn't surprised that Sherman wanted to duck the cops.

"Oh, c'mon, Train. You don't still think he had anything to do with killing those two people, do you?"

Train looked away for a moment. "I'm still bothered by the fact that all the *current* information on this mysterious Galantz comes from Sherman. I want some external corroboration."

"But how about the syringe? I mean, I saw that thing, and the look on his face when he saw it."

"We've been over this: He had an opportunity to put that thing in your car."

She shook her head in exasperation. "But why? The syringe had blood in it that matched the old man's blood type, as well as traces of a substance that could've killed him. Why on earth—"

"Because he could be playing a game," Train interrupted. "A dangerous game, but still a game. Those cops have to be wondering, too. I know," he said, seeing the look on her face, "motive. That's where I'm hung up. I can't figure the motive."

The phone rang before Karen could reply.

"Navy JAG, Commander Lawrence speaking, sir." She mouthed the name Sherman at Train.

"Tonight, huh?" Sherman was saying.

"I'm afraid so, sir. Although I haven't called him back."

There was a pause. "Okay," he said. "I'll be done here in about thirty minutes. At this hour, thirty minutes to get home."

"Let me give you directions to my house," she said, ignoring the sardonic expression spreading over Train's face. "It's about twenty minutes beyond where you live, but a lot closer for him, coming from Fairfax."

He agreed, wrote down directions, and hung up. She called McNair and made the necessary arrangements. She told him that Sherman had wanted to put it off a day, hoping she could find out why they wanted the meeting so urgently.

"Two people are dead, Commander—in a week's time. As I think I mentioned, some people here are starting to view this as a situation involving a serial killer. By the rules, we're supposed to bring the FBI into it, sooner rather than later. We want to talk to Sherman again because he's the common thread. Plus . . ." He hesitated.

"Plus?"

"I'm going to ask that you not tell him this, Commander. I need to see his reaction when I ask the question. Deal?"

"Yes, of course, Detective. I can keep a secret." Train was watching her when she said that, his eyebrows rising.

"Well, I contacted Admiral Schmidt's lawyer today. Asked him our standard questions about contacts, possible business or tax problems, et cetera.

Tried not to highlight the fact that I was a homicide guy, if you follow my drift."

"Yes. Go on."

"Lawyer said he was the executor. There was no other family. The old man left a bequest of a year's salary to the housekeeper. The rest of his estate—worth something just north of a million bucks, a lot of that in the McLean house and five acres bordering on that park—goes to guess who?"

"Oh my," she whispered.

"Yeah, 'oh my.' Looking at things in an objective fashion, the good admiral has had his net worth bumped up about a million three in one week. So one of the things we have to do at this meeting is to inform him that we need to look hard at his finances—with his full cooperation, hopefully. And I guess this is the time to inform *you* that we might be migrating to different sides of the fence."

"I see," she said. "Formally?"

He hesitated. "No, not yet. We don't have a consensus here. And it depends on a couple of things—what we find when we pull the strings on Citizen Sherman and what you guys come up with on this Galantz guy."

She nodded to herself. "Let me ask you something. Put aside the circumstantial issues for a moment. Do you, personally, believe Admiral Sherman is a killer?"

Train whistled softly from his chair and then got up and started pacing around. This time, there was a longer silence on the phone. Karen found herself holding her breath.

"Actually, *my* gut feel is no. The lieutenant keeps writing the facts up on a case board and underlining the common thread, which is Sherman. Our lieutenant is hell on facts, which is probably why he's the lieutenant. I'll say this: If Sherman is the guy, he is one cold and calculating bastard, and a damned good actor. Both Mrs. Klein and the old admiral's housekeeper swear that he's a prince of a guy."

It was Karen's turn to be silent. Stalling for time to think, she asked another question. "Was there a DNA match on the blood in the syringe?"

"Much too soon. DNA matching takes time. But on gross markers, yes. The ME couldn't find an injection point, but then again, that was a very fine-gauge needle on that syringe."

"What about potassium?"

"Total bust. The chief toxicologist wouldn't even try. They said that there was no way to detect a toxic level of potassium in the tissues, especially after embalming. So, see you at seven-thirty."

He was cutting off the questions. She reviewed the directions and he said he and his lieutenant would be there. "My lieutenant wants to meet the admiral. See you there, Commander."

Karen hung up the phone and recapped the conversation for Train, who whistled again.

"I should be there," he said when she was finished.

She looked at him for a moment. Given Sherman's reluctance to share information, Train's presence might be awkward for Admiral Sherman. On the other hand, McNair's latest information had unsettled her. Once again, she was beginning to wonder about Admiral Sherman.

Train saw her working it out and grinned at her. Then he skewed his face, hunched his back, and dangled one arm lower than the other. "Igor may have been right, mistress. Igor might be good troll to know if you're going to hang around with bad guys, mistress. Maybe let the bad guy know mistress has Igor on call."

"Oh, quit," she protested, but without rancor. "I'll admit I'm a little more worried than I was. But yes, you should be there."

He straightened up, his face becoming serious. "But not for the reason you're thinking," he said. "I should be out there because of that lockout banner on your computer screen this morning."

"I don't understand," she said.

"I promise to explain" was all he said as he reached for his coat.

Out on the GW Parkway, Karen checked her mirror to see if Train's car was still behind her. She had been trying to figure out his cryptic comment about the security lockout on the Galantz investigation file. But she had been too proud simply to come out and ask him. Maybe he was trying to show her that he was thinking ahead of her. Baffled, she refocused her mind on the problems posed by the news about Galen Schmidt's bequest. She could see the cops' point of view. Alibis aside, the only other explanation on the table depended entirely on Sherman's version of something that happened more than twenty years ago, involving a man who had, according to government records, officially disappeared in the swamps of Vietnam. On the other hand, if Galantz did exist, and if he was bent on setting Sherman up to take a fall, he was doing a pretty good job of it. McNair's use of the term *serial killer* would do nothing to soothe the Navy flag community's uneasiness about this whole situation. Maybe after this meeting it would be propitious to review the bidding with Admiral Carpenter. Remember your tasking, she thought. The big guys want to avoid surprises. On the other hand, if Sherman was innocent, the fundamental unfairness of what was going on was starting to gall.

"Not bad for a commander, USN," Train said, looking around the expansive living room.

"Not bad for an oil-industry lobbyist who'd been in the 'bidness' for twenty-six years," Karen replied as she turned on more lights in the room. "Frank was pretty good at what he did."

He wandered around the living room, looking at pictures of Frank with name-brand senators and with two Presidents. "I don't suppose you ever get over the loss of a spouse," he said carefully.

She sighed. "At some point, I guess I was able to start getting on with life. But there are days, Train . . . there are definitely days."

"And nights, I imagine," he said. She nodded almost without thinking, and then she flushed. But there was no sexual innuendo in his eyes, only genuine sympathy. It was a side of him she hadn't expected. They were interrupted by headlights in the drive. Karen looked out the porch windows and recognized the admiral's car. Another car came up the drive behind him.

"Show time," Train said.

Karen took a deep breath and went to the door to let Sherman and the two policemen in. Once inside, McNair introduced his boss.

"This is Lieutenant Bettino. Admiral Sherman, Commander Lawrence. And Mr. von Rensel of the Naval Investigative Service."

Bettino offered his hand tentatively to Train, as if not sure he was going to get it back. Next to Train, Karen thought, Bettino looked like a college kid, with modish blond hair, bright blue eyes, and a very youthful face. She noticed that he did not say anything, but he also did not appear to be upset to have a fed present.

Sherman unbuttoned his uniform jacket and dropped into a chair. "I hope we can make this short, gentlemen," he said. "I buried a dear friend today. Mr. von Rensel, I assume you're going to expedite the NIS effort to find Galantz?"

"Yes, sir," Train said.

"If I may, Admiral," McNair interjected. "I apologize for calling this meeting so soon after Admiral Schmidt's funeral. But we're concerned that there have been what appear to be two homicides in one week, homicides that have a common thread."

"Two homicides? You've established that, Detective? Galen was killed by something in that syringe?"

"It's ambiguous at this time, Admiral," McNair admitted. "Just like the Walsh case."

"And the common thread," Sherman said. "I suppose that's still me?"

"Yes, sir, it is," Bettino said, speaking for the first time. His voice was smooth, almost silky. There was an abrupt hush in the room. Sherman's face tightened perceptibly. McNair moved to fill the suddenly awkward silence.

"Admiral Sherman, are you aware of the provisions of Admiral Schmidt's estate?"

Sherman blinked. "Estate? You mean his will? No. We were personal and professional friends. Since 1977. He has a lawyer. His name is—"

"We talked to him today, Admiral," McNair interrupted. "He informs us that you are the sole beneficiary of Admiral Schmidt's estate. With the exception of a stipend for his housekeeper, everything he had is now yours. That house and the acreage in McLean, everything."

Train was watching Sherman, who was starting to nod his head. He looked first at McNair, then at the lieutenant. "I . . . I was going to say that I'm surprised. But I guess I'm not surprised after all. He was like a father to me. His own family is gone—his wife, his son. No, I didn't know about this, but . . . " He ran out of words.

The lieutenant leaned forward. "Admiral, as of now you are not a suspect in this investigation. But as you are aware, we had a strange forensic situation in the Walsh house, in that we didn't find a normal forensic background. In the admiral's house, on the other hand, we have found evidence that you had been there."

"A fact which I told you earlier," Sherman pointed out. "On Wednesday night last week. No, on Tuesday. On Wednesday, I went to Elizabeth's memorial service. Galen was there." He looked around the room as if to make sure that everyone had noted that point.

"Yes, sir," McNair said, picking it up, almost as if they had rehearsed this. "Admiral Schmidt died sometime Thursday night. You were with Commander Lawrence until what time, around eleven?"

"Yes, something like that. We left the restaurant. And then found that syringe. Called you people."

"*You* called us, Admiral?" the lieutenant asked.

"No. I meant *someone* called. I guess what I'm saying is that your patrol officer can vouch for the fact that I was with Commander Lawrence." He looked around the room again, then realized how he was sounding. "Look, I was surprised by the fact that Elizabeth had named me in an insurance policy. The situation with Galen . . . well, that's a little less surprising. But I still think I'm being set up."

"By this Galantz individual?" McNair asked.

"Yes. I've told you all this, Detective."

McNair sat back in his chair. "That's right, sir, you have. But as of now, we have no way of corroborating the existence of the threatening letter or even the existence of Galantz. Or, for that matter, the incident that supposedly set him off after all these years. All the Navy has produced is a closed-out personnel file."

"Which proves that he certainly did exist," Karen interrupted.

"Yes, Commander," the lieutenant said. "But did exist isn't the same as does exist. Admiral Sherman, we need two things: We need to find this guy, or at least to establish that he didn't die out there in Vietnam. And secondly, we would like to ask your cooperation in allowing us to examine your personal situation."

" 'Personal situation,' " Sherman repeated. "As in—"

"As in personal finances. Whether or not you are overextended or have a big tax problem. Or if there's a pattern in your bank accounts that would indicate that you're a big-time gambler, or you're being blackmailed, or you have other personal habits requiring more money than you make in the Navy. Stuff like that."

" 'Stuff like that,' " Sherman repeated slowly, his face darkening. "I see. All of which you could do with a court order. If I were a suspect, that is."

"That's right, Admiral," the lieutenant said smoothly. "But since you're not, we're asking nicely. If you have nothing to hide, your cooperation and the absence of any of these indicators would bolster your credibility. I'm sure an officer of your seniority and experience will understand where we're coming from with this, right, sir? You know, sort of an easy way/hard way situation?"

Sherman and the lieutenant stared at each other, but then the admiral composed his face and sat back in his chair. "Anything you want, Lieutenant," he said in an icy tone. "I am none of those things you mentioned. I'm not a closet gambler, I don't have any debts other than my mortgage, I'm not being blackmailed, and I don't have a drug habit—although you'll have to take the Bureau of Medicine's word for that, as we're all drug-tested in the Navy—but, yes, I'll open the books for you. I'll instruct my accountant to provide full disclosure and my last five years of tax returns. You can even have a look inside my house if you wish, as long as you agree not to tear it up. How's that sound?"

"Like the full cooperation of someone who is eager to help us solve two homicides," the lieutenant replied, ignoring Sherman's tone of voice.

"Okay. But I'd like to ask a favor in return."

"Which is?"

"That you inform the Navy JAG—that's Commander Lawrence's boss, Admiral Carpenter—that I'm not a suspect."

McNair and the lieutenant looked at each other for a moment, but then the lieutenant nodded. "We can do that, Admiral," Bettino said. McNair nodded his agreement.

Sherman stood up. "Then I think we're done here," he announced. "If you don't mind, I want to go home and have a drink and try to wash this mess out of my mind for a couple of hours."

The two policemen stood up, as well. "We'll call you to make those arrangements, Admiral," McNair said. "Tomorrow morning okay?"

"I'll call you, if that's all right, Detective. I'm trying to keep this problem from becoming public knowledge in my office."

"We understand, sir," McNair said quickly, extracting his card case and handing him a card. "I'll be in the office by eight o'clock. Commander Lawrence, thanks for letting us meet here."

Karen nodded and escorted the two policemen to the front door. Train was still perched in his spot by the fireplace when she came back. Sherman was buttoning his uniform jacket when Karen asked him to stay for a few minutes. She needed to find out something, but she had not wanted to bring it up with Lieutenant Bettino there, showing teeth.

"I can offer you a drink," she said. "In fact, I think I'll join you."

Sherman looked over at Train for a moment, then nodded. "Okay. Scotch, if you have it." They went out to the kitchen. Karen brought the admiral his scotch, Train a beer, and fixed herself a glass of white wine.

"That was a definite change of tone," she said.

Sherman nodded. He looked dejected. "And that's with me *not* a suspect," he said. "I'd hate to see how they treat their suspects."

"Well, for one thing, you'd be meeting them on their turf, not out here on yours," Train said. It was only the second time he had spoken all evening, and Sherman looked over at him. The admiral was getting that cornered look again.

"Tell me, Mr. von Rensel, what do you think about the possibility that Galantz survived the Rung Sat, a Chinese jail in Saigon, and was able to make it back to the States?"

Train shrugged. "It's possible, Admiral. But not without some help, especially in Saigon."

"Meaning?"

"Meaning that there is a government agency that did some recruiting in that manner during the Vietnam War. Think about it: A guy's officially MIA, which is the same as dead in most people's minds. He's trained in the disciplines and techniques of Special Forces warfare. He's field-experienced. And if he survived the Rung Sat, he's one tenacious sumbitch. Those are pretty formidable qualifications for the clandestine intelligence services."

Sherman sipped his scotch, absorbing what Train had just said. One of the horses whickered from a back pasture, and another answered.

"I think I'm dead meat," Sherman announced abruptly. Karen remembered Train's first reply when she told him that there was a SEAL after Sherman. The admiral's face was grim. "A guy who doesn't exist, and who is probably some kind of—what, assassination specialist or something? I might as well paint a target on my jacket and sit out on the front porch."

Train smiled then. "Think on the bright side, Admiral. Guy like that, he could have done you a hundred times by now. He apparently wants to play with you first. That gives us time to find him."

"Oh, that's just wonderful," Sherman said, but then he smiled himself. "Sorry," he said, "it's just that I'm getting this boxed-in feeling."

"Admiral," Karen said after a moment. "Who was the young man up on the hill? At the cemetery in Annapolis? Remember, you stood up right as the service was ending?"

Sherman's smile vanished. He looked first at Train and then back at Karen. Which is when she remembered the kid on the motorcycle at Elizabeth Walsh's service and realized that was where she had seen him before.

"Okay," Sherman said, getting up and finishing his drink. "Okay. I think that was my son, Jack."

Train raised his eyebrows at Karen, who was trying to comprehend what the admiral had just revealed.

"Your *son?*"

Sherman stuck his hands in his uniform jacket pockets and walked over to the nearest window, keeping his back to both of them. He looked out into the dark yard for a minute before replying. "Yes. My son, Jack, whom I haven't seen in years, as I think I told you Thursday night. Except twice in the past week—once at Elizabeth's memorial service, then again at Galen's funeral. It's as if he's come out of nowhere—to gloat over these two deaths."

"Are you sure that's who he is, Admiral?" Train asked. "I was down there at Annapolis, hanging out in the crowd. I saw him, but at a distance, and I never did see his face."

"I'm pretty sure," Sherman said, sitting back down. "Very sure about the first time; pretty sure about the second time."

"Have you detected any other surveillance?" Train asked. ' Cars following you, people in the neighborhood who aren't normally there? Noises on the phone?"

Sherman laughed. "Since that letter? Hell yes. Everywhere I go. I see bad guys behind every parked car, under every bush." Sherman's mouth was compressed into a flat line. "Karen, I told you something about my marriage, and that my only son was . . . problematical, I guess I can say."

"Yes, sir," Karen said, remembering the conversation in the restaurant. "You indicated you two were estranged."

"Yes, basically since the divorce. But I didn't tell you the whole story. I told you we were divorced back in 1981. My wife got custody, naturally, because I was in the Navy and perpetually on the move. But I didn't tell you what happened after that. The bare bones of it is that Beth hit bottom three years afterward with the drinking. She lost custody of Jack. He ended up in foster care."

"What finally happened to your ex-wife, Admiral?" Train asked gently. He had moved into a chair closer to Sherman.

The admiral rattled the remaining ice cubes in his glass for a moment. "She shot herself," he declared finally.

Karen blinked. "She shot herself? My God, that's—that's terrible."

Sherman gave her another bleak look, then looked away.

"Yes. That *was* terrible. And, of course, Jack never forgave me. As you might imagine, he felt it was all my fault. Elizabeth told me many times that Jack was being unreasonable and just lashing out at me. Because by divorcing my wife, I had rejected him." He was silent for a moment. "I can rationalize a lot of it, but I can't really blame him for how he feels. Anyway, he wrote me a letter after she shot herself. Told me in no uncertain terms how he felt about the whole thing. Never wanted to see me again. Said that one day he'd find a way to repay me." Sherman got up again and went back to the window. He stood there for a minute, his back to them, rubbing the sides of his face with his hands.

"Admiral," Train said. "Was there anything on or in the note you got last week that would positively link it to Galantz?"

Sherman turned around and thought for a moment. "He told me—that night back in San Diego—that he'd be back when I had something of value to lose," he replied. "He said he would give me one warning. The note said Walsh was the first. So I just assumed Galantz. But to answer your question, no, there was no discreet identifier. Either way."

"Postmark?"

"I didn't notice. I read the note, read it again, and then called Galen Schmidt. Went over there. Talked to him about it. Came back, did some paperwork, looked for the note and the envelope, and both were gone."

"Paper quality? Was it stationery, or a notepad?"

"Cheap stuff—something you'd buy in a Seven-Eleven if you were in a real hurry. Lined. Five by seven."

Train nodded. "Was there a stamp?"

"A stamp." Sherman wrinkled his brow. "You know, now that you mention it, I don't think so. I've been trying to conjure up an image of the postmark since you asked, but now I think there was no postmark, because there was no stamp." He looked up. "Which means he just put it through the slot."

"Back to your son, Jack," Train prompted. "You said you'd had no contact with him for several years. Longer if you discount that last letter. Did you know where he was during that time?"

"Jack's last letter came from Quantico, you know, south of here. I assumed that's where he landed when he was thrown out of the Marines, but I have no idea if he stayed there or moved elsewhere."

"Was his letter addressed here—I mean, to your house in McLean?"

"No. It came to my office in BuPers, during my second tour there."

Train nodded again. "My point is that he either knew or found out where you were stationed. He was keeping track of where *you* were, even if you didn't know where he was."

Sherman began pacing around the edges of the counters, nodding to himself. "I guess that's right," he said. "I mean, if you don't suspect you're a target, and take no precautions, somebody could know just about every-thing about you." He stopped as the implication of that reasoning pene-trated. Karen could see him visibly slump.

She got up and went to him. "Admiral, we're ranging pretty far afield here. I think where Train's going with this is that finding Galantz might be next to impossible, especially if he is a professional operative. But maybe we should go find your son instead. Find out what he was doing at those two funerals."

Sherman stood there, his eyes staring down at nothing. "He was there to gloat. He was grinning at me down in Annapolis. That's what made me stand up. He was grinning—there isn't any other word for it."

Train stood up. "That doesn't mean he's a murderer. He may have been secretly keeping track of you constantly for all these years. Sons who've become disaffected from their fathers often do that. He may well have taken some pleasure in your loss—"

"Loss*es.*"

"Well, yes, sir, losses. I think we need to find your son, talk to him."

"Does 'we' have to include the cops?"

Train looked at Karen, who shook her head imperceptibly. Implicating Sherman's son would compound the whole mess in the eyes of the Navy hierarchy.

"No, sir, not yet, anyway," Train replied, taking her lead. "Let the cops work Galantz. I will, too, and we'll feed them what we get. Meanwhile, I'll try to track down Jack and talk to him, see what the hell this is all about. What is his full name, Admiral?"

"John Lee Sherman. Supposedly there are Virginia Lees in my ex-wife's family." He paused. "And what will you do if you get the sense that he is involved in these killings?"

"Then we *will* have to tell the cops. Actually, an argument could be made for doing that right now. You do understand where they're focusing at the moment?"

"Yes indeed," the admiral said. "And you're suggesting that we give them my son's possible involvement, thereby taking some of the heat off me?"

Train started to reply but thought better of it. Sherman was shaking his head. "I'm boxed," he said. "Someone's killed my ex-lover and my oldest friend and implicated me. The powers that be in the Navy are starting to circle the wagons. The police are saying I'm not a suspect but that they want to execute a search of my life, and one of the ways out is to accuse my son of being involved in the homicides, the kid I neglected for most of his childhood? C'mon, guys!"

"Admiral, wait a minute," Karen said. "Think about it. If you're in a box with no apparent way out, someone had to set this up. I mean, it's just not likely that all of this just happened. And the police aren't stupid: They'll see that, too."

Train concurred. "A week ago, you were ops normal. Now two people tied to you are suddenly dead, under suspicious circumstances. You are under suspicion, by both the cops and the Navy flag community. Your son, whom you haven't seen for years, makes two appearances. Karen's right. This mess didn't just come out of the blue. Somebody has set it motion."

"Wonderful."

"There's more, Admiral. We should expect something else to happen. I don't know what, but somebody's stepping through a plan. The momentum is with him right now. He's not just going to stop. You need to become vigilant. Be aware of your surroundings, your exposure. Be careful. Do you own a gun?"

The admiral stared at him. "Yes, I do. But—"

"Carry it—in your briefcase, in your car. I'm serious."

"But I don't have a permit, or anything like that."

"Think of it this way, Admiral. You don't want to be facing this guy in a dark parking lot and wishing you had put the goddamned gun in your pocket that morning. Now, we could kick this thing around all night. But I recommend you go home, and Karen and I will start in on finding Jack tomorrow. We'll make sure the cops continue to receive everything we get on Galantz, and I've pulled some strings in the intelligence world to see if there is a connection there. You concentrate on being vigilant. Let us work the problem."

Sherman nodded slowly. Karen could see that he was struggling to keep his equanimity, but she thought Train had it right. Sherman was in the box. Someone outside the box would have to get him out. He straightened his uniform jacket, thanked her for the drink, and nodded good night to Train.

She accompanied him to his car. He paused by the driver's side door. "I feel like I should be a whole lot angrier about this than I am," he said. "But I feel more resigned than anything else. I guess it's because I do own a big piece of what's behind this. What happened to Galantz back there in Vietnam—leaving a guy behind in a combat situation is a major wrong."

"But certainly you had operational justification—" she began, but he was shaking his head.

"We're talking about an almost-sacrosanct law of the battlefield. You don't leave your wounded; hell, you don't even leave your dead. Men will fight on even in the most hopeless situations as long as they believe that. We did the wrong thing out there. And as for Jack . . . well, look what happened to his mother."

"Whoever's doing this is counting on your feeling that way, Admiral," Karen replied, sidestepping the immediate truth of what he had said.

"Train's right: You need to focus right now on situational awareness. You have little maneuvering room. We still do."

"Unless Carpenter gets some direction from higher up and recalls you and von Rensel."

She hadn't thought about that. He saw her look and smiled, but his eyes were filled with sadness. "Even paranoids can have enemies, right? Good night, and thank you for your help. I guess I'm in your hands right now."

She resisted a strong urge to comfort him somehow. "We'll figure it out, Admiral. Good night."

He backed his car around and drove off down the driveway. Train came out onto the front porch and watched him go. The night was clear, but there was no moon up yet, leaving the grounds and fields around the house in deep shadow. Karen wondered where Harry, the Lab, was.

"Poor bastard," Train was saying. "Assuming he is innocent, someone's working quite a campaign on him. Tell me, is there somewhere to get a bite around here?"

They drove in separate cars to the shopping center in Great Falls and went into the Irish pub. They ordered drinks and made some quick decisions about the menu.

"Have you become a believer now?" she asked once the waitress had left.

Train reflected for a moment. "Yeah, I think so. There are still some bothersome inconsistencies, but his overall situation points toward a setup. His wife shot herself. God, there's the ultimate 'I'll show you.' "

She shivered. "That son definitely sounds like somebody we need to talk to."

Train nodded. "I'll start beating the bushes tomorrow. Then maybe we both go talk to him."

"But do you think he would talk to us?"

"Ve Germans haff our methods, madame," Train intoned. She smiled. He returned the smile. It was the first truly personal smile she had seen, and she suddenly wanted to talk about something besides this baffling Sherman case.

"So, do you live in Virginia?" she asked. He told her a little of his background, then briefly described his home on the Potomac, near Aquia. She became increasingly intrigued as he described the household setup, beginning to wonder why someone with obvious financial security and a law degree would be working for the NIS. He sensed her question.

"I know it sounds a bit anomalous. But I think I'm making a contribution, and that's been a big part of our family's ethic over the generations. Can't escape our Prussian heritage, I guess, although every time I've pulled the genealogical string, things get a little vague about exactly where the von came from in von Rensel. It may have been appropriated on the way over with von Steuben."

She stirred her Chardonnay with a fingernail. "And why no family? Is that part of the master plan?"

He looked discomfited, and she realized he was basically a very shy man. "Not *my* master plan," he said quietly. "But, hell, look at me. Man Mountain Dean. Women find me—what's the word? *Exotic,* I guess. I usually see two reactions from the ladies: downright fright at the thought of being with such a big guy, or salacious interest, for the same reason. I guess nobody ever wanted to take me home to meet the folks."

She smiled at that. "When I was younger, it seemed like lots of Navy guys wanted to take me home to meet the folks," she said. "But as a Navy lawyer, I saw too many marriages like the admiral's: women left alone to cope with tight budgets, disaffected kids who thought that their daddies went away because they'd done something wrong, or the fallout from the randy sailor types who had to have a woman in every port, sometimes including home port."

"Were there no civilians?"

"Not really. You know, when you're in the Navy, you tend to socialize Navy. You were in the Marines; you didn't associate with civilians, did you?"

"Nope," he acknowledged. "Civilians were all hapless dolts who desperately needed the protection of the few, the strong, and the brave."

She hummed a few bars of the Marine Corps hymn and he laughed. "Stop, or I'll have to stand up and salute," he said. Their eyes met for a moment.

"This is much better, Mr. Man Mountain," she said. "I think we're going to do okay." He raised his beer mug in a grave salut as the evening's entertainment, a two-man band accompanied by a twenty-piece orchestra in a computer, lit off in the corner and ended any hope of further conversation.

After dinner, they walked slowly out to the parking lot. She was wondering how he would tie off the evening.

"I'm glad we did this," he said when they reached their cars. He looked as if he wanted to say more but was too shy to come out with it.

"So am I," she replied. "However this Sherman mess comes out."

He smiled, and she almost invited him back to the house for a nightcap. But the moment passed and he became all business again.

"Are there any other signs that the JAG's having second thoughts about our investigation?" he asked as he unlocked his car.

"Other signs?"

"Who else but Carpenter would have the power to lock you out of a JAG archives file? That's what I was talking about earlier."

"Oh. I never thought—you think he did that?"

"He did or someone did on his orders. I was thinking: Maybe tomorrow would be a good day to call in sick. In case he's waiting to call you up to the front office and tell you to go back to reviewing investigations. I don't know, but I suddenly have this feeling that we've been switched off the main line here."

"Well, I suppose I could." Once again, he had taken her by surprise. Carpenter?

He opened his car door. "Look," he said, "like I told Sherman, you need to be vigilant, too. Remember what's been happening to people close to Sherman. Right now, from an outsider's perspective, you qualify."

There it was, that big-brother attitude of his again, she thought. But this time, she did not resent it. She decided to flirt a little. "But I have you to protect me, Mr. Man Mountain, right?"

He gave her a wary eye. "You want me to stay with you tonight?" he asked, keeping it light by giving her a barely visible grin.

She felt a tingle of excitement, and she batted her eyes. "How the neighbors would talk."

"What neighbors are those, specifically?" he asked. But then, as if sensing this was getting a little too personal, he backed off. "Look, whoever's doing this is pretty good at it. Something strikes you as being out of whack, call me." He fished out a card and wrote something on the back of it. "Here's the number for my car phone, and my home phone and fax numbers down in Aquia. False alarms are acceptable."

She thanked him and then watched him drive out of the parking lot. She drove home, speculating on things and feelings long dormant, too long dormant. Once home, she started to lock up the house, then remembered the dog. She went back out onto the front porch and called. Nothing. The barn—the last place she had seen Harry. He had been trotting down toward his favorite sunning spot. I'll bet he's sound asleep. She walked across the front of the house and down toward the aisle of hedge between the yard and the barn. The night was cooler now, with clear skies and a sprinkling of stars. The loom of Washington's lights permeated the southeastern horizon. She automatically searched for and found Polaris; Frank had made a fetish of fixing the North Star every time he went outside at night. She could hear small rustlings in the hedge as she passed down the shadowy aisle, taking care not to hang up a heel on a crack in the mossy bricks. A car went by out on Beach Mill Road, but the sound was dampened by the dense hedge.

She came out into the barn enclosure and looked around. The horses were not visible, but there was a night-light on in the aisle. She called the dog again, but nothing happened. Funny. Normally, he would have been bounding out of the barn by now. She walked forward, into the aisleway. The familiar smells of hay, straw, and leather reeking of One Step cleaner met her as she crossed the threshold. She looked down the aisle in the dim light and saw Harry, lying on his saddle pad against the door of the tack room.

"Hey, beast, let's go. It's time to go in the house." Harry didn't move. Alarmed, she went over to him. The dog was not in his customary furry ball. He was lying against the door, breathing, but more crumpled than curled. "Harry?" she called, kneeling. The dog didn't move. His breathing sounded ragged, shallow. Then she smelled something medicinal, like alcohol, but not exactly. Sweeter, almost sickly sweet. She remembered that smell. What the hell was it? Ether! That's what it was, ether. She bent closer to the dog's muzzle, and the smell was stronger. Some bastard had—

There was a loud crash as something hit the tin roof of the barn, something hard and sharp that rattled down the slope of the metal roof and fell with a small thud into the paddock outside. She nearly jumped out of her skin and stood up, flattening herself against the door, her breath frozen in her throat.

Silence. The dog groaned softly at her feet, his rear legs twitching. There was another noise, this time at the far end of the barn, like weeds or bushes scrabbling against the retracted aisleway doors—coming toward the doorway. She panicked and ran out of the barn, across the barn enclosure, and up toward the house. But when she got to the hedge passage, she stopped abruptly, grabbing the post of the grape arbor to stop herself. The walkway between the hedges, which was nearly fifty feet long, was in deep shadow. She looked over her shoulder at the barn, but there was nothing coming or moving—yet.

She looked back into the gloom of the hedge passage and back at the barn. There were fences on either side of the hedge passage. She was in her uniform skirt and low heels. That fence would slow her down—a lot. The hedge passage was a direct shot to the house—unless there was someone in there, someone who could reach through the hedge and grab her. A night breeze swept gently through the tree branches over her head. The barn remained silent.

She made her decision: Get to the house; get to a phone. She took off again, straight through the hedge passage, staying low, bent over as she ran, grateful for every day of her workouts, her right arm held up, her hand balled in a fist. She erupted from the other side of the passage and sprinted the remaining hundred feet to the front porch in about six seconds. She hurtled through the front door, spun around, slammed and locked it. She leaned back against the door as she recovered her breath. Phone. Get on the phone. Call the cops. No. Call Train. Where was that card? In her pocket. Call his car phone. Get him to turn around and get back here.

Then she realized the house was dark. There was enough starlight coming in to see the furniture and the walls but not much else. Turn on the lights, dummy.

They had been on when she left.

She held her breath as she slowly moved her hand over to feel the bank of switches by the front door. Three of the four were up, in the "on" position.

The power. The power's out. Someone's cut the power.

She swallowed hard and moved sideways into the living room, feeling her way through the familiar shapes of furniture. She stopped when she reached the phone at the far end of the couch, then listened carefully. She thought she sensed a foreign presence in the house, then wondered if it was just her imagination. Her mouth dry, she settled into the couch and put her hand on the telephone.

If he'd cut the lights, he might have cut the phone, too. Please, please let it be working.

With Train's card in one hand, she lifted the handset. But she couldn't see the numbers in the darkened living room. This was no time to mess around. She couldn't bear to see if there was a dial tone or not. She took a deep breath and punched 911. Then she put the handset to her right ear and held her breath. Her heart sank when she did not hear a ringing sound.

Commander Lawrence, a voice whispered.

She nearly dropped the phone. Someone was on the line, and it sure as hell wasn't the 911 operator.

I know you're there, Commander.

The voice seemed disembodied, a hoarse, machinelike whisper with a faint echo, but it was unmistakably right there, right in her ear. Where the hell was he? Oh my God, the phone didn't ring: He's here; he's in the house. She fought back another surge of panic, the overwhelming urge to bolt back out of the house.

"Who is this? What do you want?" she said, her voice coming out in a dry croak.

That's not your normal voice, Commander. Funny how adrenaline can do that. Are you afraid?

She looked around the darkened room and swallowed again. If she just put the phone down and kept very quiet, she could make it to the front door. Depending on where he was. There were extension phones in the study, the kitchen, and the upstairs bedrooms. Get out of the house. Get to one of the cars, and a car phone.

Pay attention, Commander. Stop trying to figure out where I am or how to get help. I'm not here to hurt you. If I wanted to hurt you, I would have put a razor wire about neck-high between those hedges. I didn't hurt your old dog, did I? I could have snapped his neck. But I used ether, right? So sit still. And pay attention. This is important.

"Who are you?" she asked, her voice a little stronger. She eyed the front hall, gathering herself, and then thought about getting the door locks open, and about the distance to the garage.

I think you know who I am. The voice definitely sounded as if it was machine-generated, not human.

"Galantz?"

That's not my name anymore. Marcus Galantz is dead, remember? But here's the deal: You're beginning to interfere in something that doesn't concern you. You and your friend Lurch there.

She swallowed but said nothing.

I want you to back out. Go back to being a professional second-guesser in room 4C646 in the Pentagon. There's a future in that. There's no future in what you've been doing lately. None at all. Do you understand me?

"Did you kill them?" she asked. "Elizabeth Walsh? Admiral Schmidt?"

No. He did. Your precious pretty boy with the golden sleeves.

"I don't believe that," she said. "He's not a killer."

Oh yes he is. You have no idea, Commander. He kills people, especially people who depend on him. He kills people who are close to him. And you are getting close to him. Dangerous place to be, Commander. Very dangerous, in my recent experience. Others would agree—if only they could.

That silenced her. She tried to think, but that whispering voice was starting to mesmerize her—the repetitive phraseology, the short chantlike bursts of speech. The urge to bolt was diminishing. Instead, she found herself wanting to talk to him, to pay attention to the whispering sound in her ear.

You don't believe me, do you, Karen-n-n-n?

Suddenly, the whisper was much louder as he let the final syllable of her name linger in the earpiece, the echoing voice like a prolonged hiss from a large snake. Using her name now. Focus: He's using a machine to do this.

I do believe you. But she was thinking it, not saying it.

Karen-n-n-n. Here I come. Karen-n-n-n.

She realized then that she had stopped breathing and that she was holding the earpiece against the side of her head hard enough to hurt.

No. Don't come. I believe you. But she was still thinking it, not saying it.

Karen-n-n-n. The volume was diminishing.

Please. Don't come. I believe you.

He said her name again, the volume very low now, as if he had put down the phone.

And was coming.

She dropped the phone and lunged across the living room, knocking over a table and then a lamp, caroming off an upholstered chair before reaching the front vestibule, her hands clawing at the dead-bolt handle, the door handle, and then she was out on the front porch and flying across the driveway to the garage, its right-side door still open, thank God, to the first car, any car, and then she was inside the Mercedes, batting at the switches for the door locks.

Keys. Oh God, I don't have my keys!

She whirled around in the seat and looked back at the open garage door. The door transmitter was mounted to the dash. Close it? Or leave it open?

Close it and be in total darkness. Open it and he gets in, if he wants to. Then she remembered the car phone.

She smashed down on the remote transmitter button and the big garage door started to lower behind her. She stabbed the power switch on the car phone. There was a tone, and the little screen lit up. *Locked,* it read, as if mocking her.

She yelled and slammed her hand on the steering wheel, then remembered how to unlock it. The garage door settled to the concrete floor behind her with a thump as she punched in the last three digits of the phone's number. An instant of silence, and then there was another tone, and then the blessed dashed lines of a full signal. She picked up the handset and then dropped it when the phone *rang.*

She let it lie there on the seat, afraid to touch it. It rang again, then a third time. Him. It had to be him. Finally, her hand trembling, she reached down and hit the Send button, then picked it up.

Karen-n-n-n.

She closed her eyes but didn't reply. Just held the phone to her ear.

Get clear of this. Get your large friend clear of this. Don't be there when I come for him. I won't warn you again.

She squeezed her eyes shut to make him go away.

I'm going now.

The whisper grew weaker, overlaid with reverberations.

I'm going now, Karen. Don't make me come back.

Then there was nothing except the hiss of static in her ear. She hit the Clear button and let the phone drop into her lap as she slumped back against the seat of the car. Her stomach felt weak and fluttery. Her hands and even her legs were still trembling.

She picked up the phone again to make a call, then stopped. A call to whom? The cops? And tell them what? That she was sitting in her garage, locked in her Mercedes, because there was some guy talking to her on a phone? She could just hear the cops' response: Yeah, right, lady, we'll be hustling right along. Another Great Falls Yuppie princess who's overdone her meds.

But for some reason, she felt that he was indeed gone. She reached for the remote transmitter button, then hesitated. What if he wasn't? She turned around slowly in the seat and looked out at the side mirror. She could barely make out the inside surface of the garage door, but there was a thin line of dim light along the garage floor. She turned back around and unlocked the doors, wincing at the suddenly loud noise. She opened the door and slid out of the driver's seat. Opening the door turned on the car's interior light. Feeling exposed, she pushed the door shut, trying to make no noise.

Standing by the door, she had to hang on to the door handle because her legs were trembling so badly. She stared hard at the bottom of the garage door. But now she could clearly see the crack of dim light visible along the bottom. She crept back to the left-rear fender, then slowly sank down to one knee to look under the door. She froze.

There were two dim shapes that looked very much like shoes standing right by the door.

She held her breath and closed her eyes. You're imagining things. Look again. I don't want to look again. Do it. She looked again. Nothing. She bent farther down, scanning the entire crack. Nothing. Taking care to make not a sound, she straightened up and leaned back on the fender. A mouse scuttled in some leaves in a corner of the garage, but there were no other sounds, inside or out.

Call Train. Yes, call Train. But not on this phone. Use the other phone, the Explorer's. She went over to the Ford, looked inside, and got in. She turned on the car phone, then hesitated. If he had a scanner, he could listen to any car phone. He had the Mercedes's number, why not the Explorer's? The phone in the house was no good, either, as he had tellingly demonstrated. Suddenly, all the familiar, secure appurtenances of her life were turning on her. Get to a pay phone. Drive to the village of Great Falls and use a pay phone to call Train.

She locked the doors of the Explorer and reached for the garage door's transmitter before she remembered that she still had no keys. Damn. I have to go into the house. She sighed, unlocked the doors, and got out of the car. She knelt down to look under the garage door again, feeling her right stocking pop a run. Nothing. She reached back into the car and hit the remote transmitter switch. With much groaning and rattling, the left-side door rose up from the cement floor. Even though it was dark outside, there was suddenly much more light in the garage. She looked around and saw the handle of the wood-splitting maul Frank had broken and never replaced. She picked it up; then, holding it in both hands, she walked out of the garage and headed for the house.

The first thing she noticed was that all the house lights were back on. She stopped in front of the house and scanned the windows. Nothing out of the ordinary. The front door was still open. She looked around the front yard, then climbed the front porch steps as quietly as she could and peered through the living room windows. The furniture she had collided with in her dash for the garage was still overturned on the floor. Hell with it, she thought. I'm going in.

She went through the opened front door, the maul handle ready. She walked quickly through all the rooms on the first floor, through the dining room, kitchen, Frank's study, turning on lights wherever she went and opening closet doors. She stopped when she got back into the living room. The house *felt* empty, for whatever that was worth. She reached for the phone, which was on the floor. There was no dial tone. She hung it up and waited a minute, then picked it up again. Dial tone. The numbers—where was the damn card?

There was some scratching and whining at the door, and she went to let Harry in. The dog was a bit wobbly and displaying total embarrassment, his head down and tail plastered between its hind legs.

"It's okay, Harry. It's not your fault," she said, rubbing his head. "You're no match for ether." She locked the front door again and went into the kitchen, the dog glued to her heels. She dropped the maul handle on the kitchen counter and found Train's card crumpled in her skirt pocket. She reached for the phone again but then thought about it. Was it tapped? Could he be listening right now? And which number should she call?

She looked at her watch. It was 11:15. From Great Falls to the Beltway was almost ten miles. Another ten around the Beltway to I-95. Aquia was at least twenty miles beyond that. He might not even be home yet. She looked at the numbers. Phone, car phone, and fax.

Fax.

Frank had a fax in the study, on the second house line. She could send Train a fax, and there was no way *he* could listen in to that. She hurried to the study.

Train faxed back twenty minutes later: Did she want him to come back and had she called the cops?

She replied, scribbling furiously with a ballpoint, the maul handle two feet away from her. Said she was pretty sure he was gone, and that no, she had not called the cops.

"Do you have a dog?"

"Yes, but old. Found him unconscious in the barn when it all started. Ether. He's back in the house now."

"If dog can operate, take him through the house to make sure you are alone. Then lock up. I'll be out there at first light. Don't call cops unless you think he's come back. This contact must go direct to McNair, not patrol cops. In emergency, use the phone, but assume it's bugged. Got a gun?"

Frank kept that huge government-model Colt .45 auto in the safe. She was pretty sure it was still there. But she hadn't fired one since OCS.

"Yes." she scribbled back to him. It was slow going, but hopefully secure. She never wanted to pick up a phone and hear that whisper again.

"Get it out. Keep it close. Keep dog close. Barricade bedroom door. I'll contact McNair in the morning."

She nodded to herself. Keeping the dog close would not be a problem. Harry was lying across her feet, trembling, his fur still reeking of ether.

"Okay. See you in the morning."

"Hang in there. He was there to warn you, not hurt you. You are not the target," Train replied, and then the fax machine went silent.

Not the target, she thought. Not yet, anyway. She crumpled all the flimsy paper into a trash can and opened up the safe. The big automatic was at the back. There was a full clip in the butt. She racked the slide back with some difficulty and chambered a round, then let the hammer down very carefully. It had been a long time since OCS and her small-arms training, but she still knew how to chamber a round. Firing it would be something else again. Probably take down a wall if she tried it. Gun in hand, she went around the house again with Harry, but he seemed much more interested in sticking to her than in sniffing out bad guys in the closets. When she was satisfied that no one was in the house, she checked locks and lights, then went upstairs to bed.

CHAPTER 8

She gave up trying to get back to sleep a little after five. Her night had been fitful, disturbed by dreams of whispering objects, and she had started awake with every night sound. Harry looked at her accusingly when she finally turned on a light and got up, but he dutifully followed her downstairs after she had washed her face and combed her hair. She brought the big automatic with her, putting it down on the counter next to the coffeepot. It looked very much out of place.

It was still dark outside, but there were signs of light visible on the eastern horizon. First light, she thought, then realized she was still in her nightgown. She hurried upstairs and threw on some jeans and a sweater. She got back downstairs just in time to see the headlights of Train's car rolling up into her driveway.

She went outside as Train got out. He waved to her when she said good morning. Then he went around to the back of the car, where he opened the two rear doors and called softly. An enormous Doberman hopped out onto the driveway, looked around briefly, saw Karen, and trotted right over to the porch steps. She was about to flee back into the house when Train gave a command and the dog stopped in its tracks at the top of the steps and sat down.

"What is *that?*" she asked.

Train laughed as he came over. "*That* is Gutter. He's your new-and-improved security system."

"Gutter?"

"You have to admit, the name lends a certain style," he said, patting the dog's sleek black head. "His real name is Götterdämmerung, but 'Gutter' works as a metaphor for everyday mayhem."

"Will he eat Harry?" she asked as she headed back inside.

"Not if he's submissive."

She had to go get a leash before she could drag Harry out to the front porch. Harry adopted a disgustingly submissive posture in front of the statuelike Dobe, who looked down at Harry briefly before resuming his inspection of the morning sky. Karen took off Harry's leash, and the old dog slunk down the porch steps and out of sight around the corner.

"Okay, that's all we need," Train said. "There won't be any trouble between those two. Now you."

"Me what?" she said, eyeing Gutter.

"Sit down on the top step, right next to him. Do what I say. Do precisely what I say. Have you showered yet this morning?"

"I beg your pardon?" she said as she nervously she sat down next to the dog, whose head was slightly higher than hers.

"Scent is all-important," he replied. The dog looked at Train and waited. Train came up on the steps and sat down on the other side of the dog. He reached across the dog's back and took Karen's hand. Karen felt as if she was putting her hand in a big warm vise. He held her hand alongside the dog's muzzle and bent down next to the dog's face, speaking in German as he did so.

The dog looked first at Train and then back over his shoulder at Karen. Then he wiggled like an eel and was all over her, nuzzling, sniffing, making happy whimpering sounds like a big puppy. He ended up with his head in her lap, on top of their joined hands, his big brown eyes watching her face carefully. She was suddenly very aware of Train's hand on the tops of her thighs.

"Okay, now you," Train ordered, letting go of her hand. "Pet him; tell him he's a good boy. Love it up a little. We're telling him that he's to be as loyal to you as he is to me. We'll do it a couple more times while I teach you some basic commands and his rules of engagement."

She swallowed and complied, amazed at the transformation in the dog's demeanor. Every Doberman she had ever seen looked underfed and keenly interested in rectifying that problem. This one was acting as if he wanted some warm milk.

"Rules of engagement. That sounds like weapons talk," she said.

"This *is* a weapon; it's just in standby at the moment. Gutter's going to live in your house for a while. You're going to show him around inside; then later, when I get back, I'm going to show him around outside to define the perimeter. It's actually an exercise in scent, and touching. Dobes are really into touching. They're extremely intelligent, and the good news is that they readily accept human females as dominant. When we're all done, you're going to be safe from creeps who come around here uninvited."

"What would he do to an intruder?" she asked, continuing to pet the dog. His shiny black hide felt like she always imagined a seal would feel.

"If he was outside, he would bark and run the guy off, staying just behind him but out of the range of hand weapons until the bad guy leaves the defined perimeter. Inside, he wouldn't make a sound until the creep was well past any escape routes. Dobes like to do that, too. Let people in but not out. After which, he would nail the guy to the floor by his throat until someone told him to let go or to eat him. Pat him one more time and then get up. I'm going to demonstrate the bark."

She smoothed her hands over the dog's head one last time and got up. Train also got up and gave a command. The dog sprang up into a standing position. Train gave another command and the dog broke out into a burst of the loudest barking Karen had ever heard. She clapped her hands over her ears in fright, and Harry left a visible piddle trail as he decamped across the front walk, heading toward the barn. After five seconds, Train gave another command and the dog stopped.

"That's bark. Here's growl."

Another command, and the front yard was filled with a menacing rumbling growl as the Dobe leaned forward on his haunches, looking at nothing in particular. The growl was punctuated with an occasional lip-lifting grimace that revealed what looked like at least a yard of glistening canine ivory. Another command and the dog was silent again.

"I'm not sure I can handle all this," she said, looking at the dog, who was still watching Train expectantly, waiting for the next command. The phone began to ring in the house.

"You'll do fine. I've written all this down. Mostly, he's just going to be here. You better get that."

She slipped into the living room, followed by Gutter, who pushed his nose between the screen door as she went through. Her neighbor Ken Parsons, of the perpetual lawn mower, was on the phone. She reassured him that everything was fine.

She smiled as she hung up. "I think I might be able to get used to Gutter," she said, reaching down to pet the dog. Gutter looked up at her approvingly. Train then told her to take the dog on a tour of the inside of the house, room by room. "Let him in your closet, and let him get a good scent of shoes. The laundry hamper, too. I want him to know your scent, okay?"

She was almost blushing when they finished taking the dog around on his grand tour. They were back in the kitchen in ten minutes. Karen sat down in a kitchen chair, and the dog parked himself between her feet.

"Okay," Train said. "Remember that he wants to be right next to you, as you can see, or at least in the same room with you. Or anywhere you go. Make eye contact often, and show affection. He's worth it."

"Did you raise him?"

"Yes. My family's had Dobes for years. My father used to breed and show them. Gutter is four, and I've done most of his training. He even likes the water, which is unusual. You should see him go fishing in the river."

"The river is not quite a half mile that way," she said. "Maybe I'll take him fishing."

"He'd love it." Train paused. "I need you to tell me about last night again. And then I have to get down to Fort Fumble."

"Why? What's happened?" she asked as she fixed two cups of coffee.

"Checked my voice mail on the way over here. His Legalness the JAG commands my unworthy civilian posterior into his presence first thing this morning. What's the commute from here at this hour?"

"Forty-five minutes if you get out by six-forty. I'll send you the back way."

"Bad night, yes?" he asked.

She nodded, still feeling a slight tremble in her hands. "Yes, bad night. Not much sleep." She told him again what had happened. The Dobe sat attentively on the kitchen floor between them. She rubbed the back of the dog's neck absently.

"One question," he said when she was done. "The voice—is there any chance it could have been Sherman?"

She looked at him and then closed her eyes, trying to remember the voice.

"It was mechanical," she replied. "There was an odd volume to it, as if there was some kind of obstruction. And what sounded like a precursor breath before he spoke." She shivered. "It was really spooky. But, no, I don't think it was Sherman. On the other hand—"

"On the other hand, it was artificial, wasn't it?"

She nodded. "It could have been anyone, then," she said. "You're still suspicious of him, aren't you?"

He twisted his coffee cup around in his hands. "I still go back and forth. Listening to the cops last night, I found myself agreeing with their train of thought. These Fairfax guys are pretty professional, and the pros tend to go with the Occam's razor approach: The simplest solution is usually *the* solution. Then I would look at Sherman, see the distress in his face, and my heart would say, No way. This guy isn't a killer."

"So why are you still suspicious?"

"Well, you never saw anyone, except for the silhouette of those shoes through the crack under the garage door. He could have left the meeting, doubled back, parked the car out on Beach Mill Road somewhere, and walked back into the property to terrorize you. Emphasis on the *could have.*"

"And then accused himself of two murders?"

"Arrgh," Train said. "I hate it when you start getting logical."

"So, shouldn't we call McNair?" she asked.

"Let's see what the JAG wants first. I want to go after Galantz, especially after this crap. But we need to be sure of our tasking. And I want to know why you were locked out of that file."

She shifted in her chair, looked at her coffee, then thought better of it. "But why wait to tell McNair?" she asked.

"Because the cops will immediately think Sherman. First thing they'll do is pull him in and question him as to where he went last night after the meeting here. And my guess is he went home, maybe via a fast-food restaurant somewhere along the way. Which means he would have no alibi."

She nodded. "He doesn't need that."

"Tell me, can archived JAG investigation files be altered?"

"No. The investigations are official records. The system's set up specifically to prohibit alterations."

Train thought about that. "Well, if that's true, there's something in that investigation file someone doesn't want you to see. Us to see. I'm definitely going to ask the good admiral about that. Then I hope to get through to my FBI contact. See what he can tell me about Galantz. The more meat we can put on the SEAL story, the less the cops will bother Sherman."

She nodded, suddenly too tired to argue. This great big dog did seem very comforting. Train was getting up.

"I'll hit the road now. I'll come back and do Gutter's outside perimeter training this afternoon. Stay in the house and keep Gutter with you. If you do go outside, say to the barn, keep Gutter with you. Just tell him to heel. If he needs to go to a tree, he'll let you know, but then tell him to heel." He bent down to pet the dog one more time. Then he put a hand on her shoulder and squeezed gently. "Now," he said briskly, "what's the best way down to the Pentagon from here?"

She gave him directions and he left. She watched him go, surprised to find herself wishing he hadn't gone. It would be very easy to get used to having him around.

Ninety minutes later, Admiral Carpenter's yeoman announced that Mr. von Rensel was out in the front office, as requested.

"Give me five minutes and then bring him in," the admiral replied. "And don't disturb us." He hung up the intercom phone and called Captain McCarty on the secure phone.

"Yes, Admiral."

"I'm about to talk to Mr. von Rensel. I want to get his take on the Sherman business. The last update I had was from Karen Lawrence on Friday, right?"

"Yes, sir."

"Right. Okay. Based on what the DNI told me, I think I'm going to tell him to lay off the SEAL angle. But I'm not going to tell him that we've been *asked* to lay off. Basically, I want to see what he does."

"You mean you really want him to run free to see what the hell's really going on here?"

"Basically, yes."

McCarty was silent for a moment. "If von Rensel actually flushes this guy," he asked, "are we going to get across the breakers with the DNI and/or other interested parties?"

Carpenter thought for a moment before answering. "I'm not sure. I don't think so. I don't particularly sweat the Office of Naval Intelligence; they're pretty far down the food chain in the intel world. Besides, the way I'm going to frame my instructions to von Rensel, I can always claim later that he was freelancing. The lifer spooks think he's a loose cannon anyway. And if it starts to get wormy, I can always pull Karen out of it and let von Rensel and the spooks sort it all out in some dark alley."

"Suppose it gets wormy *before* you find out about it? The last thing spooks do is tell somebody when one of their operations goes off the rails."

"I'll think of something. But first I want to get an independent assessment from von Rensel."

"Independent of Karen Lawrence?"

"Yeah. He's an experienced investigator. She isn't."

There was a pause on the line. "Whatever you say, Admiral," McCarty said finally, his tone of voice implying that he wasn't thrilled with the idea of using Train to check on Karen Lawrence.

Carpenter frowned to himself. "Just so," he said, and hung up abruptly. He resumed scribbling comments on an appeal letter while waiting for the five minutes to elapse. Finally, the yeoman brought in Train.

"Mr. von Rensel, come in. Have a seat."

"Good morning, Admiral," Train said, sitting down on the sofa. The admiral remained at his desk.

"You getting all settled in here in the puzzle palace?"

"Yes, sir. I spent some time in ONI a few years back; not much has changed."

"In ONI or the Pentagon?"

"Neither, Admiral. One's a pile of old concrete; the other's a pile of . . . well . . ."

Carpenter smiled. "Yes, precisely my view, Mr. von Rensel. Our so-called intelligence community is like an onion. CIA, NSA, DIA, ONI, all that damned alphabet soup, and all rolled up in a tight little ball that makes you cry whenever you try to get into it. What's going on in the Sherman matter?"

Train paused to gather his thoughts. He wondered why Carpenter was asking him this question instead of Karen Lawrence, who was nominally in charge of the Sherman problem. Was Carpenter checking up on her? Or had the admiral perhaps detected her sympathy for Sherman? He launched into it. He took fifteen minutes to bring the admiral up-to-date, including the events of the preceding night. When he had finished, Carpenter was no longer smiling.

"Is Karen Lawrence safe?" he asked.

Train told him about taking one of his Dobes out to her house. "But if there's a rogue SEAL on the loose, no one is safe," he concluded. "The good news is that Karen is not his target. Sherman is. The bad news is that someone's been knocking off everyone who's close to Sherman."

"Are Karen Lawrence and Sherman 'close'?"

Train hesitated for a fraction of a second. Good question, that one. "Not in a personal sense, not that I know of. But she's been with him at the Walsh apartment, the Walsh memorial service, the Schmidt funeral, and two meetings with the cops, one in his house, one in her house. And somebody sure as hell knew where to find her last night."

"Did she actually see this guy?"

"No, sir."

"So nobody has ever seen this guy, right?"

"Correct. Nobody except Admiral Sherman, and that was twenty-some years ago. But I don't think Karen imagined all this. She was really scared. She put on a good front this morning, but whoever did this knew how."

"So you think this Galantz guy is for real? I mean, all the records say he was lost in Vietnam. He's even on the MIA list."

Train hesitated. "It's possible," he hedged. "As you know, that MIA classification covers everything from someone who was actually observed being blown to little bits to guys who simply went out and never came back."

"So he could be alive?"

"Admiral Sherman says he is, or at least was back in 1972. The only other possibility is that Sherman is doing it. He's had opportunity in at least a couple of these incidents. Even last night, for instance. But what's his motive?"

"So you're coming down in favor of HM1 Galantz," Carpenter persisted, ignoring Train's question.

Train wasn't quite sure where this was going. "Possibly," he said. "Or someone calling himself that. Oh, did I mention Sherman's son?"

Carpenter shook his head patiently. Train told him about Jack, and the fact that, after many years of estrangement, Sherman had seen him twice recently, both times in circumstances that suggested the son knew something about what was going on.

"Curiouser and curiouser," the admiral muttered. "Okay. We've got two problems with this Sherman situation. The first is that, given the Navy's intense sensitivity to bad PR, Admiral Sherman is becoming a political liability."

"The big guys are ready to just drop him over the side?"

Carpenter gave a small shrug. "There is an unlimited supply of eager-beaver flag-material captains in the surface warfare community who do not bring baggage of this sort along with them."

Train nodded. "Karen told me about their little séance with Admiral Kensington. I take it he's a heavyweight here in OpNav?"

"Heavy enough. Especially when the problem concerns a surface guy, and Sherman is surface Navy."

Train nodded. "And the second problem: Might that involve a certain government agency?"

Carpenter gave him a speculative look. "It might," he said.

Train stared down at the carpet. The picture was getting a little clearer, and he now understood why Carpenter was talking to him and not Karen. He laced his hands together and cracked his knuckles, then looked back at Carpenter, who was watching him intently.

"Are you telling me *not* to try to find Galantz?"

Carpenter got up from his desk and came around to sit in one of the chairs. "Not exactly, Train. I am *going to* order you to stay away from anybody's efforts to find this Galantz individual. I am *going to* tell you not to hunt down Galantz yourself."

" 'Going to'? As in orders that *will be* forthcoming soon?"

"Very soon."

"And in the meantime?"

"In the meantime, I do order you to keep Karen Lawrence safe."

Train nodded slowly. "And if that involves—"

The JAG raised his hands. "Use your best judgment on how to execute your tasking, Train. You need not bother me with details. In fact, I'd prefer you did not. But that's your tasking: Keep Karen safe while she makes a determination that Admiral Sherman is either the victim of a setup or one diabolically clever villain. And your time is limited. Remember what I am *going to* tell you—soon."

Train nodded again and got up. "Got it. And I appreciate the latitude, Admiral. I think. I suppose if this thing goes off the tracks, I can expect to be chastised?"

"Most severely, although ultimately I'll get over it."

Train nodded. This was a game he recognized.

"I'm probably doing the wrong thing here," Carpenter said equably. "But it seems to me that Sherman deserves one chance, especially if he's innocent."

Carpenter got up and walked back around to his desk. He picked up some papers and pretended to study them for a moment before continuing. "By the way, Karen had an archive request in to review the investigation records on the incident in Vietnam," he said. "I've had her request intercepted. That investigation report is highly classified. But from what I saw, Sherman did the right thing in that incident."

Train had been about to ask. He was glad the admiral had brought it up first. "Galantz may not think so," he said.

Carpenter looked over at him. "You know that. I know that. That's why I want you to keep an eye on Karen Lawrence. I have my reasons for having her on this case, but I don't want her hurt."

"I understand, Admiral," Train said, although he wasn't sure he did.

"Good," Carpenter said. "Remember, time is of the essence, especially for Admiral Sherman. That's all."

When the door closed, Carpenter sat back in his chair and thought for a moment, then punched the intercom.

"Get me a secure call into Admiral Kensington's office," he said. He punched off and waited. Kensington came on the line.

"Admiral Kensington."

"Good morning, Admiral," Carpenter said. "Further to our last conversation on the Sherman matter, I have a suggestion to make."

There was a moment of silence. "Is this thing under control, Tom?"

Carpenter thought about the DNI's little bombshell. "I think so, Admiral," he said slowly.

"Because if it isn't, we need to do something. We've had enough dirty laundry hanging out there lately. I'm not sure any of us could stand this thing getting loose."

"I understand. I think we need to take Sherman out of circulation for a few days."

"I'm all ears."

Train left the JAG's office, shaking his head as he walked back to his own cubicle on the fourth floor. Neatly done, Admiral, he thought. You want me to beat the bushes, but you can always say that I was never tasked to find this guy. If there was to be any trouble, Mrs. von Rensel's bouncing baby boy, Train, had, in fact, been told to stay away from Galantz.

He reached his cubicle, checked his voice mail, and then called Karen to back-brief her on his meeting with Carpenter. "He wanted an update, soup to nuts, on the whole case. I gave it to him."

"You told him about last night?"

"Yup. That upset him. I also got the impression the bigs are stirring."

"What did he say about that archived file?"

"That he blocked it. That it contains highly classified material. That it shows Sherman did the right thing back there, whatever that means. But we're not going to see that report."

She was silent for a moment. "Any new instructions?" she asked.

It was Train's turn to hesitate. He did not want to tell her what his tasking had been. She was nervous enough already. "Not exactly," he said. "The gist of it was to confirm that I'm to help you in your inquiries. So right now, I'm going to put on my NIS hat and enter some federal databases."

"So you agree we should concentrate on the son first and not Galantz?" There was a thread of concern in her voice.

"Galantz is complicated," Train said. "Let me explain that when we're not on an unsecured phone. There definitely might be other players in this game, though."

"Oh."

"Yeah, oh. Hold that thought. Right now, see what you can get from Sherman on Little Boy Blue. If I can get a read on where the son is, maybe we'll go see him this afternoon. If you're up to it, that is."

"I'm up to that."

"Okay. I'll get back to you."

He hung up and sat back in his chair. You really need to talk to McHale Johnson, von Rensel. He sighed and got out his personal phone book, looked up a number, and then placed a call. Johnson wasn't in, an anonymous voice said, so he left a call-back message and mentioned the word SEAL. Then he called the NIS database query center over in the Washington Navy Yard, identified himself, and asked them to call him back at the JAG IR division's secure number. The database administrator got back to him in five minutes and he gave him the name and the few general match points he had regarding Jack Sherman's military service, approximate age, and a last-known location in the vicinity of Quantico, Virginia. He told them he would have better-defined data and a Social Security number later in the day. He asked for searches within the military and FBI criminal identification and information systems, since Sherman had said the kid had been thrown out of the Marines. He put a priority label on his request and asked for a voice debrief, with a final report to be transmitted electronically into his PC address within the JAG local-area computer network as soon as possible.

"You say you'll have better definition data this afternoon?" the administrator asked.

Train's heart sank. Should never have said that.

"Yeah."

"Then come back in with that data. Then we'll do the coarse screen, Mr. von Rensel. You know the rules."

Train agreed and hung up. He sighed. He had hoped for a quick look, but the database people weren't about to do something twice. He then decided to try one of the most sophisticated search tools available—namely, the telephone company's information operator.

"Northern Virginia information, what city?"

"Woodbridge, Quantico, Virginia."

"Go ahead."

"John Lee Sherman. Address unknown. Might be Triangle, or Dumfries, or just Stafford County."

"One moment please."

He waited. About half the time he went looking for someone, the guy was in the damned phone book.

"I have a John L. Sherman."

"Let's try that."

"Hold for the number."

Bingo, he thought, as he recorded the number. Then he called the database administrator back and luckily got a new voice. He went through the identification drill again, but this time he gave him the telephone number, asking for an address trace. The database guys could do this on a local PC. He was put on hold for a minute.

"Your boy's phone is in the Cherry Hill area, right north of the base at Quantico. The billing address is a Triangle post office box, though. I can get a premises wiring locator from C&P, but it'll take a day, and you'll have to come in with a formal coarse screen request. But that phone's in Cherry Hill."

"Much grass," Train replied, and hung up. Do it like the pros, he thought. When in doubt, call goddamn Information.

He decided to check his voice mail again. One call. "For Dr. von Rensel from Dr. Johnson," the man said. "Lunch at the New Orleans House in Rosslyn, eleven-fifteen. Today. Dr. Johnson is *really* glad Mr. von Rensel called."

Train blinked and looked at his watch. It was 10:45. He just had time to hop the Metro over to Rosslyn. He called Karen, but now there was no answer. He hung up, frowning. Now where the hell did *she* go? And she did take the dog, I hope to hell.

McHale Johnson was a very tall, almost cadaverous-looking man. He had a long, narrow, and very white face with a prominent forehead, highly arched eyebrows, and a long, bony nose. He wore square-rimmed glasses, which magnified his pale gray eyes. His hair was lanky, disheveled, and going gray, like the rest of him. He did not get up when Train approached the table, but continued to look around the room as if he was trying to remember something or someone. Train pulled out a chair, tested it for strength, and then replaced it with one from the adjacent table. The two women sitting at that table just looked at each other, declining protest.

"Dr. Johnson, I presume," Train said. He was pretty sure that McHale was indeed the man's first name, but he doubted the Johnson part.

"Dr. von Rensel," Johnson replied, tilting his head back to examine Train through those huge glasses. "You've gotten bigger. That's almost hard to imagine."

"Just spreading, probably," Train replied, looking at the menu. The doctor business was a private joke between them. Johnson held a doctorate in cybernetics, and he insisted on calling Train Doctor because of his law degree. And probably because it amused him to do so. Train put down his menu.

"Your secretary intimated that my phone call was, um, timely."

Johnson nodded slowly. "My secretary. I'll have to tell him that. But considering the subject, it was indeed timely."

"A SEAL."

"Indeed. Here's the waitress." They both placed their orders, having to speak up to be heard in the general hubbub. When the waitress left, Train asked if this was an appropriate place to talk. Johnson shrugged.

"It's crowded and noisy. Tough place to eavesdrop, really. Did someone tell you to call me?"

Train shook his head. "No. I've been given some politically adroit tasking, so I decided to pull a string or two on my own. I was hoping you might be able to enlighten me with respect to a certain Marcus Galantz, ex-hospital corpsman, USN, ex-SEAL, and current MIA."

Johnson nodded slowly again, still looking slightly bug-eyed through those windowpane-sized glasses. "Never heard of him," he said finally, giving Train a friendly stare.

Train smiled and looked away for a moment. He could not imagine Johnson being an operational agent himself, but he could very well imagine him as a controller. "Let me rephrase that," he replied. "Would you perhaps like to tell me a story?"

"Ah, yes, that I would," Johnson said immediately, then paused as the waitress whizzed by to drop off Train's beer and Johnson's iced tea. When she had gone, Johnson sipped some tea.

"Once upon a time, in a faraway place," he began, "a certain organization had a need to recruit people with certain talents. There was concurrently a fair-sized military action in progress, and this organization was tangentially involved in certain peripheral, perhaps narcotics-related operations, which operations said organization would just as soon forget about. After a while, the organization in question discovered that occasionally certain persons would become available for recruitment, sometimes through rather unconventional circumstances."

"As in Americans who might have ended up in Saigon jails under questionable, perhaps even embarrassing circumstances."

"That was one way, yes. There were conditions, of course, to such recruitment."

"One being that old identities disappeared and new ones were created."

"Or that there be no identity at all, you see," Johnson said. "That could be even more useful, depending on what the individual was being recruited to do. Or become."

Train sampled his beer. "Were the people who might have been recruited in this fashion being considered for particularly dangerous work?" he asked.

Johnson pursed his lips as he thought about the question. "More often, they were being recruited to place other individuals in danger, rather than themselves. Remember, the operations in question may have involved the heroin business. Disputes in that business tend even to this day to invoke fairly rigorous sanctions from time to time."

"I love it when you talk double. What was that lovely expression back in the sixties? Terminate with extreme prejudice?"

"Something like that. Or so I'm told. This may all be apocryphal."

The waitress appeared again with their lunch. Johnson waited until she was gone before resuming his little homily. The place was noisy enough now that they both had to lean in across the table even to hear each other.

"That's an interesting concept," Train said around a bite of his BLT. "But if you recruit and train a guy like that and then employ him in that or in related lines of work, how do you keep control of him? In the event that he gets out of control, I mean. Especially if he doesn't exist in the first place? And given that the United States government has publicly and frequently disavowed the use of such individuals? I mean, what if he goes freelancing: What sanctions do you use on him?"

Johnson looked up and mimed clapping his hands in silent applause. "Very good, Doctor," he said. Then he addressed his soup for a moment. "That, of course, is the heart of the operational problem with the individuals I've been describing," he continued. "What the Roman emperor was always wanting to know: Who guards the guards?" Then he paused, staring at Train, a spoonful of soup in midair. The light from the main chandelier reflected off his glasses, obscuring his eyes. "That particular control problem requires a very special individual indeed. And that requirement has some relevance to your initial question, if you follow."

Train sat back in his chair, a chill washing over him. So Galantz wasn't just a wet-work mechanic. He was a sweeper, a very special operative whose job it was to go after a mechanic who was no longer under effective operational control.

"Oh," he said.

"Yes, indeed, oh," Johnson replied.

And then the full import hit him—why Johnson of the FBI had agreed to meet with him on an hour's notice. There must be a serious flap on within the operational arms of the intelligence community, serious enough for the FBI to have gotten wind of it. If Galantz was indeed behind two murders out in the civilian community, then his employers had a genuine crisis on their hands. It was one thing for an agency hit man to jump the traces; it was quite another if a sweeper did it. He thought momentarily of Karen and the whispering voice.

He looked back up at Johnson, who was watching him work it out. Johnson arched his eyebrows, nodded at him meaningfully, and then went back to his soup. Train had suddenly lost his appetite.

"I'm a little confused about one thing," Train said finally.

"Only one thing. How felicitous for you."

Train ignored that. "I should think," he said, "that warnings would have been passed along by now, from their graybeards to our graybeards. As in, 'butt out.' "

"Quite so. Although your own personal graybeards at NIS aren't involved. This is well above NIS's pay grade."

"I'm not at NIS. I'm on loan."

"On loan? To whom, precisely?" Johnson had the beginnings of a worried look on his face, as if he might have said too much, depending on where Train was parking his car these days.

"I'm seconded to the Navy headquarters staff. I'm working for an Admiral Carpenter. He's the Navy JAG. The bad guy we're talking all around may have iced two civilians connected to one of the admirals on the Navy headquarters staff. The cops came to see the JAG."

"Ah. Now this really begins to tie together," Johnson said, relief evident in his voice.

"Why so?"

"Because it's my understanding that the Navy has indeed been told to butt out," Johnson said. "Most emphatically, they have been. Via the Director of Naval Intelligence."

Damn, Train thought. The DNI. Had he alerted Carpenter? And, if so, why hadn't Carpenter told him this? Johnson sensed his vexation.

"Somebody holding back on you, Doctor?" Johnson said gently. "You might want to think about why they'd do that."

Train went back to his sandwich, chewing mechanically while thinking about what Johnson had just told him. "Can I assume that interested parties in the other organization are not just sitting around on this problem?" he asked.

"You most certainly can. Which is how we lesser relations in the FBI came to know about the problem—especially since your bad guy is operating domestically. The people with the problem are not supposed to operate domestically, a rule we both know they don't always observe so scrupulously."

Train snorted. "Yeah, right. Look, these homicides have brought in the Fairfax cops. What about them?"

"I give up. What about them?"

"They're investigating two homicides. Their boss is starting to talk about a serial killer. Maybe bringing in you guys even."

"Bringing us in," Johnson murmured. "Now that would be a lovely twist."

"Anyone told *them* who or what they might be up against?"

Johnson smiled. "Probably not. But my information is that they're up against one Rear Adm. W. T. Sherman," he said. Train put his sandwich down and looked across the table at Johnson. He'd known all along about the murders and their own so-called investigation. Which meant that the FBI was already in the game. What the *hell* was going on here? He thought back to the meeting with the police the night before, and the way that homicide lieutenant had been looking at Sherman. Their request for him to open his personal accounts—that was a standard FBI tactic.

"I guess that's my problem, then," Train said. "I'm supposedly tasked to determine if Sherman is clean or not. Actually, I'm supposed to help another JAG division investigator do that—one who has no idea of what she's really getting involved in."

"Then conform to your tasking," Johnson said. "Like you said, Sherman is your problem. Sherman is not *their* problem."

"But finding their problem is the best way to clear Sherman," Train pointed out, half-knowing what Johnson would say next.

"Let me tell you something, Train," Johnson said. "You stumble across *their* problem, you or your partner—Commander Lawrence, is it? You pull the bushes aside and come face-to-face with this particular Gorgon, you may find yourself dead, understand? He's the kind of predator who can tear your throat out with one swipe of his paw before you realize you're looking at a tiger. These guys, and there are very few of them, have layer upon layer of cover and resources all prepositioned against the day they are called into action. You have a reputation for being a stand-up guy. But you're way out of your league if you're thinking of trying to track down a sweeper."

"I can't just sit around. He's already made a move against my partner."

Johnson shook his head. "Consider Sherman from the IRS perspective. Right now, he's suspected of being guilty. Prove him otherwise. Let the people who conjure up monsters like this in a basement cauldron some-where deal with *their* problem. You definitely don't want to encounter *their* problem."

"You sound like even they're scared of him."

"Any normal human being would be," Johnson said. "Given the organization in question, that means we're talking about ten percent of them being scared at least. Maybe fifteen. One has to be optimistic."

Damn, Train thought. Damn. Damn. Damn. And the FBI even knows all the names. "Like I said, Commander Lawrence may already have at-tracted this guy's attention," Train said.

"Then you make my point," Johnson answered. "Circle the wagons. Protect yourselves, especially Sherman."

"Does the FBI have people looking?" Train asked.

Johnson smiled and looked around, as if concerned for the first time that someone might be listening. "One would think so, wouldn't one?" he said. "But right now, I'm not so sure. I am just a research scientist, as you know. Nobody talks to me."

"Much. But you have an impression, no doubt?"

"Well," Johnson said modestly, "I have the impression that there is some very senior FBI management addressing this problem, or at least watching it unfold."

Train changed direction. "What's the relationship between you guys and these other people these days? It hasn't always been terrific, has it?"

Johnson smiled again. "Officially? Let me see, how does the latest presidential policy memorandum put it? 'Both organizations shall strive to achieve the maximum coordination of assets, planning, and all-source information to best fulfill their mutual mission of protecting the national security of the United States.' "

"In other words, armed truce."

Johnson smiled but said nothing, concentrating on his soup.

"Because what occurs to me," Train continued, "is that the grand dragons in the FBI might be wrestling with a strategic question. Like whether to help, or to seize a precious opportunity to allow those people to be well and truly embarrassed—again."

Johnson looked as if he was trying hard to control his face. "Anything's possible, Train," he said, wiping his mouth. "This is Washington, isn't it? You still carry that Glock?"

"Yup."

"Got it on you?"

"Not right now."

"That's not carrying. These are exceptionally good times to be carrying."

Train needed to talk to Karen. He called her home number, but there was still only the answering machine. Now what the hell? he thought. Where is she? He asked the divisional yeoman if she had had any messages from Commander Lawrence. "No, sir," she replied. "Oh, Admiral Sherman's office called in, but they declined to leave a message for her." Train asked the yeoman for that number and placed the call. The admiral was not available. In fact, the admiral would be out of pocket for the foreseeable future. The yeoman in OP-32 sounded a little uncomfortable.

"He on temporary duty or something?" Train asked.

"Uh, no, sir, not exactly. Captain Gonzales said he's on leave."

"On leave?" Train frowned into the phone. "Was this scheduled? I was with him just last night, and he didn't mention going on leave."

"Uh, sir? You're asking questions above my pay grade, okay? The admiral's on leave until further notice. I can take a message if you'd like. The admiral checks in."

"Yeah, I'd like. There was a call from Admiral Sherman's office to Commander Lawrence this morning. Did the two of them connect?"

"No, sir, not that I know of."

"Okay, then *I* need some information from the admiral." He thought for a moment. "Ask him to call me at this number; I'll be there in about an hour, okay?" He had given the yeoman Karen's home number.

On leave, Train thought, as he walked down the hall. Now what? Damn, you suppose they've put him on administrative leave? Because of the police investigation? Maybe the big boys had eased Sherman into bureaucratic limbo until this mess was cleared up, one way or another. He quickened his step. He felt a sudden urge to get out to Great Falls, not liking the fact that Karen wasn't answering her phone.

Train got to Karen's house at 2:30 and parked right in front of the walk leading up to the house, so she could see who had arrived. He waited for a moment, but no one came to the door. He stared at the front of the house, scanning the windows along the porch. And he saw Gutter's face pressed against one of the windows.

Swearing out loud, he got out of the car and trotted up the steps to the porch. The front door was not locked, and he opened it to let the frantic dog out of the house. Gutter ran out onto the lawn to take care of business, then came back to Train.

"Where'd she go, Gutter? Where is she?"

At the sound of his voice, the dog immediately sat down. "C'mon, then," he said, and went into the house. With the dog at his heel, he made a quick search of the house, calling out Karen's name several times as he went through both floors. There was no sign of a struggle or any other commotion. Everything was in order.

Where the hell was she? He was trying to figure out what to do next, like maybe call 911, when he heard her voice outside, calling her dog. Gutter uttered a low growl. Train walked back through the hallway to the front door, surprising her.

"Sorry to bust in," he said. "I couldn't get you on the phone, and the front door was open and Gutter inside. I was worried."

"Hi," she said, pushing a lock of damp red hair off her forehead. She was dressed in tight tan jodhpurs and a sleeveless white shirt. "I decided to go for a ride. Just sitting in the house was beginning to spook me."

"You should have kept Gutter with you," he said, trying to keep an edge out of his voice.

"You said to keep him inside until he learned the outside perimeter," she retorted. "I was afraid he'd run off or something. I took Harry along, though." She looked down at the old Lab, who, having spotted the Doberman, was slinking under the porch. Train rolled his eyes. "I'm thinking the heavies have maybe made a move," he said, and then he explained what the OP-32 yeoman had told him about Sherman being on leave, with no other explanation.

"Those bastards," she exclaimed, getting a bottle of mineral water out of the refrigerator. "They didn't even wait for the cops to do the financial checks."

Train went over to a stool and sat down carefully. "So you think they've put him in some kind of suspension?"

"Or sent him on temporary additional duty. Sounds like that to me. He called earlier with the data on Jack. He didn't mention going TAD."

"Let me call that data into the NIS, and then I need to fill you in on a lunch meeting I just had with an old FBI buddy."

He made the call to the database administrator and then told Karen the essence of what Johnson had said. Karen was walking around the kitchen, chewing on a knuckle when he was finished.

"Sweepers? I've never heard of such a thing," she said. "They sound like some kind of vultures."

"I debated with myself about telling you any of that," he concluded. She whirled around on him.

"What's that supposed to mean? That I need to be protected from knowing the extent of the danger?" Train was taken aback by her sudden anger.

"Well, I guess to a certain extent, yes, that's what I was thinking. You had a pretty good scare last night. I didn't want to—"

She put up a warning hand. "I'm a big girl now, Train. I need to know what's going on here. I'd appreciate it if you wouldn't treat me like some kind of damsel in distress, okay?"

"Whatever you say, lady," Train replied in a brisk tone of voice. He was getting a little tired of the mood swings. She's being emotional, he reminded himself, because she's scared. Don't go getting all huffy. But Karen wouldn't let it go.

"I hear that condescending tone in your voice, the one men use when they think they're around a woman whose emotions are out of control. I just want to make sure we both know where things stand here. We are conducting an investigation. I appreciate your bringing a guard dog. I really do. But you can't go holding out on me because you think I'm just a frail little thing who'll fall apart at the first hint of physical danger, okay? I believe you were talking about my not sharing information with you just the other day, right?"

Train put both hands up in mock surrender. "I only felt that way because you're a lawyer," he said with as straight a face as he could muster.

"But that's ridiculous! And besides, you're a—oh, you bastard!" But she was smiling again. "I'm sorry. I guess I am being emotional."

He wanted to reach out and hold her hand. "It's kind of like you stepped over a black snake," he offered. "And then you find out the next day that it wasn't a black snake, but a cobra. Anyway, I definitely won't tell you what Admiral Carpenter said this morning. About keeping you safe being a big part of my mission in life."

She gave him a suspicious look. "Did he say that?"

"I'm not going to tell you anything about that, remember? Yeah, he said that. There's more. My FBI buddy told me that the Navy had been warned off the Galantz problem through intelligence channels. Carpenter, for reasons unknown to me, failed to tell me that, which I think means he wants us to stay in this game, at least for a while. He says it's because Sherman deserves a chance to clear himself."

She put the bottle of mineral water back in the refrigerator. "I should hope so. I can't believe how they're treating him. Just because he's been accused—no, not even that, because he's been *sideswiped* by two homicides. Hell, even the cops don't think he did them."

Train got off the stool and headed for the phone. "I do 't understand, either, but for now we press ahead, agreed? Let's see what the database termites can do with John L. Sherman."

He called into NIS while Karen went up to change her clothes. He asked for an urgent open-filter screen on an individual and gave the terminal operator Jack Sherman's name and Social Security number. He went on hold for two minutes. Then the operator came back to him.

"Okay, Mr. von Rensel. I can transmit all this to your PC over in the Pentagon, but they said you wanted a verbal right now, so here's what I've got on this guy: bank records, credit cards, home and work address, military service records—that's admin, pay, and health—make and mod of vehicle, prior arrest records—that was as a juvie—sexual preferences, firearms purchases for the past two years, and let's see, what else, here."

Train was astonished. He hadn't pulled a data dump from the NIS database for three years, not since the Malone case over at the Naval Research Labs. "Should I be calling you database or Big Brother?" he said. "Since when does NIS have this level of detail on a guy?"

"Since the government became a customer of the telemarketing data banks, just like everybody else is. Total access on demand. Shit, that's not the half of it. You wanna talk about people who keep score, those sumbitches know everything, and I mean *everything*. Scary, isn't it? You wanna know where he went for the past year? We'll take a look at his gas credit cards. How about how well his—lemme see, here—his Kawasaki Vulcan Eight Hundred runs since he's owned it? He's used a Visa card at the auto-parts store there in Triangle three times this year alone. Wanna know what he bought?"

Train just shook his head. "Orwell was right," he muttered.

"Who's this Orwell guy? You wanna see if he's in the system?"

Train smiled. "That's okay. Look, right now I need to know where Sherman lives, and, if possible, where he works."

"Right. He lives in an area called Cherry Hill. That's near Triangle, Virginia. No property-tax records on him, so he's a renter. Hang on one and lemme check something. Stand by. Yup, here's a catalog listing. For guns, no less. Good deal, huh? Now lemme find out which delivery service delivered and when." There was another minute's pause. "Right. The guy's actual address is number four Slade Hill Road. He also has a PO box at the Triangle, Virginia, post office. Now, work address: the helicopter-repair activity at the Quantico Marine base."

"What's he do there?"

"Lemme get his tax return up here. Stand by. Okay. His most recent tax return lists his occupation as rigger. Hmmm. The W-2 doesn't show a government check. Not sure what a rigger is."

"General roustabout job, usually on the flight line. If he's in maintenance, he'll be the guy in the tractor, pulling aircraft to and from the maintenance hangars. Something like unat."

"Okay, lemme check current wants and warrants. Hmmm. He's lucky to have a government job, given this DUI record."

"Oh yeah? A boozer?"

"Two offenses, one prior license suspension, now lifted. But carrying nine points even now on his license. And on a motorcycle, too. Brave dummy, drinking and driving a bike."

"Okay, thanks," Train said. "Shoot me a summary this afternoon if you can. The locators were the urgent part."

Train hung up as Karen came back downstairs, now in her uniform. "Who was that?" she asked, brushing her still-damp hair as she came into the kitchen. He almost lost his train of thought. She looked divine, her complexion glowing, her damp hair suggestive of what she might look like after some more convivial physical activity. His speculation on the nature of which specific strenuous physical activity caused him to hesitate just long enough for her to raise an eyebrow in one of those "Hello, did you hear my question?" looks. He had to work at it to find his normal voice. Damn woman noticed that, too.

"That was NIS database. Jack Sherman works down at the Marine Corps airstrip at Quantico. What do you say we go pay him a visit?"

"Yes, I think that's next. I wonder, should we take the admiral along?"

Train shook his head. "I think not. There's no love lost there. Besides, isn't the admiral supposed to be meeting with the police auditors today? Hell, maybe that's why he's on leave. No, I think we move first, see what we've got here. I've got pretty good locating data."

"That was fast," she said, looking around for her uniform hat and purse. "They had him on file?"

"You don't know the half of it," he replied. "And you might not want to. Let me get Gutter situated. Then we can go."

Because Train knew the base, they went in his Suburban. On the ride down to Quantico, Karen briefed Train on what Admiral Sherman had told her about his son. Then she wanted to know more about sweepers. Train was quiet for almost a minute.

"Sweepers don't officially exist, any more than the people they are used to control officially exist. I heard about them when I was on loan with the FBI, and even those guys talk about them as if they were myths. But supposedly there are only about a dozen of them, all embedded in deep cover at strategic locations around the world. Washington, Tokyo, London, Berlin—hell, probably even in Moscow. Wherever there might be a need for 'wet work,' as they call it, there's probably a sweeper hidden in a hole somewhere. During the Cold War, the other side had them, too."

"All men?"

"Don't know. Probably not. These are individuals with no identities other than the ones they assume—people with a wide range of prepositioned assets at their disposal. I'm talking cars, safe houses, surveillance equipment, cash. Because if those people turn a sweeper on, they're usually in a hurry or in a mess."

"And they go after operatives who've gotten out of control somehow?"

"Not just any operatives: They go after the operatives who kill people. This isn't everyday work. These are specialists who hunt down other specialists."

"And do what?"

"I heard a FBI guy once say that the term of art was *extinguish.* They extinguish the runaway asset. Make the problem go away. Probably in such a manner as to attract zero attention."

"Why not bring the runaway asset, as you call him, back for disciplinary measures?"

"How do you discipline an assassin, Karen? Take him to court? Look, I don't believe the U.S. government keeps a big stable of assassins. But I do believe it keeps some, depending on the international climate and the nature of our country's enemies at any given time. There are even fewer sweepers."

"And you think Galantz is a sweeper?"

"My FBI friend does. And he says that the agency in question is going quietly ape-shit over the fact that this guy is killing civilians."

"Well, if that's true, why on earth don't they tell the Navy and get Sherman off the hook?"

Train thought about that as he turned the big vehicle off the interstate and headed down toward the base. "That's what's puzzling me," he said. "Johnson said the Navy *had* been warned off—through the DNI. But I don't know whom he's talked to. If it was Carpenter, the admiral sure as hell didn't tell me—other than some mumbo jumbo about what he was going to order me to do."

"And this is a guy with one hand and one eye? Isn't that how Sherman described him?"

"A guy with one hand and one eye who crawled out of the Rung Sat secret zone with a regiment of VC on his trail, endured a year in a Saigon jail, and lived to tell about it. And if he's been working for those people for twenty years, he's an *experienced* sweeper. I think I'd prefer dealing with any number of KGB colonels."

It was Karen's turn to be silent as they approached the main gate of the base and showed their identification. Train drove through the base, remembering his Officer Candidate School days at Quantico back in 1970.

The airstrip was primarily a helicopter operating area, situated at the base to provide helicopter training services to the various Marine basic-training operations. There was a single main strip paralleling the river, five main hangars, a maintenance admin area dominated by Quonset huts, a fuel farm, and a standard flight line and tower complex. Train drove down the flight-line perimeter road, staying clear of two Marine CH-46E helicopters that were turning up on the pad in front of the operations building. He pulled up in front of the largest Quonset hut, which had a sign indicating that the maintenance division was housed inside. Even there, several hundred feet down the flight line from operations, the noise of the two helicopters was nearly overpowering.

Inside, they faced a counter that ran the width of the Quonset hut. They produced their identification, and Karen asked a bored-looking civilian woman to see the officer in charge.

"Do you have an appointment?" the woman asked. Karen just looked at her.

"Do we need one?" Train asked, his tone of voice clearly expressing his incredulity.

"I'll see if Mr. Meyer is available," the woman said. Train rolled his eyes at Karen as the woman headed reluctantly toward the back of the open room, where a large red-faced warrant officer sat. Karen just shook her head. The warrant officer saw the clerk and then Karen and Train, and he stood up. The clerk indicated that they should come back. The warrant remained standing in deference to Karen's three stripes.

"We need to interview a John L. Sherman," Karen said. "He supposedly works as a rigger on the flight line here?"

"Yes, ma'am," the warrant said. "I know him."

"What can you tell us about him?"

The warrant looked over Karen's shoulder at the clerical area and lowered his voice. "He's kind of a shitbird, Commander. Makes like a biker hood most of the time. He's on the wrapper team."

"Rapper team?" Train asked. The warrant looked over at him, sizing him up, big man to big man.

"Yeah. They fly the forty-six echoes in here that're going to depot-level maintenance up in Pennsylvania. We do the baseline check, strip the rotor blades, and then shrink-wrap the birds for the train ride up north."

"Where can we find him?"

Myer turned back to Karen. "Best thing to do is to go down to the wrap hangar. Last one on the line. You wanna maybe just peek through the side door, make sure they're done, before you go in there, okay? It's messier'n shit in there when they're wrapping."

"This guy Sherman, he a real biker? A hard guy?" Train asked.

Myer snorted. "Naw. Real bikers would put a guy like that in panties and turn him out in a heartbeat. I can't believe that guy was ever in the Corps, you know what I mean?"

They went back outside and got in Train's car to drive down the flight line to the maintenance hangars beyond the Quonset hut. The last hangar in the line was smaller than the others. There were two helicopters already encased in the white shrink-wrap coating parked out in front. Without their rotor blades and tail rotors, they looked like giant grasshoppers that had been dipped into a can of gray-white paint. The insect look was accentuated by the bulging blisters covering the front windshield of the aircraft.

As they parked and got out, they could hear a loud hissing noise from inside the hangar. The front door of the hangar had been lowered to within one foot of the sill, and there were signs up warning of flammable fumes and telling people to keep out of a hazardous-spray area. They went to the side door, as the warrant had suggested. When they cracked the door, the hissing noise was much louder. A reek of paint solvent wafted over them. A crew of three men, fully suited up, were standing on a pipe stage platform and operating what looked like a small cannon that was spraying a white foam over the front end of a large helicopter. Most of the body was already encased and they were focusing the spray on the final front quarter of the aircraft. One man operated the nozzle while the other two tended supply lines. Two stainless-steel bottles the size of barbecue propane containers fed the spray. A large six-foot-diameter exhaust fan built into the back of the hangar was roaring away to extract the strong fumes. They watched for a few minutes through the cracked door as the team finished covering the front of the aircraft. The foam seemed to dissolve upon contact with the aircraft's skin, solidifying into a thick white second skin. The team shut down the spray unit but left the big fan going.

"Help you people?" a voice asked from behind them, startling both of them.

"We need to see Jack Sherman," Train said, producing his credentials.

"NIS to see Jack, huh? What a surprise." The man was heavyset and in his forties. There were bits of foam stuck to the outer edges of his beard where the mask had left marks on his skin. His spray suit was covered in the stuff and it stank of chemical solvent. "He's the skinny guy, running the spray gun. I'll tell him you're here. Be about ten minutes. You maybe want to wait out front, okay? Fumes are gonna be strong in here, they shut that big fan down."

"That's some amazing stuff," Train said, indicating the cocoon material.

"Tougher'n nails, I'm here to tell you," the man said. "Takes me a week to get this shit outta my hair."

"How do they get it off at the rework facility?"

"Really big knives. You all better move now."

It was fifteen minutes before Jack Sherman walked out of the hangar bay. Train sized him up as Jack slouched his way across the concrete apron in front of the hangar. Five-six, maybe five-seven in boots, scrawny, wearing ancient black jeans, a wide black belt that was mostly there for decoration, and a stained white T-shirt. A pack of cigarettes was twisted into the upper-right sleeve of the T-shirt, above pronounced biceps. He carried a black leather jacket slung casually over his shoulder. Train could see some facial resemblance to the admiral in the young man's face, but a lot of the character was missing. Pale, white face, over which a scraggly black beard wandered uncertainly; long, bony nose; thin black eyebrows; and a weak, not quite chinless mouth set in what looked like a perpetual sneer. He had muddy dark brown eyes, with the purple-stained pouches of the confirmed boozer. The eyes were now appraising Karen Lawrence's body with a casual, "I'd like to take your clothes off with my switchblade" stare. Train revised the height to maybe five-eight as Jack got closer, and he resisted the urge to smack this kid for the way he was staring at Karen's body.

"So who wants to see me?" Jack said to Karen, his voice surprisingly thin, the voice of a teenage boy on the verge of breaking. Definite boozer, Train concluded. Jack flicked a quick glance in Train's direction, as if he had read Train's thoughts. Train flipped out his credentials.

"My name's von Rensel, from the NIS. This is Commander Lawrence, Navy JAG."

"Squid stuff. Big deal. So why should I give a shit?" Sherman said, fingering the package of cigarettes out from under the twist in the sleeve of his T-shirt. Camels, no filter, Train noted. Tough guy indeed.

"This concerns your father," she said.

The change in Jack's face was dramatic—an immediate hardening. With the cigarette poised to go in his mouth, he stopped and looked at Karen as if she had just invoked the devil. "Then it don't concern me, lady," he snapped.

"We think it does," Train said. "We want to know why you made an appearance at Elizabeth Walsh's funeral, and again at the Naval Academy cemetery during Admiral Schmidt's funeral."

Jack made a slow business of sticking the cigarette in his mouth and getting it lit. Then he exhaled a solid stream of smoke in Train's direction, an insolent look on his face.

"Who says?"

"I saw you at Saint Matthew's Church," Karen said. "Last Wednesday evening. On a motorcycle. Your father saw you, too."

"And I saw you at Annapolis. Up on that hill. You left on a motorcycle."

Jack shrugged. "Beats me. I get around. It's a free country, last time I checked. How about you, lady? You free?"

Train moved in closer, staring down at the kid's sneering face but turning slightly sideways so that his left forearm was in position to block any sudden moves. "Let me put it this way, Sherman," he said. "We're helping the Fairfax County Homicide Section investigate two homicide ... So far, they don't know about your little cameos at the funerals. You can either talk to us or talk to them. But let me tell you something. You don't know hassle until you've seen homicide hassle. Now, why were you there at those funerals?"

Jack didn't budge an inch under the physical force of Train's massive presence. But his eyes betrayed him as they darted from Train's looming face to Karen and back. Then his expression changed again. "Maybe," he said with a crafty smile. "Maybe I was celebrating. Yeah. That's it. I remember now. I was celebrating."

"*Celebrating?*" Karen asked. "Celebrating what?"

Jack looked at her, then stepped back away from Train. Then he looked again, a studied, staring, lascivious appraisal, from her shoes to her hair, point by point, as if he was sizing up a piece of meat, or a whore. Train got that itch in his palms again.

"Celebrating that bastard's loss," Jack continued. "You know, he lost some things of value. Yeah, that's it, man."

" 'Some things of value,' " Karen repeated, focusing on the familiar phrase. She looked over at Train.

"Yeah," Jack said. "And I suppose you're the new main squeeze, huh, lady? *Commander,* I mean. Excuse *me.* Commander, ma'am. Or is it 'sir'?

Naw, it's 'ma'am.' " He stared intently at her breasts. "Those are definitely hooters. Ma'am."

Karen never saw Train move, but suddenly Jack was stumbling forward, toward the Suburban, his right hand enveloped in Train's left hand, his middle finger bending backward and his feet arching up against the pain, cigarette and jacket falling to the ground as he was spun up against the Suburban. Train clamped down hard and put his face an inch away from Jack's grimacing features.

"You . . . watch . . . your . . . mouth . . . dickhead," he growled. "That is your name, right? Dickhead? Yes? You agree? Nod your dick head, dick-head!" Jack was almost kneeling now as Train bore down on the finger, bringing tears to the kid's eyes. Train could see Karen off to one side, staring at him. "Good boy, dickhead. Now listen to me. Listen real good. We know *you're* in this. Tell your buddy Galantz we *know* you're in this. That the whole goddamned government knows what this is all about. And you, *dick-head,* are a stupid little patsy if you're helping him, understand? Think about this, *dickhead:* What's he going to do to you when he's done screwing around with your father, huh? You think he's gonna give you a medal, huh?" Train bent down, getting eyeball-to-eyeball. "Now you talk to me, asshole. What's your piece of this?"

Jack cried out as Train gave the finger an extra little nudge. His eyes were streaming and his face was red and straining. He was almost on the ground, trying to escape the crushing pain. His pack of cigarettes had spilled out on the concrete like a handful of nails. But he was still defiant.

"Fuck you, man," he spat in a low, hoarse voice as his elbow touched the concrete. "Fuck you! I just do what my old man tells me to do, okay? So fuck you!"

Train, surprised, let him go then and stood up. He looked over at Karen, whose expression was a mask of shock. He wasn't sure if it was over the way he had manhandled this punk or if she had heard what Jack had just said.

"Get out of here, asshole," he said to the figure crouching at his feet. "And remember, you can run, but you can't hide."

Jack grabbed his jacket and scuttled backward, holding his right hand under his left armpit and clumsily wiping the tears off his face with the back of his left hand. But as soon as he was back out in full public view, he straightened up and sauntered back toward the hangar, head up, never looking back, as if nothing at all had happened. Train walked over to Karen. From the disapproving look on her face, he had a pretty good idea of what she was mad about.

"Sorry about that," he began.

"No you're not," she snapped.

Okay, so now we know, he thought. "No, I'm not," he agreed. "I just didn't like the way he was—"

"You don't listen so well, do you?" she said, those green eyes blazing. "Let me say it again. When I need your protection, I'll ask for it. We came here to find out something, and now that kid will never talk to us. Now what are we—"

Train put up his hand to interrupt her. "Did you hear what he said?"

She checked her anger. "Yes, I did. 'Some things of value.' That phrase—"

"No, that's not what I'm talking about. That last part—where he said he was just doing what his old man told him to?"

She stared at him. "*What?* He said that? Working for his father!" She sighed and looked away across the airfield. Train decided to say nothing for a moment. It wasn't as if he had any answers, either. But finally, he felt compelled to break the silence. "We need to go back to Great Falls," he said. "It's time to think. We need to get Gutter programmed for your perimeter. I didn't like that crack he made about you being his father's new girlfriend. I know, I know," he said as her eyes started to flash again. "But remember what he just said. It's time to think, Karen. That kid is definitely part of this. And as far as that little creep is concerned, you're the admiral's new girlfriend. Suppose Galantz thinks the same thing?"

At 9:30 that night, Karen was sitting in the study, doing some household paperwork, when the phone rang. Train had gone home about an hour ago.

Gutter's ears perked up when the phone rang.

"Hello?"

"Karen, this is Tag Sherman."

Karen sat up. They had agreed not to tell the admiral about their encounter with Jack until they had had time to talk to McNair. "Yes, sir. Hello," she said. "Did you meet with the police today? Is everything okay with that?"

"Peachy. They brought a consultant in, some ex-IRS guy."

"Ugh. Was it human?"

"Marginally. But I have my taxes done by a pro, and they're really not that complex. Or they weren't. Galen's estate is going to complicate life a bit. This guy was having trouble not licking his lips. Anyhow, there apparently was nothing there that the cops cared about."

"What did McNair say when it was all over? 'Thank you for your cooperation; we'll be in touch'?"

"That's exactly what he said. But I was hoping you had some feedback. And I apologize for the late-hour call."

"We haven't talked to or heard from the police," she said, wanting to minimize what they had learned at Quantico. "We've been working on building a picture of where your son, Jack, is and what he's doing."

"And?"

"He works down at Quantico, at the Marine base. He's apparently a rigger in the helicopter-maintenance section. We're waiting for some more information from the NIS database." She was getting uncomfortable with the lies.

There was a pause on the line. "I'll be interested in . . . well, how he is, what he's like, when you finally interview him. I'd thought of maybe going along." When she did not reply, he said, "Well, I guess that wouldn't be very smart."

"No, sir, it probably wouldn't," she replied, grateful that she had not had to say it. "We'll give you a debrief when we have something." Then a question occurred to her. "Admiral, you're on leave right now?"

"Sort of," he laughed, but without much humor. "I'm actually up at the Bureau, heading up a selective early-retirement board for senior chief petty officers. That's not for publication until the board reports out, by the way. Which is why my office is saying I'm on leave."

Karen wanted to ask how long this little temporary additional-duty assignment had been scheduled, but she held back. The Navy went to great lengths to keep selection-board membership confidential, so the sudden assignment was plausible. But it was also a very convenient way of putting the admiral on ice while the Galantz thing played out. He must have read her thoughts.

"Convenient, huh? I suspect Kensington instigated this to lower my visibility in OpNav while this current mess gets sorted out."

"So this had not been in the works for some appreciable time?"

"Would you believe as of eighteen hundred last night? The board's been scheduled for a while, of course. But the president's slot was supposed to be filled by another flag officer, who was suddenly unavailable. So, yes, now I'm officially incommunicado for the next three days. Any developments on Galantz?"

Karen hesitated. She wanted to tell him about what Train had found out from his FBI contact. And about the visit she had received. But Jack's last words on the tarmac had thrown them both for a loop.

"Not yet, Admiral," she said. "But Mr. von Rensel has been talking to some people."

"I hope he's getting somewhere."

"Yes, sir," she replied, at a loss as to where to go from there. He seemed to sense that the conversation was over.

"Okay, Karen. And, again, thanks for everything you're doing. I thought when I made admiral, I'd be the guy in control. These past days, I've begun to feel like a wood chip in the rapids."

"That's just what this guy's trying to accomplish, Admiral," she said. "But I think having Train von Rensel working it is going to help—a lot."

Sherman agreed, thanked her again, and hung up. Slightly embarrassed, she put the phone down and patted Gutter's head. She thought about Jack Sherman, his overtly insolent demeanor and the brazen way he had looked at her. His father had probably seen a lot of that sneer before the divorce. She dreaded the thought of finally sitting down with Sherman senior and telling him that his son was still a slimeball, or worse.

She gave up on the paperwork and got up to turn off the lights. She had told Train she would be in the office tomorrow, where they were going to have to make some important decisions. She realized as she locked up downstairs that she was only beginning to appreciate the box Galantz had fashioned for the admiral.

CHAPTER 9

WEDNESDAY

Early the next morning, Karen called into the office and left a message that she would be late but that she was coming in. She had actually overslept, courtesy of the secure feeling of having that big Dobe in the house. She checked her voice mail. There was one message, from Sally, who had not been able to feed the horses this morning because she had to take her father to the doctor's office. She asked if Karen could please feed them.

Karen groaned. Murphy's Law, she thought. She deleted the message and looked at her watch. It was almost 8:30. The horses would be standing indignantly by their gates, an hour overdue for feeding. Okay, get the horses fed and turned out, then come back in, change into uniform, grab a cup of coffee, and jump into traffic to get down to the Pentagon. Wait, better call Train and tell him she'd be late. She punched in the office number, but it came up busy. Now what? What had happened to the office voice mail? Then she remembered Harry. She'd have to get Harry into the house before letting the Dobe out, or they might fight.

She groaned out loud. Arranging both dogs was too hard. She told Gutter to stay, patting him on the head, then slipped out the front door. Harry whimpered at her from under a porch chair, but he did not join her. She could hear Gutter complaining as she walked down off the front porch and headed for the barn. She was amazed at how quiet it was as she headed into the hedge passage. If she stood still, she could almost hear the sweep of the Potomac River through the woods beyond the big pasture. Even the hedge passage, which on Monday night had posed such a terror for her, looked entirely benign in the April sunshine, its crocus borders smiling at each other across the bricks. Duchess whinnied from the barn enclosure. "Oh, all right," she said out loud, and walked down toward the barn and her starving charges.

• • •

Train went to the athletic club early, then arrived in the office at about 8:15. He opened up his LAN mail to retrieve the full text of the database report on Jack Sherman. He grabbed a cup of coffee while the report was downloading into his computer, and he asked the yeoman if he had any messages. The yeoman told him the voice mail was down but that there had been no calls for him. "Oh, and Commander Lawrence will be coming in this morning, but late," the yeoman said.

Train went back to his cubicle, wondering how late was late. They had two immediate problems to work: whether or not to tell the cops about Jack, and finding out why the warning from the DNI had been shortstopped, and by whom. The first item would provoke an argument. He was leaning toward full disclosure, having had too many bad experiences in multiparty investigations wherein information was held back for political or bureaucratic reasons. Karen, in her zeal to protect Admiral Sherman, would not agree, but it was going to be tough getting around the matter of what Jack Sherman had said about working for his father. That didn't make any sense at all, unless they had missed the whole point of what was going on. The warning that Galantz might be a sweeper, they would have to take up with the JAG himself.

Karen opened up the feed room, found three feed bowls, and measured out three rations. It had been so long that she had to consult the feed board to see what they were getting these days.

"It has been a while, girls," she said to her three interested observers, who were clustered in the corners of their paddocks near the barn, watching her through the feed room's door and occasionally pinning their ears and making threatening faces at one another. She finished the rations, then carried the three bowls out to the feeding buckets, which were hung on the fences. She watched with satisfaction as everybody piled into their buckets, feet stamping and with an occasional white eye peeled over the rim of their buckets to stare at one another, just in case.

Karen watched for a minute, then went down the aisle to the door of the hay room. Most of the hay was stored in square bales on the second floor of the barn. One room on the ground floor had been designed as the hay service room, with a trapdoor between the upper floor and the ground floor so that hay could be dropped down into the service room periodically. She unlatched the door and stepped into the semidarkness. There were ten bales stacked on the concrete floor. The trapdoor in the ceiling was closed, as it should be. She cut the strings on one bale and carried out six pats of hay to a waiting garden cart. She rolled the cart back down the aisle to the area of the feed buckets, then gave each horse two solid pats of hay on the ground near their buckets.

She rolled the cart back down the aisle, past all the empty stalls. Sally kept a trim and clean barn, she thought. All the tools were hung up neatly, and the cabinets with vet supplies and tack-cleaning stores were all closed. She was lucky to have her, and only too happy to do the feeding chores from time to time if that's what it took to keep Sally. She opened the hay service room to put the cart inside, and suddenly there was a black-gloved fist in her face, a snapping sound, and a very bright purple flash that seemed to make her eyes ring and her brain stall, and then, without so much as a squeak, she was falling backward into a fathomless black canyon.

By nine o'clock, Train decided to call Karen's house, but there was no answer. Maybe she was stuck in traffic. He asked the yeoman for the number for her car phone, but the yeoman did not have it. He sat at his desk and scanned the database report again, his mind uneasy. He called her again at 9:15, and then he realized that calling was a waste of time. Something told him to go out there. But that would be dumb if she was on the way in. They'd simply pass each other out on the road.

He got up and paced around the office, making the yeoman nervous. He asked two of the other officers in IR if they had the number for Karen's car phone, but they looked at him as if he was slightly nuts, although they were polite about it. He went back to his cubicle and thought about going to see Carpenter. No, he decided, not without Karen. Then he remembered the athletic club. Would she have gone there before coming into the office? Knowing he was waiting? Maybe she would if she was still mad at him. Women! He got the POAC phone number and asked for them to page her. They obliged, but there was no reply. But that didn't mean anything if she was in the pool or out for a run. He looked at his watch. Going on ten. Damn it!

Karen surfaced in total darkness, surrounded by a strong smell of rubber. Slowly, she realized that it wasn't really darkness, but that her eyes were blindfolded. It felt as if there was cloth or bandage material pressed against her eyelids, and a strap or tape of some kind wrapped around her head to hold the bandages in place. There was even something in her ears, something that felt like a cotton or Styrofoam plug. She tried to move but couldn't. She was on her back, her feet and hands bound, probably by tape, from the feel of it. There was even a patch of tape over her mouth, with a small hole cut in the area around her lips. She could breathe through her nose, and partially through her mouth.

She tried to gather her wits. What the hell had happened? That bright purple light, and something else. The fist, the black fist. No, a black leather glove. She had a clear image of the glove, a man's glove with something in it. He had not hit her. She felt no pain, no sensation of having been drugged. Just that purple-red flash, as if someone had popped an incredibly intense flashcube in her face, and then she had blacked out. She tried to move again, but there was nowhere to go. In fact, she could not move much at all. With the first flare of claustrophobia, she realized she was in a bag of some kind—a rubber body-length bag. Oh my God, a body bag. She was trussed up in a body bag. She had never even seen a body bag, except on television, yet instinctively she knew what it was.

She tried to move again, tried to roll over on her side. But there was something on top of the bag—something heavy, rigid, but not hard-edged. And not just on top. There were heavy objects all around the bag, on top, along the sides, and even underneath. She could feel, rather than hear, a scratchy sensation on the rubber fabric of the bag when she moved. She realized that she was breathing heavily now, and she could feel a mist of condensation hovering around the skin of her face. But there was another smell, something different from the rubber.

Slow down, slow down, she thought. Control. Get control. Where had this started? In the hay service room. Hay. Bales of hay. That's what was on top of her—bales of hay, fifty pounds each. Heavy, although not crushing. She was buried in the haystack. But probably not down in the service room; there had been only ten bales down there. In the hayloft up above, then. Whoever had done this had carried her upstairs into the hayloft, where there were four hundred bales of hay. And—what? Stashed her?

She fought a rising panic as she grappled with her situation. She tried again to move, to wriggle out of the bindings, but then she realized that each twist and turn was settling the hay bales tighter on top of her. Heavier now, much heavier. The smell of rubber was very strong. Air. How was she going to get air to breathe, stuffed in this damned bag? By going slowly, breathing a lot slower than she was now. He hadn't meant to suffocate her, or else there would not be airholes in the tape over her mouth and nose. So the bag must have an airhole in it. Or the zipper had been left open around her face. Pay attention. Feel. Yes. The scratchy ends of hay straws against her face. An aroma of last year's grass just underneath the rubber smell. The feel of a zipper up against her chin.

She squeezed her eyes shut, feeling her lids pull against the gauze. Focus. Concentrate. Breathe, but control it. Slower. Force your body to relax, stop fighting, settle into a reduced state. Squeeze the picture of where you are out of your mind. Focus on surviving until the next thing comes along. He had stashed her here. Had to mean he was coming back.

Train would come—when she didn't show up at the Pentagon. Absolutely. He would come running. Could be coming right now, depending on how long she'd been out. Her eyes hurt, even though they were bound shut. She could still see that purple-red flash. She concentrated on her breathing. Train would find the dog, and then he would come looking. Hell, the dog could probably track her down here to the barn. Maybe even find her here in the hayloft. The trick was to listen for signs of a search. Maybe he would call the cops right from the Pentagon. Somebody would find her. Had to find her. Before whoever did this came back. So keep your wits about you; be ready to make noise when you hear someone in the barn.

Except there was cotton in her ears, and tape over the cotton. You're not going to hear *anything!*

Despite all her efforts at self-control, she lunged against the bag and then swallowed hard, fighting again to get her heaving chest and wildly racing heartbeat under control as the weight on her breasts shifted, increased again, ever so slightly. Stop it. *Stop it!* One thing at a time. Stabilize. Control. Breathe—once, and then hold it. Again, and hold it. Concentrate on *feeling* the presence of someone in the barn. Train was coming. Breathe, and hold it.

By 10:30, Train said to hell with it. He made a diskette copy of the database report to take home and then cleared his screen. He told the yeoman that he was going out to Commander Lawrence's house to see why she hadn't shown up for work. The yeoman, curious, asked if he should alert the EA. Train said no, not until he called back in. It could be just a simple misconnection. He left the number of his car phone with the yeoman in case Karen showed up, with instructions to call him at once.

It was almost 11:30 when he pulled into the driveway and stopped in front of the house. The first thing he saw was Harry coming down the front walk, head down, as if the old dog were apologizing for something. The second thing he saw and heard was Gutter jumping up on the inside of the front door. Uh-oh, he thought. He headed for the house and let himself in. Gutter was all over him, frantically trying to tell him something. Train called Karen's name, then did a fast recon of the house. Her uniform was laid out on the bed, but the house was empty. He stepped outside onto the front porch and called her name again—twice. No response. Gutter wanted to go; he was dancing around in a circle and whimpering at him.

"Okay, dog, go find her!" he ordered, and the dog took off down the path between those big hedges, toward the barn.

He stopped to think. When you find a fire, first call the fire department; then do something. He went back inside the living room and picked up the phone to dial 911. He identified himself as a federal agent, gave his name and badge number, Karen's address, and requested the assistance of a Fairfax County patrol car to secure the scene of a possible abduction. Then he went outside and headed down toward the barn.

The dog was running up and down the aisleway when he got there, and he called her name again, but there was no reply. Gutter couldn't seem to fix any one spot. She must have come down here to see the horses or something, he thought. But then what? Had she been kidnapped? The dog was sniffing hard at a doorway. Train looked at the door and wished he had a gun. The Glock was in his car. "That's not carrying," Johnson had said. Got that right. He thought about going back for it, but then he reached for the door handle. It was unlocked. He snatched it open. A hay room. Nothing in it but eight or nine bales of hay. Gutter went in and circled the room, then came right back out, obviously defeated. He ran up and down the aisleway again, then back outside. Train looked around the hay room again, but that's all it was: a hay room. He closed the door and followed the dog back outside. Sure as hell, she's been kidnapped, he thought.

Gutter ran around some more, even going partway out into one of the fields. The horses were visible at the other end of the field. Three of them, so she wasn't out for a ride. Damn. He called in the dog and went back to the house, stopping to get his notebook out of the car. He got McNair's phone number and called it from the car phone. McNair was not available. He left a message with the Homicide Section's secretary that Commander Lawrence might have been abducted and that a police unit was inbound. He hung up and heard the phone in the house ringing. He ran to beat the voice mail and just made it. It was the 911 operator, verifying his original call and asking him to remain on the scene until the first patrol units responded. He told them he would, then hung up.

He took the dog out on the front porch and paused to think. Cars. Check to see that the cars are here. Swearing at himself for not checking this first, he walked over to the garage, but both doors were down and he did not have a remote opener. He got down on his hands and knees and looked through the crack at the bottom of the doors. Both cars were in place. Satisfied that he had done all he could for the moment, he went to sit in the Suburban, after putting Gutter into the back compartment.

The first police car arrived five minutes later, and two large cops got out. Train got out of his car, showed his NIS identification, and gave them a brief outline of the events of two nights ago, telling them that he had last seen Commander Lawrence the previous evening and that he had left his dog to protect her, having given her instructions not to go anywhere without the dog. She should have gone to work at the Pentagon this morning but had not shown up. Now she was missing, and both of her cars were in the garage. He also told them that there was a homicide investigation in progress and that Commander Lawrence's disappearance might be related to that. One cop asked for the name of the homicide investigator, then got on the radio.

A second patrol car showed up with a patrol supervisor, and Train went down to tell him the same story. The first cop came back and asked him if he had been in the house since returning from the Pentagon, and if so, where he had been and what he had touched. Train told him, and the cop took it all down in his notebook while the other officers stood around admiring Gutter through the windows of the Suburban. Gutter admired them back.

"If you're pretty sure she's not in the house, we're going to wait for the CSU to come out," the first cop told Train. "I've put in a call to get Detective McNair out here. Appreciate your waiting around until he shows up."

"No problem," Train replied, getting back into his car. The cops spread out and started a careful walking tour of the immediate grounds. Train got on his car phone and called the office.

"Commander Lawrence show up?" he asked the yeoman. The answer was no. He asked if there were any messages. Another no. He then called the JAG front office and asked for Captain McCarty. The EA was in a meeting. He left a message for the EA to call Mr. von Rensel's car phone voice mail for a memo, told the yeoman it was important, and left her a three-digit entry code. He hung up and then put a memo message into a mailbox of his mobile system about Karen being missing; then he assigned it the entry code he had left with McCarty. He sat back to wait for McNair, but he got tired of that after about a minute and got out to join the cops.

The CSU showed up forty minutes later, and McNair drove in behind them in a department car. He checked in with the patrol cops, sent the CSU into the house, and then walked over to Train.

"So what's this about a night visitor?" he asked, his tone implying that he should have been told about this.

Train gave him a debrief, watching McNair's face cloud as he did so. "We were going to call you guys this morning," Train said lamely. Now he didn't dare tell McNair about their little meeting with Jack Sherman.

McNair was giving him the fish eye as he made some notes. "And you left that big Doberman in the house last night before you took off?"

Train didn't care for the term *took off,* but he understood that McNair was controlling his temper. "Yes," he replied. "I brought the dog out first thing yesterday morning, because she was going to stay home. The dog was in the house when I got here, and there were no signs of a struggle or problem in the house. I'm guessing she went out of the house on her own steam and left the dog behind. I can't explain why she didn't take the dog with her."

McNair nodded, then looked over at the barn, whose roof was visible over the hedge passage. "You check down there?"

"Yes. I took Gutter, or, rather, he took me. No joy. Again, no signs of trouble down there, either. Once I called nine-one-one, I considered the whole place a scene, so I got back in my car."

McNair nodded again and scratched some more in his notebook. Train was restless just standing there, but he knew the cops would be working their standard procedures, and procedures always took time. Then one of the crime-scene techs came to the front door and called to McNair. Train followed along. They went into the house, and the tech took them to the kitchen, where the telephone had been dismantled.

"This thing's got a bug *and* a transceiver in it," he announced.

"Meaning?" McNair said.

"Meaning someone could eavesdrop remotely, in and out, and also call in, probably make her phone ring, even talk to her, all without coming through the central office. Pretty slick toys."

"Those are spook toys," Train muttered under his breath.

McNair looked at him. "And which spooks might those be?"

Train shrugged, and McNair looked faintly disappointed. "Now don't go getting all federal on me, von Rensel," he said. "I know we're all hicks in the sticks out here, but we're coming right along in the technology department. Most of us have running water and everything."

"Sorry," Train said. "I didn't mean to patronize. I guess you and I need to talk. There's a new dimension to this case, something I learned yesterday."

"Yesterday. How timely," McNair said. He told the tech to check out the rest of the phones and also to access the voice-mail system's operator to see if Commander Lawrence had any messages that might explain her disappearance. A second tech reported no signs of violence or misplaced bodily fluids in the house after a first look. As McNair walked Train out to the front porch, another car pulled into the driveway and Lieutenant Bettino, McNair's boss, got out. He joined them on the front porch, where they sat down in chairs. McNair gave his lieutenant a quick synopsis of where they stood. Bettino took it in, giving Train an occasional glance. "Mr. von Rensel here was just telling me that there's a—what'd you call it? 'A new dimension to this case.' "

" 'A new dimension.' That G-man talk?" Bettino said.

Train squirmed a little bit. The cops had every right to be upset. Except that until Karen went missing, none of what he had learned yesterday really involved the cops—especially the news that Galantz might be a sweeper. He wasn't even sure the local cops ought to know that there were such things as sweepers. So he told them that the word in certain quarters was that Galantz was indeed real, and that he might have clandestine intelligence service connections; that there might be a larger problem than the two homicides; that the chances of laying hands on Galantz might be slim to none; and that, in a related development, Admiral Sherman might be training for Olympic-level plank walking.

"Might, might, might," McNair chanted. "Tonto's beginning to wonder if the Lone Ranger here *might* be blowing just a wee bit of smoke."

But surprisingly, Bettino waved McNair off. "Okay," he said. "What you're telling us computes, because *we* got a love note this morning, passed down through a political channel who shall remain nameless. But the message was that we *might* want to proceed very carefully and very slowly—emphasis on the *slowly*—with the investigation of the Walsh and Schmidt deaths."

It was Train's turn to be surprised. Bettino smiled knowingly. "So," Train asked, "are you still looking at Sherman for those?"

Bettino shook his head. "We put Admiral Sherman with some of our audit people, who gave him what the IRS calls a 'fiscal reality check.' Basically, he's clean. Absent any new connections being made with the murders, he's off the list."

Train thought about what young Jack Sherman had said yesterday. But they just said Sherman was off the list. So should he tell them? Karen had made a big deal about not filling in the cops until they, the Navy side, could make sense out of Jack's cryptic remark. But now Karen was missing. He didn't know what to do, so he just nodded.

"Those gizmos on her phone in there make me worry and wonder," McNair said. "And they also make me want to pay attention to political advice coming from on high."

"That's not your job," the lieutenant said, surprising Train again. "That's my job. Look, von Rensel, as far as the Homicide Section is concerned, we are still investigating two unexplained deaths. We don't have any suspects—yet."

McNair opened his mouth as if to say something, but he thought better of it when he saw that Bettino was not finished. "We appreciate your filling us in on the military aspects of this case. The two dead people so far have been close to this Admiral Sherman. I'm very concerned that Miss, uh, Commander Lawrence is now missing. Any ideas?"

At that moment, the crime-scene tech from the kitchen stuck his head out the front door and saved Train from having to answer.

"McNair? There was voice mail. Someone named Sally called and asked Miss Lawrence to feed the horses. That was early this morning. Then a couple of messages from a guy called—what was it, Train? Yeah. Those were between nine and ten this morning."

The lieutenant stood up. "Thanks, Jerry. Okay, let's go play Farmer Brown." He looked over across the yard. "I'm a city boy. That's a barn, right?"

Captain McCarty knocked once and went into Admiral Carpenter's office. His face was grim, causing the admiral to put down a briefing folder and say, "Now what?"

"Von Rensel left me a message via his mobile voice mail. Karen Lawrence has gone missing."

"Missing? What the hell's that mean?"

"That's all I have. He said he went out there this morning after she failed to show up for work. Said he left one of his Dobermans with her, and that the dog was in the house and she wasn't. Her cars are there; cops are there."

"Goddamn it," Carpenter said softly, turning in his chair to get up. He walked over to one of the windows and stared at nothing.

"I made a call," McCarty said. "To Sherman's office. To see if he might know something."

"And he wasn't there, was he?"

McCarty, surprised, looked up. "They said he was on leave. Have they made a decision? Is that what's happened?"

Carpenter turned around. "Sort of. He's chairing a selection board. Short notice. The deputy in OP-32 has been made 'acting.' "

"I see," McCarty said, the obvious question lingering in the air between them.

"Okay, it was my idea," Carpenter said. "Reduces his profile while our guys and the cops work the problem. Von Rensel's on it, presumably with the cops and not in spite of them. That's as good a resource as we can have in the game right now. Put a call into BuPers. Talk to Sherman and see if he knows where Karen is. I'm going to call the DNI."

McCarty did not understand. "The DNI?"

"Yeah. I need him to drop a message down a certain hole. Say that there had better not be any spook fingerprints on what's happened to Karen Lawrence. Because if there are, I'll go to the *Washington Post* and give them the interview of the year."

McCarty closed his notebook. "Does von Rensel know that this Galantz individual may have connections to those people?"

"Not from me. But I would guess he has his own sources on the matter. Make sure he checks in when he has something. Get in touch with Sherman. See what he knows, if anything. I think I may have been wrong about what's going on here. . . ."

McCarty hesitated, as if waiting for the admiral to explain that last comment. When nothing was forthcoming, he simply said, "Aye, aye, sir," and left the room. When he had gone, Carpenter sat down at his desk and thought about this new development. He hadn't been quite honest with McCarty just then. On the other hand, he'd been hoping von Rensel might find or at least localize this Galantz individual, which would go a long way to solving his other problem. He decided not to call the DNI. He picked up the phone to call Kensington instead. He dreaded doing it. The DNI's description of what a sweeper did was sticking in his throat like a bone.

Karen awoke with a start. She hadn't realized that she'd gone to sleep. Her throat was very dry, and her right knee hurt where there was excess weight on the bag. The bag. She felt a flare of terror and immediately stifled it. She tried to swallow, but it hurt. She tried her voice, managing only a croak. She wondered what time it was and how long she had been buried. Bad word, that. Tied up. That was better. The image of being buried alive was more than she could cope with. He'll be back, she assured herself. This was done for a reason. He'll be back. She wondered where Train was. She concentrated on controlling her breathing, and on listening. But all she could hear was the thudding of her own heart.

The lieutenant, McNair, three of the patrol officers, and Train searched the entire Lawrence property, including the barn, the yard, and the surrounding paddocks before deciding that she wasn't there. One of the patrol cops rode horses, and he showed them that someone had done the morning feeding and then cleaned up. The horses were all sticking to the far ends of the fields because of all the strange humans. It was nearly 5:30 when they gave it up and gathered on the path leading up toward the house. "Somebody just snatched her up," opined one of the patrol cops. "Up by the house. Probably when she came back from the barn. Threw her in a car and went down the road and gone. Too bad she left that Dobe in the house."

"That's a great-looking dog," McNair said to Train. "Lemme ask you something. You running a pro forma investigation for the NIS, or are you sort of freelancing?"

Train looked at him for a moment, wondering where this had come from. "Freelancing, after a fashion," he said. "I'm under tasking, but not from NIS. From Admiral Carpenter, that admiral you met the—"

McNair nodded. "Yeah, the JAG. Okay. I do a little freelancing myself, like when I need another Cadillac or something. So I know about the elasticity of rules. Now, about that spook shit, and all those 'mights'—"

"I'm going to go back to Fort Fumble and pull on that string," Train said.

McNair gave him a blank look. "Fort Fumble?"

"The Pentagon."

McNair flashed a grin, but then his face sobered. "We'll do the standard deal," he said. "A neighborhood canvass. See if anyone heard or saw anything. Not likely, this area, all these estates, but who knows. And we'll put a tap on her phone, record who calls in." He looked over to where Lieutenant Bettino was standing, speaking on a cellular phone. "And, of course, if all else fails, we might have to bring in Fart, Barf, and Itch, eventually."

"Um," Train said.

"Um what?"

"There's a remote possibility that the *FBI* may already be working the edges of this case."

McNair thought about that for a moment, then looked up at Train. "Don't tell me. We're in the middle of some kind of turf fight between the housekeepers and the gatekeepers?"

Train shrugged. This guy didn't miss much. "My main concern right now is that somebody has Karen Lawrence," he answered.

"This lady mean something to you personally?" McNair asked.

Train gave him a circumspect look. "Yeah," Train replied, trying to be very careful. "Not something she's aware of, but yeah, I want to find her. Alive, and soon. And I'm willing to break some rules and/or bones if that's what it takes."

McNair looked over toward his lieutenant again. The lieutenant was protesting something, waving his free hand in the air. "Okay. I'll keep that in mind," McNair said softly. "But you keep *me* in mind, you hear things. I'm just a lowly homicide dick, okay? Personally, I don't give a rat's ass if there's some kinda heavy-side layer developing on this case. I want to know the who and the how of what happened to Walsh and Schmidt, even if we locals do end up getting shut down here."

He was looking straight at Train, his body language sending a pretty clear signal. Train said he understood. As McNair walked away, Train checked that Gutter was still in the back of the car. He waved to McNair, who was now talking to Lieutenant Bettino, got in, and backed up to turn the big vehicle around. He drove past the patrol cop who was watching the front gate, then headed for the village of Great Falls, where he parked in the shopping center parking lot. Once parked, he got on the car phone and called the office. One message—from McCarty: "Check in when you have something to report. The admiral is very upset."

Train thought about that. I'll just bet he is. The admiral had charged him with keeping Karen safe. Now she was missing. He put a call into Captain McCarty. The yeoman said that the EA was in a meeting with the admiral but that he'd left a message for Mr. von Rensel in case he called. "He said to read it to you, sir. Verbatim."

"Shoot."

" 'Orders from JAG. Back out of the Sherman matter. Focus on the Lawrence problem exclusively until you receive further orders.' "

"Say it again, please."

The yeoman read it back to him. "That's all of it, sir. Uh, the EA wanted to know that you understood."

"Okay, reply as follows: Orders understood. Will comply."

Movement. Karen felt movement in the haystack. Her heart quickened. Had the police found her? Or was this her abductor coming back? She fought down the urge to thrash or struggle. Go limp, she commanded her body. Go limp and maybe—

Definite movement. The weight on her chest eased, and then the nearest bales were being removed. One at a time, not the urgent scrabbling of rescuer's hands.

Damn. Wrong finders.

A bale was lifted off the edge of her face. Now the one on her hips. Then the one across her thighs. Breathe. Control. In. Hold it. Out, slowly.

And then all the weights were off. She could feel the solid blocks of hay all around her, as if she were lying in a shallow grave in the middle of the haystack. The image spiked her fear, but she gritted her teeth and clamped down on it. Control. She could feel but not hear. It was maddening. Total helplessness.

Then there were hands, strong hands, under her shoulders and at her feet, lifting her out of the grave—no, the cavity in the haystack. Get that word *grave* out of your mind. If they were going to kill you, they could have done it long ago. They. Had to be two of them. But they're not going to just kill you. They could have done that by simply leaving you there, trussed, taped, utterly helpless in a rubber bag, and closing the zipper.

Control. Breathe. In. Out.

She felt herself being lifted and then carried, and she tried to visualize where they were in the hayloft. There had been at least four hundred bales of hay up there the last time she had dropped hay into the service room. About twenty square feet of bare floor around the trapdoor, the rest covered in piled bales. Were they going to drop her? The trapdoor was the only way out of the hayloft, not counting the conveyor used to load the hay up into the loft. Then suddenly she was vertical, the strong hands letting go of her shoulders and holding what had to be straps on the bag, her feet no longer supported, but jammed down into the bottom of the bag by her own weight. She tensed, waiting to be dropped, but no, she was being lowered, bumping her back along the rungs of the ladder that came up through the trapdoor. She felt her feet hit the concrete of the ground floor, and then she *was* falling, sideways, into a heap on the floor. She grunted in pain as her left hip hit the cold concrete, but at the last instant, she remembered to go limp, protecting her head and shoulder.

She lay on the floor, her thoughts whirling. They were taking her some-where, but where? And how? Was there a car pulled into the aisleway of the barn? What time was it? Was it dark? Then, partially lifted by those shoulder straps, she was being dragged across the floor, her calves bouncing hard against the doorjamb of the hay service room. Out of the service room and into the aisleway. Then she was dropped again, and this time she did bang her head.

Silence. Damn them for putting cotton in her ears and then taping it. She was in nearly total sensory deprivation. Eyes, ears, and mouth taped off, hands and feet immobilized. All the movement had produced a sudden, desperate need to urinate. How long had she been in the bag? What time was it now? What were they going to do with her? Panic rising again. Control. Breathe. No point in struggling. Hold your strength in reserve. Maybe they'll free you, and then, then you can—what? One level of her mind was spinning out images of her coming out of the bag and surprising them, lashing out, hitting someone and then running away. But below that level, her cooler subconscious mind knew that was all a pipe dream. She would come out of the bag with her joints stiff and rubbery and her muscles weak and spastic. Then they picked her up again, and she was being carried, carried like . . . well, a body. She went limp, waiting to be dropped again.

Train decided to drive back to Karen's house after his call to the Pentagon. Twenty minutes later, he changed his mind and pulled into the rear parking lot of the French restaurant that Karen liked at the end of Springvale. There was a wall of Dumpsters at the far end of the lot. He parked near them to hide from any passing cops. He assumed the cops would be gone by now, but it was better to be safe. It was full dark as he shut down, and he waited to get his night vision adjusted.

He pulled a canvas satchel out from behind the driver's seat and opened it. He shucked his coat and tie, then pulled on a large olive drab Marine Corps woolly pully sweater. He exchanged his office dress shoes for a pair of well-worn high-topped hiking boots. The suit pants would just have to take their chances.

Now for the good stuff. He double-clicked on the switch of the electric door lock and a panel toward the bottom of the left-front door edged open. He removed a holstered black Glock pistol and a four-inch sheath knife from the compartment in the door. He attached the sheath knife to the top of his right ankle. He eased the pistol out of its thin canvas holster and checked to make sure there was a round in the chamber. Then he stuffed the holstered automatic into his waistband, at the small of his back, snapping a small canvas flap through a belt loop and covering the rig with the sweater. Not as good as a shoulder holster, but certainly along for the ride.

He pulled a small Maglite from the glove compartment and then stopped to think. Gloves, and something to cover his chrome dome. He fished around in the bag and then rooted in the side pockets of the front doors before finding a pair of black leather gloves and a black knit Navy watch cap. He pulled the cap over his head.

He got out of the car, released Gutter from the back compartment, told him to heel, then broke into a casual jog through the big oaks surrounding the back of the parking lot and reached the verge of Beach Mill Road. There was no sidewalk, but most of the traffic was coming from behind him, homeward-bound, so he only occasionally had to leap out of the way of a car coming toward him. He actually passed another jogger going the other way. The guy was dressed out in a Day-Glo orange vest and was looking nervously at the big Doberman trotting along beside the even bigger man in the dark sweater and watch cap. Train wondered what warp factor the jogger could achieve if he turned around and started to follow him. He pressed on. It wasn't far from here.

She was lowered, not dropped. But not into a car. What was it? They were turning her on her side and then bending her in the middle, forcing her into something, bending her trussed legs back toward her hips in an accordion fold. She couldn't figure out what they were putting her in until suddenly she was jerked up into a slant, head up and her knees wedged down against the sides of something. The cart, the big Garden Way cart that sat in the aisle. They had dumped her into the cart and now she was rolling. She could feel the bumping through the bottom of the cart, almost hear the rumble of the wheels. Then a big bump. They had to be outside now, rolling over the rougher ground. But where? Where were they taking her? It felt as if they were hurrying.

When Train passed Karen's driveway, the gates were closed and appeared to be chained. There was a strip of yellow crime-scene tape fluttering behind the gates. He jogged on past for about two hundred yards, and then, pausing for a break in the intermittent stream of cars, trotted across the road and climbed over the pasture fence. The Dobe hesitated at the fence for an instant, but when Train had the top strand of barbed wire held down, he snapped his fingers and Gutter cleared the fence in a single smooth bound. Train moved away from the road for about twenty yards and then hunkered down in the dewy grass to get his eyes further adjusted. The dog sat down next to him and waited.

The night air was clear, but there was no moon yet. The trees bordering the paddocks looked like solid walls in the darkness. He tried to remember the layout of Karen's place. She had described it as a rectangle, divided roughly into four quarters. Three of the quarters were pastures, and the fourth, nearest to Beach Mill Road, contained the house and its immediate grounds. He remembered that there was a state park that bordered the west banks of the river all the way down to the Great Falls cataracts. He could see the house clearly across the pasture because the cops had left the external lights on over the garage.

Train stood up then and started across the field toward the barn. The last phone message on her voice mail before his calls had been about feeding the horses. So if she had been snatched anywhere, it had been down at that barn, which, of course, was a great place to do it—out of sight of the road, so a car could be positioned in or near the barn. Grab her, truss her, into the car, and then drive out easy as you please.

Damn, I wish you'd taken Gutter, he thought. They might have shot the dog, whoever this was, but there would have been one hell of a ruckus, and she might have made a run for it. Karen was certainly fit enough to sprint her way out of a problem if she had some warning. He closed in on the barn, once again stopping to hunker down in the grass, this time alongside the gate leading into the barn enclosure. The headlights out on the road were not so distracting in here, and he realized he could actually see better in the darkness. The barn was entirely dark. The aisleway was a black rectangular mouth in the side of the building. Not going to just amble on in there, he thought. He sent Gutter instead.

The dog went into the aisleway like a torpedo, loping all the way through, and then came straight back to Train. Okay, no humans waiting in ambush. He went in, with the dog at his heel, and quickly made a flashlight survey of the barn. The door to the tack room was closed and locked, as was the feed room. The stalls were all empty, and the only other door led to that small hay room. As he was looking in there, Gutter made a noise. Train turned around to find Gutter circling the area around the door to the small hay room, sniffing hard at the concrete. He snapped on the Maglite. There were bits of hay on the floor. That was new.

"Whatcha got, dog? Find it, Gutter," he called, encouraging whatever the dog was up to. Gutter gave a small yip and then trotted out of the barn, nose down, ears up and forward. Train hustled along behind him. The dog had a scent, but of what? Karen? He mentally kicked himself for not bringing the dog back down to the barn after his initial look. He should have done it right, given him a piece of Karen's clothing and then turned him loose, crime scene or no crime scene. Dobes weren't famous as scent hounds, but a dog's nose beat the hell out of a bunch of cops tramping around in the weeds. The thought that Karen may have been hidden there all day gave him a cold feeling as the dog led him straight out from the barn into the third pasture. Gutter hesitated at the twelve-foot-wide farm gate, circling anxiously until Train found the chain and opened it up. Gutter shot through, prompting him to rein in the dog with a sharp command to walk. Train's night vision was very well adapted by now, but it was still pitch-dark, and he was going away from houses and civilization, down toward the dark band of deep woods bordering the river. Not an area he wanted to run toward, especially if the dog was following someone.

Karen knew by the feel of the ground rolling beneath the cart where she was—or rather, where she was being taken. The path was leading downhill, first across the relatively smooth turf of the back paddock, now along the much harder, rockier path that led into the woods along the river. She had walked and ridden along this path a thousand times, and she could almost plot her position as the cart bumped and banged over familiar ruts and rain runoff channels. It was about a third of a mile from the edge of her back paddock to the banks of the Potomac. She knew the cart would be making some noise, but she could hear nothing, only feel.

She was wedged even tighter into the cart now that it was tilting downhill. Now that they were taking her somewhere, anywhere, the dreaded constrictions of claustrophobia had retreated, for the moment anyway. Why the river? Were they just going to dump the bag into the current? From the banks of the river adjoining her place, it was about a mile downstream to the first of the cataracts for which her neighborhood was named, and less than that to the reservoir diversion dam. The river would be in full spate, especially now with the spring snowmelts from the Shenandoah Valley and the Blue Ridge Mountains. She imagined that she could feel it already, although she knew that wasn't possible, and she certainly could not hear it. There was a rotor below the reservoir dam, where drowning victims' bodies were often trapped for months. That's a feature a sweeper would like, she thought, and then squeezed that thought out of her mind. She winced as the cart hit a bad pothole, banging her head through the rubber bag. Then she realized they had stopped suddenly, as if to listen for something. She jumped as hands grabbed both ends of her body and hauled her out of the cart.

Train followed the dog into the dark woods, stumbling along a rocky, hard-packed path through the forest. The footing was treacherous, with lots of small round rocks and six-inch-deep rain gullies. The woods were pervaded by the muddy smell of the big river somewhere down the hillside in the darkness. He gave a soft command to call the dog back to him, then proceeded more carefully. It was even darker here in the woods, although he could differentiate between the cleared area of the path, about six feet wide, and the dense tangle of new vegetation on either side. At one point, he stopped to listen, but he heard only the sounds of small animals or birds disturbing the undergrowth.

He got down on one knee, causing the dog to close in on him to see what he'd found. Shielding the Maglite with his closed fist, he twisted a red lens into place and then switched it on. He traversed the path with a dime-sized pinpoint of light, looking for fresh tracks or any other sign of recent human passage. At first, he saw nothing, but then in a soft patch of mud, he discovered the tread marks of what looked like a bicycle tire. A bicycle? The track was fresh, with little granules of red clay still balanced delicately along the edges of the depression caused by the tire. A bicycle—that would be a rough-ass ride down this path. Then he realized he was looking at the left side of the path. He traversed the light carefully across the path, finding a second tire mark three feet away. Not a bicycle. A cart or wagon of some kind. And recently, very recently. He switched off the light and closed his eyes to readjust his night vision.

The dog growled then, low but distinctively. Train opened his eyes to see the dog leaning forward, looking down the path. A cart, heavily loaded, too, to make such a deep impression in this hard-packed dirt. He hadn't looked for any tracks when he followed the dog out, trusting in Gutter's nose to follow whatever had caught his attention in the barn. His mind conjured up an impression of a guy or a couple of guys grabbing Karen, tying her up, and then taking her through the woods to—what? Why go down to the river?

To a boat, dummy. Get her in a boat and take her either way, up or down the river, or even over to Maryland. The cops had assumed a vehicle. They'd be watching the roads. Nobody would be watching the river.

He got up, put away the flashlight, and hauled out the Glock. Now what? They could be just ahead, or already down on the banks of the river. Should he run down there, in the darkness? Yell at them? Dumb move. Send the dog. Let the dog get ahead of you; then get down there.

"Gutter!" he called softly, and the dog looked expectantly at him, sensing his master's building adrenaline. Train gestured down the hill. *"Schnell! Schnell!"*

The dog was gone instantly, lunging down the path and instantly out of sight. Train waited about ten seconds, then followed, not sure how far he had to go to reach the river, although he sensed that it was only a few hundred feet now as the slope began to level off. He was slipping and sliding down parts of the path, careening against tree trunks and being whipped in the face by low-hanging branches. He only faintly heard a commotion ahead of him, then the clear roar of Gutter on the attack and a man's voice yelling, "Look out!"

Ten seconds later, he burst out of the underbrush into a small clearing on the bank of the river. Framed by a black mass of low-lying trees, the shadowy silhouettes of two human figures were outlined fifty yards upstream against a silvery expanse of rushing water, grappling with something between them. As he stopped short, he realized that the something had to be Gutter. The dog simultaneously yelped in pain, and then there was a metallic clank from the riverbank, a sound Train recognized as that of a boat sliding over some rocks. He raised the Glock way above his head and fired two rounds into the air, making his own ears ring. He ducked behind a tree trunk to take stock, not knowing if Karen was up there or not, then realizing he had to get closer. At that instant, an outboard motor lit off, and then there was a loud splash.

He started running through the underbrush along the water's edge, just in time to see a small boat careening upstream, with either one or two dark figures crouching low. He aimed the Glock out over the water, but he held back as the sound of the engine dwindled. What if they were just a couple of fishermen who had been terrorized by a large dog and some nut shooting at them? And where the hell was Karen? In the boat? He swore out loud in frustration.

Then Gutter barked from the edge of the riverbank and limped over to Train on three legs. Train put the Glock back and reached for the dog, but Gutter grabbed the wrist of his sweater instead and pulled back, a gentle but firm grab. Come here. Come this way. Now. Train stumbled forward into the low rocks and fallen tree trunks along the riverbank, but Gutter kept pulling, down to the edge, backing into the water. Train pulled back.

"What is it, dog?" Then he looked out onto the river and caught a glimpse of something long and low and shiny rolling in the inshore current, sweeping gracefully downstream toward the cataracts.

Karen heard the two shots. She still did not know where she was or what they were doing with the bag, but the two pops in quick succession did penetrate through the bag and the cotton in her ears. The zipper had come open enough to expose her face down past her chin. She could smell the cold, wet air of the river. They had been moving the bag from the cart, seeming to take some care doing it, dragging its lower end across some rocks, when something large and alive caromed off the side of the bag.

After that, everything had happened very fast. There was some kind of intense struggle practically on top of her, and she tried to roll over in the bag to protect herself. Something heavy and squirming fell on the top half of the bag, making her ears ring. She would have sworn she heard a growl or a bark. Was it some kind of animal? A dog? *Gutter?* Whatever it was, her captors had their hands full in a fight right on top of the bag. Then she thought she heard the animal yelp in pain, and everything was still for about two seconds. Then she was being dragged again, this time with no pretense of care. The bag was twisted around roughly, and then there was an odd feeling that she was falling. She tensed her body for a landing, but the sensation was wrong, all wrong. She *was* falling, and then there was a shock of cold water on her face. She was bounding upward again, and then she knew, with a cold fist of fear squeezing her heart, that she was in the river— still in the body bag, in the river. She felt the sudden cold along her back, and this time she struggled in earnest, giving way to her panic, thrashing and pulling against the tape, breath hissing through the holes in the tape, eyes streaming behind the gauze taped across her eyes. The bag just rolled indifferently in the water, submerging her face again for an instant, and then the current had her.

. . .

The dog pulled once more on Train's wrist, then let go and whirled out into the water. But the leg injury quickly brought him floundering back into the shallows. Train got the picture: The dog wanted that thing that was floating down the river. But what the hell was it? He hurried downstream along the bank, pushing his way through beached snags, muddy underbrush, embedded beer cans, and wet rocks. The main current was visible fifty feet offshore, creating swirls over submerged rocks and raising a gray bow wave along a stranded tree trunk. He realized he was losing ground in his attempts to keep up with whatever that was, but the dog persisted, splashing through the shallows, half-swimming, half-leaping, trying desperately to keep up with that thing out there. The river was a couple of hundred yards wide, with a long, low island running down the center. The Maryland shore was visible only as a darker line beyond the island.

Train finally gave up trying to get through the tangle along the shore and jumped down into the water, which shocked him with its icy grip. The bottom felt like gravel, but there were unexpected potholes, and he lurched along like a drunk, head and eyes down to see what he was stepping into, trying to keep upright while catching up with whatever was out there. The dog: Where was Gutter?

He looked up and saw Gutter out in the river now, paddling furiously toward the thing, his head bounding in and out of the water as he flailed his way out into the channel. Train stopped, then pushed forward as he realized how fast that main channel current was. He was already twenty feet behind the action out there, but try as he might, he couldn't go any faster, and he knew that he would never last in that cold if he tried to swim out there. To retrieve what? He still didn't know, but he trusted the dog's instincts. He wished he could see the damn thing, but it was indistinct, loglike, but glistening in the silvery starlight reflecting off the channel currents. The rushing noise of the river drowned out his own breathing as he swatted away overhanging branches, trying to keep up while not stepping into the potholes in the gravel shelf that ran along the bank. As he pushed through the tendrils of a leaning willow tree, he thought he heard a distant engine sound, but he ignored it, keeping his eyes on the dog.

Gutter was catching up with the thing, but the cold water was also catching up with the dog. He kept going, paddling hard, but the shiny black head was coming up out of the water less frequently. Then Train's right foot stepped off into nothing at all and he was underwater, swimming hard to escape what felt like a small whirlpool, the black water shocking him again with its icy grip. He surfaced some twenty feet away from the bank and felt a moment of panic as he sensed the strength of the current, but then he saw Gutter's head bound out of the water about fifty feet ahead of him, eyes white, no longer in pursuit of the thing, but swimming for survival. He thought he saw the thing hang up on the white branches of a snag.

He yelled to the dog to hang on, more to let Gutter hear the sound of his voice, and then he began to swim in earnest. He was not going to lose Gutter. The effort of swimming was staving off the cold, although he knew that was an illusion, that the energy equation would very soon be working to kill him in this icy water. Then he heard the engine noise again, and suddenly the river's surface was awash with light, light streaming down from above. He stopped swimming and looked up to see a helicopter flaring out above the water downstream, perhaps a hundred yards from him. Then the helo disappeared in a cloud of its own downwash, a billow of spray that was rapidly advancing up toward him and already enveloping the struggling dog. The pilot evidently saw what was happening and lifted out of ground effect as Train swam harder, his energy galvanized by the appearance of the helo.

After sixty seconds of hard going, he drew abreast of the dog, and he finally could see what they had been pursuing. It was a bag of some sort, rolling slowly against the snag in the current. Rubber, from the looks of it, its sides puffing out as if it had air trapped in it. He closed in on it as the helo came back, the powerful blue-white spotlight hurting his eyes as it dazzled through the cloud of spray. He collided with the submerged trunk of the snag and reached out and grabbed the bag, then reached for Gutter, who was on his last reserves of energy. To his astonishment, something inside the bag moved, and then it moved again. Then he recognized what the thing was: a goddamned body bag.

Karen? Great God, was Karen in there?

He momentarily lost his grip on the dog's collar, then launched back out into the current to retrieve the struggling animal. He had to fight like hell to pull them both back upstream to the snag. He caught a glimpse of a face at the top of the bag, but the features were missing. Was she dead? He ended up holding on to the dog's collar with one hand and to one of the straps on the bag, whose buoyancy acted like a long, slippery life preserver, with the other while his body straddled the trunk of the snag.

The helo swept closer, the noise and the dazzling light almost overwhelming his ability to think. The cold had him now that he had stopped swimming, and he sensed that the dog was choking in his grasp. He tried to change his grip on the dog and lost his hold on the bag again, going under with the sudden weight of the dog, and then both of them rolled to the surface again, just in time to collide with a submerged rock that knocked the breath right out of Train. When he surfaced again, he was alone on one side of the rock, blinded by the spotlight and gasping for breath. The helicopter, hovering just upstream of him, was invisible in the spray, but the downdraft felt like an arctic blast, turning his facial muscles to cold rubber.

He peeled off the face of the rock and slipped downriver, backward now, spinning as he hit another whirlpool. Then he saw the bag, with the dog at one end, clamping on with his teeth, going with him about twenty feet away. Something slapped the water near his head, and he looked up. A helmeted figure was leaning out of the helicopter, with one foot out on the skid, the other inside, a wire cable in his hand. He was trying to steer a life ring closer to Train.

Train had to decide whether to take the ring or to drag it over to the bag. He wanted to direct the helo over to the bag, but the guy would never understand. So take the ring, get up there, explain what he thought was in the bag, and then go back for the dog and the bag. He grabbed the ring as it swung by his head, thrust his right shoulder into it and then his neck. But it was too small. He could not get it around his chest, and he was suddenly exhausted by the effort of even trying. He pulled his right arm out of the ring and looked helplessly up at the blazing light and the silhouette of the man on the skid. This pilot is good, he thought idly, really good. He was keeping the helo right on top as they drifted down the current. Except that it looked like they were approaching something, some dark mass downstream, and he thought he could feel the current tugging at his hips and legs, getting more turbulent.

The life ring popped out of the water and zipped up toward the bottom of the helo, where the figure on the skid did something. Then it was coming back down, slapping the water practically on top of Train's head. This time, it wasn't a ring, but a Navy-style sling collar. Recalling his Marine training, and with his last reserves of strength, Train went underwater and came back up through the collar sling, both hands and head through the sling, then gripped the attachment point where the sling was mated to the cable. He was hoisted immediately upward, his feet smacking something hard in the water, another rock. As he approached the underside of the helo, he saw the U.S. PARK POLICE painted on the belly of the aircraft. Then he was dangling next to the hatchway on the helo. He looked down and saw the bag and the dog clearly for the first time since going in the water. Good boy, Gutter. The dog had a death grip, literally, on the end of the bag, which looked like a headless porpoise in the water. But it was still buoyant.

Then he was being hauled roughly into the cabin of the helo, the rescue wireman yelling something at him from behind the face shield of his helmet.

Train tried to answer, but his face was frozen and his lips didn't work. He grabbed the front of the guy's flight suit as he felt the helo begin to lift.

"Someone in the bag!" he yelled, trying desperately to make himself heard over the noise of the helicopter's engines and rotors.

"What?" the rescue man shouted back at him.

"Someone in the bag! Someone in the bag! Get the goddamned bag!"

The crewman gave him a thumbs-up to signal that he understood, then pulled his lip mike closer to his mouth to tell the pilots. Train sank down on the deck of the cabin and tried to get control of his breathing. The helo stopped rising fifty feet above the river, the big spotlight fixed on the bag and the dog, the aircraft spinning around to stay just downstream of the bag. Too far to drop, he thought. Yeah, like you could really do anything. Have to. Have to get back down there, get a hook on that bag. Let them lift the bag. He'd stay in the water with the dog; then they could come back for him. My God, Karen was in that body bag, he just knew it. The crewman was shaking his shoulder and bending down.

"No way to get the bag! No exposure suit! You sure someone's in that thing? Alive?"

"Yeah," Train shouted back. "Put me back in. It's a body bag. It's got straps. Send down a hook. Get the bag, then come back for me and the dog."

"No way, man. You can't go back down there!" the guy yelled. "You're done."

Train looked back out of the hatch. The helo was back over the bag, maybe thirty feet above it, the spotlight drifting back and forth across the bag. Gutter was still clamped on, but his eyes were closed. The water looked black. But at least there were no rapids. The guy saw him looking, figured it out, and started to reach for him. But Train was already moving, swinging out of the cabin and onto the skids, the downwash whipping his sodden clothes.

"Hook!" he yelled. "Gimme a hook!" And then he slid off onto the skid, holding on to the cold, wet aluminum for a second before dropping into the freezing water. He cringed as he hit, instinctively trying to pull his legs up under him, waiting for the shock of hitting a rock, but thankfully, it was deep water, but goddamned cold. It felt like fire this time, painful, every inch of his skin immersed in the icy-hot grasp of the current.

Go. Swim. Move. The helo was coming lower, but there was no hook. He used a hard breaststroke to get over to the bag, then grabbed a strap. The lower end of the bag submerged, bobbing beneath the black surface. He worked his way around to the end where the dog was hanging on and yelled some encouragement to him. He patted the lumpy shape in the bag, thanking God that body bags were waterproof. He thought he felt the lump move again, but then there was a steel hook dropping close to the water alongside the bag. Train grabbed it, felt the wallop of a static shock discharging through his elbow into the water, and then the hook was yanked out of his hand as the helo lifted for some reason. Train swore, but then the hook was back as the crewman once again swung out on the skids, now only fifteen feet above the river, and worked the rescue hoist. Train dragged the hook back along the bag and tried to snap the hook onto a strap, but his hands weren't working. He stared at the dog's face, its eyes shut, its teeth gleaming white against the glistening black rubber. His own brain numbed by the cold, he tried to figure out what to do next. Then the hook was yanked again and he refocused, and with a huge effort, he pushed the moused hook over the heavy strap. He raised his right hand and gestured to lift. He was tempted to hold on to the bag as the wire tightened, but he didn't know how strong the cable was or whether he even could hold on. But the dog could. Train grinned lopsidedly as he saw that Gutter, eyes slitted open now, wasn't going to let go of that goddamned bag for anything.

And then he was alone in the river as the helo pilot maneuvered to keep the aircraft stable against the sudden weight on one side. The spotlight moved sideways, and Train relaxed, not so cold now, letting the current just carry him, no longer having to struggle quite so hard. He looked out across the water and realized he was way out in the middle of the river, the black banks on either side several hundred feet away. The helo was stationary over the river as they worked the lift, and his view became clearer as he sailed downstream. He watched as the bag, now dangling lengthwise, with the unlikely shape of the big dog holding on with its teeth near the hook, lift up to the cabin hatch and then disappear into the cabin. The helo moved even farther away and up as the crewman and the pilot worked to redistribute the load inside, which was when Train felt something, a deep, rumbling vibration behind him. He made a lazy turn in the water, frustratingly slowly, his cold-numbed senses resisting his efforts to bring them back to life, and looked downstream. Something wrong with the river. A near horizon, a line of darkness visible against a curtain of silver spray that seemed to span the main channel, a line that was maybe four hundred yards away, and approaching. He tried to think. Why was there a line in the water? He couldn't understand it. And then he did.

Then the helo was coming back, its roaring rotor noise and blazing spotlight coming in fast, the cable already back down in the water, with the horse collar skipping wildly across the water like a game fish on the hook. The pilot flared the aircraft out right overhead, perfectly positioned, the collar actually batting Train in the head a couple of times before he sluggishly reached for it. But he didn't put it on. What was that damned line? He'd just figured it out and now he'd forgotten. He turned around in the water again, looking downstream for the black line. A moment ago, he'd had it, knew what the line was all about. But he couldn't think, all this goddamned noise, that bright light; he couldn't see it, but he could feel something in the water, a different feel, a drumming against his hips and legs that seemed to be in perfect sync with the drumming of his helicopter, his own personal helicopter. Not cold anymore, really. This water's not so bad; it's just so—what? So *wet*, that's what it was, wet, yeah. He laughed, but no sound came out, not with all that damned noise above him. He still held on to the collar. Collar. The drumming feeling was now beginning to overcome the helo noise, and the water was moving faster. He could feel it, a swiftness and a strengthening grip, an embrace as it hurried, hurried—where? Toward the falls. Yeah, that was it.

The *falls*. That black line. The collar jerked in his hands. Put the damn collar on. Why? Hands don't work. This water's not so bad, not so cold. The rumbling was shaking him now, the air different, the spray cloud from the helo above him going somewhere else now, the spotlight more intense.

Put the collar on. You're close. Really goddamned close. Put the collar on. Might be interesting, see what happens. Then amazingly, he felt his boots dragging on the bottom. What the hell? Supposed to be deep out here in the middle. His upper body was being clutched upright by the rushing current, and then he actually heard the throaty roar of falling water. Shocked finally into action, he thrust his head and arms through the collar just as he felt his feet banging up against the lip of the falls. He nearly popped out of the collar with the shock of lift. His shoulder sockets screamed with pain as the winch locked and the helo rose off the river. Fold your arms, he remembered, now on the verge of passing out. Fold your arms under the collar. Then he felt his shoulder bang up against the edge of the skid and a strong, grappling arm was reaching under his sweater for his belt, and then he was sprawling across the cabin floor, sliding along the length of a slippery, wet bag and jointly into the arms of Karen Lawrence and a very excited Doberman. See, he tried to tell them as he passed out, that wasn't so bad.

It was after eleven when the docs were finished with him and McNair was allowed into the hospital room. The Park Police helo had flown them both to the Bethesda Naval Medical Center up on Wisconsin Avenue after finding out they were Navy. Train had tried to talk to Karen before she was whisked off to another room in the ER, but he really hadn't been operating all that well himself. McNair's face was a surprisingly welcome sight.

"Well, G-man," McNair said, pulling up a chair. "They say you're going to live. Feel like talking?"

"Why do I think I'm gonna have to listen first?" Train replied carefully. The skin on his face felt rubbery. His voice was a hoarse croak. He could feel some vestiges of intense cold still lurking in the marrow of his long bones.

"What, you expect me to chew your ass?"

"Yup."

"Consider it chewed. Actually, putting aside the fact that you invaded a crime scene and otherwise messed around with an ongoing police investigation, you did pretty good. We should have left somebody there."

Train shrugged, then regretted it immediately. His shoulders were very sore.

"The sixty-four-thousand-dollar question," Train said, struggling to make his lips work. "Where did that blessed helo come from?"

"Park Police. They own the river, and they have the helicopters and the crews who know how to do water rescue. You two were lucky enough to have a Park Police helicopter already up and operating a possible drowning down at Little Falls dam."

"Man, *lucky* is the word. I need to thank that guy. Is Karen okay? I forgot everything I learned about cold water out there tonight."

"Well, not everything. Yeah, she's gonna be okay. Not harmed physically. Scared shitless, mentally. That was a bad ride she took."

"In a body bag. This guy is a serious whacko."

McNair eased his notebook out of his pocket. "Speaking of whackos," he said. "How many were there? Commander Lawrence says she thinks two, but she never saw them."

"Two," Train said. "I think. It was dark out there, but I'm pretty sure I saw two figures in that boat. They went upriver, by the way."

"Actually, they went *across* the river."

"Huh?"

"To the Maryland side, where they apparently hauled their little bitty boat up to the C&O canal and then shagged ass down the canal, locks and all, back toward Washington. A Washington cop car responded to an intrusion alarm at the Washington Canoe Club and got there in time to see a boat shooting out into the middle of the river under Key Bridge."

"They follow 'em?"

"Hell no. The D.C. harbor police boat was broke-dick at the pier. Busted like everything in the District is these days. So whoever they were got clean-ass away. Commander Lawrence told us something interesting, though, about the initial grab."

"Where did it happen?"

"Down at the barn, like you figured. But she said that she was going into one of the rooms in the barn, and this black glove appeared in front of her face and then a very intense, very bright purple-red flash. Next thing she knew, she was trussed up in that bag. She thinks they took her upstairs to the haystack and carved out a burial chamber in the hay. Anyway, about that light: Any ideas, G-man?"

Train sat back against the pillows for a moment and closed his eyes. "So she was there all the time."

"Apparently. Now about that bright purple-red flash?"

Train hesitated. "That sounds like a retinal disrupter."

McNair's eyes had a speculative look in them. "Come again, Spock?"

"Yeah, I know. I've never seen one, but I've heard of them. It's an optical weapon—like an electronic flash-bang grenade, minus the bang. It emits a blast of light centered on the color frequency of a particular group of rods and cones in the human eye. Puts the brain in stimulus-overload condition. Total disorientation for about a minute. Plenty of time to disable a guy. Or wrap somebody and stuff him in a car, or a bag."

McNair was making notes. "And which government organization carries these nasties?"

"Silly question, Detective."

"I knew that," McNair said. "Okay. Docs say they'll probably let you out after morning rounds. Your dog's down at the Maryland Staties' K-9 unit kennels. That's a barracks out on the Bladensburg Road, and one of my people retrieved your Suburban. It's out front."

"Thanks. Where's Karen?"

"Down the hall, actually. They admitted her. Gave her a sedative, and they've got a shrink laid on for the A.M. Like I said, they didn't hurt her, physically. She must be one self-controlled lady. I'd a gone snakeshit, mummied up like that."

Train shook his head. "Assuming this was Galantz, I've conjured up a theory about why he snatched her."

McNair closed his notebook and raised his eyebrows.

"This guy is after Sherman," Train said. "She's been with Sherman, and he probably thinks they're an item. Maybe he thinks she's Elizabeth Walsh's replacement. Grab her, then lure Sherman to some dark and lonely place. Have some fun with both of them."

McNair grinned at him. "And?"

"And what? What's funny?"

McNair tapped his notebook once with his fingertips and stood up, stretching. "And," he said. "Optical weapons. Telephone bugs with built-in transceivers. Like you said, those are federal toys." He paused. "We found the place up in the haystack where they hid her. Probably hid themselves there, too, all day—the whole time we were there looking. Your theory doesn't read, G-Man. This is a steely-eyed motherfucker. He could have had Sherman's ass anytime he wanted to. You wouldn't be holding back on me by any chance?"

"*Moi?*"

"Yeah, you, G-man. Like, for starters, who was the second guy?"

Train let out a breath and frowned. He kept underestimating McNair. But he was also very reluctant to tell him anything about Jack Sherman. Besides, after what Galantz had done to Karen, Train personally wanted a shot at him.

"I'm not holding back, McNair," he replied. "But my bosses might be. Didn't you tell me you scrubbed Admiral Sherman's personal scene?"

"Yeah. Clean, just like he said. Except that he's now considerably richer than he was. Although it's interesting that two hundred fifty large came and went already."

"The money's gone?"

"Yeah. Says he gave it to some Catholic charity."

Train nodded, thinking about that locked investigation report. "I'm going to pull the same string, but inside Navy channels. I'll share anything I find. Promise." He put a sincere expression on his face, hoping the lie was plausible.

But McNair was shaking his head from side to side in mock wonder. "Sure you will," he said. "Tomorrow's Thursday. How's about we meet, say Friday. Pull it all together."

"We can try," Train said. "My mind has all these earnest plans, but my aging body is probably going to disappoint both of us."

McNair laughed. Then he got up, went to the door, and looked both ways up and down the corridor. He came back over to the bed and pulled Train's Glock and knife out from under his jacket. "Here," he said. "The ER turned these over to us." He gave Train a steady look, one bespeaking years of experience as a cop. He held the gun in his right hand, pointed down toward the floor. Train felt a spike of fear as he looked into McNair's eyes. For just an instant, the friendly detective had been replaced with someone else.

"Keep the Glock handy, G-man," McNair was saying. "Me, personally? I think you're in over your head." He reversed the gun, handed it and the knife to Train, then turned and left the room.

Train lay back on the bed after McNair had gone, the Glock lying cold between his thighs under the covers. Nurse brings a bedpan, he mused, it's gonna be a contest to see who pees first. This thing tonight had been close. If that Park Police helo hadn't been airborne, he would have gone sailing over that dam right behind Karen and spent the next few months rolling around in the rotor at the foot of the diversion dam, along with the six other people who had drowned there in the past year. He wondered how well Karen was bearing up. Let's go find out, he thought.

He opened his eyes and looked around the semiprivate room. The other bed was not in use; the dividing curtain was pulled back against the wall. He wasn't hooked up to anything. He found his clothes, still damp, hanging in the bathroom, but he opted for a dry johnny from the closet. He tucked the Glock and the knife between two towels on the closet shelf and went to find some coffee and then, hopefully, Karen.

Karen lay on her back and listened carefully. A moment ago, there had been a scratching sound on the door to her darkened room, as if something or someone wanted in. A scratching sound, she was sure of it. Her body was tense, almost rigid, but she was very warm, sweaty. She wanted to push her damp hair out of her face, but her arms were leaden. She worried about that sound. She could see a rim of subdued light framing the door to her room, especially at the bottom. She focused on the bottom, watching that line of light. There, a shadow. Then it was gone. She closed her eyes and then opened them again. Everywhere she looked, there was a curious red-purple halo. She had seen that before, but she couldn't remember where. She wanted to close her eyes again, but she was scared she would miss something, whatever had scratched on the door. She stared at the line of light until her eyes hurt, then remembered to breathe.

She should be safe. No more bags. Her skin crawled at just the thought of the word *bag*. Her last memories of the bag were of ice-cold water leaking in from the partially opened zipper when they had thrown her in the river. That utterly helpless feeling of being carried away, down the surging Potomac, toward the cataracts. Wondering if the ominous cold around her lower extremities was water, and if the bag would fill before she got to the falls. In her panic, she had actually managed to rip the tape around her legs, but her hands, her hands had remained stuck. She had rolled and rolled in the water, her face alternately submerged and then free, all for nothing.

There, scratching.

She forced herself to look back down at the line of light along the bottom of the door. And she stopped breathing. There were two black shadows obstructing the line of light. Someone was out there, waiting. Waiting to see if she was awake. Then there was a purple corona of light from the corridor growing all around the door, and someone was pushing it open—a man, dressed in dark clothing, maybe in black. She couldn't quite see his face—all that light from the doorway put him in silhouette—but he was familiar. And he was holding something, something long and shiny, over his left arm, like a big cape. Something familiar. Fabric of some kind. Shiny. She knew what it was but couldn't form the word. Couldn't move as the man came closer, saying something, indistinct at first, but then louder. Whispering it. Raising a black-gloved fist and whispering.

She yelled and woke up, to find that she was sitting on the edge of her bed, bare feet swung out over the cold floor, her body trembling, her hands clutching the sheets along the edge of the bed in a death grip that was hurting her fingers. The room looked as if it would start spinning if she moved another inch.

A dream, she told herself. Just a dream. She looked around carefully. A hospital room. Must be the Naval Hospital in Bethesda. She sank back against the pillows. She felt drugged and dirty. Her face hurt where the tape had been taken off, there was a bump on the side of her head, and there were some sore spots along her left side.

Alive, and lucky not to be on the bottom of the Potomac. Unable to hear anything, she had had no idea of what was happening when the helicopter lifted the bag out of the water, and for one heart-stopping moment she had thought she was in midair, going over the falls. And the incredible relief when she felt the vibrating floor of the aircraft under her, and helping hands peeling her out of that bag. She had torn the tape off her eyes and mouth as soon as her hands were free. The helo crewman had given her a quick once-over, not trying to speak in all the noise roaring through the open hatch, and then he was gone, back out on the skid, holding the rescue cable in one hand and concentrating on something below, something in the glare of large searchlights. She had been stunned when Gutter had come crawling out of nowhere to lick her face, his whole posture one of abject apology. She remembered the noise, the spray billowing up from under the helicopter, looking like white smoke from some awful fire below, the dipping and weaving of the aircraft as the pilot positioned the bouncing machine in one turbulent hover after another, a fleeting glance of rapids and distant black trees over the crewman's shoulder. Now she knew what real terror was like. It was cold, cold in your core, cold that made your insides turn to liquid and your mouth taste like old metal, like right now.

She took a deep breath and got up and ran to the bathroom as a wave of nausea boiled up in her stomach. She barely made it in time. It was several minutes before she was able to get up off her knees, turn on the bathroom lights, and wash her face with hot water. Then she realized there was a shower. She didn't hesitate, shucking her hospital gown and standing in the hot water for a long, long time. When she finally felt clean and her stomach seemed to be relatively calm, she turned the shower off and dried herself. There was a bathrobe on the back of the door, and she put it on and went back to the bed.

There was a knock on her door, low, almost tentative, but definitely someone there. She found herself holding her breath and then saying, "Yes?"

She was vastly relieved to see Train's large gleaming head poke around the door. He had a Styrofoam cup of coffee in his hand, and he was wearing a ridiculously small johnny and white socks. He looked over his shoulder and then edged through the door, which shut behind him.

"Hey, Counselor. You look, um . . . "

"That good, huh, Train?" she replied, trying to follow his lead, keep it light. But it didn't work. She felt her face get rubbery and her eyes filling. And then he was sitting on the edge of her bed and she was in his arms, wailing like a baby while he patted her back and told her that it was all right, that they were safe. When she was finally still, he grabbed a handful of Kleenexes from a box on the bedside table and wiped her eyes and face. Then he kissed her forehead and looked into her eyes. His eyes were luminous. Up close, she saw that he had pronounced crow's-feet in the corners of his eyes. He held her hands in his, and they felt like two warm, calloused paws.

"Wanted to do that for a good long time," he said. "Under better circumstances, of course."

"These are pretty good circumstances, considering," she replied. Then she reached for his face and gave him a long, lingering kiss on the lips. She felt him stir in response, but then she sensed that he was imposing control on himself. She felt slightly embarrassed as they stopped, feeling as if she should look away, but for some reason, she couldn't. The affection in his eyes was right out there, fully visible. She tried to summon up that demure look-away expression, the one she'd used to deflect the interest in men's eyes since Frank had died, but she couldn't find it, and suddenly she didn't want to. Train must have sensed what was going on in her mind, because he put a finger up to her lips. "Slowly," he whispered. "Let's not screw this up."

She smiled at him and reached for his hands again. "No, let's not," she said. "I've been in limbo for a while, Train. Observing all the proper conventions. But after tonight . . . well, I don't want to put off life or living anymore."

He nodded his understanding. There was a rattle of some kind of trolley outside in the hallway, and he stood up to pull a chair right next to her bed. "Considering the circumstances, neither one of us should ever go to Vegas. We used up every ounce of luck tonight, and then some. So, tell me what happened."

They exchanged stories. As she began hers, he extended the coffee cup and she sipped some and then handed it back. He drank some while he listened, an unconscious small intimacy, which she registered even while she was talking. When she had finished, he just sat there, his face grim. She realized he felt responsible.

"I know. I should have taken the dog," she said.

He nodded absently. "And I should have trusted my instincts and gone out there when I first thought about it. Oh well."

"We've got to talk to Sherman," she said urgently. "About what his son said. There were two of them."

Train got up and went to the window. At the moment, he was sick of the Sherman business. What he really wanted to do was take her in his arms and hold her for the rest of the night. He rotated the venetian blinds. Karen's room had the same view of the same parking lot, which was still nearly empty. There was a hint of fog hovering over the expanse of grass beyond the parking lot. Three hospital corpsmen in their orderly uniforms were smoking cigarettes out under the ER portico.

"I think we have to talk to Carpenter first," he replied. "McCarty's orders were pretty specific. Back off the Sherman matter. I don't know if that's because you had gone missing or if those were orders from Carpenter given *before* you went missing. Either way, Sherman is being isolated."

"Sherman is getting the shaft," she said, sitting up straighter in the bed.

She was silent for a moment. "On the other hand, it got awfully up close and personal today." She was starting to feel cold again. "Train."

He turned around.

"Will you sit with me for a while? I don't want to think about this case right now. I want to make it all go away until I can see sunlight again. I—"

He shushed her, going back over to the chair next to her bed. He sat down and smoothed her hair. "Let's kill all these lights. You sleep. I'll be right here."

She hit the switches for the lights, which left only the subdued rose-colored light from the parking lot suffusing the room. Karen shut her eyes and pulled up the covers, leaving her hands clenched up under her chin. He put his hand on her forehead again and smoothed her hair back away from her brow. She reached for his hand and clasped it between her own until her breathing slowed.

He watched her sleep. He was surprised to find himself fantasizing: If he was married to a woman like this, would he ever wake up at night and just watch her sleep? He thought he might. Then he smiled in the darkness. Married? The lady had been widowed for only a year. She was just feeling grateful, that's all.

He got up and pulled down a blanket and a pillow from the closet shelf and laid them out on the chair. Then he went over to the window again and looked out. It was now almost 2:00 A.M., and the parking lot was practically deserted. He stepped back over to check on Karen. She was still sleeping, her hands clutching the covers up under her chin, her breathing deep and regular now. Maybe the sedative had finally taken effect. He sat down in the chair next to her bed and pulled up the blanket. Was this place safe? he wondered. Should he wake her and get them out of there? He decided against it. He looked over at her sleeping face again. You predicted something was going to happen, and it did. Galantz had made a move against them. And Carpenter was losing his nerve, it seemed. Train slept.

CHAPTER 10

By 11:30 Thursday morning, Train and Karen were sitting in Admiral Carpenter's outer office, awaiting an audience. Train had called McCarty at seven o'clock to give him a quick debrief of the previous day's events. McCarty had seen a short article in the morning paper about a rescue out on the river, but there had been no names. He was stunned into silence when Train gave him the details. Train also told him they needed to talk to the JAG. They would spend the morning getting released from the hospital, get Karen home for a change of clothes, and then come in to the Pentagon, he said. Train lived too far south of the city to bother going home, so he was sitting there in his suit, the jacket of which was reasonably presentable. The rest of his outfit had been attracting careful glances all morning.

Karen was properly dressed, if a little pale around the edges. He had to work at it not to take her hand right there in the front office. She had seemed steady enough until the yeoman handed her a cup of coffee, and Train caught the little ripples in it when she held the cup with both hands. He watched her out of the corner of his eye. She's solidified on the surface, he thought, but underneath she's still scared. Hell, so am I. Karen stared across the office area as officers and clerks came and went. "This has gotten way out of hand," she said softly.

"That's what we're here to tell the JAG," Train replied.

The door to Carpenter's office opened, and Captain Pennington came out. Captain McCarty was standing behind him in the doorway. Pennington looked briefly at both Karen and Train, his face neutral. He nodded curtly but did not say hello, then left the office.

"Uh-oh," muttered Karen as they got up. "That's not a good sign." But McCarty was beckoning them into the admiral's office. He wrinkled his nose at Train's clothes as they went in. Admiral Carpenter was standing by one of the windows, his back to them. McCarty shut the door and cleared his throat. They all stood in the middle of the room for a moment before Carpenter turned around.

"Karen," he said. "I am so glad you're back among us. You gave us all quite a scare."

"Nothing like the scare they gave me, Admiral," she replied. Train felt a flush of pride at her quick comeback. If they were going to be yelled at, she was showing no timidity.

But Carpenter did not appear to be angry. "Please, sit down," he said. "You, too, Train. I've just been on the horn with Detective McNair, who told us some of what happened yesterday. We didn't learn any of this until this morning. McNair said he didn't see the need to wake people up. I guess he was never in the Navy."

"It was a seriously long day, Admiral," Train said. "And now I think we need to revisit the guidance."

"You do, do you?" Carpenter said with a faint smile as he sat down. "Can't imagine why. According to McNair, you did some amazing things out on that river."

"Admiral, whoever this is, he's not messing around. One, probably two homicides, a kidnapping, and attempted homicide. I think this thing has expanded well past Admiral Sherman's involvement."

"Just so," Carpenter murmured, staring at Train over steepled fingers. Both Train and Karen looked at each other.

"Admiral," Karen said, "what is Admiral Sherman's status?"

"Admiral Sherman has been given temporary administrative duty as the president of a selection board."

"So he's not on some kind of admin leave or even suspension?" Train asked.

"No. Whoever gave you that idea?"

Karen looked down at the floor. Train pressed ahead. "Can I suggest a meeting?" Train said. "I think he needs to know what's happened to Karen, and perhaps some other things as well."

Carpenter looked over at McCarty, who nodded imperceptibly. "There is a small problem with that," Carpenter said. "No one actually seems to know where Admiral Sherman is at the moment."

Karen and Train stared at him.

"Indeed. When Karen went missing, someone from the police attempted to contact Admiral Sherman to see what, if anything, he knew, or even if she might be with him." Train saw Karen color slightly at this comment. The admiral continued.

"The OP-32 front office told them he was on leave, which is what they've been instructed to say, of course. But then this morning, the secretary of the selection board called into OP-32 and asked where he was, since the board could not convene without him. Thirty-two Acting called us, but we're in the dark, too."

Train leaned forward. "Admiral, Detective McNair told me yesterday that the Fairfax County Police Department was being pressured by someone to move slowly with this investigation. Do you know why, and who might be doing the pressuring?"

"I have no idea," Carpenter replied, looking from one to the other with a sincerely neutral expression, as if daring either one of them to challenge what he had just said. Train thought of a hundred things to say, including reminding the admiral of their earlier words on this subject, but it was pretty obvious that something had changed and the admiral wasn't going to talk about it. After a few seconds of silence, Carpenter got up and walked around to his desk.

"I think it is indeed time to review your tasking. Both of your taskings, for that matter. Karen, I think Admiral Sherman, wherever he might be at the moment, has problems that are beyond the scope of your initial tasking. I want you to resume your normal duties in Investigations Review."

Karen's expression registered protest, and she looked over at Train as if for support. But Train was studying Carpenter.

"Mr. von Rensel," Carpenter asked, "you remember those things I was *going to* order you *not* to do, when we last discussed this matter?"

"Yes, sir, but—"

Carpenter cut him off. "Right. Execute. The other thing I told you that I *did* want you to do remains in effect."

Train was momentarily baffled. "The other thing." Then he remembered. Keep Karen safe. "Oh, right," he said.

"Good. I don't think we need to discuss this matter any further. Karen, you've been through a truly harrowing experience. I suggest you take a couple of days' leave. In fact, I insist on it. You, too, Mr. von Rensel. How about we see you both back here, say Monday? You've both been through a lot."

"What about Admiral Sherman?" Karen protested. "What do we do if he gets in touch with us?"

"Refer any calls from Admiral Sherman to my office. Captain Pennington will be instructing the IR yeomen to do the same."

Then McCarty was standing up, indicating the meeting was over. The admiral looked at both of them as they stood before his desk. "I'm sure it hasn't escaped your attention that there are currents in this case moving above your respective pay grades, as the saying goes. Above my pay grade, for that matter. You both did well. You two were very lucky yesterday. Now I think it's time to observe the golden rule about following orders when you don't understand the reasons behind those orders: You must assume your boss knows something you don't, okay? Captain McCarty will let you know if there are any new developments. Thank you both. That's all."

After the door closed behind Karen and Train, Admiral Carpenter instructed his yeoman to hold all calls. He then went to his computer desk and entered the JAG archive system. A minute later, the Rung Sat incident investigation report was on the screen. He read through the by-now-familiar findings of fact, opinions, and then the all-important endorsements. The archive files were, by law, read-only files. He cursed his JAG forebear who'd put that restrictive protocol into the system. Access could be controlled, but content could not be modified. Well, that would never do, he thought with a sigh. He dispatched the file back to the mainframe over in the Navy Yard across the river, and the screen settled into an undulating helix screen-saver routine.

But then he had an idea. It was a program protocol preventing anyone from altering data. Maybe, with the right kind of help, he could change the protocol, or perhaps inhibit it long enough to make one small change. He thought of the dour Kensington. Okay, two small changes—if he's nice to me. And he thought he knew right where he might get some help of that kind.

He picked up his secure phone and autodialed the DNI's office. The EA patched him in to the admiral.

"Yes, Thomas?"

"Subject is the flag officer in difficulty."

"No, Thomas, I rather think the subject is larger than that."

Carpenter, surprised, said nothing for a moment. "Okay. I'll grant you that. I want to make a deal with those people."

"Oh, they love deals. What's yours?"

"They want us out of their sweeper problem, presumably so they'll have a clear field of fire. I'm ready to accommodate them. But, in return, I want two things. The first is a complication with which I need some technical help."

"What kind of help, exactly?"

"I need the services of a hacker, a really good hacker."

It was Mallory's turn to be silent. "Do I want to know the details of this, um, complication, Thomas?"

"You do not."

"Didn't think so. And the second thing?"

"I want their guarantee that nothing bad will happen to my two people, because if something bad does happen, I'll be forced to tell the whole world. But you can also tell them that, as a measure of my good intentions, I've sent the two of them home for a long weekend, with orders to stay there."

"All right. Back to this complication. It bears on your flag officer's problem?"

"He's got new problems. No, this is much more important."

"Very well. I'll transmit the message." There was a pause on the line. "If I may ask, Thomas, are you sure you know what you're doing here?"

It was a question made just possible by that minute difference in seniority. Carpenter was not permitted to take offense.

"I sure hope so, Kyle," he said. "But a lot of it depends on how quickly they solve their problem. And after what this guy did last night, sooner would be a whole lot better than later. You can tell them that if you want to. Don't forget my conditions."

He hung up the phone and dabbed the sheen of perspiration off his forehead. This could *not* come out—not now, not ever. It would mean the end of his career, not to mention the field day the press would have with it. Why in the hell hadn't those people moved against this Galantz? What were they waiting for? The simplest and therefore the most likely answer that suggested itself didn't help his disposition: They didn't know where he was.

Karen and Train walked side by side back to IR, saying nothing. Captain Pennington was not in evidence when they reached the office. Two of the IR lawyers were outlining a case on the whiteboard, and the yeoman was threatening the copy machine with bodily harm as he tried to unjam the paper tray. Karen automatically went to her cubicle to check her voice mail. The yeoman, seeing Train, gave up on the copy machine with one last, vengeful kick and then brought Train a computer diskette.

"This came in from NIS this morning," he said.

Train thanked him and dropped the diskette on his desk. It had to be the hard copy of the database screen on Jack Sherman. He sat down and checked his own voice mail. There was one message, from Captain McCarty: "The admiral thinks it might be a good idea if Karen stays somewhere else than at her home in Great Falls for a while. See what you can do about that." Train replayed the message and checked the time stamp. The message had been recorded as they had been walking down the hall from the JAG front office, which meant McCarty had not wanted to say that in front of Karen. As he was clearing it, Karen was walking over with a yellow phone-message memo in her hand. She had a strange look on her face.

"What's the matter?" he asked.

"I just listened to a message," she replied. "From Galantz." Her eyes were a little white around the edges. Train quickly got up, looked around, and then steered Karen into the small IR conference room and closed the door.

"How do you know? What did he say?" he asked.

"It was on voice mail. It was—it was the same voice as on the phone Monday night."

"Damn. Did you save it?"

"Yes. But that voice, it's hardly human."

"So much for voiceprints. What did he say?"

She consulted the message slip. "He spoke my name. He said that I was lucky last night but that I would have to be lucky every time, and that he had to be lucky only one time."

The Irish Republican Army rule, Train thought. Man had a way with words. He took a deep breath and then exhaled. "Look," he said, "I've got to go ransom Gutter, preferably before the afternoon rush hour. Why don't you come with me. I can take you home right after that. It's on the way."

But Karen was shaking her head, her face turned away to conceal her fear. "I don't want to go home just now," she said. "Not after yesterday. Not after this." She waved the yellow slip.

Train seized on what she had just said to follow through on McCarty's suggestion. "Okay, look. I've got a six-bedroom house down in Aquia. It's a pretty secure situation. There's even a housekeeper. You're welcome to hole up there for as long as you want. Or until we sort this business out. Unless you have—"

"That would be fine," she said quickly, surprising him again. She turned away from him, her hands fluttering. "Train, I'm scared," she said. "It embarrasses me, but there it is. After everything that happened yesterday, and now with Admiral Sherman missing . . . There were two of them yesterday, at least down by the river. That means that Galantz—if that's who this is— has help. I know they're watching me. They can get in and out of houses like smoke. They—"

He realized that she was starting to unravel, her eyes shooting from side to side and her voice rising. Finally, he just reached for her, turning her around and pulling her gently into his arms as she stifled a cry. He stood there holding her, patting her on the back while she let it out, babbling through a stream of tears, her words becoming incoherent, her breasts heaving against his chest and her shoulders trembling. He comforted her and held her for a few minutes until she became still. Then, with an embarrassed expression on her face, she backed away, pushing her hair out of her tear-streaked face. Her skin was blotched with patches of red, and mascara had run down her cheek on one side. She saw his look and put a hand up to her face.

"I'm so sorry, I don't know what's the matter with me. Of course I can go home. I don't have to bother—"

"No way. You're coming home with me," he said. "The hell of it is you're right. This guy has been able to do anything he damn well pleases. There's no way you should be alone, especially isolated in Great Falls. Besides—"

"What?" she asked, pulling a Kleenex out of her skirt pocket and wiping her cheek.

"Besides, that's my tasking. Or what's left of it. The one Carpenter wouldn't say out loud when he started speaking in tongues back there."

"Train, what are you talking about?" That suspicious look was back in her eye.

"My tasking, and these are the Great Man's very words, is to keep Karen Lawrence safe."

"And what was that other business, the things he was *going to* order you *not* to do?"

"Finding Galantz and interfering in anyone else's efforts to find Galantz."

She sat down, continuing the damage control on her makeup. "Are we just going to quit? Let Sherman swing in the wind?"

"No. Galantz almost got us both killed last night. I take that personally."

She nodded but said nothing for a moment. "I guess I feel the same way," she said. "But after that, that bag, I'm not as confident as you are. We should also remember what Admiral Carpenter said: Sometimes we have to assume our boss knows what he's doing with this thing."

Train shook his head. "If he or any of these admirals knew what they were doing with this case, last night wouldn't have happened. I don't think they *do* know what they're doing. I think they're flailing, hoping like hell it will all just go away. That the people who created this monster will clean it up sooner rather than later."

"But if Galantz is out to ruin Sherman, why in the hell would he be trying to kill me?"

"I don't think he intended to kill you. Just take you off the boards. It wasn't until I showed up that you went in the river. I thought it was because he thinks you're close to Sherman, Karen. But the attack on you happened after we talked to Jack Sherman. There has to be a tie-in there, somewhere, somehow. I say let's go back and squeeze that punk again. He lives near Triangle—that's not far from my place in Aquia. Nobody's given me orders about Sherman's son."

"Spoken like a true sea lawyer," she said.

"Yeah, well. So let's go get my dog out of hock."

It was six on the nose when Train turned in through the tall brick gates of the von Rensel estate. Karen, following in her Explorer, stared in appreciative silence as they drove up along a curving gravel drive bordered by ancient river oaks overlooking a wide expanse of lawn. Beyond a low brick wall at the far edge of the lawn, the Potomac River glinted in the evening sun, almost a mile wide. Ahead, a moderately sized two-story white house surrounded by columned porches appeared from behind massive boxwood hedges.

"Wow," she said to herself. Train had told her a little bit about the family property on the way out to retrieve Gutter, but this was obviously something very special. She was suddenly glad she had asked Train to take her by the house in Great Falls to get some more clothes and her car. As they pulled up in front of the house, they were met by a slim Japanese man, who came over to her car and opened her door, bowing politely. Karen got out and bowed back, and Train introduced her to Hiroshi. She was struck by the enormous physical contrast between them, the tree-sized Train and the slim but wiry Hiroshi, who could have been anywhere from fifty to seventy years old. She could see at once that there was a very special bond between them.

Hiroshi extracted her bag and hanging gear, gave Train's disheveled clothes a lifted eyebrow, and went up the steps. Train then introduced Karen to Hiroshi's wife, Kyoko, who was waiting on the front porch. Kyoko took Karen inside and showed her upstairs to one of the guest rooms to freshen up. Train went to his own room on the riverfront side of the house and changed into clean clothes. Then he went looking for Hiroshi. He found him in the back pantry, doctoring Gutter's leg, and told him about the events of the preceding night. He explained that Commander Lawrence would be staying with them for a few days. Hiroshi, ever the great conversationalist, nodded once and continued his examination of the dog.

Train left him to it and went back in time to meet Karen as she came downstairs. He gave her a tour of the downstairs of the house. "About half the house dates back to the 1790s," he told her. "This is one of two reception rooms. Sort of eclectic in style, after many generations of taste and circumstances. Started out as a smaller copy of Mount Vernon, up the river, and then it was modified several times through the years. It's not that big, really."

"How did your family come to have this land?"

"The first von Rensel came to the United States in the retinue of the Baron von Steuben. By the end of the American Revolution, he had risen sufficiently in General Washington's esteem to be granted a four-hundred-acre parcel of land downriver from Mount Vernon. My family alternated between prosperity and near financial ruin over the generations, but a strict observance of the rule of primogeniture ensured that the original land grant survived intact well into the twentieth century, when my grandfather Heinrich finally seized the opportunity to turn four hundred acres of riverfront property into a secure family fortune. These are the original kitchens."

"This place has four hundred acres?" she asked.

"Not anymore. Heinrich struck an adept political deal with the local county government that basically secured the serenity of the family estate.

In return for the sale of the remaining acres of riverside lands to the county for a park, the county agreed never to permit development of that land. By the time I was born, only ten walled acres and the house remained of the original eighteenth-century plantation, along with a structure of family trusts, which pays for all this."

Later, over a simple dinner served by Kyoko on the screened porch, he told her some more about his own upbringing. She was curious about Hiroshi and his wife. Train told her the story of how the couple had come to Aquia.

"Before my mother died in 1959, my parents maintained a pretty full social schedule up in Washington. They kept a town house up in Georgetown and used this place for the weekends. My father had British ideas about raising a son, I think. I was a lot closer to Hiroshi and Kyoko after my mother died. When both my parents were gone, I made it clear that they were expected to stay on in their retirement years."

"I'll bet Kyoko wonders when you're going to get married," Karen said with a mischievous smile.

"Wonders and occasionally nags, in her own incredibly polite way," Train said, returning that smile. Then he surprised himself.

"Tell me about Frank," he said. "I sense a loose end there."

She looked away for a moment, long enough to take a deep breath. "Yes, there is." She told him the story, faltering when she came to the part about where he had been when his heart killed him, and the possible reasons why.

"I'm still torn about it," she said. "I think he loved me. He was certainly a loving man. And you've seen the house, the nice cars, all of that. And yet . . ."

He nodded slowly. "Now you wonder if you should pull that scab until you find the truth, or leave it be and get on with your life."

"Yes, exactly."

"Advice?"

She looked at him expectantly.

"You had ten years. If he was unfaithful, he cared enough about you to keep it very discreet. You seemed to have been good friends as well as husband and wife. He left you more than well provided for. There are worse men than that."

She nodded, visibly stifling a few dozen *buts*.

"And there are better men than that, too, Karen."

She was about to reply to that when Kyoko came in to remove the plates. Suddenly, Train was yawning. His yawn immediately triggered hers.

"Tree time in the jungle, I think," she said.

"Tell Kyoko if you need anything," Train said, standing. "Breakfast at eight, okay? Then we can kick around next steps."

"Make it nine," she replied, yawning again. "I think I'm going to sleep forever. And I assume next steps include going back to see Jack Sherman, right?" she asked.

"Yes, only this time I'm going to get some answers out of him that make sense."

"How, by beating him up again?"

"I didn't beat him up. He walked away."

She gave him an arch look. "Maybe this time let me do the talking," she said, getting up. "Remember, the objective is to find out what's going on."

Train was suddenly too tired to argue. They said good night. Kyoko led Karen upstairs, and Train headed for the library. He was exhausted but too wound up for sleep. He decided to get a brandy and review the NIS file before turning in. He was just putting away the decanter of Armagnac when Hiroshi appeared in the doorway.

"Hiroshi-san," Train said as the old man came into the study. They exchanged bows, and Hiroshi sat down on the front three inches of one of the upholstered chairs, his back straight as a board and his hands folded politely in his lap.

"So, I need to tell you what's going on." Train said.

"This is a serious matter?" Hiroshi asked.

Train knew that Hiroshi would never have dreamed of coming right out with a direct question unless he was very concerned. "Very serious, Hiroshi-san. There have been two murders. A senior naval officer is being made to look like a murderer by a man from his past. It appears to be a matter of revenge for something that happened in Vietnam many years ago. The lady upstairs, Commander Lawrence, was assigned to find out if the accusations were true. I was assigned to help her. Because she became involved, she became a target, too. She cannot be safe until the man behind all this is captured, or killed."

"It is a killing matter?"

"It is for one of the government agencies involved. But the matter is complicated by the fact that some government agencies are at war with one another. I think one agency might be trying to gain advantage over the other by exploiting this matter. This man is something like a ninja who is no longer under control."

"Ah," Hiroshi said. Ninja, he understood.

"But my military superiors have told me not to pursue this man, and not to interfere in the pursuit efforts of others," Train continued. "My military superiors are apparently willing to sacrifice the senior officer in order to avoid having the Navy involved in yet another scandal."

"Does this senior officer agree to the sacrifice?"

"No. He feels it is unfair. But in a certain sense, he is not blameless, either. And now there are indications that his son may be involved in this matter. Exactly how, I don't know. And to cap it off, the senior officer has disappeared, which will probably renew suspicion against him. It is very complicated."

Hiroshi thought about all this. "What will you do?" he asked.

"There are some aspects to this case that don't make sense," Train replied. "Commander Lawrence feels the senior officer is being unfairly set up, and I'm beginning to agree with her. We plan to talk to the senior officer's son."

"Will he talk to you?"

"One way or another, he will. We think he was involved in what happened last night. And if he was, then maybe we can expose at least him to the police, which might then force the Navy to do the right thing by the senior officer."

Hiroshi thought about that for a moment. Then, as usual, he came back to the real issue. "But what of the ninja who seeks revenge?"

"His own superiors are supposedly hunting him. But if he comes after me, or, more importantly, after Karen Lawrence, I'll do whatever it takes to keep her safe."

Hiroshi thought some more about it. "And if you remove this man, would this not please your superiors? As well as all the other superiors who want to find this man?"

Train grinned. "You have, as usual, hit the nail on the head. I thought that's what my boss had in mind. He may yet want that, but he is not permitted to say it."

"Your boss is a most devious boss," Hiroshi observed, getting up. "I will release the night dogs now. When will you leave in the morning?"

"Around ten or so. I'll need time to go over my plans with Commander Lawrence. And I badly need some real sleep."

Hiroshi nodded again. "This woman has no husband?" he asked.

"He died about a year ago. She remains sad."

Hiroshi cleared his throat.

"What?" Train asked.

"Kyoko says not that sad."

Train eyed the old man. "Don't you start, Hiroshi."

"Kyoko says Train-sama must open his eyes. Hiroshi says Kyoko is interfering old woman. Hiroshi says—"

"Hiroshi says good night."

There was the barest hint of a smile on the old man's lips. "Hiroshi says good night, Train-sama."

Train smiled to himself as the old man closed the double doors behind him. Kyoko had been after Train to get a wife for about ten years now, and old Hiroshi had probably been threatened with severe chastisement if he failed to pass along her message about Karen. *Not that sad.* He chuckled. Then he put in the diskette and forced his weary eyes to focus on the screen.

He had to enter a standard NIS access code and then his personal security identifier code before the file would open.

The file began with a biographic history. John Lee Sherman. Lee and Sherman, now there was an interesting apposition of last names. Born in San Diego, California, 11 January 1967. Parents William Taggart Sherman, Marcia Kendall, aka Beth Sherman. There followed a laundry list of residences tracking the admiral's duty stations, and a schools list, which terminated in 1986 with graduation from Washington and Lee High School. A homeboy. Right here in the Washington area.

The military service section picked up the bio. Enlisted in the Marines at Quantico, Virginia, on 5 December 1987. Four months of basic at Parris Island, three months of advanced infantry training at Lejeune, and then joins the recon battalion. Well, well, well. The recon battalion was the Marine Corps version of Special Forces troops. Kid must have done exceptionally well to be picked up right out of the training pipe. When Train had been in the Corps, you couldn't even apply for recon until you'd served successfully in the Fleet Marine Force for at least a year. And yet his father had said the kid got into the Corps via what the recruiters euphemistically used to call "a judicial referral." That didn't square with the elite recon assignment. So, young Jack must have had either a unique skill set or a unique personality. Train was ready to bet on the personality. He scrolled down to the discharge info. Hello. A bad-conduct discharge in January 1990. That meant a special court-martial and something relatively serious.

He scrolled up and checked out the last physical description in the bio: five-seven, black hair and brown eyes, 155 pounds. That was still pretty accurate, even now, except for that scraggly beard. He yawned and had to blink his eyes to keep them focused. Got to get some sleep.

The physical description dated back to Jack's graduation from boot camp. A little guy, by Marine Corps standards. And yet his pack and gear would have weighed more than one-third of his own body weight, so a very strong little guy. *Little* was the wrong word; *wiry* better described it. He paged down to the section on criminal records, which was in two parts, preenlistment and then the subsequent civilian entries. Sure enough, there was his teenage track record, with three arrests, one for breaking and entering, one for drunk and disorderly, one for possession. But no convictions. Three arrests in two years, but no convictions. A snitch maybe? His father said he ran with bad company. Maybe a gang. He windowed further into the arrest record and looked for adjudication codes. PB—plea bargain on the last arrest, the B and E beef. Off to the county boot camp. From the police boot camp to the Marine boot camp, which might explain why he had done well. Already knew how to say, "Sir, yes, sir!" at the top of his lungs. "What's the right answer, maggot?" "Sir, anything you say it is, sir!" A genius-level recruit by Corps standards.

He sat back from the screen. A high school grad, but with marginal grades. Three arrests, low-life punk type, goes to police boot camp. That in itself was a little strange, given his age, which had to have been around nineteen. Then he gets into the Corps. Thirty years ago, he could have accepted that on face value. But this had happened in 1987, and things had become a whole hell of a lot more selective by 1987. Even with his old man pulling a few strings, this just didn't sound like the kind of guy the Corps wanted.

He screened up the military record. The Page Thirteen showed assignments and promotions. Boot camp. Advanced training. He had joined the recon battalion in the fall of 1988. Promoted one pay grade June 1989. BCD seven months later. The Page Thirteen had an entry listing the special court-martial but not the charges and specs. JAG records ought to have that. Maybe Karen could get them. He thought about it. If a guy didn't work out in the recon force, he'd be shipped back to the FMF until his hitch was up. But this had to involve more than just a misfit. A special court-martial, and a poisonous discharge paper that he would carry around for the rest of his life.

And there was the post-enlistment civilian arrest record. Possession of marijuana. DUI and speeding on a motorcycle. A second DUI charge that was later dropped due to contested evidence. An assault charge, dropped because the complainant had failed to appear in court. Regular pond slime, our boy Jack. But all low-level stuff.

Train considered the current address. Most of the Cherry Hill area overlooked the Potomac, separated from the river itself by the main north-south line of the railroad that serviced Washington.

He closed the file and shut down the PC. He rubbed his eyes and then looked at his watch. It was well after eleven. Suddenly, he was very sleepy. He tried to conceptualize a pattern out of the file on Jack Sherman, but nothing surfaced. The admiral had told them he divorced his wife in 1981, when Jack would have been just entering high school. Mother a drunk, kid in the full emotional flame of male adolescence, and Pop bails to save his career. Good recipe for producing a bent kid. Yeah, like you know anything about it. Still, Sherman had achieved the pinnacle of his profession, admiral's stars, while his wife ended up eating a gun and his only son was probably hustling pot to the riffraff who hung around the main gates of the Quantico base. And even those brand-new stars hadn't saved Sherman the moment there was a whiff of scandal. That exclusive club he'd been dying to join for so many years was apparently ready to deep-six him.

Or were they? Carpenter had assigned Karen Lawrence and Train von Rensel to run some cover for him, or at least until Karen's abduction. Then the tasking had become ambiguous, as if Carpenter was suddenly scared of something more than just bad press for the Navy. Now Sherman was apparently missing, but Carpenter and company didn't seem very concerned about that. There had to be something they knew—some bits of privileged information flickering around that famous flag-protection circuit—that Carpenter, for some odd reason, wasn't going to share with them.

He stared at the glowing embers in the fireplace while Gutter snored quietly in the corner of the study. The hot coals swam in and out of focus. This whole case was being expertly steered into a box canyon of some kind. Surely McNair and the Fairfax police had access to the same kinds of information NIS did. So why hadn't they found Jack? Who was telling them to back out, and why were they so willing to go along? Local cops hated federal interference. And there was the FBI, fence-sitting, trying to decide between helping out and letting the agency they loved to hate get another political black eye.

He kept coming back to Carpenter. What did that wily old man really want them to do?

He stretched at his desk, then immediately regretted it. His shoulder muscles were sore as hell from the helo hoist, and his right leg had the makings of a really good charley horse. Then another thought struck him: If they weren't supposed to go after Galantz, did that perhaps mean Carpenter expected Galantz to come after them? Take Karen somewhere safe. And do what? Wait. Wait for Galantz to come to them. And when he does . . . what? Were they bait now?

He shook his head. He was missing something here. But more than anything, he was too tired to think. It was time to climb up in his tree and get some desperately needed sleep.

He got up to close the screen and glass doors on the fire, considered going upstairs, then flopped down on the big leather couch instead. His last thoughts before drifting off were about Karen.

Karen woke up, to find herself actually out of the bed and standing in a corner of the guest room, her heart pounding. She couldn't remember the dream, other than having a desperate desire to run. She listened for signs of life downstairs, but the house was silent except for the occasional creaks and cracks of an old house's bones. Her nightgown was soaked with perspiration from the nightmare. She took it off and went into the bathroom, where she used a wet washcloth to sponge away the film of fear. She appropriated a terry-cloth bathrobe hanging on the back of the bathroom door and went back to sit on the edge of the bed, where she stared through the sheer curtains covering the window. There appeared to be a heavy fog or mist outside that hid even the big trees surrounding the house.

She wondered where Train was. Down the hall? She had been so sleepy at dinner, but now she was afraid to go back to sleep, even though her eyes were aching. She recalled his words at dinner: that there are worse men;

there are better men. She would never quell the bitter coil of anger at the fact that Frank had cheated on her. And yet, as a philosophy for the rest of her life, the "better men" thesis would be a hell of lot more productive.

She eased the bedroom door open and went downstairs, walking on tiptoes past the other bedroom doors along the hall on her way there. There was a single night-light on in the main hall, and light showing through the open study doors. She was halfway into the room when she realized Train was asleep on the couch. He was on his back, his massive hands folded on his chest. She walked over to the couch, silent as a ghost in her bare feet, and watched him for a minute. His face looked younger in repose, the lines and furrows in his face less pronounced. She spied the brandy decanter across the room, walked over and poured a small measure into a snifter, took a sip, and made a face. Strong stuff, whatever it was.

She went back, sat down on the floor next to the couch, and breathed in the aroma of the Armagnac. So what are we doing here? she asked herself. You know full well what you're doing here. You've had the stew scared out of you and now you want a man, a big strong man, to hold you and love you and make it all go away, if only for a while. That's silly. That stereotype went out the window a long time ago. Oka-a-y-y, so maybe *he'd* like someone to hold him, love him, and make it all go away. Look at the lines on his face, the bags under his eyes. The poor beast is exhausted. Hell, we're both exhausted.

She smiled to herself in the darkness. All these rules. You're forty-four years old. Just exactly how long do you plan to abide by other people's rules? Frank is gone. They had had ten years, and if he had been unfaithful, he'd at least been discreet about it. And he'd been a pretty good provider. This Sherman mess was going to come to a head of some kind, probably behind some closed flag office doors, and then what? She would be leaving the Navy and the career and all the rest of it.

She watched him sleeping, then just let her thoughts wander for a while—about her life, choices made and avoided, her ten years with Frank. She thought about this mess with Sherman. Behind the applause of flag selection, what a shambles that poor man had made of his life. Some things of value. It was ironic that Galantz seemed to have a better appreciation for which things really were of value in this life. She looked back at Train, and was surprised to find him awake and watching her.

"Did you swipe my Armagnac?" he asked.

"Not guilty. Fetched my own."

"Anything else I can do for you, Counselor?"

She looked right at him, touching him with her eyes, and then he was swinging himself off the couch and up into a sitting position, lifting her to him, kissing her hard, no more control now, just a hungry wanting that lit her up from one end to the other like a tungsten filament. They kissed while working hurriedly on each other's robes, and then he stretched out full length on his back and pulled her up onto his body. She arched her back as he explored with his hands and his lips, and then she did some exploring of her own, stopping, almost alarmed, when she realized how big he was. She swallowed hard.

He pulled her knees forward, lifting her hips, kissing her breasts, letting her labia rub along the full length of him, keeping it flat against his belly until she started to tremble uncontrollably with her own desire.

"You do it, Karen," he whispered. "Go slow."

She leaned all the way forward and reached behind her to guide him in, moaning when she felt his heat begin to fill her up while she lifted and then pushed backward, slowly, but seemingly forever, her belly fusing finally with his. He didn't move, just let her absorb him without discomfort, and then he was unfolding her legs backward, stretching her out full length on top of him. And then he did move, slowly, carefully, until she responded, and then, the first time, it went fast, very fast, her fingers clawing at the leather of the couch, his hands bouncing her hips harder and harder as she climbed the mountain, until she stopped, her breath caught in her throat, her whole physical being suffused with the power of her climax.

She collapsed over him, muscles humming, the edges of a cramp in her legs, her breath shuddering out of her in sobbing gusts until she was able to get it under control. He was still inside, still hard, and she was almost afraid to move. But then he was pulling her knees up again, gently lifting her into a straddling position on his hips, his big hands on her breasts, massaging them, rolling her nipples through his fingers while he moved inside of her, going deeper, the flat, hard muscles of his groin pressing harder and harder against her own, summoning the fire again. As she felt him rising to his own climax, she took over, driving the rhythm while watching him though slitted eyes, her hair damp and hanging down over her forehead, the taste of sweat and his hot kisses in her mouth as she rocked above him, locking him in and going faster, feeling his hands go weak and then his breath catching, his hips lifting up in one powerful deep thrust that felt as if it would split her in two as he came, filling her belly with an intense warmth.

She leaned forward when he was spent, keeping him inside, and kissed his face, his lips, his chin, his lips again, whispering to him while he stroked her back and her hips with his hands. She stretched out full length on top of his body, with his arms wrapped tight around her. After a little while, he suggested they go upstairs to his room.

"What are your intentions, kind sir?" she asked, reaching for the robe.

"Whatever my lawyer recommends, Counselor. Unless you're out of ideas."

"Silly man," she said. "What a silly man. Only you're going to have to help me walk."

CHAPTER 11

Karen came down for breakfast just before eight, dressed in her uniform and carrying a large leather civilian purse. The breakfast table was set in the dining room, but no one seemed to be about, so she went into the kitchen, where she found Hiroshi and Kyoko having a cup of tea. As Kyoko started to get up, she asked Hiroshi if he would bring her car around to the side of the house. Hiroshi frowned but then nodded and left to get the car.

Karen sat down with Kyoko and asked if she could have some tea. Kyoko took one look at Karen's face, smiled hugely, and hastened to get it.

"Train is still asleep," Karen said, blushing. "I think he is very tired."

The old woman just looked at her over the rim of her cup, and Karen was careful to avoid eye contact. "I'm going over to the Marine Corps base at Quantico. I think it best if Train was not disturbed."

Kyoko nodded once but still didn't say anything. Karen sipped her cup of tea for a few minutes, suppressing a grin of pure pleasure. She finally looked over at Kyoko. Then they both smiled, exchanging one of those knowing looks women have been trading since the beginning of time. Karen got up when she heard the car, thanked Kyoko for the tea, and went out the back door to intercept the Explorer. Hiroshi stepped out and gave her a remote device for opening the main gates.

"Train-sama does not go with you?" he asked.

"He needs his sleep, Hiroshi. He stayed awake to watch the night before last in the hospital. I'm just going over to the Marine base. I'll be back by noon. Let him sleep, all right? He's been up for almost two nights."

Hiroshi looked unconvinced. "There is no danger where you go? Do you wish Hiroshi to go with you?"

She looked at him and wondered how much Train had told him. "I don't think so," she replied. "I'll be safe on the base, Hiroshi. There are lots of big Marines there. He has my car phone number if he's worried."

Hiroshi nodded, then hesitated, as if he had one more question. But then he bowed and closed the door for Karen. She drove off as quietly as she could, not wanting to wake Train. He'd be pretty agitated when he found out she had gone off on her own, but after last night, she was determined to do two things: first, hurry this Sherman thing to a conclusion. She knew Jack would never open up if Train was present. But if she could make him talk and establish that he was acting in concert with Galantz, they should be able to force McNair to move, which damned well ought to precipitate something. Secondly, she wanted to demonstrate to Train that she was an equal part of this team.

An hour later, Karen drove back out of the Marine base front gates and turned right into tiny Triangle, Virginia. Her trip out to the airstrip had been a complete bust: Jack Sherman had not shown up for work. And when she had asked for his home address, the civilian clerk behind the counter had refused to give it out, citing the Privacy Act. Since Karen did not have Train's database file with her, she now needed to find the boy's address. She could, of course, admit defeat and go back to Aquia, but she was determined not to do that. She checked her car phone to see if there had been any calls, but there were none. Good. Still asleep, then. With any luck, she could get back before he even woke up. Then she saw the sign for the Triangle post office.

She turned the Explorer off Route One and entered a side street that led to the post office. The assistant postmaster turned out to be a retired Marine, and he perked up at the sight of Karen's three stripes. She turned on her best smile in an effort to ease his bureaucratic conscience. After a few minutes of Navy–Marine Corps banter, the postmaster produced the box with the postal box registration cards.

"Here's your boy," he announced, pulling the yellow card out of the file box. "Shows an address of number four Slade Hill Road. Which explains why he has a box. I think I've seen this guy. Skinny, rat-faced fella."

"Sounds like him. We've interviewed him once over at the Marine base where he works. But he didn't show up this morning. How do you know him?"

"Slade Hill is a one-lane mud track, goes up a steep hill offa Cherry Hill Road. There's a pair of trailers halfway up, and then this guy. Our delivery trucks can't get in and out except when it's bone-dry, which is almost never. That's assumin' they'd want to. Buncha biker lowlifes up there. The old Slade house up on top, all falling in. Plus the snake problem." He looked obliquely at Karen. "You sure you wanta go up there?"

"I need to talk to this guy," Karen said. "And what's this about a snake problem?"

"Like I said, Slade Hill Road goes mosta the way up a snaggle-assed hill that's s'posed to be crawling with snakes. You know, it's one a those places. Lotsa rattlesnakes just happen to be there, you know what I'm sayin'?"

"Right," she replied, trying not to show her apprehension. Snakes were not high on her list of favorite things.

"This guy," the postmaster said. "He never hasta know where you got the address, right?"

"Absolutely."

"Good. Always happy to help out Navy law. But like I said, that's a medium-rough crowd out there along the river. Still kinda wild back in there. You be careful, Commander."

"Appreciate the heads-up," she said, and thanked him again. She went back out to the car. "Snakes," she said as soon as she had the engine running. She exhaled, got out her Prince William County detail map, and found Cherry Hill Road.

It took fifteen minutes to get there and locate Cherry Hill Road. She thought about the jurisdictional problem she might be creating, then dismissed it. If she could get Jack to talk, McNair could deal with any jurisdiction problems. The road narrowed as it curved around toward the river, and at one point she had to pull the Explorer to the right and almost stop to make room for a pickup truck coming toward her. The good news was that Jack wasn't likely to call the cops just because some Navy people were harassing him with questions. But she was sure she was on the right track. With Sherman missing, his son had become the vital lead. The only other wrinkle was Carpenter. He had ordered them off the case, effectively. What was that term Train used—*freelancing?*

She concentrated on her driving as the narrow road climbed into the low hills bordering the river. The twisting road became even narrower, and she had to slow, both to avoid surprises and to size up the territory. There were no developments down here, only single-home plots. Along the upper part of the road, the houses were presentable, if modest: a mixture of regular construction and prefabs, with neat, well-tended lawns, established trees, and, usually, one or two elderly vehicles. As the road canted downhill, closing in on the river, the dwellings became mostly trailers. The edges of the road became more ragged, and she had to steer around some major tank traps disguised as potholes.

"Anywhere along in here," she murmured to herself, holding the map in her lap. Slade Hill Road wasn't on the map, but it did show some lines leading off Cherry Hill along in here. She decided to ask for directions when she saw a very fat man rolling a green plastic trash barrel down to the road from his house. The man was about sixty; he was decked out in an armless T-shirt and red shorts whose tops were well shielded by his paunch. He had sparse brush-cut gray hair and what looked like a few days' growth of beard littering his jowls. There was a large tattoo of the Marine Corps globe and eagle on his biceps. He peered suspiciously at the Explorer as Karen stopped, rolled down the passenger-side window, and leaned across to talk to him.

"I'm looking for Slade Hill Road. Am I close?"

"Round the next bend, first dirt road on the left. Watch yerself, lady. Buncha assholes up there. Bikers and shit."

Karen thanked him and rolled the window back up as she pulled out. Lovely, she thought. If *he* thinks they're assholes, they must be some serious assholes. She came around the next curve in the road and saw what had to be Slade Hill Road on the left, a badly rutted dirt track leading up a fairly steep hill. The entrance was flanked by two piles of white garbage bags lying in the rain ditch, both of which had been ripped open by scavenging dogs. She put the Explorer in four-wheel drive and turned left into the muddy dirt road. The vehicle slipped sideways for a moment but then gained traction and began to climb. For the first hundred yards, there was nothing but heavy trash-littered underbrush and sad-looking trees on either side, with deep runoff ditches limiting the road to a one-way passage. There must have been a spring or seep up at the top of the road, because it was wet. Then she passed a rusting, burned-out trailer on the left, surrounded by six or so junked cars and heaps of moldering trash and blackened debris from the fire. Two scabrous dogs came yapping out of the wreck and ran after her car, then quickly gave it up. The road zigged to the right, and Karen had to maneuver the vehicle carefully over a deep erosion rut that ran diagonally across the road. The road bent back to the left, still climbing, and then widened in the vicinity of two more trailers that looked as if they had been dropped from the air several years ago and then landed haphazardly in a muddy clearing. The trailers butted up against each other at an angle, and the junction was draped in sheets of heavy clear plastic like some kind of air lock. There were signs of life, in that the trash and garbage looked fresh. A new crew of scavenging dogs, feeding happily on a white garbage bag, ignored the Explorer as it ground past. There were four large motorcycles parked under a makeshift lean-to constructed out of dirty plastic panels supported by two old refrigerators. A faint wisp of smoke was coming out of what looked like a woodstove stack cut through the roof of one of the trailers. Karen kept going, watching her rearview mirror to see if humans or otherwise had come out to check on her intrusion into this sylvan paradise.

Maybe the purported snake problem up here is of the two-legged variety, Karen thought. She was suddenly glad it was morning, guessing that all the reptiles were still in hiding. She kept climbing in first gear, the road now showing less sign of use. The lower tree branches were beginning to scrape against the top and sides of the Explorer, and the tire ruts were not so pronounced. Then the track just ended, or effectively did, because there was an enormous dead oak tree lying across the road. It had obviously been down for many years, but even half-rotten, the massive trunk meant that she would have to turn around.

She stopped but kept the engine running. This has to be the top of Slade Hill, or almost so, she thought. She looked through the windshield to see if the road continued, but it didn't look like it. She tried to remember what the postmaster had said about a house up there, but she finally decided to maneuver the Explorer around so that it faced downhill. Then she shut it down and got out, wishing she had worn the trousered working uniform instead of the skirted variety. Her toes were curling in her dress shoes until she remembered that she kept a pair of Bean boots in the back. She changed shoes and then extracted her oversized bag, slinging it over her shoulder and then locking the car.

There was hardly a sound up here among the stunted tress and heavy underbrush, as if the native fauna had long since fled in disgust. There appeared to be the beginnings of a path on the river side of the clearing. She walked a few yards down the path before spotting the top of a trailer about fifty feet off the road, back in a jungle of vines and weeds. The smell of a dysfunctional septic system competed with the odor of rotting vegetation and old tires at the edge of the dirt road. Single-wide paradise. She could imagine some covert marijuana patches out in those woods, and maybe a meth boiler room down below at the double trailer. Above to the left, there was a ridgeline outlined by old trees, where patches of gray limestone appeared as silvery smudges against all the burgeoning greenery of spring. There might have been the ruins of a house back in those trees, but she could not tell. And no birds, she noticed. Not a peep from what should have been a hillside full of birds. Did snakes eat birds?

This has to be the place, she decided reluctantly, although there was no mailbox or anything else with a number 4 on it. She started in toward the trailer along the dirt path, which was littered with an amazing variety of trash, beer cans, plastic shopping bags, and ancient oily articles of clothing. Stepping through the low underbrush, she wished she had a big stick to sweep the grass ahead of her. She felt a bramble bush put a good-sized tear in her right stocking. After about thirty feet, the path opened up into a clearing, where a badly damaged trailer lay half on, half off its cinder-block foundations. The top of the trailer on one end looked as if it had been hit by a falling tree, although the tree was not in evidence. Electricity and telephone wires snaked down from a pole on the dirt road to the corner of the trailer, so presumably somebody did live here. Off to one side, there was a motorcycle hootch built just like the ones at the trailers below. Battered packing crates constituted its sides and a plastic tarp stretched across some two-by-fours for a roof. There was room under it for a couple of bikes, but only one motorcycle was present for duty. It looked quite large, and it was partially covered by a moldy-looking shower curtain. There was a mound of bags and clothes stacked to one side of the bike. She wondered if that was the motorcycle she had seen at the church, but all motorcycles looked the same to her. She looked around for dogs. She heard a sound, and sure enough, two brown rats skittered out from beneath a pile of rotting mattresses and dived into a hole under some pallets. If there was a big snake problem up here, it wasn't big enough, she thought. Time to go bang on the door. She walked up to the front of the trailer, kicked aside a white plastic bag of trash, and knocked on the front door. There was no response. She tried it again. The sound reverberated inside the trailer, as if it was empty.

She turned around and surveyed the littered yard. He hadn't shown up for work, and he wasn't answering the door. If this was his door, that is. But the motorcycle rather made her think it was his place. The silence was a bit unnerving, though, and she began to imagine that someone was watching her. She went back to the door and banged louder, but there was still no response. She stepped back from the door to check the windows, but they were covered up inside. She caught another whiff of sewer gas coming from under the trailer, and she stepped back out into the yard again.

A thought occurred to her. Suppose Jack was more than just a bit player in this business? There had been two people putting her into the cart and dragging her down to the river. Suppose one of them had been Jack? As she stood there in the silence of the clearing, she began to think that being up here by herself might not be such a great idea. Then something moved in the pile of rags next to the motorcycle.

She walked over toward the motorcycle shelter, being careful of where she put her feet. Then, to her surprise, the pile of rags itself moved, and a pale-faced Jack Sherman sat up groggily among the rags, a confused, disoriented look on his face. So drunk last night he'd never made it to the trailer. He was wearing a filthy black leather jacket over an equally filthy T-shirt. His black jeans had been embroidered recently with the finished product of the brewer's art. Karen could see the red of his bloodshot eyes from twenty feet away. She relaxed: Jack was in no shape to give anybody any trouble. Just as long as Galantz wasn't lurking nearby.

Jack swiveled his head around until he could focus on Karen. The bright light of morning was making him squint, and she wondered if he secretly needed glasses. He managed a liquid belch, and she decided not to get any closer lest the sight of another human provoke some even more distasteful bodily functions.

"Is that you, Jack Sherman?" she asked.

"Stop yellin', man," the derelict said, his voice thick. "I'm hurtin' here, man." His eyes were closed now, and he held one hand up to his right ear, which Karen noticed was crusted with a thin line of blood. He made no move to rise from his nest of rags.

Karen moved a few feet closer, looking around to make sure Jack was alone. An admiral's son, no less, she thought. She wondered if this was a sight not unfamiliar to the admiral.

"Aren't you a pretty specimen," she said. "That man said there was a snake problem up here. This looks like a rat problem."

"Snakes," the kid mumbled, his eyes still closed, his head weaving with the effort to stay upright. Then he giggled as if he was still drunk.

"It speaks," she said. "Hard to believe this is an admiral's son, but there's no denying the facial resemblance, is there?"

The boy reacted to that, opening his eyes. "What're you talking about, bitch? I ain't no admiral's son. Never was, never will be. Fuck all admirals. And fuck you, whoever the hell you are."

Karen moved a step closer. "You're telling me that your father isn't Rear Adm. W. T. Sherman?" she asked.

Jack rolled slowly all the way over in his bed of rags, squinting hard now, staring at her, pushing himself up on one arm to look at her, and then she saw a wave of recognition cross his face.

"Hey, it's you," he said. "From the base. Where's your bodyguard?"

"Not all that far away," Karen lied. "But we thought we'd try asking our questions nicely, so he's waiting in the car."

"Well, fuck that noise. I ain't answering any goddamned questions. Even if you do have a great ass."

Karen cocked her head to one side. "You talk to all the girls that way, Jack?" she asked. "Or are you just attracted to asses in general?"

It went right over his head, and he waved a hand at her as if to make her just go away. He belched again, and for a moment, she thought he was going to be sick. But then he was looking at her again.

"Like I said, fuck you, lady. I don't hafta talk to you. Besides, you oughta be thankin' me, man. He was gonna plug your ass before we dropped you in the river. Whadda ya think a that, bitch? Hey, you like your little ride in the river, huh?"

Karen felt a wave of anger swell up inside her chest. But Jack was getting up now, staggering to his feet, holding on to one of the two-by-fours.

"Yeah, yeah, you've got a great ass, lady, Commander, ma'am, sir, whatever the hell you're called. I took a little look, see, right after my old man popped his flashbulb in your face. You don't remember? I do. Great ass, like I said, sexy panties and all. Love that shit." He was trying to move toward her, but he was still too drunk to stay upright without the help of the two-by-four. Then he stopped, looked into her shocked face, and made the mistake of laughing.

Karen lost it when she heard that laugh. She reached into her bag and pulled out Frank's .45, and, almost as if she had been shooting one for years, she snapped back the hammer in one smooth motion and let one go in Jack's general direction. The two-by-four just below his hand shattered, blowing wood splinters all over the place. Jack yelled and went windmilling backward, toward the bike.

Karen stepped forward and fired again, the huge automatic kicking up in her hand and shocking her right wrist. This round pulverized the bike's headlight, sending shards of glass into Jack's face and causing him to fall sideways over the bike. The bike tipped and then fell over in a crashing heap, with Jack now pinned under the front wheel. Karen walked toward him, the gun pointing right at him.

"What did you say, you son of a bitch? You put me in that bag, did you? So that was you, Jack?" She fired again, aiming just over his head and hitting the back tire instead, and this time Jack was screaming for her to stop. She walked up close, her own hands trembling now, and lowered the muzzle to point right at his face. Jack started to babble and cry. It was the sudden acrid smell of urine penetrating all the gunsmoke that brought her to her senses.

She backed away a step and slowly lowered the big gun. Jack was curled into a protective ball underneath the front wheel of the bike, his right arm across his face. He was blubbering incoherently, his noises blending with the hiss of escaping air from the tire. Karen just stood there for a minute, taking deep breaths, struggling to wipe away the red mist of rage from her vision. She physically had to fight the urge to bring the gun up again and blow his damned head right off, and Jack sensed it.

"Get up," she ordered. Her voice was flat and hard, and there was a strong metallic taste in her mouth.

"I can't. I can't," he sobbed, still not looking at her.

"Do it, Jack, or I'll put one in the gas tank. Get up. Now!"

It took a moment for her threat to penetrate, and then he scrambled out from under the upset motorcycle, tearing his jeans and scraping his shins on a hub nut. He scuttled back away from her, farther into the hooch, a trembling hand still up in front of his face. There were shards of bright white glass on his T-shirt, and a large dark stain at his crotch.

"I said, Get up, Jack. I want you out here where I can see you, not just smell you. Get up!" She raised the .45 again.

He swallowed a couple of times and then crawled to his feet, suddenly very sober, his eyes locked on the black maw of the .45.

"Now," she said, "we're going to have a little talk. Or rather, I'm going to ask you some questions and you're going to give me some answers. Call me bitch again and you'll have to learn sign language, understand, Jack?"

He wobbled a little but nodded. She swung the gun around in the direction of the trailer. "In there."

Jack walked carefully around her, eyeing the gun, his face pasty. He wiped his lips a couple of times on the way to the door. She could indeed smell him as he went past. He opened the front door and pushed it wide against some trash behind it. She followed him into the trailer, then told him to open some windows. The trailer stank of marijuana, with an overlay of sewage. The living room area was pretty much bare, with only a sleeping bag rumpled up on a thin and filthy mattress at one end, and two overturned boxes that apparently served as chairs. There were beer cans, wine bottles, old magazines, motorcycle parts, plastic jugs of oil, and assorted clothes scattered along the wall. A single overhead light hung by a broken fixture from the ceiling, and a telephone sat on the floor. She could smell the kitchen but could not see it, and she didn't want to. A single hallway led back to the part of the trailer that had been smashed by the tree, but the hallway was blocked by a pile of clothes that looked as if they had been rescued from a Dumpster.

Jack stumbled unsteadily over toward the mattress. Karen followed him into the room, watching him carefully. Jack flopped down on the sleeping bag, then reached under it. Karen brought the gun up instantly.

"Don't," she warned.

"Drink," he said quickly. "Gotta have a drink. Goddamn, lady, you made me piss my pants. Gimme a break here."

Karen debated with herself. Maybe let him take a hit, steady his nerves. If he was a full-blown lush, she might get more out of him if he steadied up. She nodded once. "Use one hand," she ordered.

With his left hand in the air, he carefully felt around under the rag bag and then, with exaggerated slowness, extracted a long-necked brown bottle with no label. He undid the screw cap, still watching the gun, and took a long swig. He closed his eyes, took a deep breath, and then swallowed, coughing as whatever elixir of the gods went down. Then he put the bottle down and pulled the sleeping bag over his lap. He had to put both hands down on the bag to keep himself upright. He looked at her expectantly.

Karen walked over to the stronger-looking of the two boxes and sat down, putting the automatic in her lap but keeping her right hand on it. She was aware that the hammer was still back, but she decided not to lower it. He might regain his courage after that slug of rotgut and make a move. One part of her rather wished he would.

"You move and I'll empty this thing into your face, understand?"

He nodded and then took another hit from the bottle.

"You were there," she said. "You helped somebody kidnap me and then dump me in that river. Who was it?"

Jack looked away, a glint of fear showing in his eyes. "My old man," he croaked.

She couldn't believe her ears. "You're telling me that Admiral Sherman was involved in that?"

He still wouldn't look at her, just kept staring down at the floor. "W. T. Sherman's nothing to me," Jack said. "I'm talking about my *real* old man."

What the hell was this? "You mean Galantz?"

"Never heard that name. He's always been Mr. Smith. That's all, Mr. Smith. Ever since recon training."

"Where is he now, this Mr. Smith?"

Jack glanced out the back window and shivered. "Around. I dunno. He comes and gets me when he needs me. He just shows up, man. Always at night. He's like a goddamned ghost."

"So Admiral Sherman's nothing to you?"

"Not since he did what he did. Back there in D.C.," Jack said, a hint of the old sneer coming back into his voice. The rotgut, she thought. Watch him.

"You mean when he divorced your mother."

Jack didn't say anything, just stared down at the floor. Even so, Karen could sense the enormous resentment festering in this kid.

"Why do you call Galantz—Mr. Smith—your old man?"

Jack wiped his lips again and glanced sideways at the bottle. "Because he took care of me, back there in recon school, when I was getting my ass kicked by them other guys, the bigger guys. They were gonna wash me out, but Mr. Smith, he stood up, man. He knew about . . . about what happened to my mother. Said he was gonna be the old man I never had. Said he'd get me through it. And he did, too. Them other guys, they were afraid of Mr. Smith. He's a bad bastard. Not like some a those guys, go around acting tough. He *is* tough, man."

"Yeah, real tough guy. Kidnapping women. Blinding them first, then stuffing them in a bag. Then if something goes wrong, quick, Jack, throw her in the river. A real man, that. A real tough guy."

Jack's face went blank as he squirmed around on the sleeping bag. "We was just gonna keep you. Not hurt you. That's what he said."

"Why?"

"I dunno. I don't ask him questions. He calls, I come. I owe him, that's all. I owe him big. He told me to get a boat, meet him by the Key Bridge. I did what he told me. I owe him, man."

"Why? What do you owe him for?"

"That's personal."

"Look at me," she said. He didn't move. She raised the gun, trying to remember how many rounds were in it. Not that many. "Look at me, Jack."

Slowly, he raised his head, his face a study in pain and anger in about equal proportions. "I know what happened to your mother," she said. "That she shot herself."

His eyes blazed. "Because of him, the way he was. I want him dead. You listening to me? *I want him dead!* All those years, he was always gone. Off on those ships, no time to come home, no time for us. Always the big fuckin' deal. Have to work late. On the fast track here, people. Movin' right up here. You got no damn idea, man. My mother, fryin' her brain with the booze because she was always alone. Goin' to bed drunk, gettin' up drunk, drunk when people came around, drunk when I—hell, lady, what would you know about any of that shit? You're one of 'em, aren't you? You're a goddamn officer, just like him."

Karen took a deep breath. "So you blame him for what happened to your mother?"

"Fuckin'-A, I do. She was—she didn't deserve that shit, man. Neither of us did. Don't you think we deserved a little bit of his fucking time all those years? So yeah, when Mr. Smith comes knocking, tells me he's gonna do a number on that prick over some shit went down in Nam, now that he's a big-deal admiral, and do I wanta help out a little, I said fuckin'-A. In a fuckin' heartbeat."

"Were you involved in what happened to Elizabeth Walsh?"

"Never heard of her. Oh, yeah, she was the new punch, right? My mother's replacement? Smith told me about her. How she had this little fall down the stairs. 'Flying lesson,' he called it. He gave her a damn flying lesson. Told me to go by the funeral, told me where and when. Told me to make sure I rode the bike by so *he* would see me. Yeah, I was involved."

"And the funeral for Admiral Schmidt? He told you to go to that one, too?"

"Yeah. Said it was important that *he* saw me there, too. Said it was part of the plan. Said old geezers like that, they live too long. Said he was just helping nature along."

"But you did not help to kill them?"

Jack took a deep breath, as if suddenly realizing how much he had told her. His eyes started blinking. "Look at me, man," he sobbed. "Just fuckin' look at me. Look where I fucking live. *How* I live. I'm a fucking drunk, just like my mother. For the same reason my mother was a drunk. And he don't give two shits and never has. So, yeah, I helped Smith with that deal at your place. But that's all. Whatever he did to those other two, he did what he did. None of my fuckin' business. Rest of the time, I'm usually right here, man, boiled out of my fuckin' gourd, okay, man?" He stopped and took another hit. "And I'll tell you something else," he said as he tried to get up. "He comes around again, tonight, tomorrow, whatever, asking? I'm gonna sober right up and say yes, man. Whatever the fuck it is, whatever the fuck he needs, he's got it from me, man."

"But don't you understand? You're involved in murder."

Jack, halfway to his hands and knees now, just shook his head. His face was red and flushed, his eyes on fire. "Don't give a fuck. Because he's gonna do what I always wanted to do, bring that pretty bastard down, man. Far as I'm concerned, that pretty bastard murdered my mother and fucked me up for life. Mr. Smith, man? He's the fuckin' Lone Ranger and I'm fuckin' Tonto, man. Now why don't you just leave me the hell alone, okay?"

He flopped down onto the sleeping bag, his face hidden from her, his shoulders shaking. Karen stared at him for a long moment and then backed out of the trailer. She eased the hammer down on the .45 and put it back in her purse as she walked back through the weeds to the Explorer. She unlocked the car, got in, and started it up, glancing down at the phone when it beeped. Three calls in the system for her. Uh-oh, that had to be Train. Sleeping Beauty had awakened and had probably gone hermantile when Hiroshi told him where she had gone. She decided to wait until she got back to fill him in.

She steered the Explorer carefully down the dirt hillside, keeping the bag close and open in case some of the locals at the other trailer decided to come out to play. The .45 lay right at the top, exuding a comforting whiff of cordite into the area of the front seat.

Train was just getting into his car when he heard the sound of Karen's Explorer coming up the drive. He took a deep breath and got back out, trying not to slam the door. Control, he said. This is the time for lots and lots of control. He saw Hiroshi standing in the doorway to the kitchen, his face a wooden mask. Train had awakened at eleven and realized he had slept long past eight. Upon going downstairs and finding out that Karen had left three hours earlier, he had actually yelled at Hiroshi for not waking him up. Then he banged around the house for a while, worried more than he would have thought possible, trying to decide whether or not to go after her or to wait for word. He had placed three calls to her car phone, to no avail. Anything could be happening out there. Then he had called the maintenance department at Quantico airfield and found out that Jack Sherman had not reported for work—which meant that Karen had probably gone out on her own to Cherry Hill, which was no place for a woman alone, even if she wasn't the target of some mad bastard. That had settled it, and he was on his way when she returned to the house. He tried to neutralize his face when she got out of the car.

"I got him to talk," she said in a rush. "I know you're mad at me for going off alone, but I got him to talk. Now let's go inside where *we* can talk privately." She smiled up at him, took his arm, and steered him toward the house. Damn the woman, he thought, his anger melting when she grabbed his arm, but he went along, ignoring Kyoko's efforts to erase the smile that was on her face as they went into the house. Look at Kyoko. Damned women were all in it together.

Train got up and began to pace around in the study after Karen finished telling him about her encounter with Jack Sherman. She was sitting on the couch with that oversized handbag at her feet.

"So he admits he was in on what happened to you out in Great Falls?" he asked.

"Yes. He denies having anything to do with what happened to Elizabeth or Galen Schmidt. But only because Galantz didn't ask him to. He did appear at the funerals on Galantz's instructions."

Train nodded. "We're going to have to find out what the historical connection is between Galantz and Sherman's son. You said they first met at recon school?"

"That's what he said."

"That, we can check out. I'm assuming Galantz was there as an instructor or something. I wonder if Jack Sherman's BCD had anything to do with Galantz."

"There's something I haven't talked about yet," Karen said in a tone of voice that made Train turn around. She told him about her outburst with the .45.

Train grinned in spite of himself. "Wahoo," he said. "I think I'd like to have seen that, Counselor."

But Karen wasn't laughing. "I think I wanted to kill him. Hell, I _know_ I wanted to kill him. Train, I've never had an impulse like that before."

He went over to her and sat down on the couch. "Hey," he said, reaching for her hand. "If not for some fortuitous accidents the other night, you'd be dead now, and that little piece of crap up there on Cherry Hill wouldn't be giving it a second thought. You're upset to find yourself getting down to his level, but remember, he's the one who provoked it. Now, where's the forty-five?"

She reached into the bag and produced the Colt, holding it by the slide. At that moment, Hiroshi knocked on the study door and opened it to report that lunch was ready. When he saw the huge automatic in her hand, he stopped in midsentence.

"It's okay, Hiroshi," Train said hurriedly. "Tell Kyoko we'll be right in."

Hiroshi withdrew carefully while Train slipped out the magazine and worked the slide to eject the chambered round. "We need to clean and reload this thing," he said.

"Maybe I shouldn't be carrying it," she said. "I don't have a license or anything."

Train laughed at that, kissed her on the cheek, and went over to the shotgun cabinet in the corner of the study and began fishing around in a drawer. "Given what's been going down, I'd feel better if you did have it with you. A concealed-weapons violation beats a body bag every time."

He did a quick cleaning job on the pistol and then found a box of .45 auto to reload the clip. But when he turned around, Karen had her face in her hands. He finished up with the weapon and went back to her and held her for a few minutes, telling her it was okay, that nobody got hurt, and next time to take him with her when she went out into the weeds.

Over lunch, they kicked around her idea about telling McNair about Jack Sherman and what he had said. Train was for telling the police what they knew. "McNair's been pretty straight with us," he said. "We owe it to him to return the favor. At the very least, the cops will want to sweat young Jackie boy, because they'll think he can lead them to Galantz."

Karen wasn't so sure now. "I don't think Jack Sherman can lead himself to the bathroom most of the time. The cops aren't even going to get close to Galantz through him."

"But he admitted being part of a kidnap and attempted murder—namely, yours."

"I know. But right now, that's hearsay. If you could have seen him, Train, you'd know that he is nothing but a pawn. Galantz has some kind of hold on him, but otherwise he's a dysfunctional mess. Besides, there's another problem with telling the cops about Jack."

"Which is?"

"If they pick him up, either they or we have to tell Admiral Carpenter that Sherman's son is in fact mixed up in the homicides. Right now, they have Sherman sidelined on a selection board just because there's a whiff of scandal. But if this gets out, they'll force him to resign and take his homicidal relatives with him."

Train was silent for a moment. "Yeah, but you're forgetting that Sherman himself is missing. His goose may already be cooked. Let's do this: Let's talk to McNair, tell him about the son, and lay out the political ramifications for him. That way, we're straight with him, but maybe we can mitigate any collateral damage done to Sherman senior. I think we can convince McNair that his real target is still Galantz and not some whacked-out kid."

"And what do we tell Admiral Carpenter?"

Train shrugged. "That's a tougher question. The good news is that we're supposed to be sitting here on the sidelines. I don't see that we need to talk to Carpenter at all right now. We're better off talking to McNair first—before something happens to that kid."

"Happens? Like what?"

"I don't know. But if Galantz finds out that you and Jack Sherman have had a quiet little chat, Jackie boy might become surplus gear."

Karen was folding her napkin, staring pensively across the dining room. "What I'd really like to do is find Admiral Sherman," she said.

Kyoko came in to clear the table and Train suggested they go for a walk around the grounds before calling McNair. As they were stepping out through the front door, the telephone began ringing. Train paused to see who it was. Hiroshi came through the main hallway. "Detective McNair," he announced with a stiff face. Train realized he would have to deal with the problem of injured feelings before the day was over. Karen followed him back to the study.

"McNair," Train said. "We were talking about calling you."

"Trouble?" McNair asked.

"Not exactly. But we've located a new player in the Sherman puzzle—Admiral Sherman's son. We need to talk."

"What's the connection?"

"He's been helping Galantz."

There was a moment of silence on the line. "You told your Navy people about this?"

"Not yet. I figured this is first and foremost police business."

"Good thinking," McNair said.

Karen was trying to tell him something. "Hang on a sec. What?" he asked.

"Tell him we need to find Admiral Sherman," she said. Train relayed her message.

"Believe it or not, that's why I was calling," McNair said. "How do you two feel about making a little drive?"

"Like where?"

"Like to a Saint Martha's Hospice Center, about five miles outside of a little town called Harney, Maryland, right up on the Pennsylvania border."

"A hospice center?" he asked. Karen was staring at him. "What the hell, McNair?"

"I've got an all-day court deal today," McNair said. "The hospice center is right on the main drag. I think it's Route 134, just north of Harney. Meet me there, say, five P.M. Give me the number for your car phone in case I get delayed. Commander Lawrence is with you, right?"

"Yup."

"Good. Keep it that way. I'll see you there at five."

Train agreed and hung up. He told Karen what McNair had said.

"A hospice center?" she said.

"That's what the man said. On the Pennsylvania border. Look, it's almost one. This will take—what, three, three and a half hours? Why don't we get on the road now, get north of D.C. before all the traffic starts. But first, I need to mend some fences with Hiroshi and tell him where we're going."

They found the St. Martha's Hospice Center with no difficulty, arriving just after 4:30. The sky had turned overcast and colder during the afternoon, and the air smelled like rain when they parked in front of what appeared to be the main building. St. Martha's had the look of a private sanatorium. There was a brick wall surrounding nearly five acres of wooded grounds, and all the buildings were covered in old ivy. The main building, which was distinguished from the rest by the fact that it had three stories, had a granite Gothic arch entranceway capped by a plain marble cross set back into the arch. There were several cars in the parking lot but no obvious police cars.

The glass doors of the front entrance opened into a carpeted reception area, with a front desk that looked very much like a hotel check-in counter. There were couches and chairs in the reception area, and fresh flowers on the tables. There were two nuns in modern black-and-white habits behind the desk. The younger of the two was working on a computer. The other one, a pleasant-faced woman of indeterminate age, stood up to greet them. Train signed them in while Karen went in search of a ladies' room.

McNair arrived about twenty minutes later, shedding a light raincoat as he came through the door. He saw and waved to the two of them, then went up to the desk to talk to one of the Sisters, who got on the phone as McNair signed in. He walked back over to where Train and Karen were sitting and nodded politely at Karen.

"Commander, you're looking better than the last time I saw you."

She smiled at him but said nothing, not wanting to dwell on the last time. He asked Train if they'd found the place without trouble.

"No prob," Train replied. "Although we're still in the dark about why we're here."

McNair sat down in a chair facing them both. "You recall that Admiral Sherman supposedly went missing sometime Wednesday."

Train nodded. "What's that got to do with this place?"

"In a few minutes, a Sister Bernadette will come down here to meet us. She's the head of patient affairs. She's going to show us a videotape, and then we can talk some more about the good admiral. But first, run through this business with his son. I take it you two tracked him down?"

Train gave Karen a sideways look that said, Let me take this one. Then he debriefed McNair on Jack's whereabouts, his putative connection to Galantz, and what he had revealed about his own role in Galantz's operation. McNair listened carefully, taking some notes before turning to Karen.

"And you actually interviewed him the second time, Commander? What was your estimate of this individual's general physical and mental state?"

She thought for a moment. "Physically, he was badly hungover from using alcohol or dope of some kind. Probably both. He's malnourished, very thin, but still strong enough to operate a big motorcycle."

"And mentally?"

"Filled with hate. Rage. Pretty messed-up kid. Actually, he's twenty—what? Twenty-seven, twenty-eight? Not exactly a kid, but that's the word that comes to mind: a belligerent teenage kid, resenting everybody and everything, living like the poorest white trash that ever was."

"And he admitted to helping Galantz with your abduction in Great Falls? How about the two homicides?"

"According to him, his contribution to the Walsh and Schmidt affairs was to appear at the respective funerals so his father would see him. And he doesn't recognize the name Galantz, by the way."

"Right, Mr. Smith. But for him, this all has to do with getting back at his old man for what happened to his mother, correct?"

"And to him. The night the syringe showed up, the admiral told me something of this history. He admits he's more than a little responsible for what happened to his family."

"I see. Of course this is all hearsay. Might work for a grand jury, but not so good at trial, as you know. You suppose he would tell us the same story if we pick him up? There was no coercion or anything like that, was there?"

Karen looked at Train, who arched his eyebrows at her. Reluctantly, she told McNair about losing her temper with the .45.

"Uh-huh," McNair said. There was the ghost of a smile around his lips when she was finished. Karen put the best face on it she could. "I don't know what to say. I realized that here was one of the guys who cocooned me in a damned body bag for several hours and then nearly drowned me in the river. Especially when he revealed all this with a maximum sneer."

"And you just happened to have a forty-five in your purse?"

"I did that morning, yes."

McNair glanced at her regulation purse. "Got it in there now, do we?"

Karen couldn't tell if he was being facetious. Given her inexperience in the use of the big Colt, she realized for the hundredth time how lucky she had been not to injure or even kill Jack. She decided to play it straight.

"No," she said. "Look, I was overwrought. I know I shouldn't have done that. So, yes, I left the gun home for this trip."

McNair nodded again, looking over at the desk for signs of Sister Bernadette's arrival. Train was helpfully studying the floor.

"Okay," McNair said, turning back around. "Technically, what happened up there is a Prince William County problem. It doesn't sound like the kid is the type who'll be crying to the cops. The important thing is what he's revealed. Assuming Mr. Smith is Galantz, this is pretty strong corroboration."

"And maybe a good way to locate Galantz," Train offered.

"If he'll tell you the same story, wouldn't that take care of Sherman's political problem?" Karen said.

"It might," McNair said. "But it doesn't take care of his Galantz problem, not until we can take Galantz himself off the boards."

"So," Train said, "what are we doing in this place?"

McNair nodded and closed his notebook. "We checked with the Navy when we couldn't contact Sherman. Carpenter's office said he was on a selection board of some kind and that they'd get him to call us. Then they called back, said he was not present for duty. I asked if he was AWOL. They said flag officers don't go AWOL. Anyhow, they huffed and they puffed and finally admitted they didn't know where he was. I had a patrol unit go by his house. No car. I put out a locating bulletin for Sherman's car in the tristate area. Maryland state trooper located the car at a motel here in Harney yesterday afternoon. I talked to the motel manager. Turns out Sherman is a regular."

"A regular?" Karen said. She was confused, until she remembered the prior weekend, when Sherman had gone out of town.

"Yup," McNair said. "See, this motel has a cut-rate deal for people who are visiting long-term patients at the hospice here. The sisters here set it up years ago."

At that moment, a large matronly-looking nun came out of the elevators, spotted McNair, and came over to where they were sitting. She looked to Karen like an approaching battleship in her black-and-gray uniform, with a large silver crucifix bouncing over a generous bosom. McNair made the introductions.

"Very pleased to meet you both," Sister Bernadette said. "Detective McNair, I have the videotape you requested, and a busy night ahead."

"Right, Sister, and we really appreciate this. As I explained to you, just seeing this tape will be a great help in our investigation. Then we'll get right out of your hair."

"That's fine, Detective. Everyone does understand that this particular tape is not available for release or for any court proceedings, yes?"

"Absolutely, Sister," McNair said.

"Very well. Let's go to the security office."

She led them to the elevators, where they ascended in silence to the third floor. Karen searched Train's face for some explanation of what they were doing, but he could only shrug.

"All the administrative functions are handled up here," Sister Bernadette explained as they came out on the third floor. "That way, the patients and the residents are on the lower two floors. Better for fire-evacuation purposes, you know."

As they walked down a carpeted hallway with what looked like offices on either side, Karen asked what the hospice's mission was.

"We're a Catholic charity hospice, Commander. We provide a medically staffed residential-care facility for a special kind of patient—those we term 'the mentally absent.' Clinically, these are people who are not ill—with cancer, for example—but who are no longer with us mentally and who require full-time care. These are also people who can't afford or can't get access to a commercial nursing home or hospital. Families pay what they can, of course."

They arrived at the end office, and Sister Bernadette punched in a code on a keypad. "We have one hundred and eighty beds here, a full nursing staff, doctors here during the day and on call at night. The facility is full and there's a waiting list."

She led them into the security office, which combined a clerical area with a security surveillance center. The office part appeared to be closed, but there was an older man in civilian clothes sitting at a console in front of several dozen black-and-white monitors embedded in one wall.

"That's our monitoring system," Sister Bernadette explained. "This is Mr. Franklin, who has the four-to-midnight shift." The man nodded politely at them and then returned to watching the screens while Sister Bernadette explained the system.

"We can maintain surveillance of the facility and all of the rooms. A computer generates a random sampling that gives a one-minute look into each viewing area. Or the watchman can select sites for continuous sur- veillance. The system is integrated with the call system, of course, and the nurses' station on each floor has a single monitor that can be used to respond to any calls, either from a patient's room or from the security office right here, with two-way communications."

"That's a pretty sophisticated system," Train said.

"A gift from a corporate donor." Sister Bernadette replied. "Much of our facility equipment has been donated."

"I can imagine. But suppose someone wants privacy, say for a visit?" Train asked.

"Mr. von Rensel, by the time they come here, most of our patients have achieved the ultimate privacy. That's what we mean by the term *mentally absent*. They may be alive and well as persons somewhere in their own minds, but we outsiders can no longer see them or communicate with them. The monitors are watching their bodies, for their own safety, care, and comfort. In fact, that's how we come to have the tape Detective McNair wishes you to see. This way, please."

She led them to the back corner of the monitoring area and turned on a regular television set. A picture came up, one of the local stations, but the sound had been muted. She inserted a tape cassette into a VCR and switched to the video playback channel. The tape leader created a fuzzy black-and-white pattern on the screen.

"What are we going to see here?" Karen asked.

Sister Bernadette hit the Pause button. "When our patients have visitors, we monitor. It's for our protection and the patient's. Visitors are fully informed, and they can even see the tapes if they wish to. But a visitor cannot gain access to the room until the charge nurse has confirmed the monitor is positioned."

"What we're going to see here," McNair interjected, "is a tape of Admiral Sherman making a visit—to his wife."

"His *wife?*" Karen said. "But I thought—I mean, he said—"

"She's been here for ten years," McNair said. "Admiral Sherman didn't tell us the whole story about what happened to his wife. She did shoot herself. She just didn't succeed in committing suicide. She's in what the docs call 'a sustained vegetative state.' Body is alive. Brain is not."

"We don't know that last bit, of course," Sister Bernadette observed. "Her mind *might* be alive. She might even come back."

"Has that ever happened?" Karen asked. She was still trying to absorb the fact that the admiral's wife was still alive. Ten years. My God.

"Yes it has, but very seldom. It is dramatic, though, when it does happen."

"I'll bet," Train said. "And this is a tape of a visit?"

"Yes. He's been coming here for nearly ten years. When he is assigned in Washington, he comes almost every weekend. This particular tape is almost a year old, but it is representative of what happens. I must reiterate that what you are going to see is intensely personal. Detective McNair has explained that this is a murder case. You two must assure me that you will *never* reveal to Admiral Sherman that you have seen this. On your honor, yes?"

Karen and Train nodded agreement.

"Say it please," she demanded.

They said it aloud. Train wondered if *they* were being taped. "Very well, then." She pressed the button.

There were a few more seconds of leader noise, and then a black-and-white image materialized on the screen, showing a hospital room. There was single hospital bed in the room, a chair, a dresser, and a door that presumably led to a bathroom.

There was a sound and the door to the room opened. A nurse led in Admiral Sherman, who was dressed in civilian slacks and a sweater. He thanked the nurse, who looked up at the monitor briefly and then withdrew from the room. Sherman approached the bed, where a woman lay motionless under the covers. Looking at the screen, Karen couldn't tell how old she was. She had a middle-aged face that had once been pretty, but her hair was now snow white. Her eyes were open but clearly vacant. Sherman sat down on the edge of the bed and lovingly reached out with his right hand to brush a few strands of her hair away from her forehead.

"Ten years," Train murmured.

"There are some who have been here longer," Sister Bernadette said. "Some come as children. They can break your heart."

Sherman sat there in silence for a few minutes, smoothing his wife's hair and staring into space. Then he leaned forward onto the bed, near his wife's head, and gently rolled her to face him, cupping her head with both hands. Karen was startled to realize he was saying something. She had to strain to hear it.

"I'm sorry, Beth," he was saying softly. "I'm so very sorry." He said it over and over, holding her tightly. Karen watched for a few seconds, then turned away, tears in her eyes. Sister Bernadette switched off the set.

"That's what he does," she said as the tape rewound. "The same thing each time. He stays for about forty minutes and then leaves. Usually comes Saturday afternoons, and again Sunday mornings."

"Every weekend?" Train asked. Karen noted that he seemed to have a catch in his voice. McNair, who apparently had known what was coming, waited patiently.

"Often enough. Of course, some years he's been away at sea. Sometimes he comes unexpectedly. He told me once that this place has become his refuge, too, when his official life becomes too complicated. But we have a visitor log at the front desk and we keep records for seven years. Given the nature of our patients, there are often legal actions that require our records."

"I see," Train said. "This must cost a fortune, Sister. Even an admiral doesn't make that kind of money. And he's only recently an admiral."

"We know," she replied. "As I said, people pay what they can. And in his case, he just sent in a check for two hundred and fifty thousand dollars. That happens. People inherit something, or someone dies and leaves insurance."

Karen and Train looked at each other. Elizabeth Walsh's life-insurance proceeds had found a home.

"Sister, we thank you for your time and for letting us see this," McNair said. "And we will keep what we've seen and heard here private."

"Very well, Detective," she replied, ejecting the videocassette.

"Is Admiral Sherman here now, Sister?" Karen asked.

"I don't know. You can ask at the front desk, Commander. I'll take you back downstairs now, if you don't mind."

They checked at the front desk and found out that Admiral Sherman had indeed been there but had already left. They signed out, went out to the front entrance, and stood on the steps. The promise of rain had been fulfilled as a light drizzle blew in from the northwest. The parking lot was illuminated by several tall light standards, whose tops were now veiled in a misty orange glow.

"Well," Karen said.

"Yeah, well," McNair replied. "Not that he's been a very good suspect up to now. But I can't feature a guy for murder who makes this little pilgrimage for ten years, no matter what it looked like originally."

Karen had a sudden thought. "Do you suppose Elizabeth Walsh knew about this? And that's why she left him the insurance-policy money? She had no other relatives."

Train nodded thoughtfully. "Possibly. But I think the more important question now is whether or not we want to go talk to Sherman," Train said. "Tell him what his son admitted to. That he's been part of Galantz's little program."

"Not here," Karen said immediately. "I don't think he should know that we know about this. Besides, we promised."

McNair nodded. "Once I found out where he'd gone, what he was doing here, I left a message on his voice mail at home to contact me," McNair said. "But that was before I knew that the son was involved."

"We need to find out how Galantz set this up," Karen said. "I'm beginning to think he planned to use the son in some fashion for a long time. Probably from when he ran across the kid in Marine recon school. God knows, Jack has as good a motive to destroy his father as Galantz does. Or at least he thinks he does."

"Why don't we do this," Train said to McNair. "Let us sit down with Admiral Sherman and walk through the son's status. We'll tell him that you got antsy when you couldn't contact him, tracked him up here, and discovered that his wife was still alive. You told us. We don't need to get into what he does up here. He visits, that's all. But we can tell him what his son said, since we're the ones who heard it. Maybe we'll tell him you're not in that loop yet, and see what he comes up with."

"And what good does that do? I want to move on Galantz."

"I'm not sure, but I'm thinking if we can maybe, just maybe, put father and son back together, we can maybe use Jack to trap Galantz."

McNair studied the ground for a moment. "That's a real reach, G-man. But maybe that's the best we can do. And you'll keep me cut in on what you get out of that?"

"We have so far, haven't we?" Karen said.

"Yes, you have, Commander. Which is the intelligent thing to do, when there's homicide on the table. But I'm also worried about the Navy getting ahead of us. I told Mr. von Rensel here that my bosses have been getting some heat about this case from some federal sources—as in the Sherman problem involves a federal situation best left to federal solutions. It wouldn't stun me if the Navy told both of you, for instance, to return to the fort and leave Galantz to the real Indian fighters."

Train looked sideways at Karen. McNair caught it.

"Uh-huh. Already happened, am I right?" he said.

"Sort of," Train said. "Although I'm not entirely sure what the game is. I take my orders from the Navy JAG, Admiral Carpenter, as does Commander Lawrence here."

"And those orders currently are what, specifically?" McNair demanded.

"*Not* to pursue Galantz. *Not* to interfere with the efforts of other people who might be pursuing Galantz. To keep Commander Lawrence safe from any more attempts on her life."

"And Admiral Sherman was sent on some kind of temporary duty? Is that like suspension with pay?"

"Not normally, but in this case, I'd say he was put somewhat in limbo," Train said. "It's almost as if the admirals are waiting for something to happen. But I don't know what the hell it is."

McNair nodded but remained silent. He drew his coat closer around his throat as the drizzle deepened into rain. "I think," he said, "I need to go talk to my lieutenant again. This is getting too political for us snuffies. And if the feds are well and truly in it, it's gonna get pretty screwed up." He looked up at Train with a wry smile. "No offense intended, G-man."

Train laughed. "None taken. No arguing with reality."

"So we're agreed?" Karen persisted. "We'll get in touch with Admiral Sherman, Navy-to-Navy, as it were, and see where it takes us?"

"I guess so," McNair said. "But just in case, let me confirm your car phone numbers."

Train and McNair exchanged numbers and then McNair closed his notebook. "Okay," he said. "I'm headed back to D.C. And, Commander, when you have your meeting with Sherman and Junior, leave that forty-five at home, all right?" McNair grinned again as he headed for his car. Train wisely said absolutely nothing

An hour later, Karen put the road map back up in the sunshade over her seat and switched out the map light. "Route 216 from here down to the interstate," she said.

"Got it," Train replied. "It's nice having a navigator. I usually wing it and then get to see lots of unusual sights."

"Not that you would stop and ask for directions?"

"Naw. Against all the guy rules."

"Right. Is McNair still behind us?"

Train looked in his mirror and said yes. They were headed down a two-lane state road in the darkness of the Maryland countryside. McNair had followed them out of the hospice parking lot in his departmental car. Train was maintaining a fairly constant sixty in deference to the slick roads.

"So," she said, "how do we go about getting in touch with Admiral Sherman?"

"Call him," he said. "We know he's up here at the hospice tonight. I'm going to assume he's checking his voice mail."

"And if he doesn't?"

"Then I guess we'll contact with him at the motel. I had hoped not to reveal that we know the details of this situation. I felt like a Peeping Tom, looking at that tape."

Karen had been struggling with that problem since they had left the hospice: how to regain contact with the admiral without letting him know what they now knew.

It started to rain a little harder, and Train slowed down to fifty-five. The two-lane black asphalt road glistened in their headlights between indistinct boundary lines. They appeared to be passing through some low foothills, with intermittent farmsteads fleetingly visible under barnyard security lights among the trees. The farmhouses were all built practically on the edge of the road, and the barns were enormous. Train looked back in the mirror.

"Not much happening out here in the sticks on a Friday night," he said. "We and McNair are the only people out here."

As if to make a liar out of him, a pickup truck came past in the other lane, trailing a cloud of spray. Train had to hit the windshield cleaners after the truck passed. Karen turned in her seat as the truck went past, which momentarily illuminated the car behind them. She looked and then turned around quickly.

"I don't think that's McNair," she said. "Unless his car sprouted one of those cop-car spotlights since he left."

Train looked into the side mirror and then the center mirror. "I can't see anything but headlights. You sure?"

"I think so. I'm going to look again the next time a car comes past. How far back do you think that car is?"

"Maybe ten lengths. He's been pretty constant. That's why I assumed it was McNair."

She wanted to turn around again, then realized that if she did, the driver back there might see her face. "Didn't McNair give you the number for his car phone?"

"Sure did," he said, fishing in his shirt pocket for the piece of paper. Karen read the number and dialed it up on Train's car phone. The signal was weak and scratchy, but she could hear four rings, then the recording saying the customer was not available. She hung it up.

"Not available," she reported, resisting the urge to turn around again for another look.

"That doesn't prove it's not him," Train said unconvincingly.

"So now what do we do? McNair's car was white; that one back there looks like a darker color. And there's that spotlight."

"Did you see antennas? Like a state cop car?"

Karen thought for a moment. "Yes, I think I did. On the roof. Maybe it's a state cop, or a county patrol car. Are you speeding?"

He shook his head as they entered a stretch where the woods came right down to the road on either side in a blurry embrace of rain-soaked forest. The road curved to the right and began to climb a long hill. Train slowed down to an even fifty. Karen watched the car behind them in her side mirror. The distance did not change. Whoever was back there was paying attention.

"Next paved side road on the right," Train said. "I'm going to make an exciting turn. If this guy follows us, we'll either get pulled over or we have a problem." He double-punched the door locks and the compartment opened under his left elbow. He took out the Glock and passed it over to Karen. "Hang on to this for me. If it's a cop car, I'll put it back before he gets to the window."

Karen took the heavy pistol and put it in her lap.

"That's a Glock," he said. "It's double-acting. Point it and pull the trigger. It'll fire once and then it's semiauto. Don't hold the trigger down."

Train accelerated a little, keeping both hands on the wheel as he piloted the big vehicle through the winding turns of the hilly road. There was no sign of any side roads, and she suspected they would have to get back down to flatter land before there would be any. She could still see the headlights behind them, staying right with them. The rain had stopped, but the roads were still wet. Then a loom of headlights in the opposite lane was visible over the next hill, and this time Karen had time to get ready. The car flashed by them, and Karen got a good look at the car behind them. It definitely looked like a cop car, with at least two aerials visible, a large chrome-plated spotlight on the driver's side, a single driver in the front, and maybe another figure in the backseat. She whipped her head around and described all this to Train, who was still having to concentrate on the road.

"See any blue lights? Bubble-gum machine on the roof? Anything blue on his dashboard? In the grille?"

"No. No lights."

"So maybe not a cop car. Maybe somebody who wants to look like a cop car." They were coming down out of the patch of hills now, with the terrain leveling off.

"Should we call nine-one-one?" she asked.

"And tell them what? There's a car behind us? Hang on—there's a county road sign."

Karen tightened her seat belt and gripped the Glock as Train slowed down imperceptibly. They drove down toward a bridge crossing a tree-lined creek, beyond which she could see a **T** intersection with what looked like a gravel road bisecting the two-lane one. Train tightened his own seat belt, flexed his hands, and then swung the Suburban in a noisy, gravel-spitting right turn. Karen could feel the vehicle lifting off its left wheels slightly before Train hit the gas and sent them hurtling down the county road, accelerating through the dense woods on either side. She looked back in time to see a flare of red brake lights and then a pair of high beams swinging over the trees and pointing toward them.

"Here he comes," she said as Train punched it.

"Look for cop lights," he ordered.

She almost hoped for flashing blue or red emergency lights, but there was only that steady stare of high beams coming up after them in the darkness. She turned back around as Train careened through an unbanked curve, once again throwing up gravel all over the place. The road was almost as wide as the state road.

"I was hoping for a paved road. Oh well," he shouted over the road noise. Karen punched out 911 and transmitted a call for help. Nothing happened, and then she had to hang on as Train took them through another curve. She had a fleeting glance of an embankment whipping much too close past the windows, and then they passed some kind of tower. She checked the phone and saw that there was next to no signal. She swore. Then the light behind them became much brighter.

"He's using the spot," Train yelled, squinting as a blaze of bright white light flooded into the Suburban. The car behind them was a lot closer. Train batted down the center mirror and then swore as he nearly lost control going around the next bend. The road was almost too wide, and, being unmarked, it was nearly impossible for Train to hold the center. There were also more potholes now, and the Suburban was banging noisily through some of them. Karen wondered if the road went on much farther. But it had to go somewhere, didn't it?

"He's trying to pass! Get down!" Train yelled as the white light moved up on them, hovering over on the left-rear side of the car. Karen ducked as Train swung in front of the pursuing car, trying to block it, and then careened back across the road as he overcompensated. The Suburban was too big and heavy for this sort of high-speed maneuvering on gravel. Their pursuer was holding tight on their left rear, that big spotlight throwing back blinding glare from every reflective surface, including the front windshield. Karen realized Train must be having trouble seeing anything at all.

He swung back to the left sharply, too sharply, and the Suburban began to fishtail. He instinctively hit the brakes for a second, which allowed their pursuer to surge up abreast on the left. She remembered the Glock and raised her hands to bring it to bear behind Train's head as the other car's nose drew abreast of their rear doors, the spotlight blasting white light at them like some kind of ray gun. In the light reflecting off their own left side, she saw that the right-front window of the other car was sliding all the way down, and she screamed at Train to lean forward so she could get a shot as the other car crept forward. But Train was still fighting to regain control. At that instant, the other car pulled up abreast of them, blanking out the spotlight, and she caught a glimpse of a solitary figure in the other car, one hand on the wheel, the other holding something in his hand. Not a gun. Something smaller. Shiny. For a split second, she had the ridiculous thought that it was a flashlight.

Flashlight.

Light. *Light!* She remembered that purple-red flash that had stunned her into insensibility in the barn.

"Close your eyes! Close your eyes!" she screamed at Train, clapping her left hand over her own eyes and squeezing them shut as tightly as she could. Even so, she felt the brain-stunning power of the retinal flash as it imprinted the cracks between her fingers on the underside of her eyelids. Then the other car shot past and the Suburban was slowing down as Train, groaning, slumped into a semistupor behind the wheel, his eyes staring sightlessly. Karen dropped the gun and grabbed for the wheel, but her seat belt kept her from reaching the brakes. She punched at the belt latch just as the big vehicle swerved toward the edge of the road. She fought the wheel hard, her left foot punching desperately to find the brake pedal between Train's feet. The flare of red brake lights flooding the windshield alerted her to the other car. She finally found the brake pedal and tried to stand on it. Train leaned against her, and she looked right, in time to see that the other car was close, right in front of them. Just beneath the Ford emblem on the trunk was what looked like a very large gun barrel, pointing right at her. Oh my God! She groped for the Glock as her foot slipped off the brake pedal. But now the lights and her view ahead disappeared as something spattered all over the front windshield, something opaque, something that instantly blotted out all the light from their own headlights and the other car. It sounded as if they had entered a sustained rainsquall of heavy, wet plaster as she found the brake pedal again and wrestled the Suburban away from the embankment closing in on the right-front window. The interior became cavelike as she stared uncomprehendingly at the now-blackened windshield, her right shoulder pressed up against the dashboard as the car decelerated. The drumming noise continued as whatever it was covered the front windows on both sides and then moved down the left side and back windows, the spray clattering down the side and over the back of the car like the pressure nozzles of a car wash. Then abruptly the Suburban tilted as it ran off into the ditch on the right side, banging its frame over the edge of the gravel road and screeching the right side against the embankment before finally stopping with a loud bang.

She was momentarily stunned as the right side of her head hit hard on the center mirror. The engine raced, the rear tires machine-gunning gravel out from under the chassis, until she realized she was stepping on the accelerator. She jerked her foot off the pedal, but it was too late. The big car swayed once and then settled all the way over onto its right side, almost in slow motion, in a mighty crunch. Karen screamed but was able to jam the shift lever over into the park position as she slid across the front seat and banged up against the right-front door, pursued by a small landslide of all the little things that accumulate in a car. Train sagged down toward her, thankfully still in his seat belt, although the top belt bolt was creaking ominously as she struggled to get herself upright. The engine stalled out. It had become almost pitch-black inside, with only the instrument lights providing illumination.

For a moment, she just sat there, trying to get her bearings. Train was out of it, hanging like a sack of potatoes in his seat belt. The side of her head stung, and she was disoriented. The smell of gasoline began to penetrate the Suburban's interior. Then she heard something outside. She froze.

Silence. Then another noise, behind the car, but muffled. Whatever was on the windows was making it hard to hear. Another noise. She felt around in the clutter piled up against the right-front door for the Glock but couldn't find it. Train groaned softly. He started trying to unlatch his seat belt.

"Don't undo your belt," she whispered. "We're over on our side. Someone's out there."

The smell of gasoline was getting stronger. Then she thought she heard a car start up. Train groaned, rubbing his eyes. "I can't see a thing," he whispered. "Bastard got me."

"My eyes are okay, I think," she said. She was pretty sure her eyes were working. She scrunched herself up against the dashboard and helped Train to release himself from the belt and slide his legs down to stand on the right-front door. He was rubbing his eyes furiously.

There were no more sounds from outside, other than dripping and gurgling noises from the engine compartment. Conscious of the gasoline, she switched the ignition off, leaving the interior of the car pitch-black. She reached up and turned on one of the map lights over her shoulder. She looked around at the windows, but they were covered in what looked like thick dark paint. "There's something all over the windows. It came from the other car, when I was trying to get us stopped. There was some kind of gun sticking out of his trunk."

Train rubbed his eyes again. "Everything's purple. I never saw the damned thing coming."

"You had your hands full," she whispered. "I recognized it at the last instant and covered my eyes."

They both shut up and listened. They could hear the sounds of the engine block beginning to cool, and other noises from outside. "You think he's still out there?" she said.

"No. I don't think so," he whispered. "But we're going to have to get out of the car to find out. Where's the Glock?"

She finally found the gun lodged under the right armrest. "Can you see well enough to use it?"

"Not yet," he said. "That phone have a signal?"

She recycled the phone and waited for it to go through the warm-up sequence. "Two dashes. Not much of one, if any."

"Antenna may be busted," he said. "Try nine-one-one anyway. Tell them we're overturned a few miles west of State Road 216, on a county road. I think I saw a fire tower. I don't know the county road number."

While Karen transmitted the message in the blind, Train popped the door locks and then pushed up on the left-front door. It was stuck shut. Then he reached over and tried the left-rear door, with the same results. The door latches were working, but the doors were frozen. Train then tried all the windows, but none of them would move, either. He held the window switch for the driver's door down until the circuit breaker under the dash popped. He swore again. There was a new dripping sound, somewhere in the back.

Karen peered at the stuff on the windows. "I think they're stuck. This stuff's like glue." She turned around, looking past Train's legs, but it was all over the back window, too. The right-side windows were clear, but they were compressed into the embankment. The gas fumes were getting stronger.

"We've got to get out of here," she said, trying to keep the panic out of her voice. Train tried all the window switches again. Another circuit breaker popped.

"Ignition's off, right? It may not ignite," he said, twisting to look into the darkened back of the vehicle. The back of the car looked like a coroner's vehicle, with the windows painted black. "Unless it gets to the catalytic converter. And after that run, that thing's going to be red-hot."

"We're over in a ditch, Train. That gas is going to pool. We've *got* to get out of here!"

"That stuff looks like plastic of some kind," he said. "If we could get a window open, we could cut our way out." He popped the latch on the door compartment and held up the knife.

"But these goddamned electric windows are dead," she said. "We can't get at it." Then she remembered the Glock. "What if we use this to shoot a window out?" she asked. "Break the glass and then cut that stuff."

Train thought for a moment and then nodded. "Right. Don't bother with the windshield. It's safety glass. Do the window on the driver's side. Shoot a pattern—three across the top, three across the bottom, and then one in the middle. Then I can kick it out, I hope. Put something in your ears."

Karen stuffed some Kleenex in her ears as Train did likewise. Then he suggested they get in the backseat to avoid flying glass. They ended up standing on the right-rear door panel. The smell of gasoline was much stronger in the back.

"Is this safe?" she asked. "To fire the gun with all these fumes?"

"No choice. I still can't see anything. Do it, Karen."

She tried not to think about who or what might be waiting for them if and when they got out of the car. She aimed the Glock at the left top edge of the window while Train covered his ears. She had to pull hard on the trigger before the gun fired once, and the noise was deafening in the tightly enclosed car. A starred hole appeared roughly where she had aimed. She pulled again, only now the pistol was in semiauto and she ended up firing five more rounds before she got her finger off the trigger. She was astonished to see that Train was grinning at her through the pall of gunsmoke, but then he was moving, swinging his body over into the front seat, his chest half on and half off the front seat's backrest, his massive legs kicking up at the window, dislodging a hail of glass shards. But then his foot was punching into what looked like a rubber sheet outside the window.

Karen coughed, choking. The car was now full of smoke as well as gasoline fumes. Train was coming back over the seat, his shoes crunching on shards of glass as he fumbled for the knife. He banged away at one corner of the glass with the butt of the knife and then cut a line through the plastic skin covering the window aperture. Karen crouched low in the backseat to get away from the smoke and the gasoline fumes, fighting the urge to scramble past him and out that hole.

Suddenly, the air above her head cleared and she looked up. Train was slashing at the rubbery coating now, making the hole bigger. Then he leaned back down into the backseat.

"Give me the Glock," he said. She passed it up to him, and he stuck his head and right hand out of the hole. Immediately, he ducked back down. "Forgot. Can't see. Everything's still purple. You look."

She squeezed up against him in the space between the front and back seats, poked her head out of the hole in the rubbery substance, and looked around. There was only the pale stripe of the gravel road cutting through the dark woods. The other car was gone. But the stink of gasoline was even stronger outside. She ducked back down into the car.

"Looks clear," she said. "But there's definitely gas pooling somewhere."

"Okay," he said. "I'll boost you through the window. You cut the stuff off the door, 'cause there's no way I can fit through that window."

She nodded, handed him the Glock, and squeezed her head and shoulders through the hole. He hunched down on the right-side door, wrapped his arms around her legs at the knees, and straightened up. She felt like a Polaris missile coming out of that hole, and she promptly lost her balance as she scrambled to find a handhold, finally grabbing the edge of the luggage rack on top of the car. She tore her skirt sliding over the bottom edge of the car but landed on the gravel more or less upright. Train popped his head and one arm out of the hole right after her and gave her the knife. In order to free the front door, she had to climb back up on the side of the car to cut away the rubbery dull white film covering the whole left side of the car. The film was thin but very strong, and it would not peel off the side of the car, so she had to cut through to the seam of the left-front door before being able to yank it open. The rubber clung to the door like a shroud.

Train climbed out, and together they scrambled wordlessly around the front of the car. But just as they started up the hill, they heard the sound of the car phone ringing. They looked at each other. The phone rang again.

"Who the hell—" Train said.

"McNair. I'll bet it's McNair. We called him, remember?"

"But—"

"There must be a signal now," she said. The phone rang again. Karen handed him the knife and ran back around to the side of the car. But there was no way to reach the phone inside without climbing back up on the side of the car.

Train was about to help her when something at the back of the Suburban caught his peripheral vision. A whiff of smoke? A tiny white object, back by the bumper. Purple-white. Everything tinged with purple. He squeezed his eyes shut and then opened them, desperately trying to see as he moved carefully toward the back of the car. Karen was stretching, trying to lean into the car.

"Karen, wait a minute," he called as the phone rang again. And then he froze when he recognized what was on the rear bumper. A lighted cigarette was dangling from a string tied to the bumper, about eighteen inches over the shimmering puddle in the ditch. The ash had burned almost back to the string.

"*Karen! Karen! Get out! Get away, now!*" he shouted, and then began to backpedal sideways across the hill, trying to get to her.

Karen had been halfway into the hole in the driver's window when she heard him yelling. She turned, saw the look on his face, dropped back off the car, and bolted up the bank, where Train grabbed her. Together, they scrambled up the hill. An instant later, the car exploded behind them in a bright red-and-yellow fireball. They both hit the ground as the hot compression wave seared the night air over their heads, and then bits of hot metal and flaming plastic were clattering around them on the wet hillside. Down on the road, the remains of the Suburban burned furiously, hot enough to keep them backing up the hill, hands held by the sides of their faces to ward off the intense heat. The road and the surrounding trees were thrown into stark visual relief in the yellow-orange glare. They stopped about fifty yards up the hill and sat down in the underbrush.

Karen examined her torn skirt, ragged stockings, and mud-daubed uniform jacket. "Remind me never to go parking with you in the woods again," she muttered.

Train grinned weakly in the firelight. "Well," he said, "I try to give all the girls a hot time. The good news is that fire ought to bring somebody."

"The good guys this time, I hope," she said, trying to cover her thighs with the torn skirt. "I've got to go buy some fatigues if you and I are going to keep seeing each other like this."

He grinned again and put his arm around her. But then he grew serious. "We were lucky. Very damned lucky. Again." He described the cigarette hanging off the bumper. "It's the oldest time-delay fuse in the business, and it leaves no trace. Once the cigarette burns back to the string, it drops. In our case, into that ditchful of gasoline."

"Then he meant to kill us this time."

"No doubt in my military mind," Train said, shifting his bulk in the grass. She noticed for the first time that there was a cut on his forehead. Down below, the burning hulk was settling now as the frame deformed and bits of the interior fell out onto the road. The hood popped open as they watched, revealing several glowing engine components. The night breeze was raining soot all over the hillside where they crouched under a small tree. Finally, the fire began to diminish.

"How did he know where to find us?" Karen said.

Train rubbed his eyes and thought about that. It had to be the phone lines at his house. McNair had described where the hospice was, and he'd also intimated that Sherman would be there, that they would all be there. "He got it from McNair's phone call. My phones must be tapped."

Karen nodded in the flickering light, knowing the feeling. Then she realized what had been tickling the edge of her memory. "That stuff—on the windows. I know what that is. It's that plastic compound they were using to cover that helicopter—at the Quantico air base."

Train looked at her and swore softly. A jet of intense green-orange flame hissed out of the engine compartment when the fire found the air conditioner's Freon flask. Karen shivered in the wet darkness.

"So young Jack Sherman did his old man another little favor," she said. "He said he would. I wish I'd shot him when I had the chance."

Train squeezed her hand. "McNair will have to move now. After this."

Twenty minutes later, they heard a siren approaching, and then a second one. Train got up, helped Karen get to her feet, and put his arm around her. They began to walk sideways down the hill, keeping their distance from the burning hulk. The distant flickering of blue and red lights over the trees was a welcome contrast to the glowing metal carcass on the road.

Three hours later, they were in McNair's car, headed back to Washington. Karen was lying crosswise in the backseat, her legs up on the seat, her sleeping form wrapped in one of the Fenster County EMT blankets. Train sat up front with McNair, who had been listening carefully to Train's debrief of the incident on the county road for the second time. Train finished with the arrival of the first EMTs. Their clothes still smelled of char.

"Pissed me off," he said. "Burning up my Suburban."

"Goddamned lucky you both aren't toast," McNair replied, accelerating to pass a semi. "This wasn't a warning. You know that, don't you? This was for real."

"Message received," Train said. He looked back over his shoulder at Karen, but she was still sleeping. "I think it's time we went over to the offensive. I'm beginning to feel like the settlers barricaded in their cabin. I want to get out in the woods and start killing some Injuns."

McNair shot him a skeptical look.

"Yeah, I know," Train said. "But we need to break the pattern here. We need to act instead of always reacting. What I can't figure is why he upped the ante."

"Maybe the commander's little courtesy call on the Sherman kid had something to do with it."

Train nodded silently. He had been thinking the same thing. "Okay," he said. "Let's look at that. Galantz wants us out of the way now because we've attracted daylight to Sherman's son. If this is still all about Sherman as the target of revenge, why's the kid important? Guy like Galantz surely doesn't need help."

McNair did not reply. Train let him think about it.

"Okay, I give up," McNair said. "I can see the 'what' part of it but not the 'why' part."

"My theory," Train said, "is that Galantz has been planning to fold the kid into his little scheme for a long time. From what the kid told Karen, they met back when Jack was still in the Corps, at recon school, where Galantz was probably an instructor. That'd be a good stash for a sweeper. Then something happened, maybe even something his new 'old man' engineered, and then Jack was out with a BCD. The only friend he's got in the world now is the guy that got him through recon training."

"But what's the game?" McNair said. "Like you said, it's not like Galantz would need the help of a shitbird like that to off the admiral."

"It's not about killing Admiral Sherman," Train said. "This is about destroying him. Ruining his reputation. Provoking a Navy rubbed raw by a string of scandals to force him out, right when he's made it to the top. Using the guy's son would be icing on the cake in that program."

"But how?"

"Picture the headline: ADMIRAL'S SON A MURDERER. Galantz has been thinking ahead of us. He *knows* you guys will never catch *him,* so you'll settle for what you *can* catch—Sherman's son. Hell, it's already working. Sherman did nothing but attract a homicide cop, and they've stashed him sideways over in the Bureau. Then he gets spooked and bolts for the hospice. Goes AWOL. An admiral, for crying out loud. And after this caper tonight, you guys are going to *have* to move. And you'll move against Jack Sherman, because you know you can pick him up anytime you want. Arresting Jack Sherman gives the Fairfax County cops a 'suspect in custody,' and any potential political heat dies away."

McNair shot him a look. "We're desperate guys," he grunted. "But not that desperate. And we're just supposed to forget about Galantz?"

Train glanced back at Karen, but she was still asleep. "Isn't that what certain federal agencies have already asked you to do? You've got two probable homicides, and two attempted homicides. You grab up a viable suspect, your face is saved, and you can leave Galantz to the spooks and hope he doesn't get Sherman, about whom the Navy no longer cares."

McNair nodded again in the darkness. "It reads," he said finally. "Except for maybe when I take it to a commonwealth's attorney. Which leads me to believe that this is a really good time for you two to hole up somewhere."

"Yes and no," Train said. "After tonight, I'd rather be the finder than the findee. I think this guy just wants us dead." He looked back over his shoulder. Karen's face was illuminated momentarily in the light of some passing headlights. "I don't want her exposed to any more of this, and I also want a crack at the real bad guy here. Especially if you guys are gonna back off."

McNair didn't answer. He patted the pocket of his suit coat and then sighed. "Goddamn, I'd like a cigarette. Quit two years ago, and not a day goes by that I don't crave one. Look, I'll make a deal with you. Give me a day or so. You two get your heads down and stay low. Take her back to your house. I'll get Stafford County to put some protection on for you, whatever. But basically, you agree to stay put. In return, I'll see what I can do about putting some heat on Galantz."

Train thought about it. "Why are you doing this?" he asked.

"Because he's killed two people on my turf, and tried for two more. That pisses *me* off—personally. I want his ass. Deal?"

Train thought about it. As they approached Washington, the traffic out on the interstate was heavier, even at this late hour. The stream of red and white lights still had a purplish corona to them. "Okay," he said finally. "Deal. Two days."

"Okay," McNair said. "And leave Sherman to me. I'll break the news to him about his kid's involvement."

CHAPTER 12

McNair dropped them off at Karen's house in Great Falls. Karen needed some clothes, and with the Suburban destroyed, they needed a car. Karen's Mercedes was in the garage. McNair stayed in his car to make a call while Karen extracted a spare key from its hiding place. Once they were in the house, McNair left. He had given Train a beeper number in case something came up over the next two days. Twenty minutes later, they were out of there and headed for Aquia.

Karen, refreshed after her long nap in McNair's car, was elected to drive, while Train kept watch behind them, the Glock stuffed between the front bucket seats. He was not going to be surprised by this bastard again. The sodium-vapor lights along the highway still had a reddish purple tinge to them.

"I'd be happier if McNair had come with us," she said as she pulled the car onto the Beltway.

"He's just as tired as we are," Train said. "Actually, with all this traffic out here, I think we're reasonably safe." We hope, he thought.

"Nobody's safe on the Beltway," she said. "But at least there's a phone signal."

At which point, the car phone started to ring, startling both of them. After a moment's hesitation, she reached down and hit the button so they could both listen.

"Hello?" she said.

Congratulations.

Karen actually closed her eyes for a moment before she remembered she was driving. Train leaned over to speak into the remote microphone. "Gonna try again, Galantz?"

You were lucky. Again. As I think I told you, you have to be lucky every time. I have to be lucky only one time.

"You some kind of ghost, Galantz? Only come out at night?"

Not a ghost, von Rensel. A grotesque, to be sure. I have one eye, a scar that bisects my face, a stainless-steel hand, and a Teflon larynx. I am memorable.

"So what now, Galantz? Calling to tell us you have the admiral tied up somewhere?"

There was an audible wheeze, a precursor breath each time before the voice replied.

You don't understand, von Rensel. If I'd wanted Sherman dead, he'd have been extinguished a long time ago. That's what I do. What I've done for years.

"So what do you want?" Karen asked, speaking for the first time.

His destruction. At the hands of his own kind, Commander. I'm provoking his precious Navy to turn on him at the peak of his professional success. I'm going to take away everything of value to him and leave him to contemplate that for the rest of his life. And there's nothing you two can do about it.

"The Navy knows what's going on here, Galantz," Train said. "They're not going to fall for this." But as he said it, he wondered.

The admirals will do precisely what I want, von Rensel. In a manner of speaking, they're part of this. That's why you're going to Aquia now. And that's why I'm making this little courtesy call—to reinforce your orders. Stay out of this. Stay out of this or I'll extinguish you both, understand?

How in the hell did he know that? Train wondered. He tried to think of something to say, but he sensed that Karen was getting truly frightened. Hell, so was he. There was absolutely zero emotion in that machine voice.

You listening, von Rensel? I've been setting this up for years. Years of watching Sherman. Years of cultivating his wretched son. But time is growing short. My employers are a little upset with me just now, and I don't need any distractions in the endgame. Go to your pretty little estate. Stay there. This will be over soon. Now, look behind you.

Train snapped his head around. Their Mercedes was all alone out in six lanes of the Beltway. There was a wall of headlights farther back, but all of the traffic was holding back because of the police car that was a hundred feet behind them.

"Oh no," Karen whispered.

Train reached for the Glock, but then he saw the police car begin to fall back, signaling an exit, merging into the phalanx of headlights a half mile behind them.

Go to Aquia. Live a lot longer. Then there was only the hiss of static.

"Now what?" Karen said.

"We call the cops, that's what," he replied. "What's this number?"

She gave it to him while he reached for the phone, recycled it, and dialed the beeper number McNair had given him. The beeper tape came up, and Train punched in the car phone's number and hung up. The phone rang one minute later.

"Von Rensel," Train said.

"You called us," a male voice replied.

Train hesitated. Us? Who the hell was us? "I have a message for Mc-Nair," he said.

"Go ahead."

"Tell him Galantz caught up with us on the Beltway, gave us a friendly phone call. We're headed for Aquia."

"Your ETA?"

"An hour from now. Maybe less."

"Your route?"

Train hesitated again. Who was this guy? But then, if they wanted protection, the cops would have to know their route. He told the voice they would take the Beltway to I-95, and then straight down to Aquia. "Us" broke the connection without replying. Train hung up the phone.

"Who'd you get?"

"An ops center, from the sound of it. They knew McNair, though."

"That voice scared the hell out of me."

"Me, too. Rock and roll, Karen." She kicked it up to seventy.

An hour later, they arrived at Train's estate. Train had called ahead and raised Kyoko to tell her they were coming in. Hiroshi was waiting for them at the front steps when Karen pulled the Mercedes to a stop. The two Dobermans, who had accompanied the car up to the house from the front gates, sat attentively on either side of the car until Hiroshi gave them an order that sent them back out into the morning twilight. Karen slumped behind the wheel and turned to look wordlessly at Train, her eyes betraying her exhaustion.

"For the moment, I think we're safe," he said, not entirely believing it even as he said it.

"Only for the moment? I thought McNair said we weren't targets anymore."

"Yeah, but what does he know." When they got out, Hiroshi signaled that he had something to tell Train. Karen took her bag and went into the house to use the bathroom. Hiroshi waited until she had gone into the house. "There is a visitor," he announced.

"Visitor?" Train asked. "At this hour?" And then he knew. "Admiral Sherman."

Hiroshi nodded. "Arrived three hours ago. He is asleep in the study."

Train was wondering where the hell the good admiral had been all night. He was still bothered by what he thought of as the feasibility problem. Then he dismissed his suspicions: As Galantz had said, Sherman was in endgame and didn't know it. He took Hiroshi aside.

"Go in and wake him up. Take him some coffee. When Commander Lawrence comes back out, we'll take a little walk around the grounds, give him a few minutes to get himself together. Then we'll come in."

Hiroshi gave a short bow, then hesitated.

"Yes, Hiroshi-san?"

"He has a gun, I think. In his coat pocket."

Train nodded. Why not, everybody else was packing tonight. "It's been a long night, Hiroshi," he said. "We were ambushed up in Maryland." He told Hiroshi about what had happened.

"Ninja," the old man murmured thoughtfully. Train caught the note of approval. But then he realized that it was respect being given to a worthy and capable opponent and not admiration for what Galantz was doing.

"Yes, ninja," he replied. "But a ninja without honor. He kills women and old men. His real objective is the destruction of this senior officer, this Admiral Sherman, the man inside."

"Ah. *This* is the senior officer? The ninja will kill him?"

"I don't think so. I think he means to disgrace him and then let him live with that disgrace for a long time."

Hiroshi gave another nod. Disgrace was much worse than being killed.

"Commander Lawrence and I interfered. I think the first attack on her was meant to neutralize me. The second time was meant to remove both of us. Now I think if we were just to stay here, nothing more would happen to us. Or to anyone else here," he added pointedly.

Hiroshi gave a dismissive snort. "Let him come here. Life is sometimes boring."

Train laughed out loud. "Not with this guy, Hiroshi-san. But my other problem is that my superiors are playing at some kind of game."

Hiroshi was silent for a moment while he absorbed this news. Then he gave Train a sideways look. "You will remain here?"

"I'm not sure. When I was in the Marines, we were taught not to sit still and wait for the enemy. Waiting in one place just simplifies his problem. There's another factor: The senior officer's son is involved in this matter. He has been helping the man who is behind the killings."

Hiroshi shook his head. "The son helps the man who would destroy his father? What kind of son is this?"

Karen was coming back out of the house. There was a hint of sunrise across the river. "There's history, Hiroshi-san. The father treated the son very badly long ago. The father is not entirely innocent here. Send Gutter out, please."

Hiroshi bowed and went back into the house as Karen walked up, carrying two mugs of hot coffee. A moment later, Gutter came trotting out from behind the house. Together, they walked across the front lawn and down a gravel path toward the river oaks. Train was amused to see that Gutter was staying closer to Karen than to him. Dogs figure stuff out, he thought. There was a thin band of red light defining the silhouette of the Maryland hills across the Potomac. They could hear the honking of some Canadian geese upstream in the park; the sound made the Galantz problem seem remote.

"Have you figured out what we're going to tell this poor man?" she asked, taking his hand.

"I'm getting the inklings of a plan," he replied, kicking a dead branch off the path. "Although McNair might not like having his hand forced. I think we need to tell Sherman about his son's involvement. Then maybe suggest we put the two of them face-to-face, see what happens."

"What about your deal with McNair?"

"So far, we've kept it. Sherman came to us, not the other way around. But here's the problem: McNair knows the kid's involved. He may have told the Navy. If he has, what use does Galantz have for the kid now? Jack's served his purpose—another nail in Sherman's political coffin."

"Which makes Jack expendable?"

"Yeah, I think so. I think he plans to kill the kid and heap final insult to injury. Things of value, remember? Galantz knows that, despite the estrangement between father and son, it would just about crush Sherman if his son became the final victim."

Karen shivered in the predawn air. "And we're the ones who told McNair. I'm beginning to feel a little like a puppet, aren't you?"

"And the son thinks Galantz is more of a father to him than his real father. He'll never see it coming."

"Wow. Like he said, years of planning."

Train nodded. "I'm starting to regret our deal. This stinks. We ought to *do* something."

Karen paused to watch the morning twilight play on the broad silvery expanse of the river. An alert catbird discovered them and began to scold from one of the oaks. "We have company," Karen said, glancing back over her shoulder.

Train looked. Admiral Sherman was coming across the lawn. Karen quietly disengaged her hand from Train's. Even from a distance in the dawn twilight, they could see that his face was haggard and his eyes unnaturally bright, almost as if he might have a fever. He was wearing his navy blue uniform trousers, shirt, and black tie, but he had a beige civilian car coat on over his uniform. Karen felt Train tensing up as the admiral came across the wet grass. She felt a pang of disappointment that Train was still suspicious of this man.

"Good morning to both of you," Sherman said, the fatigue audible in his voice. There were dark pouches under his normally youthful eyes. "Hiroshi said you were out here. Mr. von Rensel, I hope you'll forgive this intrusion."

"Good morning, Admiral," Karen replied, jumping in before Train could say anything. "I hope your night wasn't as interesting as ours."

Sherman stared down at the grass for a moment and then out over the river. "I've been driving," he said. "All night. Never done that before. Just got in the car and drove. All the way east to the north side of Baltimore, then back down to D.C. Trying to sort some things out."

"How did you end up here?" Train asked.

"McNair," Sherman said. He looked from one to the other. "We need to talk. I want to know what my son has to do with all this."

"Did McNair tell you about our being attacked last night?"

"Only that you had been. That you would fill me in—on that and on Jack. *He* said that you and I needed to talk."

"Where were you last night, Admiral?" Karen asked as gently as she could, trying not to sound accusatory.

Sherman frowned, but then he answered. "Where? I was up in Maryland, near the Pennsylvania line. A little town called Harney."

"So were we, Admiral, courtesy of Detective McNair," she said, giving him a moment to comprehend that they knew, that McNair also knew. "We do need to talk. Train, let's all go back up to the house."

Over coffee, fresh fruit, and hot rolls, Karen told the admiral about what had happened since Wednesday. She finessed what they knew about the hospice situation, limiting it to the fact that his wife was still alive. With one eye on Train, she told the admiral about Jack's admissions. Train dutifully kept silent. Sherman's face was grim when she was finished.

"Great God," he snapped, tossing down his napkin. "I had no idea. This guy is on a goddamned rampage." He looked from one to the other. "How much of this does the JAG know?"

Karen looked at Train for a brief second. He picked right up.

"He knows about what happened out on the river," Train said. "To my knowledge, he doesn't know about the attack on the road last night, or your situation at the hospice. I'm not sure he knows of your son's involvement."

The admiral let out a long breath. "If he doesn't, he will," he said. "McNair will probably be filling him in shortly. Perhaps it ought to come from me. Technically, I'm probably AWOL right now, anyway."

"Why did you bail out, Admiral?" Karen asked.

His face tightened, but then he relaxed. "I felt everything closing in. Usually, I go up there out of a sense of responsibility. She's there because of me." He stopped to take a deep breath. "But the second reason I go there is to seek refuge. It's the one place in this entire world I can go and never be judged."

Karen nodded slowly. Train continued to study the tablecloth.

"Now tell me, what Jack's role is in all this? Did he help Galantz kill those two people?"

"From a legal standpoint, I think the police would say he was an accessory after the fact," Train said. "But he did admit to being part of Karen's abduction."

"He was there? At Elizabeth's? At Galen's?"

Karen gave Train a reproving look. "He says he wasn't. He claims his only role was to show up at the funerals, so that you would see him. But we think he's definitely working with Galantz. The attack on us out on the highway involved a machine Jack uses at work."

"Damn," Sherman said, rubbing his face. "And McNair knows this?"

"Yes, sir, he does," Train said. "But we're not sure what exactly he's doing with it. Galantz is the guy McNair really wants."

"My God," Sherman muttered. "My own son."

Train leaned forward. "We think that's part of the plan, Admiral. Galantz has been contemplating revenge for years. He encounters your son at the recon training school, realizes who he is, befriends him, then sets something up that gets Jack thrown out of the Corps. Once Jack's out on his ass on civvy street with a bad discharge and a drinking problem, here comes his old buddy from recon school to make life interesting again."

"And fold him into his master plan to destroy me."

"We think so. Use Elizabeth's homicide to frame you, or at least to get you in trouble with the Navy. We think Galen Schmidt became a target of opportunity."

"Because I went to see him when I got the note," Sherman said, his face gray.

Train sidestepped that remark. "And if that didn't do it," he continued, "Galantz puts Jack in our faces. We focus on Jack, the cops are right behind us, and now you and your son are involved in homicides."

"Jack was a hater," Sherman said softly. "I never figured him as a dupe."

Karen reluctantly began to shake her head. "No, sir. I think he's in this willingly. I'm sorry, Admiral, but that's what I took away from talking to him."

The admiral stared down at the ground. Karen's heart went out to him when she saw the desolation in his eyes. Galantz has won, she thought.

"Jack's not exactly—how shall I say this—socially functional?" she said. She described the living conditions at the trailer, and Jack's physical state when she first found him. Sherman shook his head and pushed back roughly from the table, causing Gutter to sit up. Sherman got up and stared out through the windows for a minute while Kyoko came in and silently cleared away the dishes.

"I told McNair I need to go resolve this," he said finally. "I'll call the

JAG. I had thought of maybe going to see Jack, alone, to try to sort this out. But . . ."

He didn't finish this thought. Karen looked at Train. She could now see at least two problems with what Sherman was suggesting. If the police found the two of them together, the implications might be very disturbing for the police. But worse, she wasn't sure the admiral would stand up under the emotional assault of his son's boasting about helping Galantz, as he surely would. And then of course, there was Galantz. She was relieved when Train stood up.

"The phone's in the study, Admiral," he said. "Then if you'd like to shower and shave before you go in, Kyoko will show you to a guest room."

The admiral rubbed the sides of his face with both hands, his characteristic gesture, and then nodded absently. He followed Train to the study, where Train showed him the phone. Then Train came out, closing the door behind him. Karen met him in the hallway.

"He's at the end of his rope, I think," Train said. "Taking him to see Jack doesn't seem like such a good idea just now."

"I agree. If the police showed up, they'd be very suspicious if they found the admiral there, especially if Jack seized the opportunity to deny Galantz's existence and point the finger at his father."

"Damn. He would, too."

"That three-star is going to force Sherman out," she said. "And he knows it."

"I hate to say this," Train said, "but maybe you should go in with him. He's going to need a friendly face."

She smiled up at him. "About time you were nice to this poor man. And why, exactly, do you hate to say that?" she asked.

Train actually flushed a bit under her direct look. "I don't want to let you out of my sight. Things of value, you know?"

She smiled again and squeezed his hand. But then she thought about Sherman's situation. "If they agree to see him this morning, on a Saturday, they're not going to want any commanders in the room," she said. "Especially commander lawyers. This will be a flags-only meeting. No mere mortals allowed. At least not until they get all the blood off the walls."

"Yeah, but I'm worried about what he might do afterward. Like try to go to find Jack, and maybe walk into Galantz in the process."

Karen was not fooled. "And while *we're* gone, kind sir? You will be staying right here like you promised? Like a good Train, right?"

Train was looking over her head and squirming perceptibly. She grabbed his elbow and steered him away from the closed study door. "You promise me, Train von Rensel. No Lone Ranger stuff. You be here when I bring this poor man back out here. You promise, right now, or I don't go with him."

"I wasn't thinking of—"

"Oh yes you were," she said. "Now you promise me—"

The study door opened and the admiral came out, running his left hand through his hair. They turned to see what he would say.

"It's show time," he announced. "At noon, I'm to meet with Admiral Kensington in his office. I think they've made some decisions."

"Admiral, Karen thinks she should go with you," Train said before Karen could speak. "Moral support, if nothing else."

Sherman gave Karen a weary smile. "This isn't going to be a pretty sight, Karen," he said. "They'd probably invite you to wait out in the hallway. And if you did come in, I have to warn you that commanders who get in the middle of a flag-level gunfight do so at their professional peril."

"I'll take my professional chances," she replied, shooting Train a look. "Besides, I have firsthand knowledge of the facts, and the law."

"Well, I'd appreciate the hell out of it. Not that they're likely to let facts or law get in the way of a little purge. Mr. von Rensel, may I take you up on that offer of a guest room?"

"This is Admiral Kensington."

"He's coming in. At noon."

"Have you solved our problem?"

"Yes, I have. Those people sent someone over this morning. He was able to lift the protocol long enough for me to edit the file and then replace it. Then he put the protocol back in place. I've lifted the access restrictions as of Monday morning and returned it to the archives. Until then, there's a security trap on it."

"You're telling me more than I want to know. Very well. You told him to come to my office?"

"At noon."

"Good. I'll send everyone home before then. Is this going to be easy way or hard way?"

"That's not knowable, Admiral. But that detective has been in touch. It seems Sherman's son is involved in the homicides somehow."

"His own son? Well, that does it. This isn't going to be any problem at all, Thomas."

"I hope not. I'll see you just before noon, then."

At eleven o'clock, Hiroshi brought Karen's Mercedes and then the admiral's sedan around to the front of the house. Train thought the admiral looked impressive as always in his blues, the single broad gold stripe glowing in the morning light. Kyoko had done his shirt, and a shower had done the rest. Except for circles under his eyes, he looked almost ready for a fight. When Karen came out on the porch, he felt his heart do a little flop. She, too, had prospered from an hour's rest, and a treacherous voice in his head pointed out what a good-looking couple they made, both handsome people in uniform. And you suggested they go into the Pentagon together to face the lions. Good move, bud. Really great thinking. But then she winked at him and he felt a whole lot better.

Karen went to get in her car. The admiral came over to Train. "Mr. von Rensel," he said, offering his hand. "Thanks for everything. You have a lovely home out here. I assume that after this morning, the Navy's official role in this investigation will be finito."

"Admiral, that may be true," Train said, taking the admiral's hand and shaking it. "But I'm not ready just to let this thing go, even if the Navy is. This guy has tried to kill me once and Karen twice. If the cops don't get him, and soon, I'm going to take a shot."

Their eyes met. Train got the impression that the admiral knew precisely what he was talking about. "If this goes the way I think it will, call me," Sherman said. "I'd like to go along when you take that shot."

Train went over to the Mercedes and Karen lowered the window.

"Did I ever tell you I'm a sucker for sailors in short skirts?" he said.

"This is not a short skirt," she retorted, although sitting in the front seat of a car in a straight skirt was making a liar out of her.

Train grew serious. "Look, I'm not thrilled with your venturing out alone. We promised McNair—and this guy's already tried for you twice."

"*You* promised McNair," she said. "And besides, this was your idea, was it not?" Then she put her hand on his. "You're right about this. Somebody has to be there with him. And one of us should be here in case McNair tries to contact us."

"I hope to hell someone besides us is working this problem. Any sign of trouble out there on the road, you get onto nine-one-one. And remember, your car phone is not secure."

"Everybody knows that. And I promise to yell if something starts. And you promised to stay here, right?"

The admiral's car started forward around the circular drive, heading for the gate. Train stepped back from the car. "You better roll. You've got Saturday shopping traffic to get through up at Springfield."

"Train, you promised!"

"I know. I won't do anything stupid."

She gave him a warning look and then started the car and followed the admiral out.

Train watched them go and then walked thoughtfully back into the house. He yawned. He had slept a little bit last night, but not restfully. Need to call McNair again. Tell him that Sherman and Karen are headed to the Pentagon. Then I'm going to go put my hands on that kid.

He went into his study to make some calls. The first was to his insurance company, and the second was to the Chevy dealer in Fredericksburg to order up a replacement Suburban. Then he called McNair's number again. It being Saturday, his call to the Homicide Section was diverted to the police department's general operator, who promised to relay the "Call me" message. He hung up. Saturday. Then he thought of something: that number McNair had given him. He had to go find his suit coat to retrieve the card, but there it was, a beeper number. He called the system, prepared to leave the house number. Instead, he got the phone company's hideous "you just screwed up" tone in his ear, followed by a taped message saying, "The number you have dialed is no longer in service. Please check the—" He hung up. What the hell? He had assumed that the beeper system connected with a police operations unit. No longer in service? They must change it all the time for security purposes.

He leaned back in his chair and rubbed his eyes. So, where the hell was McNair? He put his head down on the desk for a few minutes. Not to go to sleep, of course; just to rest his eyes for a minute.

Karen was surprised to see how many cars were in the South Parking lot. Lots of eager beavers here today, she thought. Polishing that all-important career. What was it someone had once said? The word *career* was also a verb? She parked beside the admiral's Ford and got out. He was putting on his uniform cap and buttoning up his service dress-blue jacket. It was a lovely spring day, with clear, bright sunshine everywhere and a leafy breeze blowing in from the green slopes of Arlington Cemetery across Washington Boulevard.

"Too nice a day to go in there, isn't it?" he said, glancing over at the drab concrete pile that was the Pentagon building.

"It'd be a good day for a run," she replied, locking her car.

"If I went for a run, I think I'd keep on going," he said. "Karen, I've been thinking. I'd like to keep the hospice situation out of this, if I can."

"They'll want to know why you went off like that, Admiral. And where."

"Why, maybe. Where is something they have no need to know. They may just seize on the fact that I checked off the net for a couple of days. Couple that with this Galantz business and I think they'll ask me for my retirement papers." He gave her an intense look. "If that's how it comes out, that's okay, as long as I can protect Beth."

"I thought you were going to fight something like this, Admiral. You've given up an awful lot for those stars."

"Haven't I just," he said bleakly. "But if the big boys want me out, practically speaking, there's nothing I can do."

"You could refuse."

"Yes, and then what? Orders to a tour in charge of the Antarctic research station? No thanks. I'm either a player in the surface Navy or I'm not. Let's go, Commander."

"You're going to have to sign me in, I'm afraid," she said. "My ID card burned up in the fire."

Sherman did the paperwork at the South Parking guard station and then they walked quickly up to the OpNav area. When they arrived on the fourth floor, the admiral stopped and looked up and down the deserted corridors.

"Not quite noon on a Saturday, and yet everybody's gone," he said. "I think somebody's cleared the decks early in the OP-03 area. Don't want any snuffies walking in on a kangaroo court." He gave her a wry look. "Sure you still want to come along on this ride, Commander?"

She nodded firmly, although as they walked into Kensington's office, she wondered if she should have checked in with Admiral Carpenter before doing this. But Admiral Carpenter was standing in Admiral Kensington's front office, talking to Kensington's deputy, Admiral Vannoyt, when they arrived. The normal front-office staff was also present, including the EA and the flag lieutenant. Carpenter stopped in midsentence and greeted them.

"Admiral. Commander," he said, nodding at each of then. Vannoyt just looked disapprovingly at her but said nothing. Karen felt the social temperature in the room dropping. The office staff was suddenly concentrating very hard on their paperwork.

"Admiral Kensington's on the phone with the Vice Chief right now," Carpenter said to her in an abrupt, almost unfriendly tone of voice. "We'll go in shortly. Are you here for some special reason, Commander Lawrence?"

Karen had to swallow before she found her voice. "I'm here because I know some aspects of this case with which Admiral Sherman may or may not be familiar. Have you heard from Detective McNair, sir?"

Carpenter stared at her as if she had said something grossly impertinent. "I don't think your presence is going to be necessary at this meeting, Commander," he said in clipped tones. "Admiral Vannoyt, what do you think?"

"I quite agree, Admiral. Feel free to wait here, Commander. Or better yet, outside in the passageway."

Karen felt her face flushing. "In the passageway, Admiral?" No senior officer had ever talked to her this way.

"That's what I said, Commander," Vannoyt replied acidly. "Or in the parking lot. Or at home, if you'd like. This meeting was called at the flag level. There will be no need for staff legal officers."

The venomous intonation Vannoyt put on the term *legal officers* evoked a raised eyebrow even on Carpenter's face. Sherman's mouth was set in a tight line, but he remained silent. Karen, her heart racing and her face turning red, wasn't sure what to do next, but she was saved momentarily by the intercom buzzer on the EA's desk. The EA, a polished-looking young captain, stood up and nodded once at Vannoyt. As Vannoyt and Carpenter began to move toward the inner office door, Karen grabbed Sherman's arm.

"You need a lawyer for this," she whispered urgently. "You really, really do."

Carpenter overheard that, and, sensing what might be coming, he stopped dead in his tracks. "Karen," he began, but she turned her back on him. Sherman looked into her angry eyes, understood, and then nodded once.

"You have to ask," she said. "You have to request counsel, formally— from the JAG."

"Karen, what the hell are you doing?" Carpenter said, visibly angry. Vannoyt looked confused, and he was still trying to get the group moving again. Kensington was waiting.

Karen turned back around to face Carpenter. "As Admiral Vannoyt just pointed out while he was inviting me to cool my heels in the passageway, I'm a navy lawyer. What I'm doing is my job, Admiral."

Sherman stepped past her. "Admiral Carpenter, I hereby request Commander Lawrence be appointed as my counsel in these proceedings. I believe that's my right if these proceedings are going to be adversarial."

Carpenter was staring at Karen, and she realized that for the first time since she had been working for him, he didn't know what to do. He looked from her to Sherman and then back at her. He started to say something but then snapped his jaw shut.

"Gentlemen, the admiral is waiting," Vannoyt said.

"Well, Admiral?" Sherman said.

Train sat up with a start at his desk and instantly regretted it. He had a sharp crick in his neck and his left arm was asleep. He looked at his watch. It was 11:30. Damn it. He looked across the room. The study doors had been closed. Gutter was on watch in the corner of the room. That sneaky Hiroshi.

Coffee. He needed coffee. He got up and stretched, then sat back down again. He lifted the phone. The dial tone stuttered in his ear. One message on the voice mail—from a Detective Davison, Fairfax Homicide Section. "Detective McNair is on leave. If someone else can help you, call back."

Train put the phone down slowly. On leave? Now what the hell? He tried to rationalize that bit of news, and then it made sense. If there was political heat coming down on the Fairfax cops to back off this case, then having the lead detective slip off on leave might just solve everyone's problem. McNair was probably working off-line, much like he and Karen were. And if McNair turned up in the wrong place at the wrong time, he could always be severely chastised. Absolutely severely, County Commissioner, sir. It'll never happen again, sir. A smoothy like Lieutenant Bettino would be quite capable of that.

He got up and went out to the kitchen, where Kyoko was poring laboriously over the household accounts through a pair of oversized reading glasses. Train realized with a pang that she was getting old.

"Any coffee left?" he asked.

She got up immediately and went to fetch the makings for fresh coffee.

He carried the coffee back to the study and waited for the caffeine to do its work, still speculating about McNair. Then he had another thought: Suppose McNair was freelancing and had gone directly after Jack Sherman. He called the maintenance division at Quantico. No answer. Saturday, stupid, he reminded himself as he hung up. So then Jack ought to be at that trailer up on snake hill or whatever it was called. I'd still like to drag that little prick back here and let the good admiral have his confrontation after all. Although, from what he had seen of that little viper, he didn't give much for the admiral's chances of achieving any sort of reconciliation. But over and above that, he felt a strengthening need to do something and not just sit here waiting for the bogeyman, or for McNair.

You promised Karen not to leave the house, an inner voice chided.

He thought about that for a minute. Actually, I never did. Promise, that is. She just thought I did. He got up and beckoned the dog. "C'mon, Gutter. Let's go rat hunting," he said. He wondered how they were doing at the Pentagon.

"Very well," Carpenter said, glaring at her. "Commander Lawrence is so appointed." He appeared to be ready to say something else, then turned on his heel instead and followed Vannoyt into the inner office. Sherman gave Karen's arm a little squeeze and they followed the two flag officers in.

Kensington was, as usual, in full uniform, but he was not at his desk. He was standing with his back to them by one of the large windows overlooking the Pentagon helipad. Vannoyt walked to the center of the room, cleared his throat, and announced that Admiral Sherman was here as requested.

"Directed," Kensington said, continuing to face the windows. "Not requested. I don't desire. I don't solicit. I don't request. I *direct.*"

"Yes, sir," Vannoyt said, sounding to Karen like a chastened ensign. Kensington turned around and fixed Sherman with an eagle eye, and only then did he see Karen.

"Why is she here?" he demanded.

"I'm Admiral Sherman's counsel, sir," Karen said.

Kensington looked at Admiral Carpenter as if to ask why he had not been told that Sherman was coming with his lawyer. The JAG's face was tense.

"I just found out about this, Admiral," he said. "Admiral Sherman is within his rights to request counsel under these circumstances."

"I don't want her in here," Kensington snapped.

"Um," Carpenter began, but Kensington shut him off with a gesture and turned to Sherman.

"Admiral Sherman, I want to talk to you privately. Off the record, if that's what it takes. I want you to listen to what I have to say, and then you can decide if you want your lawyer here to hear it, in which case I'll say it again, for the record, and in her presence."

Sherman looked to Karen. Her first instincts were to refuse to leave. On the other hand, that would just provoke an impasse. These senior officers could get Sherman by himself anytime they wanted to, just by issuing some well-timed direct orders taking her out of the building. She had to swallow to find her voice.

"I advise you to commit to nothing beyond what the admiral has just proposed," she said to Sherman. "And if you don't want to go along with this, you have the right to request formal proceedings."

"If you do, those proceedings might be called a court-martial," Carpenter said. "I advise you to listen to what Admiral Kensington has to say. I remind you that he just got off the phone with the Vice Chief of Naval Operations."

"Very well," Sherman said. His voice was firm, but he had that mouse-trapped look on his face again.

"Then I'll wait outside," Karen said, looking at Vannoyt. "In the outer office, if you think there's room."

Vannoyt glared at her and Karen left, closing the door forcefully behind her. The EA looked up at her with the beginnings of a smirk on his face, saw her expression, and retreated back to his paperwork. Karen went to the far end of the outer office, over by the front door, sat down, and tried to compose herself. Her professional talent and good looks had carried her a long way into the inner and senior circles of the Navy JAG world, but she had just learned that there was at least one private club of which she was definitely not a member.

And her move to become Sherman's counsel—where the hell had that come from? It changed everything. She was no longer working for Carpenter as far as the Sherman case was concerned. It also split her efforts from Train's: Train *was* working for the JAG. You better call him. Tell him what's happened.

She got up and asked to use a phone, and one of the yeomen turned his telephone around on his desk. She dialed Train's number in Aquia. Hiroshi answered.

"He's not here," Hiroshi said. "He took your car."

Karen swore softly under her breath. "Going where, Hiroshi?"

"Cherry Hill. He took Gutter."

Karen thanked him, hung up, and went back to her seat. I knew it. He is going after that kid. At least he has the dog with him. She hoped that the kid was all he ran into up there in the weeds. She concentrated on summoning up what she knew about the military law of individual rights. That's almost an oxymoron, she thought.

Train drove slowly up the dirt track, finally coming upon two more trailers sprawled across a muddy clearing. He saw three large motorcycles parked under a makeshift lean-to. Two men were changing the rear tire on a fourth motorcycle by the side of the dirt road, and the larger one of them straightened up as the Explorer came into view.

Train slowed as the big man moved into the lane to block the way. He looked to be in his early forties, and he was dressed in greasy jeans, combat boots, and a filthy sleeveless undershirt. Emphasis on *big*, Train thought as he stopped. Gorilla-sized, maybe slightly less intelligence. He had a full flowing black beard that reached his chest and an oily ponytail of equal length hanging down his neck like a drowned rat. His glaring eyes bulged dangerously.

The other man looked positively anorexic, with thin, pale arms showing below an olive drab T-shirt that flapped over ancient Army fatigue trousers and scabrous sandals. There was something wrong with his face, as if it had been knocked sideways a long time ago and badly reset. Train thought he saw a thin line of drool visible on his chin. He remained crouching by the bike, watching the bearded one the way a smaller dog watches a larger one around the food bowl.

Train stopped the Explorer and ordered Gutter, who was lying in the right-rear seat, to stay down. Then he got out, leaving his door open.

" 'The hell you want?" demanded the big man after spitting a brown glop of chewing tobacco into the dirt right in front of Train. His pawlike hands were twitching as if they were longing for the feel of an ax handle.

"I'm going up this hill," Train said equably. He concentrated on Beard while keeping an eye on Drool.

Beard hunched his considerable shoulders and leaned forward. " 'The hell you are, Bud. This here's private. Turn that piece a Yuppie shit around and git your ass outta here."

"Or?"

" 'Or?' " The man exclaimed in mock surprise, straightening up. "Or!" He grinned down at Drool then, as if his morning had just been made. "Or I'll throw your ass and that Ford down the goddamn hill. How's that sound to you, asshole?" As he spoke, he reached down to pick up a tire iron and then began to smack it gently into his left palm. Train spoke one word, and

Gutter came out of the car to stand next to Train, who quietly gave him the growl command.

When Gutter rumbled, Drool dried right up and began to scuttle backward, away from the motorcycle, on his hands and heels. Beard frowned.

"Which one of you is rare?" Train asked.

Beard was still frowning. " 'Fuck's that supposed to mean?" he asked.

"Dog here likes his meat rare," Train explained, eyeing Drool. "So which one of you is rare?"

That did it for Drool, who bolted for the trailer, not stopping until he was safely through the flimsy metal door. Both Train and Beard heard him lock it.

"Sounds like he locked it," Train announced. "Guess that means you're rare." He raised his hand as if to give Gutter a command, and Gutter obliged by notching up the volume and showing another yard or so of teeth. Out of the corner of his eye, Train saw a shade flutter across the single front window in the trailer.

"Hey, man, hey, wait a goddamn minute here," the big man complained, backing up now, the tire iron dropping conspicuously out of his hand. "You wanna go up the goddamn hill, play in the snakes, that's cool. You go right the hell ahead. We didn't mean nothin', awright?"

Train silenced the dog and flashed his ID. "I'm a federal agent," he said. "You go back in your trailer with your girlfriend there, and you stay in there until you hear me leave. I'll be leaving the dog on watch when I get up there. You or anybody else goes up there will be disemboweled. You understand disemboweled, do you?"

The big man continued to back up, his eyes still locked on the dog. "Yeah, right. Got it. No problem." Then he turned and walked quickly to the door and beat on it for Drool to open up. The whole trailer shook. He was still banging on the trailer when Train got back into the Explorer and resumed his climb up the hill, with Gutter outside, trotting conspicuously alongside the car.

After fifteen minutes of cooling her heels in the front office, Karen was startled when the buzzer went off on the EA's desk. He picked up a black handset, listened attentively, and then said, "Yes, sir. Right away, sir." He hung up the phone and looked over at Karen.

"The DCNO would like you to come in," he announced.

Karen took a deep breath, got up, and walked back over to the closed door leading into Kensington's office, ignoring the curious stares from the office staff. She knocked once and then opened the door.

Kensington was now sitting at his desk, his uniform coat still buttoned up. His face was tight with anger. Sherman was standing in front of the desk, and the other two admirals were sitting in adjacent chairs to one side. The tension in the room was palpable, reinforced by Sherman's expression of defiance. Karen walked over to stand beside Sherman, trying to keep the nervousness out of her own face.

"All right," Kensington snapped. "She's here. Now I want an answer."

Sherman turned to her. "They want to know where I was on Thursday and Friday. I don't think they need to know that."

"Why does it matter?" Karen asked the room at large, stalling for time.

"Because the admiral was technically an unauthorized absentee from his place of duty—to wit, the selection board," Carpenter interjected. "We assume he had a good and sufficient reason for being so absent, but that assumption rests on his willingness to tell us what that reason was. Beyond so-called compelling personal circumstances, that is."

Karen did not like the fact that she was coming into this conversation cold, but she made her decision. "You do not have to reveal the reason, especially under these circumstances," she said, making it clear that she thought "these circumstances" had something of the flavor of a kangaroo court to them.

"Now look here, young lady," Kensington began, but she ignored him. "I need to confer with Admiral Sherman," she announced. "Privately. Excuse us, please. We'll be right back. Admiral?" She took Sherman by the elbow and steered him toward the door.

"Goddamn it, JAG, she works for you. Do something," Kensington protested, but Admiral Carpenter had a peculiar look on his face and was starting to shake his head. Karen propelled Sherman through the door of the inner office and then out into the A-ring corridor, pulling the outer door shut as she went through.

"What's the deal?" she asked.

He sighed. "McNair's told them everything. They want me to put my papers in. Ask for early retirement. If I don't, they're going to proceed against me for disappearing without notice. It would probably start with some kind of psych evaluation at Bethesda. Kensington started in with some kind of bullshit about how concerned they were about this Galantz situation. How they had lost confidence in my ability to focus on my duties with this extreme personal threat hanging over my head. How it would make the Navy look bad if I were to be hauled into a courtroom, an admiral in uniform, for being involved in two murders."

"But Carpenter knows that's a lie," she argued. "He knows full well you're not a suspect and that you were never involved."

Sherman nodded as two commanders walked by, trying hard not to stare. "I pointed that out. But strangely enough, Admiral Carpenter has had very little to say in there," he said. He paused for a moment. "And I'm not about to beg him to speak up. If this is a setup, then he's part of it."

Karen recalled what Galantz had said about the admirals being part of this. "But why?" she said. "You're one of them. You're a flag officer. Why aren't they protecting you? Why are they so ready just to let you go over the side?"

"I don't know. I haven't done anything, other than bolt the other day. And that wasn't from fear of Galantz, but from overwhelming disappointment. You make flag, it's not supposed to be this way, Karen. Hell, at this point, I'm ready to do what they want."

"You shouldn't do that. You should fight them."

"But how? I don't know where I stand. Kensington said he just got off the phone with the Vice Chief. If there's a four-star against me, there's no point in fighting it."

Karen tried to make him look at her, but he resisted. "You don't know that," she said. "He may just have said that. He may have been talking to the Vice about something entirely unrelated. You said it yourself: You worked for all those years to wear these stars. At great personal cost, may I remind you."

He looked at her then, and she saw in his eyes that he had crossed an important psychological bridge and was now prepared to burn it. He took her hands. "Karen, that's the whole point, isn't it? The career has been everything. For all those years, it was my career, my advancement. I was always so very important, so very busy. And now my wife's in an institution, and my son is in league with my worst enemy. All for what? Preserving my almighty stars?" He dropped her hands, and the emotion seemed to leak out of him. "To hell with these people."

"Is there anyone else you can talk to?" she asked. "Any other flag officers?"

He laughed. "My contemporaries are all guys against whom I competed for the first star. Now we're competitors for the second star. If that three-star in there has put the word out, nobody in this building is going to return my calls."

The door to the outer office opened, and a yeoman stuck his head out. "Sir? The admiral was—"

"Yeoman?" Sherman barked.

"Yes, sir?"

"Bring me a pair of scissors."

"Aye, aye, sir." Looking baffled, the yeoman retreated back into the office.

"Where's von Rensel?" Sherman asked.

"He's . . . he's gone looking for Jack, I think. He was supposed to wait at his house until we got back or he heard from McNair."

Sherman nodded. The yeoman returned with a pair of scissors. Karen could see the EA standing at his desk, trying to see what was going on out in the corridor. Sherman pulled out his wallet and extracted his ID card. He took the scissors and cut the ID card into four pieces. He handed the pieces and the scissors over to the yeoman. "Give these to your boss. Tell him I've gone to look for my son."

"But, sir, the admiral—"

"Tell him what I said, young man. Tell him *Captain* Sherman left with his lawyer."

Train stopped short of the clearing containing the decrepit trailer and checked his watch: just past 1:00 P.M. He looked around. He was standing behind a large scraggly bush, which put him mostly in the shadows. There were no sounds coming from the trailer, and the woods both above and below the trailer were silent and strangely devoid of birds and insects. He wondered briefly about all the talk of snakes. Gutter stood by his left side, ears up, eyes alert. Train eased the Glock out of its waistband holster, checked the chamber, and then sent the dog forward to scout the place out. Gutter trotted into the clearing surrounding the trailer, stopped, and then put his nose down and began to cover the ground between the trailer and the plastic-covered hootch to the right, where Karen had said she first found Jack.

Train considered crouching down but then dismissed the idea. He was simply too big to hide behind anything much smaller than a house anyway. The place felt abandoned. He had thought he had seen the dark silhouette of a fallen-in house up there among the trees near the top, and there were signs that there had once been a road or a driveway, now entirely overgrown, beyond the dead tree. Gutter disappeared behind the trailer and then reappeared a minute later on the far side.

Train considered his options. The dog would find anyone hiding outside the trailer, although not necessarily someone *inside* the trailer. Karen said the guy rode a motorbike, and there was no motorbike in sight. As the day warmed up, the aroma from all the trash around the trailer was becoming stronger, accompanied by the whine of flies. He could not imagine someone living like this, and yet he knew that there were lots of other trailers just like this in these parts. The dog came loping back to him, and Train, satisfied that no one was lying in wait ahead, decided to go check out the trailer itself. He looked over at the huge dead tree lying across the road, then took Gutter back to it, instructing him to stay down underneath the trunk. Train was pretty sure he could handle Jack if he was in that trailer, and while he would have preferred to keep Gutter with him, he wanted the Dobe between him and those two thugs down below. He could always call him in if there was trouble. Gutter flopped obediently onto his belly, giving Train a mildly resentful look.

Train patted him, reinforced the command, and then walked down the path leading to the trailer, proceeding carefully, with the Glock in his right hand but held down by his side. He went straight up to the door, knocked, and then stepped back, holding the gun behind his back. He kept looking around the clearing to make sure no one was moving, hoping that Gutter still had a view of the clearing. He knocked again and called out Jack's name. Nothing moved inside the trailer. He knocked a third time, more forcefully, making the side of the trailer rattle. Then he tried the door handle and found the door unlocked.

He looked around again and then pushed the door in, hard enough that it banged all the way back to the wall. He called Jack's name again and then listened carefully, but there were no sounds coming from the trailer. The gun pointed up now, he went into the trailer. He felt the floor sag beneath his feet as he took shallow breaths against the stink of rotting food and filthy clothes. The interior looked a lot like the exterior, and the trailer had a definite sewage problem somewhere. But it felt empty. He checked out the other two rooms and the bathroom, staying out of the tiny kitchen for fear of the mess he would find there. He looked around. The place was little more than an aluminum cave; all it needed was a pile of bones in one corner. But there was no one here.

He went back to the clearing and checked on Gutter, who was still on command, then focused on what looked like a ruined house a hundred yards or so up the hill from the downed oak tree. It took ten minutes to push through all the undergrowth, and he was careful about where he put his feet. It was only early afternoon, but already there were shadows forming under the trees. The house was a total wreck. Two enormous stone chimneys at either end were the only things vertical about it. It appeared to have been a two-story wood-frame house with porches running around three sides, but the second floor and the roof had long ago subsided into the ground floor. The porches sagged and dropped like old spiderwebs. The steps were long gone, although the stone supports were still there. The ground-floor window frames were deformed and empty of glass and sash, and he thought he could see parts of the ground-floor ceiling sagging down into the front rooms. The front door was missing, leaving an asymmetric black hole facing the dying trees out front.

He walked around three sides of the house, but there were no signs of life or the detritus of vagrants. Huge old vines roped up the remains of the porches, and some had even gone inside. He was about to go back down the hill when a squirrel burst out practically from beneath his feet, giving him a good scare. The squirrel hightailed it up one of the old trees and Train watched it go damned near all the way to the top, which is when he saw the antenna. At first, it didn't register. He moved closer to the tree, peering through the branches, and there it was, a radio antenna of some kind. And a wire, cleverly concealed in the ragged bark of the tree, descended the tree and disappeared in the underbrush. He rooted around the base of the tree, found it, saw which way it was pointed, and followed the route with his eyes until he found it again, disappearing under one of the porches. Well, well. Ruined, but not necessarily abandoned.

Still holding the Glock, he made his way around to the front steps. Balancing himself, he climbed up the stone step supports and then tiptoed across the bare floor joists of what had been the front porch and approached the open doorway. The old wood creaked ominously under his weight, but just inside the door, he hit pay dirt again: There was a piece of plywood resting over the open floor joists about six feet inside that doorway. He eased his way through the doorway and saw that both front rooms on either side were filled with the wreckage of the second floor. Heaps of plaster and broken boards pointing every which way were all piled onto the ground floor. But straight ahead, in what looked like a main hallway, there was more plywood, ending in a closed door that seemed to be surprisingly intact.

He listened carefully, but there were no sounds. No smells of human habitation, no candy wrappers or beer cans. But that wire had to go somewhere. That wire was new. And this plywood was new. He stepped out onto the first sheet and it held, although broken plaster scrunched underneath as he took the next step. The hallway got darker as he moved across the plywood, and he kept looking over his shoulder at the frame of the front door, where the glare of the afternoon light outside etched every detail of the front porch. He was about six feet from the closed door when he looked up and saw something shiny above the door—something round and glinting, as if made of glass. A camera? Oh Lord, was that a video camera?

The flash went off in his face, a sickeningly familiar purplish blast of light that overwhelmed his brain circuits even as he recognized it. As he reeled back, his brain paralyzed, he thought he heard an ominously familiar inhalation sound.

"Let him go," Carpenter said after the yeoman brought in the pieces of the ID card. "He's just mad right now. He'll come around."

Kensington dismissed the yeoman and waited for him to close the door. "Are you completely sure those archives are clean?"

Carpenter wasn't sure of anything. He had been truly unsettled when Karen Lawrence turned on him like that. And God only knew what that von Rensel guy was doing. "Yes, sir, but I'm going to keep a security trap in place until we have Sherman's papers."

"You said it was clean."

"It is, but I don't trust computers, or the weird bastards who can get into their brains and manipulate them. Like that guy those people sent over."

Kensington nodded thoughtfully. "Do you realize how bad that whole business would look in today's climate?"

"I don't want to even think about it. Leaving a guy behind was one thing. Not trying to get him back was something else again. In today's climate, the Navy'd be torn apart over this little story."

They were interrupted by the EA. "Admiral Carpenter, your office has patched down a call from a Mr. McNair? Says it's urgent."

As they walked quickly away from Kensington's office, Karen's mind was spinning. Why was Carpenter doing this? As a woman, she could understand Sherman's decision to throw in the towel. But not why Kensington and Carpenter were doing this. Unless, of course, Sherman wasn't the scandal they were really afraid of. She stopped short in the corridor, thinking about that locked file. "Admiral, there has to be something more behind all this than just fear of a public-relations problem. And I think I know where we might find it."

Sherman gave her a weary look. "Do we have time for theories, Karen?"

"I think we ought to make time for this one," she said. "I'd like to divert to my office before we leave the building, and hopefully before Admiral Carpenter gets back to his office. I need to get to my computer."

"Will the office be open? And what are we looking for?" he asked as she turned down the sixth corridor, heading toward the Investigations Review offices. Their voices echoed in the empty hallway. Stern portraits of CNOs past frowned down on them.

"This whole thing began in Vietnam," she said. "A week ago, I asked for the archive file of the original JAG investigation, when Galantz was lost. But when I tried to pull it up, there was a security block. Admiral Carpenter told Train that he had read it, and that it corroborated your version of what happened out there in Vietnam. But I'm wondering if there isn't something else in that file."

"Did von Rensel see it?"

"No, sir," she said, turning into the D-ring corridor and quickening her pace. "He obtained the NIS file on Jack. But he thinks Carpenter is behind the security block."

They arrived at the IR office door, whose opaque glass window was dark. She punched in the code and opened the door. Sherman followed her in and closed the door behind them as she turned on some lights. "Why would NIS have a file on Jack?" he asked.

She hurried over to her cubicle, debated with herself about turning off the lights, and decided against it. She went over to the yeoman's desk and booted up the network server, and then she went to her desk to bring up her own system.

"I'm not sure they had a file on him, per se. They apparently have access to multiple databases, and they can do what the telemarketers and the credit checkers can do, only with some federal muscle."

"What a concept," he muttered.

"Okay, system's up." She sat down at her desk and put through a request from the IR system to the JAG local-area network. Sherman paced around the empty office while Karen's fingers flew over the keyboard.

"Any luck?" Sherman asked from across the room.

"Almost," she replied, opening the access screen and keying in her original request number. The screen asked for her personal identifier. She keyed that in. A red banner exploded across the screen. It told her that her access was invalid and that the restricting authority was being notified.

"Uh-oh," Sherman said from across the room.

"Uh-oh is right," she said. "Access denied. And I'll bet Carpenter's office is getting an alert right now telling them I'm trying to get into this file."

"Maybe we should shut down and get out of here, then," he said. "Before the rent-a-cops show up. Or worse, some of the CNO's Marines from OpNav security."

"I can't imagine anything like that," she said. "It's not as if I was doing something illegal. This is a system I use all the time."

"See if you can log into your division's LAN E-mail system," he suggested. "See if this denial is file-specific, or user-specific."

She frowned but then exited the archive system and opened E-mail. Another red banner. "It's me," she whispered.

"I was afraid of that," he said. "Let's go. Now."

"I have to shut the system down. If I don't, the server will—"

"Screw the server," he said, reaching down to hit the computer's power key. "We need to get out of this building and down to Aquia as quickly as possible."

Karen got up hurriedly and turned off the office lights. They opened the door and looked out into the empty corridor.

"No sounds of approaching jackboots," Sherman said. "Follow me."

"Where are we going?" she asked, hurrying to keep up in her skirt and heels.

"Don't think we ought just to waltz out the South Parking entrance," he said over his shoulder. If that was a network trap, there'll be a security alert. I'm not sure what's going on here, but somebody's locked *you* out of the system, and recently. We'll take these stairs right here."

He ducked sideways into a small stairway in the middle of the corridor. Karen followed, her heels clattering on the concrete steps. "Where does this go? I've never used this one."

"Spend enough years in this building, you learn some shortcuts. This'll get us down to the first floor, and then we'll go around the B-ring to corridor four. Stay out of the A-ring in case security vehicles are on their way. Damn, I wish it weren't Saturday. The building's empty as a tomb. We're going to be conspicuous."

"Where will that take us?" she asked. "And I may have to take these shoes off."

He turned around to look and then apologized. "Sorry. I forgot about heels. I guess there's no need to run."

But even as he said that, as they were about to cross the sixth corridor through the B-ring, they heard the urgent beeping sound of an approaching electric security vehicle coming down the A-ring to their left. They stopped and ducked back into the B-ring, flattening themselves against an office door. There were two large glass doors across the sixth corridor, where they could see the reflection of the security vehicle, a large electric golf cart with a rotating amber beacon, go humming by. There were four armed men riding in the vehicle.

Sherman swore. "Reaction force. Probably on their way to the main entrances. That may or may not be for us, but if it is, we're going to have to hurry."

Karen popped her shoes off and began to trot in her stockinged feet. As long as they were on the polished corridor floors, it wasn't too bad. They moved quickly along the angled segments of B-ring, across the fifth corridor and then into the fourth corridor. She had to put her shoes back on to get across the garage and utility street between D-ring and E-ring, and she left them on as they went back up a small stairway to reach ground level. Sherman paused just inside a doorway.

"Okay," he said. "What we're trying for here is the heliport door. It's an exit that's open only on workdays. Usually, there's a guard, but probably only an alarm system right now. It opens directly into the heliport area, and from there it's only a hundred yards or so to South Parking. It's all I can think of."

She nodded. "I can't believe there are police after us. I didn't do anything I don't do routinely."

"That's when you were persona grata," he replied, keeping an eye out into the corridor through the glass door. "Now you're keeping bad company. Sure you want to keep going with this, Counselor?"

"I'm sure," she said with a small smile. "I think."

"Right. Remember that the forces of truth, justice, and the American way are all behind you. Way behind you. Let's do it."

He took one more look through the door for amber strobe lights, then pushed the door open. They stepped out into the fourth corridor, which was darker than usual. In the perpetual effort to save money, the Pentagon building's management turned out half the overhead lights in the corridors on weekends. Trying to act normally, they walked together the final eighty feet to the small doorway at the end of the corridor. The guard table by the door was unoccupied, but they could see a red sign chained across the door.

"Definitely alarmed," she said, keeping her voice down as they approached the door. "Won't that bring the reaction force?"

"Probably. We can only hope they come from the inside and that no one thinks to simply step out of the South Parking entrance to see what's happening back on the heliport. Wish I had a helo out there."

"You're an admiral. Can't you just call one?"

"Remember the guy in *Henry the Fifth* who claims that he can call forth spirits from the vasty deep? And the other guy says, yeah, but do they come when you call them? That's me. I used to think I could, though," he said.

The chain across the door was there to hold the sign, not to secure the door. The door itself had a fire-escape bar on the inside, which meant they could get out, although not back in once that door closed. Two black boxes with shielded wiring were positioned on either side of the top-left crack between the door and the doorjamb. There was also an amber strobe light mounted ten feet high in the ceiling and it, too, was wired to the black box.

"Definitely alarmed," he said. "Okay. Once outside, we turn left and walk quickly but normally toward South Parking. If someone stops us, we did see a man in civilian clothes headed for the River Entrance."

"He went thataway, Sheriff?"

"Right. Unless they're specifically looking for us, my admiral's uniform may do the trick. Ready?"

"I guess," she said, adjusting her shoes. She was wishing she could see through that door.

He stepped forward, unhooked the chained sign, and then pushed the bar. Karen expected an audible alarm, but the only thing that happened was that the amber light began to flash over their heads. They went out through the door, pushed it shut, walked quickly down the steps to the heliport area, and turned left for South Parking. Traffic out on Washington Boulevard whizzed past just beyond the heliport. The bright sunlight was almost blinding.

They headed down a sidewalk right alongside the building and made it almost to the edge of the heliport before two armed guards came around the corner of the building.

"Good, they're Marines," Sherman murmured.

Karen couldn't quite figure out why that was good, but then she began to understand when the Marines trotted up to them, assumed rigid positions of attention, and saluted in unison. Sherman returned the salute casually and asked what the problem was.

"Intruder alarm, heliport door, sir," the smaller one said.

"I saw a guy come out of there as we were walking past," Sherman replied, pointing down toward the other end of the building. "Civilian? With a briefcase? Seemed to be in a hurry?"

"Yes, sir. Thank you, sir. Good afternoon, sir!" they shouted in unison as they took off down the side of the building, unslinging submachine weapons.

"Let's go, Counselor," Sherman said, looking over his shoulder. "That'll be good for about another ninety seconds if we're lucky."

They walked rapidly to the corner of the building and then stepped across the empty perimeter street toward their cars. Karen could see other guards standing around the South Parking entrance doors, one of whom was using a radio. They made it to their cars, and Karen slipped into the Mercedes while the admiral opened the door to his car. She reached down to finger a pebble out of her right shoe, and when she straightened back up, the cars were surrounded by armed guards. A huge man in a uniform she didn't recognize was gesturing for her to get out of the car. He was emphasizing his command with the barrel of his gun. She rolled the window down, keeping her hands in sight.

"Get out of the car, please, Commander," the guard said. Two other guards were between her car and Sherman's, and she could see Sherman getting out of his car. She did the same, and they walked her around to the back of Sherman's car. Three Army majors who had been about to leave for the day were watching in amazement from the next row of cars. Karen was grateful not to see the two Marines they had encountered along the side of the building.

A Marine captain walked up to the group of guards and saluted Sherman.

"OpNav security, sir. Sir, did you just come through the heliport door?"

"Yes, I did. We did."

"That's an alarmed door, Admiral," the captain said in a tone of voice that clearly indicated he was pointing out the obvious. "May I see your identification, please, sir?"

"Sure," Sherman said, reaching for his wallet. And then he paused for a second and looked over at Karen. She felt a cold wave of dismay. He had cut up his ID card up there at the DCNO's office. He fished out his wallet, looked inside, and then shrugged his shoulders. "Well, Captain, I seemed to have misplaced it."

"I can identify this officer," Karen said.

"May I see your ID card, then, Commander?" Which is when she realized she didn't have an ID card, either.

"Uh" was all she could manage to say.

"Yes, ma'am," the Marine said in a gotcha tone of voice. "Why don't we all go back to OpNav Security and straighten this thing out. Admiral Sherman, this way, please, sir."

They know who we are, Karen realized with a sinking feeling. Train, we need you.

Train was blind, again. He had been looking directly into that lens, his eyes wide open, when the retinal flash exploded down his optic nerves. He was only vaguely aware of a sharp sting in his left arm. He tried to think of what to do next, but his brain was just idling quietly in place. He realized that he was still standing, leaning against the wall in that hallway, but that was about the sum of it. There were still two intense purple suns pinwheeling in his eyes. Seen those puppies before. And then a wave of something else took over, a warm, almost-comforting tide of sleep washing over his brain, diminishing those purple suns, filtering all that bright light, causing his knees to buckle, and then he was going down like a stunned ox, his right hip and elbow hitting the plywood, but no big deal, tuck and roll with the best of 'em, so nice to rest, so very nice just to sleep a little while. He thought he heard a voice say something about getting his arms.

Karen was starting to get angry. They had been cooped up in this small room for nearly three hours since their apprehension in the parking lot. The Marines had escorted them up to OpNav Security on the fourth floor, given them a perfunctory airport-style search for weapons with a magnetic wand, and then deposited them in this office without another word. The room was about fifteen feet square, with a small table and four chairs in the middle. The door to the main operations area of the security office had a partially opaque glass panel, and they could see people moving around out there but could not hear what they were saying.

The walk through the Pentagon had been embarrassing, as it must have been obvious to anyone passing them in the main hallways that they were under police escort of some kind, even with only four guards. The Marine captain had accompanied them as far as the security office, but then he had disappeared. A policewoman escorted Karen to the bathroom the one time she had asked, but there had been no other contact. At one point, Karen started to ask Sherman how long this would go on, but he had put his fingers to his lips and pointed to the ceiling. She automatically looked up. There was nothing up there but a fluorescent light fixture. And then she understood. The room was probably bugged. She had nodded and then made herself as comfortable as she could while they waited.

But three hours? She was ready to go bang on that door and demand something, although she wasn't sure what. The only actual crime they had committed was to breach the security door by the heliport. Okay, so sue us, or give us a building traffic ticket, or whatever. Carpenter and company had to be behind this somehow, but for the life of her, she could not understand why. And she was worried about Train. She didn't want to think about that prospect. She looked at her watch for the hundredth time. Sherman gave her a wry smile when he saw her do that. He motioned for her to pull her chair around so that she was sitting next to him. Then he began to print invisible letters on the table with his finger.

"There's a point to this," he scrawled.

"What point?"

"Something else is happening. We are being held out of the way."

She nodded, and then thought about Train going to Cherry Hill. She reminded the admiral of this fact.

"Going to find Jack?" He traced the question, his eyes alarmed.

"Yes."

"To arrest him?"

"No. To bring him back. Train feels Jack is in danger."

Sherman got up then and began to pace around the table. She watched him while he considered the possibilities. Then she saw an idea come over his face. He pointed up at the ceiling and mimed that there was somebody listening hard somewhere. Then he started talking to the ceiling.

"Damn it, I'm getting tired of this," he announced. "Don't these people realize that von Rensel is out there right now? That he's probably going to shoot Jack as soon as he finds him?" His voice startled her as much as what he had just said. But he was motioning for her to play along. Quick, what to say? she thought.

"You're right, Admiral. He's out of control," she said. He was nodding vigorously. "If they'd let us out of here, maybe we could stop that. But they're probably too dumb to do that. I hope it's not too late."

"Von Rensel's more than just out of control," Sherman said, looking up again at the ceiling and the presumed microphone. "He's going to go public when he's finished with Jack. Some people in this building are going to be pretty embarrassed if he does. He's much too close to those Fairfax cops. You know NIS. They'll just screw it up."

They went on like this for a few minutes, then subsided into silence. Twenty minutes later, the door was being unlocked and the Marine captain was back.

"Apologize for the long delay, Admiral, Commander. We've had some trouble verifying your identity. Saturday and all that. But you're free to go now, sir. Commander, next time don't let the admiral here go busting through security doors. Use the regular entrances, okay, ma'am? And you need to get that ID card problem squared away."

Karen just stared at him, but he maintained an entirely sincere expression in the face of her obvious disbelief. She was half-expecting Sherman to go through a "how dare you" routine, but he was touching her elbow. "Let's go," he said urgently.

The admiral was in a hurry. Suddenly so was she. They needed to get down to Aquia. But more than that, they needed to get to a car phone. A single Marine was detailed to escort them back out of the building, since it was illegal for them to be in the Pentagon without ID cards.

Out in the parking lot, Karen called Hiroshi from the Mercedes while Sherman stood by her door.

"Hiroshi, this is Commander Lawrence. Is Train back?"

"Not back yet. No calls."

"And he's in my Explorer?"

"Yes, your car."

She thanked him, hung up, and looked at her watch. A little after four. There were only about thirty cars left in South Parking. The sun was starting to set behind the Arlington Annex buildings overlooking the national cemetery. The dark band of an approaching weather front lurked in the west.

"Nothing?" Sherman was asking.

"Not a word. No calls. He should have been back by now."

"He take your car?"

"Yes."

"Call your car phone. See if he's there."

Why didn't I think of that? she fumed, and punched in the number for the Explorer.

One ring, two rings, a pickup, and then the voice: *Hello, Commander.*

She almost dropped the phone when she heard his voice again. She mouthed the name Galantz at Sherman, her throat too dry to speak. Sherman reached for the phone.

"What do you want, Galantz?" he shouted into the phone.

Your dripping bloody spine on my kitchen table, the voice said. *If you had one.*

"Where's Jack?" Sherman said, his voice not quite so forceful. Karen felt an icy fist grip her insides. If Galantz was in *her* car, then where the hell was Train?

Jack's with me. Want to see young Jack, do you, Admiral?

"Let him go, Galantz."

Let him go? He's here of his own free will. Although that might change, of course.

"Let him go, Galantz. You've done enough damage."

Nowhere near enough damage. But I will. You want Jack? You come to where von Rensel went. Tonight. Come alone. No helper bees. Let's say about nine. That suit your busy calendar? We can finish this tonight. Just you and me. But remember, come alone. Or we just keep playing.

Sherman swallowed as the phone hissed at him. He handed the phone back through her window.

"He's offering to trade Jack for me, from the sounds of it. Wants me to come to wherever von Rensel was going this afternoon. Says we can finish this tonight."

"Damn!" she exclaimed. "We've got to tell McNair. We need—"

"No. I have to go alone."

"That's crazy, Admiral. I'm sorry, but you're no match for this guy."

"Don't you see, Karen, this is never going to end until I face him. And Jack." Sherman looked away for a moment, and she suddenly had the impression that he no longer cared what happened to himself. "Did he say anything more about Train?" she asked.

"No. So we'd better get down to Aquia."

It was nearly 5:30 when they arrived in their separate cars. An obviously worried Hiroshi met them in front of the house.

"No calls?" Karen asked as soon as she got out.

"One call. From a Mr. McNair."

"McNair!" exclaimed Sherman, joining them next to Karen's car. Hiroshi turned to face him.

"It was for you, Sherman-sama. He said don't go."

"That's it?" Karen asked, frowning. Then she looked at Sherman. "But how in the world—"

"The phones," Sherman said, kicking gravel at a tire. "They must have all the goddamn phones covered. Here and the cars, too. Was that the entire message, Hiroshi?"

"No. He said he was sorry about Jack. But Galantz was more important."

Sherman's face paled in the evening light, as if Hiroshi had slapped his face. "Sorry about Jack? *Sorry about Jack!* What the hell is that supposed to mean?"

Karen took him by the arm and steered him away from the cars. Hiroshi waited patiently behind them. "McNair *is* the police," she said. "He knows that Jack has been helping Galantz commit murder. He's obviously willing to sacrifice Jack to get the mastermind here, Galantz. But what he doesn't know is that Train may be up there."

Sherman shook his head. "He should know if he can listen to all these damned phones. How did you find out Train went wherever he went?"

"I called Hiroshi from OP-03's office. Oh, right. If they've got devices on the phones here, he would know." She stopped for a moment. "And you're sure Galantz didn't mention anything more about Train?"

"Nope. Nothing other than to say that I should come to where von Rensel went. Where is that, Karen?"

Karen felt her heart sink "A place called Slade Hill," she replied. "It's near the river. Did he imply he had Train, as well?"

"No. Just that one oblique reference."

It was Karen's turn to think hard. But then an odd thought struck her: Could McNair have been behind their three-hour detention in the Pentagon? McNair working through those two admirals? If he knew that Train had gone to Cherry Hill before they were detained, might he have arranged their detention? But how would he have found that out? Easy, the phone call she made from OP-03's office, when Hiroshi had told her where Train had gone. And then, when he overheard Galantz tell Sherman to come to Cherry Hill, he had left this new message. Which meant the police were finally moving against Galantz.

"What?" Sherman was asking.

Karen shook her head. "An off-the-wall theory," she replied. "But I think the cops are about to make their move."

Sherman sighed in exasperation "At this moment, Karen, theories don't interest me. I want my son out of there. I have to talk to him. I have to know if he really was part of this, or if he was just a dupe. Look, the rest of my world is in pieces. I've got to know this. Do you understand? I can't just sit here."

"I do understand," she said. "But if McNair has a police operation under way, and we go up there, we could screw that up. Run into a SWAT team up there."

"McNair wants Galantz. I think he's made it personal. Jack's just excess baggage to him. Well, Jack is blood personal for me. I've got to get face-to-face with him, just once."

Karen was wavering. If Jack were to be killed, either by Galantz or by a SWAT team, Galantz would have succeeded in destroying everything of value to Sherman: his lover, his mentor, his career, and now his only son.

"Karen? Train's probably up there, too." He took her arm. "I can't do this by myself," he said. "You've been there. You know the ground. And you've got something of value up there, too, Karen. Either Galantz has him, too, or he's been hurt. The cops will treat him as another cop. They'll try to recover him. But McNair is focused on Galantz, and sometimes cops get hurt."

That did it. "Hiroshi," she called. The old man walked over, his eyes alert. "We need some weapons."

Train rose toward consciousness, aware now that he had been chemically silenced but not able to remember why, or where. He opened his eyes slowly, seeing nothing but a purplish halo in the darkness. He tried to rub his eyes, only to discover that his arms were constricted. Then he realized that his hands were taped back-to-back, and his wrists felt like they had been taped together and then fastened by more tape to his belt buckle. His ankles were also taped together. His whole body was constricted, enveloped in something that had him wrapped loosely from head to toe. Only his face was exposed. He smelled rubber, and immediately he recognized the shape of the thing that held him. And he remembered where he had been when he saw it.

He turned his head, but then his face slid under the aperture in the bag left open for him to breathe, the rough edges of a zipper scratching his cheek. He didn't do that again. The darkness was complete. He had a vague sense of being underground.

Okay. Karen managed to get through this. So can you. Breathe. Regain sensory control.

But then a wave of torpor insinuated itself as a last vestige of the chemical washed across his forebrain, sinuous molecules urging sleep, a resumption of the comforting nothingness that took away the fear of being cocooned like this.

No. Fight that. You know who did this. He has plans. He doesn't want you. But he'll use you to bring Sherman in. You have to be ready when he comes back. Breathe. Exhale the poisons. Reinvigorate the bloodstream with fresh oxygen.

After a few minutes, the deep breathing began to work, and he felt the insidious chemical recede. Then he tried the tape bonds on his arms and feet. Tight, unyielding. But he knew about tape. The secret to tape was steady pressure. Tape was plastic fabric. Hard to break with brute force without first tearing it, but ultimately, it was stretchable. This was an exercise in isometrics. Put on steady pressure, then relax. It was difficult with his hands being back-to-back, but the sword exercises had built unusual strength in his forearms. Push out, like trying to do the breaststroke. Relax. Then do it again. Keep doing it. Push out. Relax. Get one hand free, then the other, and then get out of the bag. But first the tape. Push. Breathe. Relax. Push.

Hiroshi drove them in Sherman's car. It was fully dark by the time they reached and went past the entrance to Slade Hill Road. Sherman had Karen's .45; she carried a Browning .380 semiautomatic, which Hiroshi had produced from the gun locker. She sat up front with Hiroshi, with the admiral perched on the edge of the backseat like a kid trying to see everything out the windows.

"That's the entrance to the road that goes up to the trailer," she announced quietly as they drove past the familiar trash piles in the ditch. They had talked about how best to approach the trailer on the way over. They decided to go past the entrance, turn around, and get out somewhere above the Slade Hill Road entrance, on the premise that it would be easier to walk downhill to the trailer than climb up to it in the darkness. She had told Sherman about the postmaster's snake stories. Hiroshi drove back up the hill until Karen signaled for him to stop abreast of what looked like an abandoned trailer pad. "We should be about a quarter mile above the entrance to Jack's road," she said.

"Okay, then it's show time," the admiral announced, hefting the big Colt. They each had a flashlight, whose lenses the admiral had darkened by using a red felt-tipped pen. Hiroshi's instructions were to drive back down to the entrance to Slade Hill Road and park the car facing out on the road. Karen and the admiral got out, closing the car doors as quietly as they could. Hiroshi drove off, with one further instruction: to call McNair thirty minutes after he had parked to tell him that they were on the hill.

Karen waited to get her eyes adjusted to the darkness. The sky was overcast, with a low scud blowing down toward the river. She realized they would be walking across the face of Slade Hill rather than down any slope. She suggested they bear left, partially up the hill, so that they would come down on the trailer and traverse the dirt road rather than have to climb any part of it.

Sherman nodded in the darkness. He pushed the light on his watch. "Nineteen-thirty," he said. "We'd better go."

They set out into the woods, where immediately they found themselves enveloped in a tangle of vines and thick vegetation. Sherman led the way, and they both soon picked up sticks to use to push the brambles out of their faces. She hoped they were going in a straight line across the hill, but there was really no way to tell in the darkness. The ground was soft and rocky, with patches of ankle-deep mud in places. Karen tripped and fell at one point, and then realized she had lost the .380. They spent five minutes searching for the gun in the weeds, and this time she put it into a zippered pocket of the windbreaker. The admiral paused periodically to listen, but the woods were silent, with only some night insects and the occasional rustle of small game getting out of their way. The night air was heavy and humid as the front approached, compressing the atmosphere.

After twenty minutes, they could see a single dim light below and to their right, which Karen assumed was the bikers' trailer. Something snapped a stick up ahead of them in a grove of trees. They froze and listened for a few minutes, but there was no other sound. Finally, the admiral motioned that they should go on. Karen checked that she still had the gun, and she was about four paces to his left when the snake let go, an alarmingly loud buzz that sounded as if it was coming from just in front of her. She froze.

Sherman turned around in the darkness. "Where is it?" he whispered. "Can you tell?"

"To my right. Can't tell how close."

The snake buzzed again as Sherman stepped closer to where Karen had assumed her one-legged stance. He probed the bushes where the noise was coming from, then stopped when he realized he didn't know how close the snake was to Karen.

"I'll try to distract it," he said, probing very carefully now with his stick. "If I feel it hit my stick, I'll sing out, and you jump backward, okay?"

The snake stopped buzzing, and Sherman froze. "Now what?" she said, her throat dry. Neither one of them was properly dressed for rattlesnake country. Sherman swore and then began tapping his stick on the ground. Nothing happened. Karen felt her first real surge of fear. As long as it was buzzing, she knew about where the damned thing was. Now, she could only imagine it slithering between her feet, or gathering to strike.

Sherman stopped the tapping. "In theory, they're as scared of us as we are of them. Supposedly, they'll escape if allowed to."

"In theory, huh?" she said. Her leg was getting tired, and she hated not being able to move. She put all her weight onto her left leg and moved her own stick to the right in the damp grass, probing for the dark patch where the buzzing sound had started. There was no response. Then she described a circle in the grass within two feet of where she was standing, still with no response.

"Hell with it," she said, putting her foot down gingerly. "I think it's gone."

Sherman beat the bushes between them more aggressively with his stick. "I think you're right," he said, and turned around to proceed. He took one step, and a loud buzzing erupted right in front of him. It was his turn to freeze.

"Damn it," he said. "Now it's right in front of me."

"How close?" Karen asked, trying to see around him without moving.

"Close enough," he said, his voice tight as the snake buzzed again. "I'm even afraid to move my stick. Circle around! Come in from ahead of me and distract the damned thing!"

Karen went sideways, probing carefully ahead with her stick, moving uphill of where the admiral was frozen in place. She stepped very carefully, not placing a foot until she had swept the ground ahead and to the side. She had heard the old tale about rattlers traveling in pairs. That sounded like a big snake. She had just about made it halfway around him, at a distance of about six feet, when another snake let go, this time in front of her. As Sherman swore out loud, she froze again, focusing her senses, trying to detect the snake's position. It's a god-damned minefield, she thought. Then her heart gave a leap when the tip of her stick hit something that did not feel like a tuft of grass. The snake buzzed louder, and she realized she had stopped breathing in anticipation of a strike.

She pulled the stick back, but it caught momentarily and pulled something off the ground. She jumped back then, throwing the stick off, certain that the damned snake was on it. She stepped back and to the left, but to her horror, another snake started up to her left, about five or six feet away.

She froze again, not sure of what the hell to do. Sherman was calling to her as the buzzing stopped.

"Karen! Stand still. We've disturbed a nest!"

"I am standing still! There're three of the damned things out here. I don't know which way to go!"

He had no answer for that, and they both stood there for a minute, immobilized, listening carefully. They could hear nothing but the wind.

"Karen," he said.

"What?"

"Did you throw your stick?"

"Yes."

"Why?"

She told him. He asked if what her stick had caught on could have been a wire. She thought about it. Something had caught her stick, but had it been heavy enough to be a snake? "It might have been a wire. I thought it was a snake."

"Okay, hang on a minute."

She could barely see him in the darkness, but he was probing again with his stick. After thirty seconds, the buzzing started, and he stabbed down hard with the stick and then pulled the tip straight up. There was a loud buzzing noise in front of Karen, and another one off to her left. It actually sounded as if there might be even another one to Sherman's right, down the hill about ten yards.

"Got it," he said. "It *is* a damned wire. These 'snakes' are electronic devices."

"Are you real, real sure of that?" she asked, embarrassed by the sound of her own voice.

"Come over here. I have it in my hand."

She took a deep breath and stepped sideways toward him. When she got up close, she could see the dark wire in his hand, as well as a small black object embedded in the wire that was putting out a really good rattlesnake noise. He jerked hard on the wire, and the others in the reptilian chorus let go for fifteen seconds before going silent.

"Pretty damned effective," he said. "The good news is that we know what it is. The bad news is what might be listening at the other end of this wire."

"Where does it go?" she said. "Up there?" They looked up the hill. Galantz was more likely to be at the end of that wire than at Jack's trailer. She recalled seeing the glimpse of a fallen-down house up above the trailer that day she had talked to Jack. But if that's where the wire went, they were way off course.

"That light," she said. "That might have been Jack's trailer. We might be closer to the top than we realized." She told him about having seen what looked like a ruined house at the top of the hill.

"Jack's trailer," he asked, "did it look like two people were living there?"

"It didn't look like a human lived there," she said, and then regretted it immediately. "I'm sorry."

He took a deep breath. "Then we need to follow this wire," he said, looking up the hill into the darkness. "And we're going to be expected."

Train was making progress with the tape, a millimeter at a time. The skin of his wrists was getting raw, and he could feel the tape getting warm as he applied pressure. He was now convinced he was in some kind of basement or underground room—something about the temperature and musty smell of the air. But the tape was giving way, little by little.

He alternated pressing his hands out and then his feet, intent on restoring as much circulation as he could. He was wary about moving around or trying to see in the darkness, in case Galantz had another one of those blinding devices attached to a motion detector. He tried to think. Galantz would contact Karen or the admiral somehow and offer a trade. More than likely, he wanted to get the admiral in the room with his son, make sure the father knew that the son had been part of it, and then perhaps execute the son to finish his lethal head games on Sherman. Galantz didn't want Sherman dead. Quite the opposite: Galantz wanted Sherman destroyed, and then left alive to contemplate his ruination.

And what would happen to Karen if she came with the admiral? And what was Galantz going to do with him, for that matter? He stopped pushing as a small wave of nausea swept through him, a fleeting vestige of the sedative. Galantz had been able to move with impunity throughout this whole business. Granted he had had years to prepare, all the time in the world to plant devices and scout the ground. Plus Jack's help with some of the dog work. And tradecraft at the level of a sweeper. No wonder McHale Johnson had been impressed, and FBI guys didn't impress easily. He was also pretty sure that the FBI had decided to sit on the sidelines if the agency they loved to hate was showing its ass. But why hadn't the Fairfax police been more effective? McNair should have been able to find Jack, so why wasn't a SWAT team in these woods? The cops should have picked Jack up and squeezed him for information about Galantz: where his base of operations was, what was going down next. They must have known almost from the start that Walsh and Schmidt had been homicides.

You are seriously in the dark, Bud, he thought. He stared out into the darkness. Well, duh, Sherlock. So push harder. His left hand was getting looser.

They crept together to the edges of a shadowy clearing that revealed the remains of a house. Sherman had followed the wire up the hill, lifting it periodically to make sure where it was headed, provoking a battle line of rattlesnake noises all the way up. Karen followed thirty yards behind, a new stick in one hand and the .380 in the other. Sherman had insisted on the separation: If someone fired on him, she would have a chance to escape. When he stopped at the edge of the clearing around the house, she sank down on one knee behind a bush. With her eyes fully night-adapted, she could just see him up ahead in the darkness. He stood there, apparently waiting to see what happened next.

She fought down the urge just to cut and run. If Galantz was up here, there was zero chance they were going to surprise him. Once they picked up that wire, someone had to know they were coming, or at least that Sherman was coming. He might not expect Karen, in which case she wanted to go to that trailer, on the chance that Train was down there, maybe disabled. She didn't want to think about the other possibilities. Damn the stubborn man for going out on his own.

Sherman was moving again, toward the front of the house. Then he was climbing carefully up the zigzag step supports. She couldn't make out much about the house, other than it had fallen in on itself. Sherman appeared to stop in front of what should have been the front door. She put the gun down on the ground near her right foot, turned her left forearm away from the top of the hill, and slipped her sleeve back to see what time it was. The fact that she had her face turned downhill saved her from the searing visual impulse of the retinal disrupter firing above her. Even so, her night adaptation vanished in a millisecond, and she could only gasp and sink down on her hands and knees while her brain reeled from the purple flash a hundred feet away.

Train gave one last pull, and his left hand, minus all the hair on the back, came stickily out of the tape. He immediately stripped the tape off his right hand, and then, flexing his hands rapidly, worked them up to where he could grab the zipper on the bag with his thumbs and pull it down. He kept his eyes tightly closed in case there was another disrupter set up in this place. But so far, none of his struggles had set anything off. He shed the bag like a snakeskin, then rolled over on his side to get the circulation going back in his legs and knees. The tape around his ankles proved to be a tougher proposition. Without a knife, he was forced to find the edge of the tape and start unwinding it.

He rolled up onto his hands and knees, experiencing a wave of dizziness as he did so. He reached out to see what he could touch. The room or wherever he was remained in total darkness. He tried to stand up and almost fell over. The chemical wasn't entirely gone. He could still feel the puncture wound on his left bicep. He sat down on the floor and began stretching and breathing. He ignored the total darkness. He was in a basement, or at least underground, at night presumably, although he had no idea how long he'd been out. He felt for his watch, but it was gone. Of course—his watch had a light.

He waited for a few minutes for the dizziness to subside, then started crawling, until he ran into a wall. Stone wall, from the feel of it. He turned right and followed the wall, proceeding carefully when he ran into a big spiderweb. Visions of black widows in long-empty basements flitted across his mind, and he decided to turn around. He kept one hand on the wall as he reversed course, not wanting to lose his bearings any more than he had to in total darkness. He had crawled about three feet back toward where he'd started from, when he heard that dusty inhalation, and then the metal voice came laughing out of the darkness.

Big man like you, afraid of a little bitty spider, is he?

Train froze in place. Galantz! He'd been in the room with him all along? Watching him get out of the bag? There was more metallic laughter. Son of a bitch must have a night-vision device, Train thought.

That's right. I'm wearing a night set. I've been admiring your physical discipline. Why don't you just wait there, von Rensel. We have one more visitor; then we can do what we came to do.

"What's the game, Galantz?"

Endgame, I think. I've invited the object of my affection to come up here. Told him I'd let his boy go in return for some quality time with the father.

"And then you'll kill the kid in front of his father? Finish what the Navy is doing to him?"

You have no idea, do you? Why the Navy is cutting him loose?

"They're tired of getting black eyes in all the national papers. They've probably figured out that you're going to kill and tell."

I certainly am. But that's not why they're cutting him loose, von Rensel. They're cutting him loose so he can come to me. They're counting on me to kill him.

Train moved sideways a little, trying to locate the metallic voice. But it seemed to be coming from all around him. "Why kill him? I thought you wanted him alive. To savor his fate."

You figured right, von Rensel. I want him to live with this for a long, long time. But you need to find out why certain very senior officers in the Navy might actually want him dead. Then you'll understand why he's free to come here tonight. Now sit tight. Stop scaring my spiders. My time is unfortunately limited.

He sensed motion across the room from him, a stirring of the musty air, a brief thinning of the darkness diagonally to his right, and then what sounded like a trapdoor being dropped quietly into place. Train sank back down on his haunches, reaching out for the stone wall and then settling his back against it. So what the hell was Galantz talking about? What was this stuff about the admirals? He stared out into the darkness, massaging his wrists and ankles, and waited.

Down on the hillside, Karen could see literally nothing but a purple haze, whether her eyes were opened or closed. She crouched motionless in the grass for a few minutes. She was at the very least night-blind. But she could hear. The words *Help me bring him in,* intoned in that mechanical, gasping voice, floated clearly down the hill. Galantz! She froze at the sound of that voice, then settled down onto her stomach in the wet grass behind a mound of vegetation, held her breath, and tried to control the shaking in her knees. The night air was oppressively warm. It was starting to rain, and she thought she heard the distant rumble of thunder. She felt around to find the .380.

Train tensed when he heard sounds above him. Someone moving around—no, two people moving. Another sound: a dragging sound, like a sack of some kind being pulled across the floor above, toward the area of the trap-door. A rattling noise that sounded like boards being shoved aside, then the noises stopped. A clatter of boards and sticks from above and then, there: Something hit the floor over there and groaned. A man's voice. Sherman? Was that Sherman?

The trapdoor closed audibly this time, a heavy wooden thump, and there were steps coming down, two sets of feet. A metallic clank.

Hide your eyes, von Rensel, said the machine voice. Train did as ordered, afraid of another disrupter blast. But instead, there was the noise of a small engine starting, over to his left, and then the room was filled with a pulsing red light, a red strobe light, coming from some device set up on the steps. It actually wasn't very bright, but compared to the absolute darkness, it was initially almost blinding, and he uncovered his eyes only slowly. But at least he could see—sort of. It was as if his eyes were taking pictures with a red flash unit.

The basement was rectangular and, for the most part, empty. Roughly fifty or sixty feet long and about thirty wide. Stone walls, an empty expanse of hard-packed dirt floor. At his end, he recognized the remains of an enormous coal-burning furnace, its large insulated ducts reaching up through a mass of cobwebs into the house above. The grate door to the furnace had been removed, and what looked like the controls of a portable generator glinted in the furnace's combustion chamber. Extension cords ran the length of the basement to the other end, where there appeared to be a cot with a single mattress, a table, and a folding chair. There was a PC sitting on the table, and three racks of other electronic equipment next to the table. There was a tangle of wiring on the floor.

He shielded his eyes against the strobe light, trying to adapt his eyes. It was like watching a film through an antique projector, flashes of darkness punctuated by flashes of the scene in the basement. On, off. On, off—about two times per second. Train shook his head, trying to clear his vision. The strobe effect was really disorienting, like watching the dancers in a discotheque, where disembodied faces flashed in and out of view, each time their expressions and attitudes slightly altered. Only everything down here was blood-red, not white. Red made sense, if Galantz had a night-vision device on.

The ceiling was made up of large, heavily cobwebbed wooden joists that sagged ominously into the basement in places. Near the bottom of the steps was one recognizable figure: Jack, in T-shirt and jeans, leaning insolently against the wall, his eyes hooded in the red strobe light, his arms folded across his chest. Not drunk this time, but casually alert, his eyes two black circles in the pulsing red light, his studied pose that of a street thug waiting for a knife fight to begin. On the steps was the silhouette of a man, barely visible because he was standing very close to the strobe source. Bigger than Jack, heftier, thicker. Galantz. Train couldn't get a focus on the face because of the strobe light, which was placed conveniently just to one side of Galantz's head. There was just the silhouette, standing there, arms hanging down, holding what looked like a bulky automatic pistol in his right hand. The left arm, which ended in a glinting metallic device of some kind, was held casually across the figure's hips. But no face. Only the shape of the man's head, distorted somewhat by something he was wearing. The night-vision device, Train thought.

And there was Sherman, crumpled on the floor near the bottom of the steps. Train put up an arm to shield his face from the disturbing pulsing of the strobe. He had thought Sherman was unconscious, but he wasn't. He was lying on his right side, his hands up to his face, covering his eyes. Know that feeling, Train thought. Bet he was out there in the dark, irises wide open, when Galantz popped his little flash toy. Sherman groaned again and tried to sit up. Train could see Jack staring down at his father's helpless figure, and the expression on his face was not a pretty one. They appeared to be watching Sherman, waiting for him to come out of it.

This bastard was a master of light, Train thought. Galantz had a gun, and Jack might have one, too. And somewhere was the disrupter, ready to disable anyone in the room who didn't see it coming.

Sherman groaned again, and this time he managed to sit up. He dropped his hands from his face, then slapped them back up there again when the strobe light hit him.

Where's your girlfriend, Sherman? Galantz asked. Train tried to see Galantz's throat, but there was only shadow. The combination of the synthetic voice and the slowly pulsing red light created a phantasmagorical image. And who was he talking about, Elizabeth Walsh or Karen?

The admiral did not reply. Galantz instructed Jack to go outside, see if Sherman had come alone. Jack moved immediately and wordlessly up the steps, heaved open the trapdoor, and closed it behind him. It was evident from the sounds that the trapdoor was hidden under a pile of wreckage on the ground floor.

"She's not my girlfriend, you bastard," Sherman said. "You murdered my girlfriend."

Now that you mention it, yes, I did. Let me tell you about it while we're waiting for Jackie boy to come back, okay?

After five minutes, just when she was about to get up and try to move downhill, Karen thought she heard something, something or someone moving carefully through the grass up by the house. Then the noises stopped, somewhere uphill of her position. It was hard to tell, as the patter of the first large raindrops began to mask the woods noises. She clutched the .380 and tried to remember if she had chambered it. Yes, she had. But this one had a safety. She felt along both sides of the gun until she found the small latch down on the left side of the slide. Because if someone was coming down here to get her, he was going to get shot at a lot. She realized she was breathing too fast, and she put a clamp on it. She tested her eyes on a hand held up in front of her face, but all she could see was a purple silhouette. The poor admiral, that thing must have dropped him like a stone. She waited, putting all her mental energy into listening very carefully.

Then she heard the sounds again, definitely footsteps, someone working slowly, carefully, across the hill above her now, one, two, three steps, soft crunching sounds in the grass, punctuated by intervals of silence. She remained absolutely still. If whoever this was had been near the flash, even behind the disrupter, his night vision would not be terrific, either. You fervently hope, she thought.

She conjured up an image of a man standing up there in the woods, looking and listening, probably with a gun, or even that disrupter thing in his hand. Somewhere to her left, maybe fifty, sixty feet away, up the hill. There were some big trees up there, but the ground was badly overgrown. There shouldn't be a clear field of vision down here—unless he has a night-vision device. She flattened herself even harder against the ground. He would be on the edge of the trees, just inside their cover, looking down the hill. Don't move. Don't even twitch.

He was moving again. She tried her eyes; she thought she could see something now, the outline of her right hand, holding the gun. She very slowly turned her head, individual blades of grass tickling her nose, and looked up the hill. There, a darker shadow among the black tree shapes. Everything was still outlined in a purple halo, but her vision was coming back, although she had to look just to the side of objects to see them. The shadow moved again, going left across her field of vision, obscured now by the mound behind which she was hiding. He was staying in the trees, crossing a dozen yards of ground, until suddenly the buzz of a rattler erupted near him. The deadly sound made Karen jump. She closed her eyes and fought for control. She had never heard a rattlesnake before tonight, but there had been no mistaking it. She opened her eyes, then raised her head again to look. The shadow had stopped at the snake sound. Then, making no more effort to be stealthy, the figure crunched back up the hill and disappeared into the darkness surrounding the ruined house.

Train couldn't believe what Galantz was doing. He had ordered Sherman to move back, to crawl back over toward Train. Then, staying in front of the strobe light, he had recounted in a cold, clinical manner how Elizabeth Walsh had died. *It's easy if you know how, Sherman. Not my first one, of course. Turn the head sideways, then pull straight back. You can actually hear it. It's like a rattlesnake: an unmistakable sound.*

Sherman's hands had dropped as Galantz told his story. Train could not read his eyes in the strobe light, but everything in Sherman's posture spelled total defeat.

And her only crime was to have been your girlfriend. Just like the old man: He was really your only friend, wasn't he, Sherman? Did I get that right? I felt a twinge about killing the woman, but the old man—well, he was on borrowed time. I think he actually had a heart attack, when he saw my face. Not the first guy to do that, either. The face you gave me, Sherman. You remember, don't you?

The rhythm of Galantz's voice was almost hypnotic—the strong inhalation, the stream of words through the voice box, with that wheezy harmonic. Sherman was shaking his head slowly, as if unwilling to hear any more of this. There was a rattle of boards above, and then the trapdoor opened and Jack came back down the steps.

"The yard area's clear," he said. "Can't tell what's out there on the hillside. If they're out there like you think, they haven't moved any closer."

Galantz moved to the other side of the strobe, passing directly in front of it. Train got a glimpse of his face in the reflected light. He definitely had some kind of mask on. Train wished he could fire a disrupter right about then. The light amplifier of a night-vision mask would really do a number on him.

That woman is out there somewhere, Jack. Your father here isn't brave enough to come alone. Get me the flip phone. Jack went to the desk, sorted through some things, and then brought Galantz a small flat object. Train chose that moment to begin creeping very slowly along the wall, an inch at a time, toward Sherman. He didn't have a plan, but he couldn't bear just standing there anymore. He had gone about two inches when he sensed

Galantz looking at him, and then there was a bellowing blast from the .45 and something hit the wall next to his head, stinging his face with stone splinters, followed by the sounds of a bullet ricocheting around the stone walls. Everyone in the room except Galantz ducked down instinctively, including Jack. Train straightened up and put a hand up to the right side of his face. It was wet, the blood making a black smear in the red light.

"Is that like 'Don't move'?" he asked.

"Sit still, you crazy bastard," Jack hissed, rising from his own crouch, his tone of voice clearly intimating that Train wasn't the only crazy bastard in the basement. Sherman had ducked his head almost down to the concrete floor, and he was only now raising it. Galantz was talking into the phone as if nothing had happened.

Karen waited ten minutes before moving, keeping her eyes closed to let them rest, listening hard while fighting back the urge just to get up and run full tilt down the hill. She was almost sick with worry about Train. He had to be up there, too, which gave them two hostages. But Hiroshi was down there on the road, with a car and a phone. Finally, she put her head up and looked across the hillside. But there was nothing moving out there, just the stationary shapes of trees and bushes couched among the sounds of the night insects. The rain had petered out for the moment, although the thump and rumble of thunder in the distance was getting more frequent. She thought about going up the hill, then quickly discarded that idea. The best thing she could do was get help, and help lay at the end of that car phone down the dirt road.

Staying on her hands and knees, she crawled carefully down the hill, trying to remember where that damned wire was, with all its venomous voices. Another ten minutes and the undergrowth thinned out as she crept closer to the huge downed tree blocking the top of the dirt road, near Jack's trailer. And then she froze, her skin crawling, when she heard a low, rumbling growl.

Animal there. Big animal. Dog. Huge dog.

She raised the gun. She couldn't see the dog, but there was no mistaking that noise.

Familiar noise.

"Gutter?" she called. The rumbling stopped immediately, replaced with a eager whining noise.

"Gutter, come," she called, trying not to say it too loudly. The dog bounded out from behind the downed tree and ran straight to her, a hundred-pound mass of sleek, wriggling canine. She hugged the dog with more than just a little relief. She stood up and walked straight down the hill, around the fallen tree, and discovered her Explorer parked to one side. Train. She looked inside, then hurried down the path toward the trailer.

She was pretty sure that she had heard Galantz tell someone—most likely, Jack—to bring Sherman in. So Jack's trailer should be empty. She had to find out if Train was in there, although she was pretty sure she knew where Train really was. With the dog at her side, she wasn't worried anymore about what might be lurking in the bushes.

She went to the trailer and found the front door open. Gutter bounded inside and made a quick sweep, then started whining excitedly. So Train had been here. She followed the dog back out, but then she called him back, her heart sinking, when he started up the hill. All right. So Galantz had them both. Now, get to a phone.

It took her five minutes to get down the hill, with only one delay when she twisted her ankle in a rut she failed to see. The darkened sedan was parked across the entrance to the dirt road, pointed uphill on the edge of Cherry Hill Road. But the car was empty when she peered inside. When she looked up, Hiroshi was standing up across Cherry Hill Road, where he had been hiding in some bushes. He cradled what looked like a sawed-off shotgun in his arms. Gutter ran across the road, wiggling a greeting to his old friend.

"Hiroshi, thank God," she said. "I need to get on the phone. They've taken Admiral Sherman. And I'm sure Train's up there, at the top of the hill. There's an old ruined house up there."

Hiroshi trotted over, unlocking the car doors with the remote key set. Karen jumped in on the passenger side and powered up the phone while Hiroshi waited outside with the dog, scanning the dirt road. Now, who to call? McNair was the obvious choice, but she hesitated. McNair already knew that Galantz was probably up on this hill. He had sent a message for Sherman to stay out of here. So why in the hell weren't the woods full of cops?

She stared down at the lighted keys on the back of the car phone's handset, increasingly aware that critical seconds were passing, but also sure she was missing the big picture here.

Hell with it, she concluded. I'm going to call 911, bust this thing wide open. Even better, call 911, then call the nearest television station. Start a media circus. But then she hesitated again. That last bit was not such a great idea. It might provoke Galantz to do—what? Shoot them both, the kid, too, and vanish? She groaned in frustration, finger poised over the keys.

Then the windshield suddenly filled with headlights, from ahead and from behind, accompanied by the sounds of cars skidding to a stop. She was blinded by all the white light, and she heard Gutter start barking outside, but now the lights were everywhere, all pointing at high beam into the car, and then there were several men outside, shouting some tense orders to Hiroshi to drop the gun, someone else shouting about tranquilizing the dog. A large man was opening the door on the driver's side and sliding in. Before Karen could say anything, he told her to put her seat belt on, and then he was autolocking the doors and starting up the car. She looked frantically for Hiroshi, but he was gone, and the other cars outside were already starting to pull out.

"Who the hell are you?" she asked, ignoring the order to put a seat belt on.

"The cavalry, Commander. You've done your part; now we're taking over, okay? Put your goddamn seat belt on." He slammed the car in gear and pulled out onto Cherry Hill Road, headed uphill. It looked as if there were two cars in front and another behind.

"But what about the admiral? And—"

"Not your prob anymore, Commander." The car swerved around the next curve, going up the hill at much too high a speed. Karen grabbed a handrest on the right-front door as the car almost went into the ditch. She decided she'd better put her belt on.

"Who the hell are you, goddamn it?!" she yelled, struggling with the seat belt. "Where are you taking me? What have you done with my dog?"

"FBI," he answered, swerving again, again almost missing the next turn. There was a roar of gravel from the left-rear wheel. "*God*damned road!" he yelled, looking back in his rearview mirror. The car behind had backed off to avoid all the gravel. "We're handling the secondary. Another agency is working the primary. That there's a kill zone, lady, back on that hill. Our orders were to pick up you or anyone else who came back down that hill. The dog's okay; they've just tranked it. This guy Galantz—he's got von Rensel?"

"I think so, yes."

"He was a good man. Too bad." The two cars ahead were slowing down now that they were well away from the dirt road.

" 'Too bad'? 'Was'? What's going to happen up there?"

He didn't answer her, concentrating on the road. She repeated the question. He still didn't answer, but he looked over at her for an instant, and she was shocked to read sympathy in his face. She faced forward then, realizing now that Sherman, Train, and Jack had all become expendable. Someone was going to solve the rogue operative problem once and for all, and any bystanders be damned. The cars up ahead were slowing down even more, apparently preparing to turn off into a large driveway that was visible up ahead on the right. The car behind them had already pulled over, its emergency flashers going. The "secondaries" were going to wait here until the "primaries" had finished whatever was planned up on the hill.

A decision crystallized in her forebrain like a bright sunrise. She didn't give it a second thought, just like when Jack had run his mouth.

She pulled the .380 out of her right pocket, pointed it right in front of the driver's face, and blasted two rounds through his side window, sending the rounds about one inch in front of the big man's nose. The window exploded.

With a shout of fear, he slammed on the brakes, bucking up against the wheel as he did so, because he had not put *his* seat belt on. She fired again, this time behind his head, screaming at him, "*Stop the car! Stop the car. Now, get out! Get out of the goddamn car! Now! Do it!*"

She fired once again just past his head. The man was white-faced and screaming back at her, a series of "*Hey! Hey!*" and then he was babbling incoherently. She could barely see in all the gunsmoke, but he got the car stopped, and then he was pushing the door open and rolling out onto the pavement, still yelling as he scrambled away from the car's rear wheels as it continued to roll forward. Karen unsnapped her belt and grabbed the wheel to pull herself into the driver's seat. She slammed the door and pulled the big car around in a tire-screeching U-turn, the right-front tire banging off the culvert. She caught a glimpse of the terrified agent rolling into the ditch, and then she was blasting back down the hill, nearly losing control as she floored it.

She had to stomp on the brakes—thank God for antilocks—to maintain control through the first curve, ignoring the flare of headlights and taillights from the chase car that had pulled out of her way. Goddamn them! God-*damn* them! Absolutely typical. They'd lost control of one of their super-goons, and now innocent people had to die so they could cover up their latest mess. The whole thing had been a setup, right from the beginning. Goats staked out in the jungle, that's all they had been. Bait for the tiger—Galantz.

She saw the white blur of the trash piles just in time to slam on the brakes. She barely made the hard left turn onto the dirt road. There were more lights behind her now, but she didn't care. She had no plan, no idea of what she was going to do up there, but she was god*damned* if she was going to let them just nuke the place to get Galantz. She blasted bags of trash all over the entranceway as she made the turn, and the big car's V-8 screamed when she lost traction momentarily in one of the ruts, but then she was banging up that hill, accelerator mashed flat down. The car flew past the bikers' trailer, went off the road into a stand of small trees, and then back onto the road briefly before swerving off on the other side. She fought the car's wheel viciously, then realized she still had the accelerator mashed all the way down. Control, she thought. Control—slow the hell down!

The car fishtailed three or four times as she took her foot off the gas, and then it settled into a banging, bumping track up the dirt road, until she finally saw the big dead tree. Again, she didn't hesitate. She hauled on the wheel and drove off to the right, around the tree, fishtailing again in the bushes; except this time, the right-rear wheel hit a soft spot and started spinning helplessly. She banged her fist on the wheel and gunned it, but it was over. Her headlights were pointed directly up the hill, unnaturally high. She cursed the hill, the car, the FBI and every other government agency she could think of, and then shut the car down, tears of pure frustration in her eyes.

After a minute, reality settled onto her shoulders like a cold, wet towel. What the hell was she doing? She was a commander in the Navy, a commissioned federal officer, an officer of the court. She had shot at an FBI agent, driven through a law-enforcement cordon, and now what? Going to charge up San Juan Hill here, guns blazing, like Teddy Roosevelt? And accomplish what, exactly?

She suddenly felt a wave of nausea sweep through her as the adrenaline started to crash. She punched off the headlights and opened the door. A small cloud of gunsmoke puffed out of the car, along with a few shards of glass from the shattered window. She reached over for the .380 and wondered if there were any rounds left. She swung her legs sideways and sat with her head down, half in, half out of the car, holding the smooth steel of the automatic against her belly and taking deep breaths of rain-cool air. She never heard the man who stepped out of the woods until he called her name.

She looked up in shock. It was McNair, walking carefully through the rain toward the car, his hands held out at his waist, one eye on her face and the other on that .380.

"Commander Lawrence? Karen? It's me, McNair."

She stared dully at him. He was dressed in khaki pants, a white shirt under a dark bulletproof vest covered by a khaki windbreaker, and what looked like combat boots. He had some kind of automatic weapon strapped across his back, the barrel just visible over his right shoulder. He wore a khaki baseball cap on his head. He stopped a few feet from the car and showed her his hands, wiggling his fingers to make sure she saw they were empty. But his left hand wasn't quite empty, there appeared to be a flip phone in it.

"Commander?" he said again in a soft voice. "We okay here? This is just a phone, okay?"

She stared at him, her fingers closing unconsciously over the automatic in her lap. He saw her hand move, and he stopped short, his eyes locked on the .380.

"What's going on up there?" she spat. "And who and what the hell *are* you, McNair?"

He nodded slowly, acknowledging that he had some explaining to do. She was dimly aware that there were cars and some flashing blue lights down at the base of the hill, although they did not seem to be coming up. She had to wipe her eyes, but she never took them off McNair.

"I know, I know," he said. "But look, there isn't much time. He's holding Sherman and von Rensel. The kid's in there, too. Galantz is offering a deal."

"A deal? A *deal!*" She shook her head to clear the sudden wave of fatigue sweeping over her, compounding the nausea. "What the hell are you talking about, McNair? Aren't you people about to drop a bomb or something up there?"

He took a step closer. "We will if we have to," he said, his voice a lot less solicitous now. "But he says he'll come out—on one condition."

"Which is?"

"You have to go in. He says he needs you as a witness."

"A *witness?* To what? And if I don't? I mean, why the hell should I put my life in that killer's hands again? Or yours, for that matter? I can't trust him, and I sure as hell can't trust you people, can I? You get us all in there, then drop your bomb or whatever it is you're planning, and all the potential talkers are in the grave, right?"

"We wouldn't do that," he said. "We can't do that."

"No? You cops have let this guy run loose so far, ever since this crap started. Why should I believe you?" And then it hit her with the force of a hammer. "You're not a cop, are you, McNair?"

"Actually, I am. I told von Rensel that I did some moonlighting." He looked right at her. She was shocked by the transformation in his face. No more congenial detective. Somebody very different, with steely eyes and the flat, hard-edged face of a killer. Then she really understood.

"Oh my God, you're one of them, aren't you? You're one of those sweepers!"

McNair shrugged and looked down at the ground for a moment, the leftover rainwater spilling off the bill of his cap. She couldn't read his expression in the dim light from the car's cabin, but she could see he was struggling with something. She sensed now that there were other people out in the woods, out of sight, but not far from the car.

"Okay," he said, looking up at her. "You're right. You can't trust Galantz, although I know the guy, and I'd trust him with this. Hell, he knows it's over. This has to do with Sherman, not you, or von Rensel. But we won't move against all of you. There's a lock."

"A lock? Stop talking in code. What the hell's a lock?"

"Your people know what's going on here. That one of our guys has gone seriously wrong. Our people know the real reason *why* your people pulled the plug on your investigation. But we made a deal that neither of you would get hurt."

"By you or by him?"

"Well, we can't speak for him, but since nobody wants any of this to come out, that's a lock."

Carpenter, she thought. The blocked file. "And what's the FBI doing here?"

He sniffed in contempt. "They've horned in, mostly to watch us squirm and, someday, to extract something for their silence. We have this tradition."

"If you knew where he was, why didn't you move? Before we even got here?" She could hear the shrill note of frustration in her own voice.

"Because von Rensel is in there. And because we had to work some stuff out with the Feebies. Perimeter, comms, who would do what to whom." He had the grace to be embarrassed. "What can I tell you, we're all just a bunch of armed bureaucrats."

She shook her head in disbelief. Two innocent people had been murdered, and all they cared about was protecting their turf? "And on the basis of that, I'm just supposed to go up there?"

"That, and the fact that he says he'll kill von Rensel if you don't. Look, Commander, time is kinda short. There are some people here who really *are* disposed to use a bomb."

She felt the icy hand of fear grip her stomach. She had actually forgotten about Train. So she really didn't have any choice, did she? She stood up, her legs shaky. McNair put his hand out, and she hesitated, but then she handed over the .380. McNair actually grinned then, the way a coyote might. "You should have heard the Feebies on the radio," he said. "That guy's still shittin' and gittin'."

But Karen just stared at him, dry-mouthed and wanting the gun back. He saw her expression and his grin died. She looked up the long, dark hillside. The dark bulk of the ruined house was almost invisible among the trees. "I just walk up there?"

"I'll call him. Tell him you're coming in. We've got long guns all around it, so if it looks hinky as you get close, they can do something."

"But once I'm inside?"

He just looked at her. He didn't have to say it. Then the phone in his hand began to chirp. He flipped it open and answered it, then listened for a second. "She's coming up the hill right now," he said. He listened for another moment and then snapped the phone shut. "He said come in the front door and then close your eyes. Said you'd understand why."

"Oh yes," she said, and started up the hill. Close your eyes, or he'd fire that damned disrupter again. She wanted no more of that. Her eyes still hurt a little, and she hadn't even been looking at it.

"Commander," McNair called. She turned around, wiping her forehead. He was coming up the hill.

"Take this." He handed her something that looked like a television remote, only thicker.

"What is it?" she asked, but then she knew.

"It's a retinal disrupter. There are two buttons. The big round button charges it. The little sharp button fires it. Charge it, wait two seconds, and then it's ready. Like he said, close your eyes."

She took the thing from his hand and examined it. It was heavy, dense with latent energy. She looked up to thank him, but he was gone.

As she climbed through the tangled weeds toward the house, she tried to think of what might happen in there, and why. Obviously, Admiral Carpenter had been running her—no, had been running them like a couple of lab rats in a maze. And Sherman, too. Galantz's owners had been desperate to corral him once the Walsh woman was murdered. McNair, the sweeper, perfectly positioned in the Fairfax Police Department, had been activated. But how had Carpenter known what was really going on? The only one the cops had ever talked to in detail was Sherman. Unless there was some connection between the thing back in Vietnam and the admirals.

She found herself taking smaller steps as she got closer to the house, which was taking definition now that she was moving into the dripping trees. She could make out the sagging chimneys, but the crumbling mass between them was in deep shadow. She slipped the disrupter into her pants pocket.

The wood planks on the porch were rotted through, for the most part, but she discovered a piece of plywood had been placed near the front door. The front door itself was missing, and the doorway loomed ahead like the entrance to a mine tunnel. She hesitated. She really did not want to go in there. She looked back over her shoulder, but there was only the spidery trace of the trees showing against the night sky. The sound of the rainwater pouring through the holes over the porch obscured all other noises.

Taking a deep breath, she stepped through the doorway, placing her feet carefully, but it felt as if there was more plywood inside the door. The interior of the house smelled of dry rot, insects, and bird dung, in equal proportions. She was in a central hallway. Ahead, to the left, a stairway led up to the second floor, but the stairs themselves had long ago fallen in. Beyond the stairwell, the hallway ended in darkness. Probably a door there.

She waited for her eyes to adjust to the darkness inside the house, then remembered that she was supposed to close her eyes. She squinted, keeping them open just a crack, dreading another purple flash but not willing just to stand there with her eyes shut. The skin on her back was crawling, and she had to fight back her own imagination as to what might be approaching, or coming behind her. Then she heard a noise ahead—something being opened, a soft clatter of boards and debris, then silence. Then the darkness at the end of the hall dissolved into a grayness. Someone was standing there. She held her breath and kept her eyes just barely cracked open.

Karen-n-n.

She stopped breathing. Him, right in front of her. She surprised herself by wishing she had that big .45 right about now. He must have sensed her thoughts.

Open your coat and show me your hands. That horrible wheezing voice. She did as he asked. The shadow seemed to get smaller, and then she realized he was backing up.

Walk straight ahead. Keep your eyes closed. I can see just fine, by the way. But if I see your eyes, I'll use the disrupter. You remember the disrupter, don't you?

She nodded wordlessly, remembering very well, the urge to grab the thing in her pocket almost overwhelming. But he had one, too. She took one step, then another.

Keep coming. Straight ahead. You're going through a doorway. That's good. Now stop. Feel behind you. Find the door. Shut it.

Karen felt behind her, encountered what felt like a vertical sheet of plywood, and swung it shut behind her back. The voice moved closer.

Now, step sideways. More. Once more. Good. Stop. Now, there's a lot of debris in here. I'm going to open a trapdoor. Keep your eyes shut. Step carefully. Take two steps forward. There will be steps going down right in front of you. As you start down the steps, you can open your eyes. There'll be a strobe light. Go down the stairs and find von Rensel.

She did as she was told, opening her eyes on the second step down, then immediately squinting again as the red strobe light penetrated. She put up a hand and tried to see into what looked like a large basement, but the dazzling strobe made it very difficult. But she did see Train, hunched against a side wall, and Sherman, sitting down in the middle of the floor. She didn't see Jack with the gun in his hand until she got to the bottom of the steps. He gestured for her to get over against the wall and move down to where Train stood, looking like an angry bear ready to spring out at something. Not looking back, she moved across the cement floor and took Train's hand. It was all she could do not to hug him, but the tension in his hand reminded her of where she was. She turned around when the trapdoor banged shut, and the silhouette of Galantz came down the steps, disappearing into the penumbra of the pulsing red light.

Sherman was just sitting there, not looking at anything. She thought she could smell gunsmoke in the basement. A small generator was putt-putting away inside the remains of an old furnace. Galantz was saying something.

Jack. Come over here, next to me.

Jack obeyed quickly, keeping the gun in his hand pointed out into the middle distance between Sherman and Train. He moved over to the stairway and stood just below where Galantz was perched above him on the steps.

Hey. Sherman. Look over here. It's time to finish this.

Sherman looked up slowly, as if he had been asleep. He turned his head to face the strobe light. "I can't see," he said. Karen felt Train tensing up even more. Galantz apparently sensed it, too. She saw the .45 pointed at them in the next flash of red light.

Sit still, von Rensel, and your lady friend there won't get hurt. Your job here is to listen and watch, nothing more.

"I can't see," Sherman said again.

Yes you can. Recognize your son, Jack, here, don't you, Admiral? He sure as hell recognizes you. You do know he's been helping me all along with this, don't you? That he hates you just about as much as I do?

Sherman put a hand up to his face to shield his eyes against the light, but he said nothing. The two of them, Galantz and Jack, had merged into a single shadow right next to the pulsing strobe light.

You two over there, listen up. Did Yellowbelly here tell you why I've hunted him down?

"Yes," Train said. "He failed to make a pickup when his boat ran into a mining ambush."

That what he said? "Failed to make a pickup"?

"You didn't make the rendezvous, and then they ran into the ambush."

Oh, but I did make the rendezvous, didn't I, Sherman? I saw you at the controls, when that mine went off. And you saw me, too, didn't you? Didn't you, Sherman?

The admiral, still squinting into the light, said nothing. Galantz leaned forward and fired the .45 again, this time down onto the concrete floor an inch from Sherman's hand. The admiral yelled and spun sideways as the bullet went spanging around the stone walls. Train pushed Karen down to the floor and tried to cover her from the ricochet round. Amazingly, through all the noise, she thought she heard Jack laughing. The pulsing light clearly illuminated the gunsmoke in front of the strobe.

Right, Sherman? Answer me, you yellow bastard!

The admiral was picking himself up off the floor, and then he stood up, his legs obviously shaky.

"Yes," Sherman whispered.

Yes what? Tell them!

"I did see you. You were there."

Where did you see me?

"Under a mangrove tree."

But you ran away, didn't you? Answer me—goddamn your eyes!

A moment of silence. "Yes."

Train helped Karen get back up. She tried to control her shaking knees. Her hand brushed over her pocket, and she slipped it inside.

But that's not what the final investigation said. It said the SEAL never showed. The SEAL never made the rendezvous. Missing and presumed lost. Isn't that what it said, Sherman?

"I did tell them."

Bullshit! Because if you'd told them that, your precious career would have been down the tubes, wouldn't it? Panicked under fire and left a guy behind. No stars for that kind of cowardly shit, are there, Sherman?

"I did tell them. They didn't want to hear it."

See, Jack, you were right all along. Your daddy here is not only a coward but a liar, too. Hey, Sherman, know what? Jackie here remembers the night I came to see you. Used to have bad dreams about it. Because he knew, even as a little kid, that his daddy had done something wrong. But you didn't give a shit, because you never liked him very much, did you, Daddykins?

Sherman sighed. "I was wrong about that. Jack, I was wrong about a lot of things. About your mother, about—"

"Don't you even *talk* about my mother, you bastard," Jack hissed. "It's because of you that she's dead."

Sherman looked up, raising his hand again to shield his eyes against the strobe. He started to say something, but Jack cut him off. "I was there, you bastard. Did you know that? I was there when she did it. Took that damned gun and blew a hole in her head."

Sherman seemed to shrink when he heard that. He shook his head. "I didn't know that, Jack. They didn't tell—"

Jack cut him off again. "They wouldn't even let me see her. Goddamned cops took me away, never let me see her. And you didn't even come, did you? Away somewhere, being really busy and important with all your Navy shit."

Sherman said nothing, just hung his head.

Tell him, Sherman.

The admiral snapped his head around and stared into the light, but then he began to shake his head slowly. Galantz said it again, raising the Colt for emphasis.

"Tell me what?" Jack said.

Karen held her breath as Sherman hesitated. Then he said it. "She's not dead, Jack."

There was absolute silence in the room except for the muttering of the generator. Even in the strobe light, Karen could see that Jack was stunned.

Give me that gun. He's mine, and I don't want you doing anything to screw that up. Give it here. That's a boy. Good. Now ask him where she is, Jack. Ask him what really happened to your mother.

Sherman nodded slowly, his gaunt face a study in defeat. He told Jack where his mother was, and in what condition. Jack just stared at him, open-mouthed. Karen began to feel sick to her stomach. Train put his hands on her shoulders, and she flinched when she saw Galantz looking.

You two getting all this, are you? Because that's why you're here. When we're done here, you're going to be the only ones who know the whole story, once all those people outside do what they came to do. It's going to be interesting, living with this knowledge. Life's all about choices, isn't it? Well, I'm going to leave you two with some interesting choices. But we're not done here yet. Not quite done yet. Jack, step over there, against the wall, would you?

Jack looked up over the strobe light, a puzzled look on his face, and then straightened up when he saw the Colt pointed into his face. Sherman started to move forward, but he froze when the .45 swung his way.

You know what's coming next, don't you, Mr. High-and-Mighty Admiral? I killed your woman, and I killed your best friend in the whole world. And I made your only son an accomplice, not that he resisted. Now you've surely figured out how this thing is going to end, right?

"Don't," Sherman began.

"Hey, man," Jack said, his voice uncertain. "What are we doing here? Do him! You said you would. You even said I could watch. You don't want to do him, then I sure as hell do!"

Galantz laughed. Karen shuddered at the horrible sound coming through the electronic voice box.

Sherman had his hands up. "Don't do this. Shoot me instead. But let him go."

Ah. Choices again. What do you think of that, Jack? Him for you?

"You're gonna shoot me?" Jack asked in a plaintive voice. "I thought—"

"Jack, listen to me," Sherman said, the words tumbling out of his mouth. "I know you think I've despised you all these years. That I despised your mother, too. That's not true. I know I didn't do this right. I was wrong. All those years, I was wrong. My career was all I thought about. That was wrong."

Jack just looked at him, his mouth working soundlessly. Karen saw tears in Sherman's eyes. Galantz was strangely silent, as if he was enjoying all this.

"That's why I couldn't marry Elizabeth Walsh, Jack. I've been going to see your mother every weekend in that hospice for many, many years. Elizabeth never knew. I told her I had to work those weekends. She had no idea. The Navy never knew. Galen Schmidt didn't even know. I've paid a price, too, son. Not like she has, but I've paid."

"Jack," Karen spoke up. "Don't you see it? This bastard never was your friend. He's used you. He stumbled across you in recon school, and he realized he had the way to get back at your father. That's been the plan all along, Jack: to use you and then kill you, too, to complete his revenge."

But Jack wasn't listening. He was staring at his father, his expression unreadable in the pulsing red light. Sherman was pleading with him.

"I don't hate you, Jack. I . . . I love you, son. I forgive you for helping this . . . this *thing* to kill those people. I'm asking you to forgive me for the way I treated you and your mother. Please."

Galantz stood up behind the light. *So, Jackie boy, what's it going to be?*

Jack looked from Galantz to his father and then back again.

"You were gonna shoot *me?*"

That's right, Jack. But now your father's made a more interesting offer. All along, I've wanted him to live with the knowledge that I'd taken every-thing of value to him. But maybe I ought to let you decide, Jack. You said you were ready to do him. Are you, Jackie boy?

Karen, holding Train's arm with her left hand, gripped it twice, trying to alert him that she was going to do something. Train was staring at Jack, but then he was looking sideways at her, trying not to attract Galantz's attention. She felt with her thumb over the smooth plastic surface of the disrupter, searching for the big round button. She found it and pushed it once. She felt a tiny vibration, which stopped after two seconds. Then she moved her thumb over to the sharp, smaller button and began to extract the disrupter from her pocket.

C'mon, Jack. We have an offer on the table. His life for yours. This is even better: You choose him, he dies knowing you did it. Or you could choose yourself, Jack. Make him live with it. What do you think, Jack? Life been that good for you?

Karen tried very hard to move her arm without showing movement, but it took supreme concentration, and that damned pulsing light was driving her nuts. Jack kept looking at his father, then at Galantz. His hands moved.

Hey, Jackie, not thinking about making a move here, Jack? Did you forget something? I've got your gun, Jack. Galantz held up both hands, Karen's Colt in his right and Jack's bulky automatic in the other hand. The red light glinted off the goggled mask he was wearing.

Karen had the disrupter just about out of her pocket as Galantz pointed the .45 over at Jack. Then she screamed and pulled hard on Train's arm, spinning him around, away from the disrupter, which she raised and pointed right at Galantz's face and his light-intensifying night-vision goggles.

NO-O-O-O! the voice box squalled, the guns starting to swing around, and then there was that terrible ripping blast of light. Karen closed her eyes at the last possible instant, and then Train was pulling Karen and himself flat onto the concrete as there came a barrage of gunfire, the blasts from Galantz's two guns hammering against their brains in the confined space, the whine and howl of bullets smacking stone and wood and concrete, and even the furnace. Karen tried to melt into the concrete floor with each blast, every shot punctuated by a high keening noise from the steps. Then came a sudden silence, followed by the sound of the trapdoor opening and banging shut. She realized that the strobe light had stopped and that the room was in total darkness. She couldn't hear anything after the intense hammering of the gunfire in the enclosed space.

Train rolled off her and they clutched each other on the concrete, coughing in all the smoke. They heard a moan from the direction of where Jack had been standing, and an ominous gurgling noise coming from where Sherman had been. As the strobe light died, Karen realized the generator had been hit, its smooth puttering sound replaced by a distinct knocking sound. She wanted to call out, but she was afraid to. Her ears hurt from all the gunfire.

Train was signaling her with his hands to move with him, away from where they had been when the strobe light had last been on. The smoke was very strong, but she realized it wasn't gunsmoke. It was something else. Then they both found out precisely what: There was a bright orange glare accompanied by a whooping noise from behind them as the generator burst into flames. But at least now they could see.

Sherman was down on the floor, both his hands to his head, and there was a shiny black pool of blood around his hands and head. Jack was slumped against the wall, his eyes open. He was holding his stomach and breathing through his mouth. There was a pool of blood expanding beneath his legs. Karen crawled first to Sherman, then turned to check Jack. Train ran for the steps and tested the trapdoor, but it was either blocked or locked. He had to jump down off the steps because of the bank of dense oily smoke that was accumulating along the ceiling of the basement. The diesel-oil fire in the furnace was gathering strength.

"Karen, we've got to bust out of here somehow," Train shouted. "See if you can shut the furnace door, stop the smoke, while I look for something to break through the trapdoor!"

Karen, bending low to stay out of the choking band of smoke swirling across the ceiling, got as close as she could to the furnace door, but the fuel fire inside was getting very hot. The generator's carry handle blocked the furnace door, and the fire was making a roaring noise now as it sucked the oxygen out of the basement.

"I can't get near it," she called. "The door's blocked."

Jack slid over on his side with a low groan. Karen was horrified to see how much blood there was on the floor, under both men. She heard a crash from the other end of the basement. Train came back into view, holding a timber from the wreckage of the collapsed flooring at the other end.

"We've got to get them out of here," she shouted over the noise from the fire.

"We gotta get *us* out of here," he shouted back. "Help steady this table."

She joined him at the table where the computer had been set up. Train swept everything off the table onto the floor in one big crash and then got up on the table. Using a four-by-four, he began battering the floorboards above his head. She held the table with one hand and his leg with the other as he became a human pile driver, smashing the four-by-four into the rotten flooring up above, choking and coughing in the writhing cloud of smoke that was banking up against the ceiling. Then he was through, and the hole widened as the smoke shot up through the hole into the room above. The furnace box and the ducting began to shake as the airflow reversed, feeding fresh oxygen to the burning diesel fuel. When he had the hole big enough, Train turned around and grabbed Karen, and in one great swing he thrust her through the hole in the ceiling, shoving her hips and then her legs up until she was able to roll out on the floor above.

"Get outside and call for help," he shouted as he got down off the table. "You can't lift us out of here!" She nodded and ran outside to the porch.

Down in the basement, Train dragged Sherman and then Jack away from the fire and closer to the hole. His hands became sticky with blood, and he wondered if either of them was going to survive this. Then there was a face in the hole, but it was quickly withdrawn as the stream of smoke immediately blinded the man. A minute later, there was a crash of timbers above the trapdoor, and then it burst open and several men in vests came tumbling down the stairs.

"Head wound!" Train yelled to the first one to reach him, pointing at Sherman. "Gut wound on the other guy."

"We got 'em," someone yelled. And then there was a general commotion as everyone tried to help. Train saw Karen briefly at the top of the steps before someone topside grabbed her and took her out of there. He helped carry Sherman up the stone steps, through the hallway, and out onto the front porch and into a blaze of headlights, radio chatter, and blue flashers littering the side of Slade Hill. A helicopter was hovering over the trees east of the house, shining a large spotlight at something on the ground. Several men were gathered in the vicinity of the spotlighted area. Karen ran to meet Train as the first signs of the fire appeared in the front window sockets of the old house. He embraced her, but then, to his surprise, she was pulling back, looking behind him. McNair materialized out of the darkness.

"Well?" she said. "Did you get him?"

McNair looked over his shoulder at the crowd of police and FBI agents milling around the house. A small fire engine was trying to get up the hill below them, but it appeared to have become stuck. He turned to face them.

"Get who?" he replied.

Train stepped forward. "You know goddamn well who," he said. "Just what—"

But McNair had his hand up, signifying silence. "This would be a really good time," he said, "for you two to walk down that hill and get in that Explorer and get the hell out of here. A really good time. The commander here will explain it to you. We're all done up here. But you two might have a loose end or two to work out." He turned back to Karen and gave her a slip of paper. "The guy at the other end of that number will be expecting your call. He did a little computer work for your boss. The thing you should know about him is that he can undo anything that he's done."

Train started to object again, but McNair only pointed down the hill. Karen touched his arm. "We'll be knee-deep in cops all night, answering questions," she said. "Let's just get out of here. There are some things I have to tell you."

McNair nodded at her and walked back into the darkness.

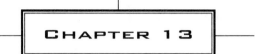

CHAPTER 13

On Monday morning, Train signed Karen through the Pentagon security checkpoint. They walked in silence through the corridors, along with a steady stream of civilians. Train had to remember not to hold her hand as they walked down the A-ring, heading toward the escalators to the fourth floor.

"You still think this will work?" he asked. Sunday had been a day of rest and recuperation, and planning.

"It had better work," she said grimly. "If Sherman makes it, I want to be able to tell him why they were so hot to force him out of the Navy."

Captain Pennington was waiting for Karen when they arrived at the IR offices. "The admiral wants to see you, Karen, as soon as you get in."

"But not me?" Train asked innocently. The other officers were keeping their heads down.

Pennington frowned at him. "I think you are going to be reassigned back to the Navy Yard, Mr. von Rensel. I'm not privy to all that went down this past weekend, but there's been something of a shit storm going on up front since I got in, and your name was featured often and rudely."

"Oh my." Train sighed. "And I was beginning to like it here."

Karen was not amused. "I'm not going to see anybody until I've had a chance to get into my PC. There's an archive report I want to see."

"Um, well," Pennington began, but Karen walked past him to her cubicle. Train went to his and turned on his PC. He could hear Pennington trying to talk to Karen, but she was answering in monosyllables while she booted up her own machine. When Train was sure Pennington was fully engaged, he got on the phone and called the NIS database administrator.

"What is it now, von Rensel?"

"I need you guys to get into the JAG archive database."

"JAG? We don't normally target specific—"

"I know," Train interrupted, keeping an eye on Pennington, who was starting to get worked up. Karen was supposed to stall him long enough for Train to make this one phone call. "But this one should be easy. I need you guys to pull up a specific investigation file." He gave the administrator the cite number.

"What the hell, von Rensel. Aren't you right there in JAG?"

"I am, but I need an external query. And then I need you to attach the report and E-mail it to me at this address, and I need this done ASAP, like anytime in the next ten minutes, if that's humanly possible."

"Ten minutes! That's ridiculous! That's—"

Train cut him off. "Two people have been murdered," he said. "An admiral has been shot in the head, and his son has been shot in the stomach, and my car's been burned up with me in it, and I think you should really do this thing, and now would be really nice, okay?"

"Holy shit, why didn't you say so?"

"I just did. Here's the E-mail address. And this is a real fire, okay? Get that thing over here right now."

"Coming at you." Train hung up. Pennington was stomping off across the office to his cubicle. Karen watched him go, and then looked over her shoulder at Train, who gave her the thumbs-up signal. She turned around and kept going on her PC. Train stood up and rearranged the privacy panel on his cubicle so that no one standing next to Karen's desk could see him across the room. He heard Pennington call one of the other commanders into his cubicle for a short conference, after which he came out and started telling the rest of the people in the office that there was going to be an urgent all-hands meeting across the way in the main conference room in five minutes. Nobody would even look at Karen or Train as the commander shepherded everyone else out of the office. Pennington remained in the entrance to his cubicle, looking meaningfully at Karen, but she ignored him. Train ducked back into his own cubicle and waited for the E-mail banner.

Five minutes later, the office door burst open and Admiral Carpenter stormed in, followed by a worried-looking McCarty. Train watched through a crack between the privacy panels, but he kept out of sight, resisting the urge to shake his PC monitor to make the E-mail arrive faster. Carpenter went directly to Karen's cubicle.

"Commander Lawrence, I am not amused," he said "When I summon a staff officer, they damned well come to see me, not the other way around!"

Karen stood up respectfully and pointed down at her screen, where a large red ACCESS DENIED banner was displayed. "I want to see that investigation report," she said. "I'm not going anywhere, and I'm not talking to anybody until I've seen that investigation report."

"What goddamned report?" Carpenter shouted. "Pennington, out!"

An astonished Captain Pennington backed out of the office, giving

McCarty a "what the hell?" look. He got a nervous shrug in return. He closed the door behind him forcefully. Karen hadn't budged.

"You know what report, Admiral," she said. "The JAG investigation on the loss of the SEAL back there in Vietnam. The one you told Mr. von Rensel you had seen, where Sherman was adjudged to have done the right thing when he abandoned that man back there on the river."

Carpenter started to say something but then faltered.

Train tapped his monitor with his fingers. C'mon, C'mon, he thought. She couldn't hold this guy off forever.

"Sherman told us, Admiral. Before he was shot up there on that hill. He admitted seeing the SEAL. That's not quite the story he told us before, but he admitted it to Galantz. He also said that he *did* tell his bosses back there in Vietnam that he *had* seen the SEAL on the night of the incident, that they knew he *had* been left behind."

"That's not what the investigation says," Carpenter declared.

An E-mail notice bloomed across Train's screen, and he quickly switched screens to the communications program. One message—from NIS—file attached. He accepted the message and then ordered the attached file copied for retransmission and forwarding. The system asked for the forwarding addresses. Train consulted the OpNAV directory and then sat down to type them out.

"Then let me see it, Admiral."

"It's classified. You're not cleared."

"It was over twenty years ago, Admiral. And after what I've been through, I am more than cleared. In fact, I feel like telling the whole world about my fun weekend. Then everyone will be cleared."

Carpenter stared at her, but then his expression changed. "All right, Commander. Since you insist. Captain McCarty will remove the lock."

Karen got up, and McCarty slid into her chair. After a minute on the keyboard, he got back up. "Call it up," he said.

Karen sat back down and accessed the archive system. This time, the file appeared on screen. Carpenter just stood there, looking as if this was just an enormous waste of time, the beginnings of a triumphant expression on his face: the admiral humoring the commander.

Karen began to scan the investigation report as fast as she could scroll through it. The basic letter report, followed by the appendices: the appointing order, the interview list, the findings of fact, the findings of opinion, the substantiating documents. She was looking for two things: the Swift boat division commander's statement and the all-important reviewing authority's first endorsement.

There. The DivCom's statement. Interview with Sherman. The mining ambush. Subsequent actions to extract the boat from the kill zone. Damage to the boat. Injuries to personnel. A brief mention of the skipper thinking that he had seen the SEAL by the riverbank at the time of the engagement. As Galantz had charged, and as Sherman had admitted.

Carpenter was looking at the screen over her shoulder. "Well," he said. "I guess it does say that. So what?"

"That's only part of it, Admiral," she replied. "Now I want to see the final endorsement. Because whoever approved this investigation essentially covered up the fact that Galantz had been left behind."

Carpenter stood back and took a deep breath, his eyes flitting from side to side for an instant. But then he gestured to McCarty, as if to say, Beats me. Karen scrolled down through the document to the final section. The final endorsement appeared on the screen. The reviewing authority, Commander Naval Forces, Vietnam. The major conclusion: concurring in findings of facts and opinions, with the exception that the COMNAVFORV did not concur that the SEAL had been at the rendezvous. That in the heat of an engagement, the skipper could not have seen the face of a man as mines were exploding and heavy machine-gun fire laid down on the banks of the river. That the SEAL had, in all probability, never made it to the rendezvous. That the division commander was directed to take no further action with regard to the SEAL.

Carpenter again read over her shoulder. "Well," he said, "I'm not sure that's what I would have recommended. Seems kind of coldhearted. But I guess that's what they recommended, whoever they were. Are we finished here, Commander?"

"Just about, Admiral," Karen said. "I just want to see who signed this thing out."

Carpenter again stood back. "I'm not sure why that would be of interest, after so long a time. Most likely some names who are long gone."

Karen turned to look at him. "Are you sure, Admiral? Because if the approving officers were still on active duty, and the Navy opens an investigation into why Admiral Sherman is lying in Bethesda with a gunshot wound, these names might be of burning interest within the flag community."

Carpenter looked exasperated. "I think I'm getting bored with all this, EA. Why don't you—"

"Ah, here they are. Approving for Commander Naval Forces, Vietnam. Captain McCarty, want to take a look?"

"Me?" He looked at Carpenter and then leaned down. "Son of a bitch!" he exclaimed.

Carpenter pushed him aside and looked at the screen. His face went white as the names jumped out at him. The two lieutenant commanders at headquarters of Naval Forces, Vietnam—the ones who had approved the investigation report: Lieutenant Commanders Kensington and Carpenter. Carpenter for JAG approval, Kensington as the operations officer. The fact that it was signed "By Direction" made it even more damning, because that phrase meant that the admiral commanding in Vietnam had never seen it.

"What's the meaning of this?" Carpenter spluttered. "This shouldn't—I mean . . ."

"Shouldn't be there, Admiral?" Karen asked softly. "But this is an archive file. Read only. No one can change an archive file, can they, Admiral?"

Train stood up in his cubicle and pushed the privacy panel aside. Carpenter, visibly shaken, turned around to look at him, as did McCarty.

"Commander," Train said formally. "I've got what you need. The NIS query went through. I've got that Vietnam incident report right here."

Karen started to walk over toward Train's cubicle, but Carpenter stepped in front of her. "What's the meaning of this, von Rensel? You have no right to access restricted JAG information. That report is classified. That report—"

"In light of the upcoming investigation that will be conducted into the injuries sustained by Admiral Sherman, your NIS liaison officer thinks this report is undiluted dynamite, Admiral," Train said as he pushed two keys on his keyboard. "Especially that approving first endorsement. It's a great thing, that archive system, the way it preserves the facts. Preserves and protects them. And so is this E-mail system."

"E-mail?" Carpenter squeaked, his voice rising. "What are you doing?"

"Why, I'm E-mailing this to the CNO's office," Train announced, pushing two more keys. "And to the Vice CNO's office." Two more keys. "And to your buddy Kensington. And to the Deputy JAG. And to my bosses over at NIS. And to CHINFO—he should know all about this, don't you think, before the press gets into it? Before people start asking why this deranged ex-serviceman shot an admiral, committed two homicides in Fairfax County, and tried to kill two federal officers, all because two staffies in Saigon were afraid to tell their boss that one of their skippers had abandoned a guy in the Rung Sat zone?"

Carpenter seemed to shrink. He started to say something but then shut his mouth. McCarty was glaring at his boss.

Train picked up the unspoken question. "How did the file get changed back after you altered it? Well, see, you didn't keep your end of the bargain, did you? You told those people that you'd keep your two operatives out of the way. If it had been just Galantz and Jack in that house, they could have just nuked it or something. But once the two of us were involved, not to mention Sherman, well, that was too many people in the loop. So the guy who helped you alter this file came back and did this super undo routine."

"Why?" Carpenter whispered, his face gray. "Why would they do that? They wanted to limit this thing more than we did."

"What thing is that, Admiral?" Karen asked.

"Galantz was theirs."

Train shook his head. "Who's Galantz, Admiral? If you bring up Galantz, they'll say he was an ex-*Navy* man, and that he was shot and killed in a hostage-rescue operation up on Slade Hill. Their guy McNair, in his capacity as a Fairfax County homicide cop, will corroborate that, and you better believe Fairfax County, who wants no part of this tar baby, will back him up. No, sir: The only question remaining is *why* this all happened. And I believe you and perhaps the vice admiral down the hall will be called front and center directly. Of course, he being a three-star, he may just ask you to explain it."

"We're leaving now, Admiral," Karen said. "We're going over to Bethesda."

Carpenter sagged into a chair, looking even more bewildered. "Sherman?" he said. "He's in a coma."

"Which the docs say he should come out of. As his lawyer, I want to be there."

Train and Karen left them there, the admiral and his EA, looking at each other.

CHAPTER 14

Two weeks later, Train pulled down the windshield visor to block out the sun setting over the West Virginia hills. They were headed west on Route 50, straight out of Washington, in Karen's Mercedes. Karen was dozing in the passenger seat. He glanced over at her and felt that familiar flutter.

The past two weeks had not worked out quite the way they had predicted to Carpenter. The Chief of Naval Operations had cobbled up a quick joint intelligence commission and had convinced the other players that this was one of those times when the national interest might best be served by a fully coordinated version of events. Train mused on the subsequent fun and games. The joint commission had been chaired by Admiral Vannoyt, of all people, who, speaking for the Navy, emphasized that incidents involving special operations in a war long ago and far away were, in the judgment of the highest levels of the Navy, matters best left to history. The Navy would therefore, however reluctantly, interpose no objections to closing the files on this matter at the earliest opportunity. And the slab-faced lady who spoke for those people made the point that sometimes the human resources best suited for certain kinds of extremely difficult operational situations become occupationally dysfunctional over time, especially as changed circumstances arose. She had actually said that without reading from any cards, which had impressed the rest of the joint commission members no end. The FBI sent over a smug-looking associate director, who sat through the entire proceedings, saying almost nothing, serene in the joyful knowledge that the FBI was going to be able to blackmail those people into all sorts of interesting modalities of intragovernment cooperation for years and years to come after this little fiasco, or at least until all the principals were safely retired, their pensions intact.

With this level of understanding achieved on the first morning, the rest of the week had been devoted to layering enough investigatory paperwork on the problem so as to ensure its total obfuscation. Train had been approached by the deputy director of the NIS during the first coffee break of the second day to sound out his level of understanding of what was supposed to be taking place here. Just for the hell of it, Train speculated aloud on his prospects for getting a year's leave of absence, with pay, of course, to explore some continuing educational opportunities, and the deputy director allowed as to how that should present no problem whatsoever. The deputy director then speculated on how the NIS party line might possibly evolve with respect to this matter, a homily to which Train paid rapt attention.

Train had spent several hours explaining to Karen how the dance was going to come out and why a restoration of various federal glossy surfaces was probably in everyone's best interest. Karen finally agreed, remarking on the irony of Galantz's comment to them in the basement about whether or not they would tell the truth when this thing was over. The good news was that Sherman was recovering from his head wound. Upon Karen's advice, he had asked the Navy for early retirement, provided it was in the grade of rear admiral, in return for two concessions. The first was his silence, which was, of course, the most important thing. The second was that he be allowed to supervise his son's rehabilitation, under whatever circumstances a court might think appropriate. The joint commission had taken just under ten minutes to endorse that deal. Carpenter and Kensington had met a less-generous fate. Carpenter had lied about telling the CNO, leading necessarily to one of those surprises of which the CNO was not so fond. The two admirals were going to join Sherman on the retired list, each minus a star.

Train looked over at Karen again. Soon to be Commander, USN (Retired) Lawrence—now on preretirement leave until the clock ran out at twenty years. During dinner one night, she had reiterated her intentions to go away for a while, and, after about thirty seconds of serious thought and mental girding of loins, Train had worked up the nerve to ask if she might like some company on her walkabout. Karen found an unusually expressive way of answering his question, actually managing to embarrass Hiroshi, Kyoko, and even Gutter.

The only loose end was Galantz. McHale Johnson had called Train two days before they left town to get his version of the story. There were, he said, some utterly fascinating rumors circulating around the various agency grapevines. But one question caught Train's attention.

"Did you see a body?" Johnson had asked.

"Never did, actually," Train replied. "Lots of activity around what I thought was a body, but no, I never did."

"That sort of confirms what I'm hearing," Johnson said.

"Oh man. You mean he's still alive?"

"Well," Johnson said, "better than that, really."

"What do you mean? I should think they'd—"

"They'd what? Execute him? Why should they? Don't you see—now he's twice dead. Once in Vietnam, again on Slade Hill. That's what I would call really deep cover, wouldn't you? Those people would never waste an asset like that."

Karen stirred in her seat and made a small noise in her throat. Train reached over and took her hand. If Galantz was still alive, he might be back, although he had achieved what he wanted. Some loose ends will just have to stay out there, he thought. Small faceless terrors back there along the Potomac River, among the many degrees of purple.